The Pride

John Campea

DEDICATION

This book is dedicated to my family. My wife, my mother and father, my brother and my sisters, my grandparents, uncles, aunts and cousins. Collectively I have watched them my entire life endure, survive and even thrive in the midst of great adversity. I've watched them in awe, I've watched them in wonder and I've watched them in gratitude. They've taught me what determination is. They've taught me what sacrifice is and most importantly they've taught me what family is. Family doesn't mean always getting along. It doesn't mean talking daily on the phone and it doesn't necessarily mean being very close all the time. But in the Campea clan, what family does mean is when one of the family is in need, in trouble, in pain or in mourning, we close ranks. Differences are put aside, the limited number of times phone conversations were shared becomes irrelevant and conflicts are suspended. I've watched my dad and mom, my grandparents, my uncles and aunts do this over and over again. In many ways, the definition of family I've learned from my own has inspired THE PRIDE. Many of the things The Pride holds dear is a direct reflection of the example I've seen set. In many ways, The Pride is an extension of those lessons. So to my pride living up in Ontario, Canada: I love you all and thank you.

PROLOGUE

NOW

Summer

Summer smiled as the four others waved, still looking at her like she was crazy. Marylyn put her hand to her head, mimicking a phone call and Summer nodded. She wouldn't call, of course, but that was the ritual. Her friends dropped her off for what they thought was a weekend of solo survivalist adventure every month, and every time they came up with new horrors awaiting her, new terrors she'd find in the forests or the islands or, in this case, the mountains. Every time they received assurances she would call at the slightest hint of danger. Summer watched as the old coupe reluctantly obeyed the steering wheel and turned around. She kept watching until they were out of sight and then lifted her backpack from the ground, slung it over her shoulder, and turned away from the winding road, pausing as her senses became momentarily overwhelmed by the sounds and smells and life of the mountain. It happened every time, and she thought it strange though it really wasn't.

She spent three-hundred and thirty days every year keeping her senses in check, forcing herself to conform to the sterile—tame—environment of the city. Three-hundred and thirty-one days on leap years. Tame. That was the problem, really. There was so little opportunity to be anything other than exactly what she was supposed to be during that time. Sure, it was right. It was exactly what made things work, and it really wasn't a great sacrifice though she often felt jealous of those freer than herself, those who lived in rural expanses or in cities that stood hand in hand with the wilderness so that life was impacted by the wild. That wasn't her, though. She had no such freedom.

But she did now. She did for three days. Every month, two or three days. This month, three.

She made her way to where the shoulder met the trees and sloped up sharply, choosing her steps carefully but not too carefully because she was already lost in the joy of the freedom. The upward slope lasted only a few dozen yards before it leveled out, followed by another upslope that brought her about a hundred feet above the road, thirty or forty feet above the tops of the evergreens on the first rise. She kept going, almost seeing them already, the herd of elk she knew would be there. She thought also there might be a bear or two but she stopped wondering and instead stared in wonder when she reached the crest stood on the edge of a great valley. The elk, indeed, were there, a vast herd that had to include two or three hundred animals. Most of them were cows but she was surprised to see a dozen males. She thought she'd remembered reading something about that.

No matter. She was here now. She took the backpack from her shoulder and started to strip but thought better of it and picked her backpack up. She could hear cars occasionally passing. She carefully made her way down the sloping forest toward the valley, thrilled with every step and finding urgency growing with every step. Already, the sounds of the cars grew distant. Already the world was wild and loud, and not the loud of the city where cars and sirens and music and people, so many damned people, seemed to draw all silence from wherever it hid and transformed it into cacophony. No. Here the sounds came together in chorus. In the distance an elk bull bellowed, the strange screaming noise a signal to a cow as strong as the urine that covered its belly. Birds sang and chirped and clucked, and each of the sounds echoed and bounced upon the leaves and branches until they formed a soft melody of life that fell upon Summer and only increased her wonder.

She reached a slightly steeper downslope and smiled broadly, laughing silently as she let herself fall so that she slid down the bed of pine needles and brush, disturbing a squirrel with reddish-brown fur that chirruped angrily at her before leaping to the trunk of a conifer and scurrying up. She twisted her body to avoid three rocks protruding from the ground and then twisted it again to avoid a burrow hole that might have been a rabbit den or a badger den or the den of just about anything. The air rushed through her face and the elation was great enough to ward off disappointment as the slope evened out and the trip ended a few feet from the side of a rotting log. She laughed, this time out loud, and she heard the sound of leaves parting and wings flapping as birds shot away at the sound. Finally, she calmed herself and stood.

2

A moment later, her backpack lay against the log as she stared up at the trees and the sunlight filtering through the canopy like water through a sieve in brilliant droplets that played out another melody altogether in the air and on the forest floor and on her body. She breathed deeply and as she exhaled she realized the bull wasn't bellowing anymore. He'd taken his cow and was enjoying the fruits of his labors. She smiled and listened also to the sounds in the distance. Coyotes, perhaps, or perhaps wolves circled the herd, hoping to catch a sick elk or a young elk unaware. She laughed again. It was instinct, she knew, but the pack was a hell of a lot more likely to find bulls and cows unaware at this time of year.

The feel of the ground beneath her and the air above her and the trees surrounding her was simply wonderful. She kicked off her shoes and then kicked them toward the log next to her backpack. She slid her left foot into her sock on her right foot, and once she had that off she hooked her toes into the left sock and got that off as well. She paused as she felt the crumbly and soft vegetation and soil beneath her feet but she paused very briefly because the urgency was overwhelming. She pulled at her jeans and then cursed herself for wearing the ones that buttoned up instead of zipping. It took too long before they rested crumpled at her feet. She kicked them toward the shoes and socks and lifted her shirt up and off. She grabbed at the elastic band that held her hair back in a tight ponytail and then shot it like a rubber band at the backpack as she shook her head to free her hair. Already, her heart beat harder, faster.

Better.

She unclasped and then shrugged off her bra, delighting in the sudden loss of constriction and the feel of the air over her skin. She tossed it with the other clothes and then walked to the pile. She opened up her backpack and stuffed the clothing inside, at the end reaching for the waistband of her panties and sliding them down over her thighs and then her ankles, putting them on top of the other clothes before pulling the drawstring tight and looping the strap through its buckle. She considered covering the backpack with leaves or dirt but in the end decided getting it up to the trees was safer. But not yet. Not yet. Free from the damned clothes than trapped her like a second skin over a second skin, she lifted her arms and extended them outward from her shoulders, parallel to the ground as she twirled and listened to the orchestra of the mountain.

It might have been hours.

It might have been minutes.

She finally brought her arms down and reached for the backpack. She imagined any tree would do for her and any tree would do for the backpack so she put it on again and walked toward the nearest. She smiled. A black bear was near, watching her, trying to understand the strange creature. She ignored it and made her way to a tall pine with a thick trunk. It wasn't as thick as the redwoods in California. She'd spent a weekend there years ago and loved it but decided against ever returning. Too many tourists explored there, too many tourists and too many eyes. She reached above her head and grabbed hold of the bark, lifting herself up effortlessly and then moving her legs and arms in concert. It would be an easy climb.

When she felt the tearing in her shoulder, she thought first a broken branch had somehow eluded notice but she turned her head and saw the gleam of metal. Metal. Metal and string and wood—no. Not wood. Fiberglass. Sharp metal in the shape of a spade attached to the fiberglass rod with string. Sharp metal glistening with blood and something else. She stared in shock, the pain not registering so much as surprise. Along the edges of the blade something gleamed. Diamonds. There were diamonds because diamonds would be necessary to...

She felt the second arrow slam into her back and then a third into her other shoulder. She tried to cry out but the arrow in her back had pierced a lung, and blood flowed from her mouth. She turned and fell, catching a glimpse at her attacker and trying, but failing, to fly from the violence. Another arrow sent diamond, steel, and fiberglass into her flesh, this one hitting her at her throat, which she thought was silly and unnecessary. The arrow in her back and the damage to her lung had already killed her, and her body would figure that out shortly. She lifted her head, the arrow at her throat making the movement excruciating but by this time such pain was distant, a phenomenon to be observed rather than experienced.

Her attacker had another arrow nocked but he held the bow without firing, studying her face instead, and she stared back in wonder and tried and failed to speak. She managed a gurgling sound but couldn't determine a way to get her lips and tongue to form a single word.

Why?

Blackness closed in and her attacker answered the unasked question anyway. "There's no other way."

CHAPTER ONE

THEN

Agathon

The early morning mountain mist clung to the needles on the lower branches of the evergreens and left damp the piles of dead underbrush and detritus that piled around the surface roots and between the trees but already the mist burned away higher by the branches. The brook fed by a spring at a far higher elevation seemed never to sleep but nonetheless awakened with ripples of insects and leaps of brown trout as the water warmed in its descent to the basin formed eons ago from a comet or a meteor or some movement of the earth. At the edge of the basin, the mud gave way to orange-red clay and the earth breathed deeply of the sun.

Somewhere within the soil a stirring grew as the warmth heated channels formed by burrowing grubs and the steady rippling of the stream's music gave way to silence punctuated by tiny percussive explosions as the brook ended and the basin filled. The bellows of bullfrogs disappeared, replaced by the calls of birds and the chattering of tree squirrels. The stirring grew but the ground remained still even as a solitary crane descended to the edge of the shore to dip its beak into the water for a morning meal. The crane hunted at the mouth of the stream, which allowed it to snap up disoriented minnows adjusting from the rapid movement of the brook to the sullen and leisurely ebb and flow of the pool. The bird paid little attention to the soil just beginning to crumble into the basin except to hop left to where the water wasn't murky. The edges of lakes, large or small, always crumbled.

The crane took note, though, when the ground itself began shifting but again only to move its body from the suddenly uncertain land to a section of shore with more purchase so it could continue its pursuit of food. Still, the ground shook and soil danced atop the surface so the crane stepped into the water, wading several feet outward to avoid the growing muddiness and keep up its assault on the darting flashes of silvery light near the surface of the water. It continued its breakfast undeterred, and if it took note of the shifting ground that made up the shores of the small lake, the crane's focus on its meal was not to be outdone by something so easily avoided by flight. A sudden larger flash of

5

silver shimmered past and the bird struck, capturing a full size fish almost as long as the crane's beak. It lifted its head up and began the jerky swallowing motions that would send the trout down its neck when the ground exploded.

As soil shot up and then rained down, transforming the basin into a boiling collection of splashes and darting fish, the crane leapt into the air, still swallowing frantically to keep the fish from disgorging. The attempt, however, was doomed and a strong jerking flap of the trout's body sent it careening back down. The crane turned its head as if indecisive but didn't slow at all as it rose straight up, bypassing the trees as pebbles, soil, dust, and clay alternately shot and billowed out. Its wings caught the current and it extended them, pausing for only a moment as it glanced at the mayhem in the basin before traveling upstream to finish its meal on quieter waters.

The trout was not as fortunate as the bird. It fell through the air but never reached the water as a sudden snapping strike from the shoreline closed strong jaws around the glistening form and old memories fought to form but failed. The taste of the fish was familiar but to the creature on the soil the familiarity made no sense at all. There was something hiding in his mind, something that would explain the fish and the clay and the long sleep in the soil but knowledge of its existence wasn't enough to distract him from the sudden newness of the world around him. He shook his head and then dipped it into the water to clean it. There was still murkiness but it was settling, and the creature stared in wonder at the algae, the weeds, the tiny minnow, the larger bass and trout, the colorful carp, and the little crustaceans crawling from cracks and rocks. Slowly, he lifted his head from the water. The chaos at the water's edge had cleared enough that he could see the surface of the water, and on it he could see himself reflected.

The glistening drops of water traveling along his brow seemed to magnify the deep red of overlapping scales and the darker, almost brownish-red ridges that framed his eyes and his snout. He didn't know this place. He didn't know why he was there. He didn't know the soil and couldn't recall knowing of the existence of soil. For that matter, he couldn't recall if he knew of the existence of water or of crustaceans or minnows or fish, though the insistence of memory about the taste of the trout in his stomach suggested he had to.

He was not alone. Gradually, he became aware of movement and turned to see others like him.

Like him.

Not him.

Again, desperate memories fought to rise from deep within but none of them broke the surface as he looked from figure to figure along the banks of the basin. There were a dozen or so, great ancients that stood two or three times taller than he stood along with hatchlings about half his size. He closed his eyes and willed himself to remember why he knew to call the larger creatures ancients or elders, why he knew to call the younger hatchlings. There were greens and blacks and blues along with a few, like him, whose scales gleamed in red splendor.

Splendor.

How did he know that each of them believed his own color was perfect?

He closed his eyes and took in a deep breath, willing himself to remember. He could feel the thoughts fighting to break out but became distracted by the scents and the temperatures in the air. Far from the lake, a creature filled with heat loped patiently behind a smaller, skittish creature upwind and unaware of its presence. The creature knew that as long as the hunter kept silent until it closed the distance, it would likely make a meal of the other. Within the basin, a great fish swam, a fish that had lived decades in the basin, a fish four or five times larger than the largest of the others of its kind that fed from the bottom. He could smell it, could feel the ripples of its movement, and could even sense the respect and distance afforded it by other fish. By far, though, the fish were more wary of threats from above, the cranes and eagles and gulls and ducks that hunted them, diving through the air like—

Like me.

Again memories tried and failed to surface. On the shore, the creature felt his shoulders tensing and then stretching as he spread his wings. They weren't like the birds. The birds' wings were lighter, more controlled. His wings were membranous, not quite like the bats but—bats? How did he know of bats? They weren't like him, either. Hot blood flowed through bats and fur rather than scales covered their skin. His wings were not like the wings of bats. His wings weren't modified arms. He had hind legs with knees and forelegs, arms, without. He had wings that erupted from his shoulders.

And his wings were stiff, almost painfully stiff.

Without consciously deciding to do it, he opened and closed them. He felt dirt falling from them as he did and felt them gradually grow limber. His wings were powerful but for his kind they were weak, would be weak for years until he was older. Until he was elder. Until he was ancient. He spread them wide and thrust his body into the air. Force from his wings sent loose soil back into the basin and sent waves over the surface. He felt the wind cascade over his face as he ascended and felt the familiar exhilaration of the air as he somersaulted above the basin before finding the air currents and beating his wings at the right speed to remain stationary in the sky.

How was the exhilaration familiar? Again, there was no hope to recover the memories but thoughts of the great fish stole from him any desire to do so. He dove, tucking his wings against his body and bulleting into the water. He reached the fish in a second, snatching it from where it lay on the bottom as he arced back up, using his legs to kick the muddy floor before bursting through the surface and somersaulting triumphantly again as he swallowed. It wasn't trout. The trout was a clean, fresh taste and familiar. This was familiar, too, but deep and rich and thick tasting. He realized the fish was bigger than the prey in the forest but smaller than the creature hunting it. He decided he didn't like the taste. The meal was satisfying, though, and he beat his wings to dry them. He stared at the basin. The creatures, his creatures, his kind—they stood around the shore. Most paid him no heed at all though a few of the hatchlings looked in his direction. He wondered what they were. Wondered what he was.

He hovered again as the water in the basin cleared and saw himself on the surface, his body somehow conveying grace and power and danger and majesty. His body seemed like the body of a great, crimson serpent but with strong, broad shoulders and strong, broad haunches more like the lizards from the islands of the ocean to the south even though those lizards were tiny, hunched, and slithered along close to the ground with no majestic outbursts of glorious wings that filled with the air and stretched tautly against the flexible bones that framed them, and his eyes were deep and purple and seemed somehow to convey wisdom and recklessness at the same time because—

How in the world did he know about islands in an ocean to the south? How in the world did he know about lizards? How in the world did he even know to think of a phrase like how in the world? He didn't know any of that. He didn't know why he remembered the taste of trout or why he could fly. He didn't know how he'd come to sleep at the side of the basin, and he didn't know how long he'd slept. As he stared at the distorted reflection of the creature flying above the little lake, he know only one thing. He knew himself.

He was dra'acheck.

He was dragon.

He was Agathon.

He was awake.

Agathon

His wings weren't stiff anymore, and outside of the amused looks his flights would elicit from the ancients and the jealous looks they'd get from those his own age or younger, flying now brought the exhilaration without any of the awkwardness, awkwardness made apparent shortly after he caught the fish and in his moment of triumph plummeted into the pool when the current shifted. He laughed inwardly at himself as he soared with just enough movement in his wings to keep slow forward progress. Below, a dozen or so other dra'acheck— that was what the elders decided to call those who woke but Agathon had already called himself by that name—walked along the floor of the clearing. They'd reach the tree line soon so Agathon let himself fall slowly toward the Earth until he landed in front of the group.

"Show off." Agathon turned lazily and peered at the speaker. It was Bethusula, a sinewy green youngster not much bigger than a hatchling at all. "At least you don't just lie around all day trying to remember."

Agathon nodded. The elders spent an inordinate amount of time trying for force the memories all of the dra'acheck felt buried beneath their conscious minds to the surface. It was a waste. The world was beautiful, almost overwhelming in its kaleidoscope of visual stimulation, it's cacophony of sounds, and its opportunity for exploration and adventure. He'd explored before ever communicating with the others, disappearing into the forest to find the loping hunter and the skittish prey. To some extent he'd been eager to disappear from the humiliation of his flying mishap. He hadn't found the two animals. The hunter killed the hunted within a few minutes of Agathon setting out and he'd instead followed a strange smelling trail until he came upon a large group of tiny creatures. They'd scattered and then disappeared into holes in the ground, and the scattering had amused him so he'd grown silent and waited for them to emerge once more so he could scatter them again.

He'd returned to the lake in the basin to discover hundreds rather than dozens of dra'acheck. They'd awakened in other nearby areas as well, most at slightly higher elevations. None offered help understanding the nature of their existence and after days of pondering, Agathon left to explore. Bethusula left with him and they explored for days before returning. More youngsters joined him for the next outing and more for the next. They'd awakened on a mountain, the tallest mountain in a range that spanned for what seemed like forever. It didn't, though. The range bordered a large forest in an expansive valley that ended with a series of tall hills. Agathon hadn't yet explored beyond the hills. "How long since the awakening?" he asked.

There were a few noncommittal grunts but Bethusula answered, "The sun rose and fell one-hundred and twelve times."

Agathon stared at him. "You counted?"

"Nobody else wanted to." That was Bethu. He took certain things so seriously. It was almost comical except for the sincerity of his intensity. It was he who realized their practices were unsustainable. Game disappeared in a radius surrounding the foot of the mountain. The ancients could eat once and then go without for a great deal of time. In fact, Agathon imagined most of them had fed only three or four times since the awakening. Youngsters and hatchlings, though, had far greater need. Agathon ate when he was hungry, and that meant every five or six days. Hatchlings typically whined for food every other day. The youngest ate daily.

Bethu advocated hunting in different areas of the valley rather than concentrating in one area. Agathon agreed with him. The elders seemed disinterested but gave their blessing on the concept and individual hunting ended with hunting parties instead, hunting parties led by Agathon with Bethusula always at his side.

"Do you sense them?"

"Nothing," Bethu replied.

Agathon looked the rest. Alcheen, Velerak, Fortenesk, and the rest shook their heads but then Bethu's eyes grew wide. "Wait. Wait!" He inhaled deeply through his nostrils and then shook his head. "I thought I did but I can't smell anything."

Agathon laughed. "They're very far away. Of course you can't smell them. Don't try to smell them. Don't try to hear them. Just try to feel them."

Bethusula closed his eyes and Agathon waited. "They're small but not too small. Enough for one of us or two hatchlings, maybe. There have to be a hundreds of them, maybe more. They're moving constantly, just pushing their faces into the ground for food all along the way." He paused. "Not just into the ground. They eat everything. One just ate a lizard or a snake. If it's there, they eat it."

Agathon smiled. "Where are they?"

Bethusula closed his eyes again and when he opened them he nodded to the right of Agathon. "They're that way."

"Then lead the way," Agathon said. He fell into step behind him as the younger dra'acheck led the group into the forest. Bethu was wrong. He was leading them to where the creatures had been about an hour ago but Agathon hoped he would discover his mistake along the way. If he had to, he could lead them to the colony but something about the awakened having to rely solely on him frightened Agathon. He didn't feel afraid of the responsibility so much as he feared the entire community relying overly much on any one of them. Frankly, it didn't feel right for all of them to be gathered, as though a group of such size went against their nature. As often happened, the old memories rose but as always they refused to form and Agathon distracted himself by staring at the effortless way Bethusula snaked over the forest floor in silence.

Bethusula stopped suddenly. "They're not this way," he said.

"Go on."

He turned to the right at a sharp angle and Agathon followed after him smiling. He'd found the right direction, and—

One was dead. It was a straggler and wandered away from the rest of the group but it was dead, pierced by something like a sapling thrown by a creature Agathon had never sensed before. It was a mile away, maybe a mile and a half, and its blood had flowed from its body, inciting it into a rage that died, as it did, before it could reach its attackers. Agathon turned his head to investigate but before he could, the squeals and snorts of the prey signaled the hunting party's success. He felt power surge through him as he leapt into the fray with the others, grabbing one of the creatures in one hand and one in another. They squealed but his grip was far too strong for them to escape. He snapped out at a third with his jaws and felt another rush of excitement as his teeth tore into it. He paused momentarily as he considered his options. The others were attacking as well, and taking his lead to heart, the larger ended up with one in each clawed hand and one held tightly in the jaws. The smaller fumbled a bit and he spit the wounded animal from his mouth and said, "Go after the younger ones."

The wounded creature tried to scramble away but collapsed. Agathon swung his arm, connecting with a tree and ending the squealing of a second. A moment later, his other arm was free as well. The entire hunt took only a few more minutes before a pile of the animals lay on the ground and Agathon roared a triumphant roar. The others joined him, one by one ending their pursuit of the fleeing game and depositing their last trophies on the pile. They'd killed about seventy of them, enough to feed everyone for long enough to allow the creatures to replenish.

Agathon roared again, and when he did he felt a strange burning in his stomach. For a moment, he thought he was ill or weak or something along those lines but the burning grew and as it did it felt right instead of wrong. He roared again, louder and the burning felt like it would burst from him, like it would detonate in all-consuming heat until the forest itself was reduced to ash and smoke. He roared a third time and again the burning grew, until he felt that he and the heat were one, that his wings and legs and claws and eyes and teeth and tail were only fire, fire that could sear the mountains themselves. He roared a fourth time, and when he did the heat exploded.

He felt the fire burn from his gut to his throat and then to his mouth and then outward in a stream of light and heat that tore through the tops of the trees and into the sky as the celebratory roars of the others ended in sudden, shocked silence and blackened branches fell among the carcasses of the meat. Part of him recoiled in terror but the greater part of him opened his mouth widely and willed the stream to flow faster, wider and hotter into the heavens until the sky itself glowed red and shed molten heat like raindrops. It ended as abruptly as it started, though, the burst of fire suddenly disappearing through the trees with nothing but the softly falling ash remaining as evidence it had ever erupted from him.

He closed his mouth as he tried to understand what had just happened. He turned and stared at his companions, who stared back in awe and fear until Bethusula leapt forward, cried out, "Agathon!" and lifted his head to roar at the heavens. The others joined in again, shouting his name in between roars as he stared at the smoldering tree tops in wonder. When he finally broke free of his thoughts he said quietly, "We need to get this food home."

They were halfway to the basin lake, the carcasses dragged on three sleds of woven branches by three of the older members of the party who'd been granted the right to eat one each before the journey started, before Agathon remembered the stray, the one killed by a sapling thrown by the other, different animal.

Yara

The taste of the blood was maddening and to taste it time and time again as they filled the pile with the carcasses that would feed all of the awakened made him ravenous but to Yara, the thought that he would eat before any of the others back on the mountain made no sense. He felt something seething as he watched Bethusula wolf down one of the creatures. Did he not understand that the group hunted for all of the dra'acheck on the mountain and not just for themselves? He saw others eating and the seething seemed to erupt into a dark blur that only calmed when Agathon's face suddenly appeared in front of his.

"Eat, Yara," he said. "We will eat now so we can enjoy the sight of the others eating by the basin." Yara hesitated still. All should eat together, surely, but Agathon seemed to understand his recalcitrance and added, "We have to find a way to bring all of this food back, and I'd like to do in one trip. If we eat our share here, it will help us do that. Less for us to carry." Yara nodded and made his way to pile, selecting the smallest he could find, not out of duty or continued reluctance but simply because he was the smallest who'd joined the hunting party. He'd almost been refused but eventually Agathon relented, and Yara felt pride at the reasons. They were simple. He was a very new hatchling but he was beyond all of the others and beyond most of the younger dra'acheck as well. Perhaps only Agathon was faster and perhaps only Bethusula was brighter.

He pulled the carcass from the pile and it was still more than would fill him so he tore a hind leg from the body and brought it to a softly-colored green dragon, one of the larger ones, and dropped it. "My portion is more than I can eat," he said by explanation and then turned around, suddenly nervous that he might be thanked and somehow concerned that the thanks would almost invalidate the gesture. He was thanked but he was already a short distance away and pretended he hadn't heard it. He felt strangely out of place among the others. He wondered if it was his age, wondered if he would become more individually driven rather than so... so what? Community driven? Was what they had a community? Dra'acheck driven. That was a good enough description.

Agathon.

He was dra'acheck driven. He explored, and there were times when he seemed consumed by his own pursuits but it was Agathon who took it upon

14

himself to teach, to lead. Of course, nobody seemed interested in following for the good of the dragons so much as just to be around him. Yara could understand that. There was something about being in his company that meant traveling with greatness. Still, the others followed him for the excitement and, to some extent at least, for the honor. Why was it Yara alone who followed him to become better, to make the group better?

He shook his head and ate, and the final satisfaction that came with the meal was surprising. This meat was good, better than the fish he'd eaten, and better than the small animals he'd snapped up. He watched the others eating and celebrating. They'd return to camp and all bask in the glow of the appreciation of the others. They'd likely tell stories to the others to impress them, likely treat the hunt as though it were some glorious thing to do instead of simple responsibility to everyone. The elders taught. They had wisdom and life to impart. Why did nobody congratulate them? It was duty.

Duty.

Yara wondered if it were too early to decide to make his life a life of duty. He wondered if others could understand that real honor lay in protecting, serving, contributing to, and leading his kind. He wondered if Agathon would agree. Surely Agathon would. The others? Probably not. They were eager to learn but also eager to be their own dragons, eager to learn so there was no more need to learn, so they could strike out on their own and be free of any obligation. Already some of the larger dra'acheck spoke of moving on, of finding a home of their own.

He understood. Even as young as he was, he understood that there seemed too many in this place. Still, to change locations couldn't be an excuse to eliminate all responsibility to his kind, could it? He leaned down to finish his meal and realized he already had. It was strange to think so much, to contemplate so much. Other dragons didn't seem to. Even Agathon didn't seem to think deeply about anything but instead seemed naturally to instantly arrive at conclusions that made a great deal of sense. Perhaps he misread it. Perhaps Agathon agonized over decisions and then revealed them in a way that made it appear spontaneous.

Perhaps Yara would learn to do so. Perhaps it wasn't a skill that could be learned. Perhaps Agathon really came to conclusions with no effort. Yara leaned down to finish his meal and realized he was done. Realized again. Was it youth? Did he spend such time lost in his mind because of his youth? He sighed. He was young now. He would not always be young.

But he would always remember his duty.

CHAPTER TWO

NOW

Petros

"Patricia, my dear, you're no longer dating a pre-med student. Instead, you're listening to the voice of the newest MD-PhD scholarship recipient. I'm so damned good it took two universities to get me. Anyway, Indiana here I come. But tonight…well, I think congratulations are in order so feel free to be naked on the bed when I get there."

Patricia, my dear?

What the hell was that?

Petros tossed his cell phone onto the passenger seat and shook his head. Already pompous. Maybe that would make him a better doctor. Still, Indiana University only accepted a half dozen students into this particular program, and it offered the program in concert with Purdue. When he finished he'd have a medical degree and a medical research doctorate.

He felt a brief flash of panic when he thought about Patricia. He was pretty certain she'd go to Indiana with him. He'd just worked up the courage to ask his father for a loan to buy an engagement ring, and telling his father immediately before the request that he landed a scholarship to one of the oldest and most successful medical schools in the country, a scholarship that included tuition and also a stipend, would help make the loan happen. Damn, that would make five grand for the ring a pretty easy yes. How easy would the yes be for Patricia, though?

Naked on the bed.

Geez. Was he some kind of teenage horn dog? He could be forgiven for thinking of Patricia's body. Hell, she was perfect. She was here on a track scholarship, and her body reflected it. She was trim and fit and her ass was… "Perfect." Petros felt his cheeks warm in embarrassment as he realized he'd spoken the word aloud. "I guess you are a horn dog, asshole. She's more than her ass." Patricia was a lot more than her ass. She was beautiful, sure, but he was pre-med and beautiful college girls were pretty damned easy to come by. No. That wasn't what made Patricia perfect. She was funny. She was warm. She was sweet. She was caring. She was brilliant, not necessarily in the same way that Petros was brilliant but brilliant nonetheless.

Of course, few people were brilliant the way Petros was brilliant. He skipped first grade, fourth grade, and then seventh grade before his mother refused to allow any more. She kept him from enrolling in college until he was seventeen, and since she frowned on it, he didn't just finish his undergraduate work in two years but instead triple-majored in pre-med, business, and economics. He'd never received any grade other than an A and graduated high school with a 4.38 grade point average. He maintained a 4.0 in college and found no classes challenging at all. In fact, nearly nothing challenged him intellectually.

Patricia did, though. God, she was perfect! She called him a dumb jock just because he was tall and built, even though he didn't play sports competitively. That, too, was something he didn't have to work to accomplish. He'd wrestled the captain of the wrestling team on a dare and actually had to hold back, afraid he'd hurt the guy. Yeah, Petros. You're the picture of manly perfection. He smiled as he realized it was Patricia's voice, laced with sarcasm, he heard say that. Others looked at him like he was some kind of a god, and not a god to be worshipped but a god to be kept at a distance. Sure, there were always girls who wanted to trade favors—his ability to write term papers as fast as he could type for their abilities to induce orgasms—but that wasn't intimacy. Anyway, he stopped taking advantage of that his second year of college when he was paired with Patricia for a project in intercultural communications and his smarts didn't impress her at all.

He laughed out loud as he remembered her rolling her eyes when he tried to take control of the project. "So you're going to do all the work? You're going to write it all by yourself? I'm just gonna look pretty for you?" she'd asked. He hadn't been able to tell if she was joking or serious and he'd paid for that awkwardness with two and a half years of teasing ever since. She wasn't impressed. For eighteen and a half years everyone around him had been impressed and she wasn't. Now, two and a half years later she was the only person he cared about impressing.

Okay, sure—he still wanted his mom and dad to be impressed but that was different. They'd taught him to think of his intelligence as a responsibility, his physical gifts a responsibility as well. Wanting to impress them was different than how he wanted to impress Patricia. Impressing mom and dad basically meant not screwing up. Impressing Patricia meant… well, who knew how the hell he could do that? She sure as heck wasn't letting him coast, that was certain. Frankly, there was something remarkable about being challenged, about finding himself uncertain about every move, finding himself actually seeking approval.

So would she be naked on the bed when he got there?

That was the crazy thing. She was just as likely to react to his voicemail with instant agreement as she was to dismiss it. In fact, she was just as likely to not only be on the bed but to accentuate her nakedness with some kind of sexy lingerie as she was to roll her eyes at him for suggesting it. It was so damned strange. She was giving and loving and kind in all ways—sexually, emotionally, intellectually, and more. On the other hand, she made it clear that Petros didn't have what it took to influence when and how she chose to be any of those things.

It was wonderful frustration.

He exited the freeway and actually kept himself from yelling at the jerk who cut him off. A right turn took him along the access road and three quarters of a mile later, he turned right again past the suburban self-storage facility and then left into Patricia's apartment complex. He felt a sudden and desperate need to forget about the ring and just propose now. Anyway, no ring would impress her. He dismissed the idea, though, because she deserved a ring whether or not she gave a damn. She deserved anything. Everything. He pulled into a space next to the station wagon her grandfather had left for her and turned off his car.

"Oh God. That's good, Charlie." Her voice was strained and distant, and Petros stared at her door. Then, he looked at the radio display. It was off. He shook his head.

It couldn't be her.

He couldn't have heard her anyway.

"Yeah. Like that. Fuck. That's good." That was a man's voice. What the hell? Petros got out of his car and stared into the station wagon, expecting in a sickening way to see her with some asshole named Charlie in the back. Nobody there.

"Yes!" Jesus. Petros had never made Patricia respond like that. What the hell? He made his way to the door, red anger rising up behind his eyes.

"Jesus, how can you even twist like that?" However Patricia was twisting, Charlie wouldn't be enjoying it for long. Petros felt like every bit of his body would explode, like every muscle was wound and ready to spring. He reached for the doorknob, turned it, and pushed it open just as he heard, "Yes! God! Yes! Like that!"

The crashing, snapping sound cleared the red from behind his eyes, leaving him stunned and bewildered. From the look on her face, Patricia felt the same way. She stood about four feet away in sweat pants and a tee-shirt, a stack of mail in her hands. Her eyes were wide with confusion and indecision, indecision about whether the appropriate post-confusion response would be anger or fear.

Petros looked at her for a moment and then down at his hand. He held the door.

Held it.

He'd pulled it from the door jamb with one hand.

"God damn, Charlie. That was so damned hot." The voice wasn't strained anymore. The voice wasn't Patricia's anymore.

He set the door down against the wall just as Patricia asked, "What the hell just happened?"

He gulped hard. "I don't know. I mean, I didn't kick the door or anything."

"Yeah but you have a key so why didn't you use it or just knock?"

He exhaled slowly and said, "I thought I heard something. Yelling." That was almost the truth. "Someone named Charlie yelling and a girl yelling back. I thought you were in trouble."

Her face transformed instantly and she smiled, "I'm fine, Baby. She stepped forward and put her arms around him. "I'm glad I'm leaving this place in a few weeks, though. First my garbage disposal and now the damned door." She leaned against him, resting her head against his chest. "Baby. Calm down. Your heart is beating like crazy." She suddenly pulled away. "Charlie? Did you say Charlie?"

Petros nodded. "Yeah, I thought—"

"That's Hillary's boyfriend. She was afraid their fights would get violent. Come on." She grabbed Petros' hand and pulled him through the open doorway and then left to the staircase. She took the stairs two at a time until she reached the third floor. "Hillary's the only one left in this building. Everyone else is already heading home for the summer." She stepped in front of a door and began banging on it with her fists.

A few minutes later, the door opened and a mousey looking brunette in a bathrobe stared out in fear. When she saw Patricia the fear disappeared from her face and she asked, "What's wrong?"

"Are you okay, Hillary?"

The girl nodded. "Yeah. Is something happening?"

"Petros heard something. He heard fighting. Was Charlie at it again?"

"At it again? Oh! You mean… Sweetie that wasn't Charlie. That was David and he and I broke up. Charlie is the new one, and…" The girl blushed terribly, and Petros felt himself blushing as well. She bit her lip. "Um… sometimes I can be pretty loud."

There was silence and then Patricia gasped. "Oh, God!" She turned to Petros, and he prepared for the inevitable assault but Hillary rescued him.

"That was so sweet, though. I mean, if I had been in trouble, I would have had you guys here to help."

Mortified and mollified, Patricia said, "Yeah, but he'd better learn the difference between… well, you know." The girls hugged and Hillary closed the door. Petros followed her down the stairs. When they stood in front of the broken door again, she said, "Well, that was weird."

Petros nodded. "It must be, like, the echoes or something because the building's empty. I thought it came from your apartment. I don't…" His voice trailed off because Hillary and Charlie were at it again. He looked at Patricia. "Can you hear that?"

"Hear what?"

"You don't hear anything?"

"Am I being kidnapped by a serial killer this time?"

He shook his head. "Keep it up and I might have to kidnap you."

"Give me your phone," she said.

"My phone?"

She smiled. "It's the communication device you use to text people and call people and check email and get information."

He rolled his eyes as he handed it to her. "At least I don't use it to look at cats. Where is your phone anyway?"

"Left it at work. We're going to go pick it up as soon as we fix my door." Using his phone, she called the landlord and after a short argument making it clear she didn't care how recently the doors were installed, how expensive they were, or how architecturally sound they were; she hung up and handed Petros his phone. "He's sending the handyman right over. He bitched at me until he watched the video."

"The video?"

"It's a recording device, new technology that—" She laughed as Petros sighed. "All of the buildings are monitored. He tried to say you broke the door down on purpose and I had to pay and, well you heard everything. Anyway. He saw you just tried to open it and it fell apart so that's that."

Petros nodded. "You want to get out of here?"

She smiled. "Are you kidding me? I have to wait to get the door fixed and then we're getting my phone and coming back. We're staying in tonight. Sure, you were a total dork but you were a total dork because you thought you were being a hero." She stepped forward and kissed his cheek. "Hero's get rewarded." Petros tried to fight back a grin and Patricia giggled. She turned around and he stole a quick glance at her rear end. It was a beautiful as ever, and the sweat pants were a bit tight, accentuating the beauty. Still, he found himself strangely unaroused.

No. There was nothing strange about it. He could still hear Hillary and Charlie. He could hear them as clearly as if they were right there on the walkway in front of Patricia's door.

Petros

Petros stood on the stage, the last words of his speech hanging in the air. It wasn't a particularly good speech, he thought, except for that last exhortation to balance the memories of college with the need to move on, to explore, to develop, and to make a mark in the world. Of course, that part came from Patricia. He stared awkwardly at the crowd and then suddenly the graduating class leapt to their feet, cheering wildly. It was over. For seventy-two years the university nestled in the mountains in Colorado had ended its graduations with the Valedictorian speech. He knew the cheers were for the end of the ceremony as much as for his speech but as the other stood up and cheered as well he pretended they cheered for him.

He stared out at the crowd and suddenly came upon his family. He blinked hard because they were half a football field away and he shouldn't have been able to see them so clearly. Nonetheless, his father's square jaw and choppy, sand-colored hair was set in complete focus and his mother's soft eyes and wavy brown hair right next to him. Uncle Philip was there, of course, as was Uncle Hartford, Uncle Aldous, Uncle—Jesus, everyone was there, cousins and uncles he knew were actually related as well as what seemed like an eternal line of men and women he called uncles and aunts but were really close friends of his parents. He stared at Uncle Philip who, impossibly at this distance, seemed to notice his stare and return it. Petros looked away. Nothing up close looked different. He stared back at his family, and again they seemed focused, like they were just a few feet away. He shook his head violently.

Hillary and Charlie, the broken door, and now this? That was bullshit actually because when he'd left Patricia's apartment the next morning, still reeling from the power of her touch and the intensity of the "hero reward" he'd received, he'd heard shouting when he reached his car. It took him a moment to realize he recognized the voice and then a moment to realize it was a movie star and the shouting was part of a movie he'd seen a few months back. Someone was watching it on Television and he could hear it though he couldn't see any open windows. Later in the week he'd turned a corner and an elementary aged boy had rammed into him with his bicycle. Petros hadn't moved at all and barely felt the impact but the boy had flown through the air toward the street and Petros had leapt forward and then back, catching the boy before he hit the asphalt and making it back to the sidewalk as the traffic sped by.

He looked back at the crowd of relatives and friends but this time instead of focusing on the remarkable fact that he could see them all so clearly at this distance, he instead focused on their presence. He didn't know of any other families that had so many relatives and close friends. They took up three rows by themselves. He stared at his mother's face. She was happy. She'd always been happy. She wasn't giddy or flighty or anything like that. She was just happy. She loved her husband and loved her family and loved her life. His father was happy, too. He could be distant and even hard but when he looked at his wife, his eyes softened in an almost enraptured sort of way. If Petros were ever forced to describe the meaning of love he'd describe his parents.

Could he have that with Patricia?

He pulled his eyes from the sight of his family and ducked as a graduation cap sailed by his head. He laughed as he stood back up and briefly considered throwing his cap but then felt a sudden blinding pain come over him, centered over his forehead but pulsing at his temples. He froze as hurt and nausea washed over him. The headaches. Those had come over the last week as well, and they were terrible. He'd imagined them to be something to do with the stress of graduation or nervousness about his next steps but in concert with the crazy things happening to him he wondered if there was something seriously wrong. Brain lesions could create auditory hallucinations. Every second year student knew that. If he had a tumor, it could impact his vision, his hearing, his—

"You gonna just stare into space or are you gonna congratulate me."

The sound of Patricia's voice brought him back and he smiled at her. "We made it," he said, laughing as joy welled up at the sight of her smile.

She rolled her eyes and said, "We? You had it down before you ever took a class."

He laughed. "Well then you made it."

She put her hands on her hips. "That surprises you?"

He laughed again and felt suddenly gripped by the thought of life without her. What if she didn't go to Indiana? What if the ring wasn't bright enough or if his parents disapproved? He swallowed hard. "Marry me," he said softly.

Patricia stopped laughing. "What did you say?"

"I can't give you anything but another four years of school and maybe six if I decide on multiple specialties and even then if I become a research doctor I'll never be one of those jet set rich guys. I don't have a ring. I was going to borrow the money from my dad but I haven't talked to him yet. I don't have a ring, don't have a diamond. This isn't romantic and it isn't perfect and there aren't flowers or violins and everybody is so damned loud that I can't even hear myself. I can't live without you, though. I can't imagine going to sleep tonight without knowing that I'll see you tomorrow, that I'll see you every tomorrow. I can do anything, anything, and I've been able to do anything since I was little and it's never work and it's never hard but I don't think I could tie my shoelaces anymore without you. I should have planned this and I should have made a speech and I didn't and I suck at this but I can't leave this stage without asking. Marry me, Patricia. Marry me."

She stared at him, her mouth open in shock and for all of his strange senses of late he couldn't see well enough to read her expression, couldn't listen well enough to hear her thoughts. He did, though, see tears well up in her eyes and his heart sank as he prepared himself for her to refuse him.

It leapt instead as she whispered single word.

"Did you say, 'Yes'?"

She nodded?

He stared at her, shock and disbelief suddenly crashing over him. "Yes?"

"Yes," she whispered.

"Yes?"

She stared at him and then the Patricia he knew was back. "Yes, you dumb jock! Yes!"

"Yes!" he shouted as he twirled around. "She said, 'Yes'!" As he twirled, he passed by the microphone, and still live it sent his words out to the celebrating students, faculty, and family. They erupted in applause as she rushed forward and threw her arms around his neck and twirled with him. He held her tightly and when he stopped twirling he saw his father beaming, his mother crying but smiling, and Uncle Philip looking at him pensively.

Justin

"It will have to be a practical demonstration, Justin." Daniel's voice was soft but there was steel within it.

"You think we need to take him to Nevada? You think we need to take him to the desert?"

"I can't tell, Steward," Daniel answered. Steward. That was a title. The conversation had just transformed into something official, something related to the group as a whole. "He is not himself or perhaps who he was isn't who he is now. I saw it at the ceremony, and now the pain has come. If it's as we suspect we must show him, we can't just tell him.

Justin sighed and stood. He made his way to the hutch cabinet, opened it and pulled out a highball glass. He took another, gestured to Daniel, and put it back when Daniel shook his head. He poured himself three fingers of Pernod and took a sip before turning back to the conversation. "What then?"

"How can you drink that? You have a cabinet full of scotch and bourbon and vodka and you drink that candy. My God, Justin, I'll never understand you."

Justin. So, they were back to friends again. Justin laughed and said, "It reminds me of France, and I suppose France is still what I call home."

Daniel smiled. "There are good memories in Paris but there are horrible memories as well. I'll take that drink now." Justin nodded and reached for the bottle. "No! God. Not that stuff. I won't taste anything else all day. Bourbon maybe. Scotch. I don't care. Something strong that doesn't taste like I bought it at a candy stand."

Justin smiled and reached for another bottle. Once he'd filled the second glass, he walked back to Daniel and handed it to him. "Are you sure? I know you're close. You're godfather to him, and you took that seriously. I get that, but you also thought he was going to get into heroin when he was sixteen, and—"

"Well, Jesus, Justin! What other kid has a box of hypodermic needles as part of his science kit? I mean, what the hell was I supposed to think?"

"Okay. Listen. I don't want to force something on him or worse, try to force something on him if we're not sure. He could get hurt."

26

Daniel didn't hesitate. "He smells different, Justin. Haven't you noticed it? Philip and I have both found that he smells more of us, and less of them." He paused and then took a long breath. "What if he's changing?"

Justin stared for a moment and then took a long drink, the sweetness and the licorice almost overwhelming. He put the glass down, empty, and then picked it up again. He walked back to the cabinet and poured another. "I don't remember that being in France when we were there."

"It wasn't. But there was absinthe, and when it was banned, this is what Pernod replaced it with."

"But you can buy Absinthe again."

Justin sighed. "What are you saying?"

"Yeah, I can go pick some up at Beverage Depot right now, it's—"

"No, Daniel. What are you saying about Petros?"

"Yeah," Daniel said. "I know." He drained his drink and said, "If he's changing, he needs to know. I think he is."

"Nobody changes in that direction, though."

"He's not like anyone else. You know that."

"Ah, you've been saying that since he was born."

Daniel shook his head. "I'm not talking about how smart he is or his brightness or anything like that. I'm talking about... Justin. You know what I'm talking about."

"So you think we have to take him to the desert?"

"Would you rather it just happened out here, Steward?"

Steward. It was back to business. Justin sighed. "Have you said anything to him? Has anyone?"

"No. But he'd already be at a doctor's office if he didn't have just enough knowledge from school to be terrified of what they might tell him."

Justin took a deep breath. Naturally, a doctor was out of the question. He'd never been. None of them had. There had never been a need for Petros before, and none of the others ever got sick in a way a doctor could help.

But that was going to be difficult to explain without giving him a reason.

"So, what then are we supposed to do? We just sit him down and say, Petros, you're a—"

"We have to tell him." Cheryl stepped into the room. Justin recognized the look on her face. She was immovable, utterly. Immediately, Philip and Daniel stood, hands at their sides. She smiled at them and gestured for them to sit.

Justin took a breath. "Honey, this is complicated. We've never dealt with this. He's the first, I mean. There's nobody before him that's like him."

She raised an eyebrow and Justin instantly regretted the comment. "Complicated?" she asked. "Well, I suppose I don't know anything about complications. Of course not. I had my whole life planned that one day I'd be rescued by a man who turns out to be—"

"That's not what I meant."

I don't care what you meant. You want him to find out while he'd driving? While he's flying? While he's kissing Patricia? We need to tell him and we need to tell him right away."

"Think about it." That was a new voice. Philip stepped into the room, immediately heading for the liquor cabinet. "It's not fair that he should leave this place without—"

"Without what?" All eyes turned to see Petros standing in the doorway. He looked better somehow but he looked weak as well.

"What have you been doing?" Cheryl asked as she rushed to him.

"I can't stay in my room in the dark every day. I went outside and stayed outside until I could handle it. Without what, Uncle Phil?"

Phil smiled. "We were just talking about you."

Petros rolled his eyes. "I got a perfect score on the PSAT, the SAT, and the MCAT. I was just smart enough to figure that part out on my own."

Phil gestured to Justin. "Your father will have to tell you."

Justin tried desperately to hide his nervousness but fortunately spoke without thinking. "You've been home all this time and we haven't been to a game. I was thinking you were too sick with the headaches. Everyone else says it wouldn't be fair to not go to at least one." He immediately felt guilt over the deception but lost the guilt with his son's response.

Petros brightened up at the words. "I'd love to go. I'll just bring a few bottles of ibuprofen in case."

Cheryl took Petros by the arm and turned him away. "Come on. You're eating and then you're sitting down." As they walked from the room, she glared at Justin. He lifted up his hands, palms up.

"You deserved that look," Daniel said.

"No I didn't."

"She's right, Steward. We're right."

"Yeah." He handed his glass to Daniel. "I know. Pour me another. Let's plan a demonstration."

CHAPTER THREE

THEN

Agathon

As the sun rose and his body warmed, Agathon stretched lazily on the shore of the lake and then sighed contentedly. The pigs had resulted in feasting and celebration for nearly two weeks. Pigs. That was what Tynboleth called them. She looked confused after she said it, and Agathon knew the look. She'd just used knowledge for which she couldn't account, had called into memory information she didn't know existed and didn't know how she'd learned it. She was older, an ancient, and she spent her time with all of them trying desperately to remember what all of their kind seemed to have forgotten. The hatchlings only occasionally showed any sign of the hidden memories but those closer to Agathon's age seemed to have more of the moments even though, like Agathon, such concerns were fleeting and the call for exploration and adventure almost always cut concentration short.

It was likely for the best, he assumed. The elders concentrated for hours at a time, for days, and never seemed to make any progress toward recall. He turned his head and saw Bethusula talking to a group of hatchlings. He didn't really pay attention to the words but he knew he was regaling them with tales of the fire. They pestered Bethu for the story constantly since they learned the fire wasn't something unique to Agathon but instead a trait common to the dra'acheck, something they would all some day be able to do. He considered joining the group but decided against it. If he did, he'd likely end up escorting hatchlings into the forest and he didn't really feel up to it.

The hatchlings adored him. In fact, almost all of the dra'acheck did other than the elders. They didn't dislike him, at least he didn't think they did, but they were different than the rest, far more subdued and almost reluctant to act in any circumstances. All of them but Tynboleth. She'd been kind to

30

Agathon, beyond kind. While other ancients seemed dismissive of his exuberance, she'd instead encouraged him and even if sometimes her encouragement was more indulgence than anything else, he still appreciated her sincerity and her love.

Love.

That was the word. He realized she loved him, realized she protected him and encouraged him because she loved him. A curious thought occurred to him and though he feared she'd be asleep, he stretched his wings and flew toward the rock outcroppings she favored higher up the mountain. He passed over Godon, who slept in a depression Agathon believed the ancient had borrowed out himself. Godon was immense, his deep indigo so dark it was almost black. He was the oldest of them, so old that the power within the elder was tempered by frailty. Godon rarely ate, and when he did he ate only because someone brought him food. Agathon wondered why he would have awoken to have only a short time in this world. Of course, he had no idea why any of them woke, young or old. But despite whatever his age, one undeniable fact stayed ever present. Godon was powerful. Beyond powerful actually. Perhaps time will claim his life before any of the others, but nothing else in creation could do it. No creature in the waters nor beasts of the land could compare to Godon. Agathon doubted even the 3 strongest of their kind combined would be a match for Godon. He considered returning to the basin and bringing back a pig for him but decided against it. Perhaps later he'd bring one or perhaps he'd hunt and return with something else for Godon.

He continued upward, a strange wistfulness filling him as he realized the ancient might have little time before he left them. He tried not to think about it and instead focused ahead on the spot Tynboleth favored. He landed on thick ledge a few lengths from her, disappointed because she indeed still slept.

"You're up early, Agathon," she said without opening her eyes.

He chuckled. "I don't understand why the elders sleep so much of the day away but what I really don't understand is how hard it is to tell if you're awake or asleep." She grunted noncommittally and he asked his question. "Are you my mother?"

Her eyes opened then and her head came up and around as she stared at him. He felt a moment of almost overwhelming awe. It was strange, almost like the feeling that first day when he'd lost flight and fell toward the lake. He felt a flash of panic before it passed as it always did. Almost any of the elders had that effect when they stared intently at the younger dra'acheck. He had that effect on some of the hatchlings. He was no better at dealing with it than he had been the first time. "No," she said. "I am not your mother."

"How do you know?" he asked.

She stared at him for a moment longer and said, "How do I know anything? How did I know you brought us swine? How did you know to gather your fire? How do—"

"I didn't know how to gather my fire. I roared and it just escaped."

She smiled at him and put her head back onto her legs. "I am not your mother."

"Do you know my mother?"

She tilted her head. "I know only the dra'acheck here, Agathon."

"But you protect me. You treat me like I'm your son."

She smiled. "Shall I be your mother, then, Agathon? Shall I be a mother to you and shall you be a son to me?"

"Are you? Am I?"

She laughed softly, and the sound sent musical ripples through the air that seemed almost perfect in pitch and filled him with an almost overwhelming sense of well-being. "I am if we choose it to be. You are if we choose it to be."

"Then I choose it."

She didn't respond and after a while Agathon decided she slept again so he stepped over the ledge, caught the wind, and soared down. It was strangely comforting to have decided things despite the curious way he and Tynboleth went about it. He flew faster, suddenly energized. He'd intended to return to the basin but instead he continued his flight, circling above the valley and exalting in the sounds and smells and sights. He could sense the pigs. There were already seven young born since the hunt and they behaved as though the hunt never happened. He could sense larger animals, tall animals with horns like branches on their heads who walked around the outskirts of the valley but lived beyond the hills. Of course, the smaller animals were everywhere, the same hopping ones he'd scattered before, the squirrels that filled the trees, the tiny creatures that scurried on the forest floor. There were insects and fish and more.

But there were no dra'acheck. They all gathered on the mountain, the young and the hatchlings just stirring but not yet recovered from the unexpected and enormous meal. The ancients, though, slept as they always did and would stay close to where they woke all day. The valley was clear of his kind but that didn't concern Aragon at all. He wasn't searching for dra'acheck. He wasn't searching for pigs or elk or wolves or mice or any of the other denizens of the valley.

He was searching for the other animal, the strange one that didn't kill with teeth or claws but instead with sharpened saplings.

Agathon

Agathon turned his body just a yard or two from the gap between the boulders, and as he glided through the narrow passage he considered just how automatic flight had become, how the joy of the air seemed distant now, not because it held no appeal—there was still overwhelming power and grandeur in soaring over the trees and the land—but because the newness, the discovery was gone. The risk, Agathon. The risk is gone. He shot from between the boulders and straightened up with a laugh. It was the risk. In the beginning the possibility of falling was strong, a terror that gradually became a fear and then a worry and then an afterthought but now it wasn't even a consideration, and without the risk of consequences there just wasn't much fun to it, he supposed. He heard wild sheep, hairy beasts that strayed over the hills and into the valley about… when was that? He wished Bethusula was with him to tell him how many thousands of times the sun had risen and fallen since the ram with enormous curving horns led his harem on eleven females and seven young over the hills and into the valley.

How many thousands of sunrises since the Awakening?

Bethu would have a number. He'd deliver it without hesitation. There were many thousands. Tens of them. Perhaps hundreds of them. Those who awoke on the mountain numbered fewer than a hundred dra'acheck. Three generations had come and already the younger paired off for a fourth generation. Now, the mountain held four or five times the population but that number represented only a portion of the race. It had been with the first generation after the awakening that the migration had come, Bethusula, actually, taking his mate and his young hatchling, over the hills and away. He persuaded an elder, a thin and sinewy but brilliant ancient named Horchak to accompany them as a teacher for his son and they set off.

Something about that felt right.

It felt right the way the unknown memories felt right. Understanding seemed to fall over the dra'acheck. They were not a race given to community but instead to solitude. Others soon took the same path and with each successive generation they made their way out of the mountains of the awakening and out of the valley and past the hills. Dra'acheck with no interest in mates left to live solitary lives. Mothers with children but no males took their children and left. It was right. It was good.

But they returned. They always gathered, traveling every second or third summer or every fifth winter or just sporadically, traveling back to the mountain of awakening. Day to day life was solitude but longing for other dra'acheck grew over time until the desire to see others became longing and the longing became need. They returned unannounced and they returned for great gatherings that seemed to spontaneously erupt from nothing Agathon could place. He traveled to one such gathering now, and the familiar smells and sights of the valley filled him.

When Agathon left the valley, he travelled west with two others. Artemi, one of the awakened who'd explored the valley with him in the early years of the awakening, was a fierce hunter, particularly skilled in tracking and almost as perceptive as Agathon when it came to the strange, long-range perception that sensed prey from miles off. The second was Justinian, one of the first generation of dragons born after the awakening. Agathon had watched as Elenda and Ffirth, two of the younger dra'acheck who'd awakened, took great joy in their new son. Two years later, Justinian was orphaned when his parents explored a cave on the far side of the mountain range and it collapsed over them. Artemi, who'd been close to Elenda and Ffirth, took responsibility for raising Justinian but it was Agathon that molded the hatchling into the dragon he became. The two were likely already at the basin but neither knew of Agathon's purpose. In this case, the visit to the mountain wasn't a social call, not really.

Their travels took them to untouched wilds filled with creatures that seemed magnificent and impossible. None could compare to the dra'acheck but unlike the others of his kind, those who treated the others as beneath notice except for food or as another predator reducing the opportunity for food, Agathon found them fascinating. Two creatures might serve the same purpose, like the birds and the dog-like creatures that both ate carcasses. They both dealt with the dead and kept their bodies from polluting the waters or bringing sickness but they were so different! He once spent five decades watching a river. In the first years, a disease killed a group of large cats, and the grazing creatures ran free, devastating the vegetation. Before long, there wasn't a river but several, banks collapsing and reforming in different ways without the stability of the shrubs and trees. Twenty-two years later, a fire miles away drove more cats from a scorched valley to the same river. He watched as the antelope and deer and sheep and other animals fled from the river to the forests. He watched as the trees re-grew and the plants stabilized. He watched as animals that had disappeared when the river became streams suddenly returned again.

He watched as the entire area became something different just because the cats returned. There weren't very many of them but they'd altered the area forever. There was something to that, some balance that was worthy of attention.

He wasn't headed to the gathering to share that, though. He already had, years before. He was heading to the gathering because the he'd finally discovered the strange creature, the one that had captured his attention. From the plains and the river, Agathon and his companions travelled high into the mountains of the north, delighting in the snow and it was there Agathon saw the village of creatures who had no fur of their own so dressed in the fur of animals they killed with sharpened sticks and slings. He watched them for a year, never revealing himself to them or them to his companions. He silently followed them as they hunted creatures not unlike the grazers by the river, killing far more than they could eat but smoking some of the flesh and storing more on the icy peaks for against winter time. He watched as they cultivated plants and watched as they used fire to temper metal tips to their sticks.

How these creatures had come to the valley so long ago, he didn't know. Nonetheless, Agathon felt drawn to them. They didn't act like the other animals. There were animals that built shelters and even animals that herded other animals in their way, and there were even animals that cooperated with one another but these were different. They didn't act on instinct alone but made choices, and some of the choices appeared to be self-sacrificing choices. He could hear them speaking to each other and not like the other animals spoke, not just warning grunts of chest-puffing indications of size and territory and sexual prowess. These creatures that killed with sticks were unlike the rest. They behaved like the dra'acheck.

As he felt the familiar swirl of the air currents of the mountain, he quickened his pace. He looked down and saw the small clearing where he'd first wrestled with Vertina, an awakened just slightly younger he'd believed for a time would be his mate. It wasn't to be, though. They'd enjoyed each other but in the end Vertina wanted a perch, a cave, a basin, a home. She wanted everything Agathon didn't. They'd parted on friendly terms and she remained at the basin, eventually leaving with a younger dra'acheck and heading far to the east. He turned his head and was surprised to see one of the familiar landmarks gone. An earthquake or something else had sheared off the face of a cliff, leaving it jagged and ripped instead of smooth. How long had it been since he'd visited the valley? He felt strange about time. He knew it passed and he knew even ancients aged unto death. One had already died in her sleep. Jaanan was mate to Godon and had passed shortly after Justinian's birth. Perhaps more were gone.

He dove suddenly, crashing through the trees and splintering branches as he slammed through the canopy and raced among the trees, swerving and veering as he moved. It would have been foolish if he'd intended to hunt but he wasn't interested in game but simply in recapturing the excitement thoughts of Jaanan's death had stolen. He darted around a bear which roared for a brief moment before the sound disappeared in a terrified squeal and it dashed madly through the underbrush to safety. He startled a pair of pigs and a pack of wolves as well before he shot up and out of the forest in a cascading detonation of leaves and wood. In the air again, he spun a few times, heart beating faster and his mind filled with wonder again. He was only a mile or two from the basin now, and he flew forward, thoughts of Tynboleth suddenly front and center.

Agathon

There was already a great deal of excitement in the air when he passed over the basin lake and it came not just the sudden flood of memories, memories built over centuries, but instead the sights and sounds of so many dra'acheck in the same place. They basked or moved like an ocean of blues, greens, yellows, purples, reds, and more. Hatchlings dotted the shore of the lake, some so new they only tentatively tried to enter the water, and Agathon smiled at the thought of all of them someday careening through the air or roaring in the trees.

He made his way up to Tynboleth's ledge, the ledge she made her home for four generations of the dra'acheck, and softly landed. Tynboleth lifted her head lazily and, as was typical, treated him as though they'd spoken just yesterday and not been parted for decades. "Have you eaten? There is a flock of sheep on the south slope generally unmolested by the young."

Agathon smiled. "You look well, Mother."

"I look old. I look tired. That makes sense because I am both." He didn't think she looked old and there was nothing in her behavior that seemed particularly tired or in her look that seemed any way different than she always looked.

"Then you've been old and tired since we met."

She nodded. "I suppose I have. You want something, Agathon. You're not just paying your respects."

"I have watched the world, seen creatures, and begun to understand things. I've learned how we over hunted the foot of the mountain and how Bethu and I rotated our grounds kept food available. We didn't know it when we did it but I saw it in a place miles from here. I've learned no creatures, not even the biggest of the killers, can compare to us, not in power. There are none that live as we do, either. Except one. But it's not big. It's not even a killer, though it kills. It lives like us, though, I think. It lives like us and speaks and cooperates." She looked amused by his words but then again Tynboleth always looked amused at his words. "They don't cooperate like we do. We hunt together. We celebrate. They do that. But they also grow plants and build dwellings and burn their food over fires. They talk and—"

"What do they say?"

The question seemed odd, and it took a moment for Agathon to respond. "I… they don't use the same words we use. I don't know their language."

Tynboleth smiled indulgently and said, "You saw creatures and you don't know what they are and you don't know how they speak and you don't know anything about them. Do you think I have some magic that will let me tell you all you want to know?"

"No! I just… well, yes. I guess I do."

Tynboleth laughed, and for a moment Agathon felt warmth like when he was a hatchling, which was impossible, of course, since he awoke older than that, but the feeling was powerful and comforting, even as it made him feel foolish. He said softly, "Mother, I must know what these creatures are. I sensed one years ago in the valley. Just one. When we found the pigs right after we woke. It hunted the pigs, too, but it found one that wandered from the herd and killed it with a stick. I've never come across another one of them until now."

Tynboleth arched her neck, her scales clicking slightly as she moved and she turned to stare at him with another smile. This time, the awe, that all-consuming desire to flee didn't come. One of her eyes opened a bit, and Agathon wondered if she knew he'd not been affected. "Why do you presume to think I would know, Agathon? Why do you come to me for answers to things far away when you know I make the stone wear away right here under the weight of my body because I'd rather perch atop my rock for years at a time than move? Why do—"

"Enough, Tynboleth," a stentorian voice sounded. Agathon turned and his eyes widened at the sight of Godon, the ancient who defined the very idea of ancients. His skin was deeper now, even deeper and darker than before so that to look at the purple of his scales wasn't to see color but to peer into the darkness of the night sky or into the depths of a cave with no light. He moved with grace despite his age and settled next to Tynboleth. "It was man, Agathon. It was man, and you're fortunate you survived."

Agathon realized he'd expected Tynboleth to know about them, and it made perfect sense that Godon would know about them as well but the warning made no sense at all, as though he'd just been warned to avoid hunting pigs because some of them had tusks, tusks that might devastate a wolf or another boar but couldn't even penetrate the skin of a new hatchling. "They are not our friends," Godon continued, his deep rumbling voice ominous, adding even more gravity to an impossible suggestion. "We must avoid them, must stay out of their sight."

"I don't understand. How could they hurt us? I'm not even as large as I will be but I'm larger than six or seven of them together. How could they pierce my scales? How could they harm me?"

The ancient dragon shook his head slowly. "The humans are an old race, older even than ours, and their size is not their strength any more than the largest among us is the strongest. They are clever and cunning and with bodies that can't withstand the elements they nonetheless carve lives for themselves wherever they choose." Agathon thought of the snow, of the men, even their young, thriving in the cold. "They build their claws and their teeth, and they attack and if they fail more come and they attack and if they fail more come still until they don't fail."

"But how do you know…" His words trailed off. How did any of the dra'acheck know what they knew?

"You will know soon enough, young one. All of us will, and some who have left have already learned and suffered for the lesson but we need not hasten that day. They are filled with lust for everything, greed for what exists rather than for what is needed. They will come and will keep coming and we must not reveal ourselves to them."

Agathon was silent for a moment and finally breathed out, "But they were not like that, the human's I saw. They worked together. They communicated. They were like us. I don't understand. How can we know? Could not some be as you've described? I once saw a cat by a river kill more than it could eat, as though it killed for the hunt and not for itself, and I thought it cruel but most of the cats didn't do that. Perhaps these humans are like the cats."

Godon inclined his head slightly and again, Agathon was struck that the normal and almost overpowering sense of awe was faint instead. "We have lived among them, Agathon."

"What? But you said we—" He turned to seek Tynboleth in his confusion but instead gasped at the sight of a human, a female human. He had seen them before, covered in furs and plants but before him, the woman was unclothed, and other than a long, flowing mane of golden hair that cascaded over her shoulders, and a wisp of the same between her legs, she was bare, completely bare. She was tiny, so frail, prey and not predator, and Agathon shook his head. They were wrong. How could—? "Mother!"

He reared and would have leapt toward the human if she hadn't lifted her hand and said in the language of the dra'acheck, "I am here, Agathon."

CHAPTER FOUR

NOW

Petros

"Keep up, Petros."

Petros could hear the chuckle in his father's voice and he made sure his own chuckle was filled with as much mocking as he could. Unfortunately, it came out as a stupid kind of cartoonish giggle instead of the derisive laughter he'd intended. He tried to recover. "You're just pissed because I was right."

"Don't say pissed. I'm still your dad."

This time, the laugh was natural and worked as he wanted. "Sorry. Please allow me to rephrase. You're just irritated because I was right about the bullpen and you pinned all your hopes on a rookie who needs another season in the minors at the very least."

"Be a good winner, smartass."

"Don't say smartass. I'm still your son."

Justin laughed. "How the hell do you miss a save when you're three ahead? Anyway, I buy tonight but we can just stop talking about the game now."

"I'm ordering the most expensive thing on the menu."

"I'm taking you to a hole in the wall burger joint, so be my guest."

"I guess I'll have to eat nine or ten burgers then." When his father didn't respond, Petros changed tone. "Why the hel... heck do we have to walk after every game? I mean, we could take the Metroline or just drive."

"You've always liked the walks."

He had liked the walks. Things felt strangely tonight, though. They'd felt strangely for a while, and not for the first time, he felt the recent but all-to-familiar fear rising up. "Dad?" He paused but Justin didn't reply. He waited but there still came no reply. They reached Sunset Boulevard and turned right, and that allowed Petros to change the subject. "Where are we going?"

"How's your head?"

Petros didn't respond right away. His head hurt like hell but he'd almost gotten used to it. The headaches, occasional before graduation, had become constant upon arrival at the family's Bel Air estate. He'd been home a month, and it was strange to fall right back into the routine. Breakfast every morning with his mother about an hour after Justin, his father, left the estate and then every other week a trip with Justin to a ball game. The move home had been easy although leaving Patricia had not been. She'd be flying out in a few weeks but for now she was busy planning the wedding with her sisters and her mother. She'd stay a few weeks and return home and then they'd meet together in Indiana. As of now there was some controversy among her sisters about the wedding date with one faction demanding a snow-filled January wedding at her family's cabin in the Rocky Mountains and another faction holding fast for a June wedding locally. Thankfully, he'd suggested they ought to elope to his mother before mentioning it to his fiancé. Cheryl had piled on an extra helping of sausage gravy over his biscuits and hash browns and told him to shut up and suffer.

The routine, though, was clouded by constant pain. Before long, there was no escape from the pain. When it wasn't sharp, a shooting pain he thought would split his skull, it was dull and throbbing. Nausea made eating near to impossible after his first two weeks. Nothing worked as the pain took him and when he could make his way downstairs in the morning, it was only to stare without eating at the plate that would have delighted him before. It kept up for two weeks until he looked in the mirror and didn't recognize the person staring back. Where he'd been bright and energetic, the face in the mirror was gaunt and hollow. He'd forced himself outside and endured hours of torture in the bright light of the sun until he learned to accept the pain.

"It's better, Dad. I think it's just stress from finishing up, starting up again in the fall, and of course about Patricia."

"Patty's a good find, son."

Petros smiled. He hadn't told Justin just how much Patricia hated the shortened version of her name. Of course, at graduation she hadn't seemed to mind. In fact, she'd been wonderful. She'd moved from relative to relative and hugged and shook and behaved about as perfectly as he could have hoped. She had a kiss on the cheek for Uncle Daniel and Uncle Philip and told them both how Petros talked about them enough she almost felt she knew them. He hadn't asked his father for money for the ring because shortly thereafter, Philip had taken him aside and promised out of the blue to take him to a jeweler friend when they all got back to California.

"Where are we going, Dad?"

"Fifth and Crocker."

"Isn't that, like, skid row?"

"Poor people can't eat? Besides, I'm thinking there might be a way to help with your headaches."

They walked for a while in silence. Finally, Petros spoke. "I… do we have any history of mental illness in our family? I mean back in Greece?"

Justin stopped. "Greece? What makes you think I'm Greek?"

"Well, you have a Roman name and lots of Greeks ended up with Roman names and I have a Greek name and—"

"Why didn't you just ask?"

"Are we Greek?"

Justin began walking again. "Your mom's dad is Irish and her mom is French."

"Yeah but what—"

"I'm a little more complicated."

"Look, Dad. This is important to me. I—"

"What? You want to know if you're descended from Hercules or something?"

"No!" His voice came out a lot louder than he'd intended, and he took a deep breath as he realized it. The immediate narrowing of his father's eyes, the certain response to any open act of disrespect or rebellion, didn't come, though. Instead, Justin seemed, if anything, sympathetic. Emboldened, Petros said, "I think I'm going crazy. I read online that schizophrenia can start right about my age, and I don't know if…"

Justin turned and kept walking. "Follow me. I'll show you something before we eat."

Petros stood. Justin got six or seven steps away before anger seemed to surge. What followed, if not quite a scream, was certainly loud. "Didn't you hear what I just said? Didn't you hear a damned thing? What the hell is—" He stopped instantly when his father turned and stared, this time with eyes narrow.

"Are voices talking to you?"

"No. But sometimes I can hear them. I mean, sometimes it feels like I can hear people talking even though I'm too far away to hear them."

"Do you see things that aren't, smell things that aren't there? Hallucinations?"

"No. Maybe. I don't know. I mean, sometimes things are a lot more vivid. Sometimes mom brings dinner and it's like the first time in my life I ever smelled anything. Sometimes I'm driving and I can read a billboard two miles down the road. I don't..." He gulped hard. "I don't know if it's real or not. I just. Do we have crazy people in our family?"

Justin smiled. "We have our share but not the kind of crazy you think we have." His eyes softened. "You know you can trust me, right Petey?" Petey. He hadn't called him that in years, maybe more than ten years. Sure, his mother still used it often enough to irritate him but not his father. He nodded. "Then let me show you something when we get closer. It might help with everything." With that, Justin turned again and began walking. He seemed faster now but Petros wasn't sure if he followed a bit more reluctantly and therefore more slowly.

They turned on Figueroa and walked a mile or maybe a mile and a half to Second Street. Petros pulled his cell phone from his pocket and swiped the screen. It was ten to eleven. Though Figueroa had been well-lit, Second Street was dark but Justin walked as he always did, as though the darkness held no danger at all. They weren't walking down Sunset to eat at some chain restaurant, though. They were headed right into the poorest area of all, not on a busy street where the biggest threat was drunk kids from UCLA or even from one of the Orange County colleges out for a night on the town.

He would have complained but just musing about it slowed him down, and by now Justin was almost a block ahead. He sighed and began moving faster but before he could get his bearing, his father disappeared. Petros blinked twice and caught a flurry of movement up ahead and to the right, which made no sense because the street was far too dark to see anything. Nonetheless, he rushed forward, shouting, "Dad!"

"Behind you, son." At the sound of Justin's voice Petros whirled around and then stood, confused. He was at least ten yards past his father and

45

at least fifty or even sixty yards away from his starting point before he rushed forward. It couldn't have been more than a five or six seconds from the time he ran. His father stood in front of an alley, and again it seemed impossible that he could see him clearly.

But he could.

He could see clearly, clearly enough to distinguish the weathered red brick of the building on the west side of the front of the alley and the mottled concrete tilt-up wall of the building on the east. His father stood staring impassively. Behind him, he could make out graffiti but couldn't tell what it said. He stared back at his father, and Justin must have noticed the incredulity on his face because he smiled gently and said, "Come here."

"But how did—"

"Come here."

Petros walked slowly back to the alley. At least, he tried to walk slowly. It still felt like he arrived at the mouth of the alley far faster than he should have. He squeezed his eyes shut, shook his head, and reopened them. His father leaned against the side of a somewhat battered car.

"You ever seen one of these?"

"One of what?"

"These cars."

"Have I ever seen cars?"

Justin laughed. "No, I mean one of these. It's an old Town Car. It's what people would…oh, never mind." He stood and put his hand under the rear quarter panel. "This is really gonna suck for a little while but remember I love you."

"What? What sucks? Why won't you tal—" His voice stopped. It just stopped. He saw his father. He saw his father's hand. He saw the car. The sight was arranged impossibly, though. The car was on its side, or at least pretty damned close to on its side, leaning at eighty degrees or so, the passenger side on the ground and the rest of the car… The rest of the car was against his father's hand.

"Let go," Justin said, and he followed his own advice, taking a step back as he moved his hand out of the way. The car fell with a crash that seemed to echo along the alley and reverberate through Petros not only audibly but also physically, as though the impact of the car and then the bouncing as its shocks

46

gradually steadied it send waves through the asphalt, waves that translated into sensation in Petros' legs.

"What the hell is going on, Dad?" As if in response, Justin disappeared. At least, he seemed to disappear. Vaguely, Petros understood he'd just moved quickly, quickly enough that he couldn't immediately distinguish the individual steps.

"Let go, son," he said as he reappeared directly in front of him. Petros felt his hands on his shoulders and then he was flying.

No. Flying suggested some active participation. He was shooting, shooting through the air, and for the first time since they'd stepped onto Second Street time seemed to slow rather than to speed up. Petros watched as he arced upward, his father standing impassively and gradually getting farther away in an almost comical way. He watched as the car entered his vision and disappeared, watched as another line of graffiti became visible, this one legible, although "D4 Homeys" meant nothing to Petros. He watched as he sailed past two dumpsters, the first overflowing with cardboard boxes and the second almost empty. He watched as a broken shopping cart came into view and then felt the impact of a wall on his body and time rushed back to normal.

He fell to the ground and landed impossibly on his feet. The shock of the wall was profound but strangely the primary reaction wasn't pain but disbelief. He turned and looked where he'd hit. There were broken bricks in a squarish block where his back had hit. He could feel his head pounding and he fought back rage and then gave in as he whirled around. Before he could speak, though, his father was there, lifting him up again and staring calmly at his face. "Relax, Petros. Just let it go."

"What the hell am I supposed to let go?" Petros screamed. "You just threw me across the alley." Across the alley. He stared back at the car. It had to be thirty or forty feet away. He turned back to his father but before he could ask anything, he was sailing through the air again. This time, though, time didn't slow at all. Instead he saw the concrete wall approaching at impossible speed and lifted his hands too late to offer himself any protection as he smashed against it. He felt his breath leave him and felt the pulsing pain in his head grow unbearable as he crumpled down, landing first on the vulcanized rubber half-lid of the empty dumpster and then bouncing to the right to fall inside.

The pain in his head seemed to explode until it became all-encompassing but instead of consuming him it energized him, transformed somehow until it was less than pain or more than pain or not pain at all and he roared as he leapt from the dumpster and landed on his feet in front of his father.

And Uncle Philip.

And Uncle Daniel.

He stared at them and they stared back. He felt power fill him, power unlike anything he'd ever experienced.

"What the hell is going on?" he asked.

Justin didn't speak. Philip didn't either. Daniel walked to the town car and simply tore the side mirror from above the passenger door. He walked back and held it up. Petros gasped at the reflection and lifted clawed almost metallic-grey hands in front of his face.

"What the hell am I?"

"We're dra'acheck, Pete," Daniel said. "Dragons."

"I'm a dragon?"

Daniel shook his head and gestured to Justin and Philip. "No. We're dra'acheck. I don't... Aw, damn, Pete. I don't know what the hell you are."

CHAPTER FIVE

THEN

Agathon

Balance was the key, the thing most impacted by the transformation. Sure, he could stand on his hind legs and when flying only rarely used his forelegs at all. These humans, though, balanced and moved so strangely, and he felt the lack of his wings with more intensity than he might have imagined. Awkward. That was the word. He felt awkward, and it was strange to feel something he couldn't remember feeling, at least not for centuries. In fact, Agathon was fairly certain he hadn't felt this emotion since the first weeks of the awakening. It troubled him but simultaneously, it heightened the newness of the situation, the thrilling excitement of the remarkable discovery. Almost immediately upon seeing Tynboleth robed in human form he'd realized he could do the same, realized it with the same strange hidden knowledge that alternately confused, plagued, and liberated all of his kind. He'd immediately tried, concentrating on the golden hair cascading down over the small shoulders, resting in waves over the pillowed breasts. He concentrated on the curve of her body, the way her hips flared, the tiny details like the coloration her skin, pale with flecks of brown in random spots. He focused and tried to change but couldn't.

When he expressed his frustrations, Tynboleth (or at least the human Tynboleth) laughed and asked him why he'd want to change into her. It took him some time to understand. Changing form was one thing but changing into a specific form? There was a human counterpart to the dragon? He wanted to understand it better but with that knowledge came sudden ability, and a brief moment of concentration changed the world into heat and a shimmering blue. In seconds he stared at small pink hands were claws had been and felt as though the pressure of containing all of himself in the tiny form would rend his body, tear it into pieces in an explosion of force.

And then he was Agathon again, and the sudden shift caught him off guard so he fell from the ledge and had to flip over and extend his wings to keep from plummeting. He lighted back in front of Tynboleth and Godon and stared in amazement. Tynboleth, still human, walked to Godon and put her hand on his neck, and the sight of her tiny form next to the deep purple bulk of the eldest of elders was at once contrary to all rationality and somehow perfect. "It usually takes a great deal of concentration and effort to affect a transformation, Agathon. You accomplished it in seconds. Remaining transformed requires even more effort, though it becomes easier with practice. Some of us have remained in human form for weeks at a time." Agathon's eyes widened at the statement. He couldn't imagine remaining in that form for even minutes at a time.

Of course he did now. He did now and he was fairly certain the effort to remain human had less to do with concentration than it did with relearning to function, from moving from a body capable of nearly anything to a body capable of so much less. There were advantages, of course. There was dexterity the smaller hands afforded no dragon could achieve without the transformation. There were places a human body could go too small for a dra'acheck. There was something wondrous, too, about seeing the world from a smaller perspective, to understand how even a raccoon, when cornered, could pose an almost terrifying threat.

But couldn't it be easier to walk?

He'd realized right away what Tynboleth and Godon confirmed. The elders weren't as idle as the rest of the dra'acheck assumed but had explored farther than any of the others, explored and used the human form to spy. It still made no sense to him. The humans Tynboleth feared and Godon reviled were nothing like the humans Agathon saw in the snow. They didn't kill for sport and knew nothing of dragons, certainly nothing enough to suggest they held any ill will. Agathon said nothing of his uncertainty, naturally. Perhaps he might have argued a bit had Tynboleth been alone but with Godon there it felt disrespectful to even question him.

Openly.

He questioned him now or at least questioned his conclusions as he walked along the narrow game trail, scouting for a place to sleep for the night. He'd need somewhere with shelter and somewhere safe from predators. On the first leg of his journey, he'd simply slept in an open field and it not only rained but a sudden growling of wolves sent him scrambling toward trees. The wolves caught up, and though he'd promised himself months as a human he had to transform and send them yelping and screaming away. That had been months ago.

Months.

In this form, months had meaning. As dra'acheck they had none. He appreciated it, oddly enough, because somehow he felt more connected to the world around him when he shared if not the actual, then the theoretical burden of the short lifespan of the other inhabitants. He'd kept human form for almost four months, now, walking toward his home and trying to make his way there using only memories of his flights, aerial perspectives he hoped could translate into landmarks he'd recognize while walking.

He missed his dragon form. He desperately desired it during the day as he walked and ached for it at night as he tried to sleep. He'd learned, though. In fact, he thought he knew more now about this form than even the elders. He thought back on the men he'd seen in the village and realized now their strange chattering had meaning, recognized the meaning. He wondered if perhaps the language of men was only mysterious before a transformation. He recalled the conversations now, recalled discussion of hunts and chewing skin to make it pliable, of keeping fire burning at all times.

Fire.

He'd always loved fire, of course, and he had long since come to the conclusion that all dra'acheck did but it was strange to realize how much more the humans loved it. They huddled near it at night to keep from freezing. They didn't eat their meat raw but cooked it over burning wood. They place sharpened sticks in the fire to harden the wood and they heated rocks and dropped them into snow gathered on a large stone to melt it into water. After walking for months, Agathon could understand the veneration. On more than one occasion, his greatest temptation was transformation just to light a fire.

Of course, he was ravenous for the first month. It took far too long to learn how to catch game, and he'd eventually become skilled with thrown rocks and stealth, catching birds and then rodents. Later, he fashioned a club from a limb he broke from a fallen tree. His stealth worked in his favor but he found the club still only allowed him success with certain animals, fawns for the most part. A close call with a boar sent him racing for high branches after his club simply bounced off the things head. It was there in the tree that he realized he still had qualities from his other self. He'd remained in the tree, frustrated that one of the tiny pigs, the very creatures that had made his reputation centuries ago when he'd singlehandedly killed two dozen and led the others in his party to dispatch with four or five times that number. He'd leapt from the tree in a moment of stupidity and grabbed it, rending it in two. Now, he was reasonably certain of food on any given day. It was raw, though, and except for certain fish, raw didn't appeal to his human form.

He rounded the corner and stopped.

They were there.

Men. Male and female. One man and three females.

Yara

He let his wings catch the currents and purposefully made his way over the gorge and then down between the sheer walls that seemed to erupt from either side of the river though Yara knew a better description would point of that the river sank into the ground and wore the rock away as it did. Perhaps some movement of the earth opened the ground and the river came later. It didn't matter. Yara flew and contemplated such things only because he didn't want to arrive at his destination. It had to be done. Surely it did. Still, if these confrontations continued it was certain that one day either he would kill Bethusula or Bethu would kill him.

No. That was disingenuous. He would kill Bethusula. There were few dragons who equaled Yara's strength and prowess. Agathon could match him, and it was possible some of the elders could but there were few. One day, these skirmishes with Bethu would become battles and then the battles would become war and then Yara would stare down at his rival's body, the first dra'acheck to kill another. It was possible, Yara supposed, that dragon had killed dragon before the awakening but Yara wasn't fully convinced there was a before the awakening in the first place. He was fully convinced that the current path meant Bethusula's death, though.

And for what? Alliances and agreements about game? Would a dragon die over pigs and sheep? He almost roared as he thought about it but caught himself. He had to be rational. He'd had enough battles with Bethu and this last time, holding back from a killing blow was a challenge far harder than it should have been. Frankly, he couldn't understand the reasoning. They'd settled a bit too closely to each other. Fine. So what? Extend Bethu's hunting grounds in one direction and Yara's in the other. Problem solved.

Except it wasn't. The game didn't seem to care about the arrangement at all and one season Yara's land flourished while Bethusula's land remained all but barren. The next year the situations reversed, and while Bethu and Yara acted with restraint, in general, the other dragons, the younger dragons, were impulsive. Yara had hunted and seen the young dragon with the dull coppery scales, one of Bethu's colony, get a sheep not five miles from Yara's cave. Five miles! And this was a year where game favored Bethu's territory!

Yara still didn't understand why so few seemed to take their responsibility to others seriously. He'd argued with Agathon for weeks on end about it, and it seemed so strange that Agathon could be the dragon he was but still urge Yara to act with discretion. Yara smiled. He argued with Agathon almost every time he saw him but his arguments with Agathon were arguments born of respect, arguments between equals.

Equals.

The very thought warmed him. Agathon believed in understanding. Yara believed in action. Both, though, behaved with the same purpose, with the same desire to protect the dra'achek and to serve them. The methods were different, and the disagreements were contentious but the arguments never led to violence or even the possibility of violence, as they did with Bethu. He didn't have to wonder why. He knew. Agathon's love for his race was clear and obvious even though his methods seemed alien to Yara. Bethusula, though seemed intent only on himself, only on his own.

Perhaps I'm too harsh.

Agathon certainly thought that. He'd said time and time again that Yara was all hard edges. He was claws and fangs instead of thought and heart. Perhaps he was right.

Perhaps.

He saw a large shape in the water, one of the swimming lizards that fed on fish or small animals that got too close to the shore. Yara lifted himself up over the edges of the gorge and then flew back down, following the meandering course but ignoring the lizard. He was hungry but a quick glance at the hills to the south had indicated he'd already crossed into Bethu's territory. That lizard didn't belong to him. He wondered why he felt no temptation. He felt hunger, sure, but he felt no temptation. Why was that so strange among him kin?

He followed the river until it abruptly ended in a great lake many times the size of the basin on the mountains of awakening. He skimmed over the surface, moving slowly, dreading the possibility that the impending confrontation would finally be the one that resulted in tragedy. All too soon, though, he crossed the lake and began the ascent up the mountain slop that would lead him to the cave Bethu called home.

He realized the thought of turning back, of letting the transgression with the sheep go, never occurred to him, and he wondered why. He'd certainly rather lose every piece of game in his territory and all territories before being the cause of another dra'acheck's death, an impossibility made more possible with every confrontation with Bethu. Why then was it impossible to turn around? Why was the confrontation inevitable? He sighed as he landed a few dozen yards from the mouth of Bethu's cave. It didn't matter why. It just was.

He took a deep breath but instead of shouting for Bethusula, his voice caught in his throat and he instead heard himself say quietly and almost pleadingly, "Bethu?" He didn't realize the cause of his sudden uneasiness right away but then his mind filled with images of a hatchling from a century before, a hatchling only hours into its life that wandered to the edge of a cliff and fell before anyone could see. Its fledgling wings could do it no good and when its mother realized it was missing, she raced to the cliff just in time to see his body break upon the rocks.

It was death he sensed. It was death he smelled.

A dra'acheck had died, and Yara felt paralyzed. He forced his legs to take a step forward and tried to convince himself he was wrong. He smelled the blood of another animal but the closeness to Bethu's cave mingled the smell of dragons with the blood and all of his fears were empty and wrong. He knew it wasn't the case but it offered him a few seconds of hope until Hotilla stepped out of the cave, the blood of Bethusula, her mate, still gleaming red on her soft amber scales.

"Oh, Yara... Yara..." she whispered but no additional words came as he rushed to her. She was unharmed but she was non-responsive now. He recognized the grief. He'd seen it in the mother who lost her hatchling. He'd seen it among some of the elders as the years finally claimed one of their own.

"How?" he said softly. "How?"

"It was the humans," a tinny voice said, and Yara turned to see the young dragon with the golden scales who stolen a sheep and started his journey. "We were in the forest this morning. He called it exploring. He told us how he would follow Agathon into the forest and how joy was to be found just in finding. He... he saved us."

"Who are you, little one?"

"I am Phineas. Bethusula is my father." The young dragon's eyes suddenly welled with tears but he choked back sobs as he said, "Was my father."

Yara felt rage building but he forced it down and asked quietly, "What happened?" Phineas didn't respond right away, and Yara realized he was ashamed to cry, probably especially ashamed in the presence of his father's adversary. "Tell me, Phineas," he said softly.

"They appeared out of nowhere, it seemed. Father was tracking a group of pigs and telling us about how they were the very first hunt, the very first hunt in the valley by the mountain where he was born. Suddenly, they were everywhere, and they had sharp things they threw and stabbed and…" He lost the battle, weeping. Yara imagined if his anger wasn't growing so intensely he'd likely join Phineas to weep as well.

"Where is your father, Phineas?"

Phineas choked down the sobs and said, "He killed many of them, ten or eleven, maybe more. There were too many, though, and he ordered me to leave, ordered me to take mother with me, to get her away and safe. I didn't want to do it but he ordered me, and…" Yara knew. No dragon as young as Phineas could defy a dragon of Bethu's age.

Hotilla spoke. "I took to the air, and Phineas joined me. There was no way to call fire down on them without… There was no way." She stopped talking again but Phineas took over.

"Father was too close. If they hadn't stabbed him the fire would have been nothing to him but there was blood everywhere. The sticks, their sharp sticks, were inside of him, dozens of them. He was weak and I watched as he stopped struggling altogether. And then I just…"

Yara understood the hesitation. He'd just left his father to die. "Then you obeyed your father and brought your mother to safety, Phineas. That is what you did." He felt pain raising in his chest, pain rapidly changing to anger and from anger to rage. He felt it grow to bursting and lifted his face to the skies as he roared.

He roared.

He roared and heard birds across the lake leap from the trees and take flight in panic. He roared and heard sheep miles away huddle skittishly at the sound. He roared and then stopped roaring, turning his gaze upon Phineas and then back at the sky. "Where?"

Phineas didn't answer but Hotilla did. "To the East."

Yara leapt into the air just as Phineas cried out, "Where are you going?"

He didn't answer. He simply turned east. He didn't answer but Hotilla did. Yara heard her tell him, "He's going to get your father, to bring him to us."

She was right. Bethu would not spend even one night where he was slain or if they took him he would not spend even one night with his killers.

Yara would bring him back but as he opened his senses to the path ahead, he knew that was only half of his task.

The other half was revenge.

Agathon

Agathon took the pottery bowl filled with steaming liquid and Nallal smiled at him. "Drink, Stone." He smiled back as he took a sip and she took her place in front of him, kneeling, as he knelt, and reaching for her own bowl. She took her sip and then they exchanged bowls. At first, Agathon found the custom strange but after almost three decades, he appreciated it. Humans were filled with ritual. He imagined it had something to do with the average lifespan of a human, the tiny window of time so brief as to be meaningless without them. He took a drink from her bowl, and he the strength of the broth, the fattiness and the herbs no longer distracted and unsettled him. He still couldn't understand the blandness of everything they did. He wondered if they found broth as satisfying as he found a freshly killed boar.

Freshly killed.

She, too, took a longer sip. They would drink more deeply from the other's bowl than their own. It was fitting, and he wondered, as he often did, why he could behave as though the feelings he felt in this guise seemed somehow right, somehow more apropos to his very existence than he'd felt as Agathon. He fought the urge to transform right then and leave. Curiosity kept him in place, though. Thirty years with her and more with others and he still didn't understand them entirely.

"You are kind and strong, Nallal," he said. It was ritual but he again felt struck by the significance of the statement. Nallal was kind. She was strong. Among humans, she was a prize. Among dra'acheck she was an insect.

"As are you, Stone," she said as they exchanged bowls again. Agathon drained his, and Nallal did the same with hers.

"You truly came from Ehr-tu, my husband."

Agathon smiled and said, "I am just of the Earth, like you." The lie came easily to him, though he technically told the truth. To the Ehr-Alani, of the Earth meant human. Still, he woke in the Earth, and though the lie weighed heavily on him of late, he brushed aside the guilt as he always did and rose.

"What shall I bring you today?" he asked.

"You bring whatever Ehr-tu gives you. He favors you."

"Why do you say that? I am just a man."

Nallal laughed. "You are no man." Agathon's heart beat crazily at the comment and he found himself fighting to keep from trembling. "You are as I met you, exactly. Thirty times I have celebrated the return of the deer but you are still the same. I have grown old and now the younger women now look on you with eyes full of desire."

Agathon smiled. "Only one woman matters to me, Nallal. She and I shared a meal just moments ago." He pulled her to him and covered her lips with his. He wondered why humans didn't venerate the beauty of age as did the dra'acheck. He wondered if she understood how desperately he wished he might appear older. He kissed her and led her to where furs lined the floor, gently pushing her back onto them and following himself.

She kissed his neck and said, "I wonder why you would give your life to me when there were others more beautiful." He didn't respond. What could he say? How could he tell her that the decades with her were nothing more to him than if she gave five minutes of her time to another?

Tynboleth and Godon were wrong. There were no two ways about it. They were just wrong. Humans weren't mindless beings with nothing but avarice and violence in their hearts. He found them more than willing and ready to live their lives in peace, the vast majority wanting nothing more than to wake, eke out a living from the land, enjoy the living as well as they could, and then sleep to begin all over again. In that, they and the dragons were identical. Humans certainly looked at the world with more wonder, with more trembling. Of course they did. They were fragile and even if they lived a long and productive life, they disappeared from the earth after no time in it at all.

They were diverse, more diverse as the dra'acheck but unlike the dra'acheck they naturally formed into large groups and societies, naturally worked together to accomplish their goals and their hopes and their dreams. Certainly, that made a group of humans more formidable than the sum of its parts but it was wrong to suggest that meant they were a threat as a species, as a race. Certainly individuals were threats but how could a whole race be dismissed? There was nothing about them that suggested they were anything but interesting, if sometimes annoying, creatures.

He stared at the leathers stretched over the saplings that formed the frame of the tent. For a hundred years, he'd heard rumors of dragons, of the great flying snakes that breathed fire and hoarded treasure. He'd listened intently but to him the tales were no more real than the stories hunters would tell of wolves the size of horses. There were elements of truth distorted into caricatures. None of the humans he'd met, lived with, or interacted with had ever seen one. Well, none had ever seen one they knew to be a dragon. They were harmless. They were richly diverse but they were harmless.

He stood and stared at the tent, understanding it was time to leave Nallal and her people. He felt the longing again for the companionship of dragons but it always felt a bit bittersweet to leave. There was more he wanted to learn even though he had almost no confidence he'd be able to gain anything else from another decade. Hell, he hadn't really learned anything useful for the last hundred years and two dozen tribes. Justinian and Atheni surely waited patiently in the snow-covered mountains for his return. He could be with them in a flight of only a few days. He sighed, and the woman leaning against him misinterpreted and leaned over to kiss him again. He patted her back and then kissed her cheek. "I'll be right back," he said.

Nallal laughed softly. "You want to look at the sky. I think you come from the sky. I think Ehr-tu sent you from the sky."

Agathon got to his feet and made his way to the flap that served as a door to the tent. "I am just a man."

The night air was cold and beautiful, and he marveled at how wonderful the temperature felt on his skin, how oblivious he sometimes felt to it while in dragon form. He knew it was weakness, really. A dragon could essentially fly through rain, snow, ice, hail, and sleet without the slightest irritation and could fly for days under the most blistering sun with no discomfort at all. His first forays into this weaker form were filled with the exploration of new sensations, sensations he might never have believed important had he not transformed. Now, though, he valued them. The first weeks he'd spent in the elements taught him more about mankind than all of the studying. How could the dra'acheck fear humans? They were almost like a herd of sheep.

Almost.

Almost but he was dra'acheck and the form called to him constantly. In many ways, Agathon supposed, taking human form wasn't unlike the study he made of the grazers and the predators so long ago. It was wonderful to explore and wonderful to learn but if forced to choose between the bipedal weaklings and the glorious form of the dragon, he wouldn't hesitate at all. He felt the calling potently. He turned to the left and then to the right. The small community slept within their dwellings. There was nobody awake. Nobody to see him. He breathed deeply of the night air and thought of Justinian and Atheni. It was time.

It took only as long as making the decision. The moment the thought occurred to him he felt his body changing. He felt the strange translucence, saw the burst of heat, and wondered briefly why his senses reversed rationality during the change but only briefly because he was Agathon again and he leapt into the air, gathered the wind beneath him, and flew off to find his companions. He thought briefly of Nallal as he'd thought briefly of all who came before her but those thoughts didn't linger but became lost as he waded through the sudden cacophony of smells, senses, sights, and sounds.

He briefly considered traveling right to the mountains, of telling Tynboleth what he'd learned and what he'd seen but the longing for Justinian and Artemi was too strong so he kept his original path, traveling directly over the steppes and then over the hilly country. Gradually the ground grew beneath him as he made his way to the frozen lands he still called home. He was dra'acheck. He was dragon. He was Agathon.

The wind carried him and he breathed deeply of the clouds and the sun until the ground beneath him was white and sparse and he quickened his pace until he saw the peak ahead at which time the pace became frenetic until he lighted at the mouth of the cave and stepped inside. Justinian smiled at him but there was something strange in his demeanor.

"Is he here?" It was a new voice, and Agathon turned to see a lithe dragon, barely adult. Her scales shone softly in the reflection of the cave mouth, a beautiful hue the color of rose crystals.

Justinian said, "This is Linara, Agathon. My mate."

Agathon smiled and stepped closer into the cave. "Well, then. It is time for celebration."

Justinian shook his head. "It's not. Artemi is dead."

CHAPTER SIX

NOW

Alec

Alec stared at the chain link fence, the way that the wires crossed together and how they seemed to create patterns so that instead of seeing a mesh he instead saw lines that seemed constantly shifting and changing. Changing. Always changing. That was Alec, too, he supposed. He was impulsive, even by human standards, and that certainly meant an abundance of concern from his parents and his friends and his relatives and just about every single dra'acheck he ever came into contact with.

But damn! They were so slow! They all thought so ponderously making their way through an idea, and they never seemed to care. At least there'd never been urgency. He could hear above him the sounds of the giant air conditioning units working atop the office building. Nine-hundred and eighty-seven dollars. That's what it would cost the management company to have those on over the weekend. He knew that because his parents owned this building, or rather his pride owned the building through his parents. They'd sent him to work for the property management company, and he'd let the air run. It did seem pretty damned strange for it to run at two or three in the morning on a Friday night.

He turned and, just to be safe, looked again. The office building was four stories tall. There wasn't a single light on the side facing him. He began a circuit of the building even as he felt foolish. The air was on because he left it on. Nobody was working over the weekend because they'd have to tell him to ensure he alerted the security company so there wouldn't be any false alarms. Nobody was there but he still did his circuit and satisfied himself.

It was risky.

Worse than risky.

If his father caught him, there was be punishment, severe punishment. The truth was even if the punishment wasn't too severe, the shame would be terrible. He already lived under a cloud of it that seemed to follow him everywhere. Hell, he had his own studio apartment and could still feel his father's stare, his mother's pained looks as if to say he just wasn't dra'acheck enough.

He was dra'acheck enough all right.

He was more than enough.

And that was the problem. He couldn't help himself. He didn't understand how others found it so easy to fight their nature. He made his way around the building. There wasn't a single light on. The security guards had left at eight and he'd stayed in his office for hours. He walked back to the rear of the building and leaned against the wall, feeling the coolness of the concrete and listening to the sounds of the cars on the freeway.

It seemed cars filled that freeway at all hours and he supposed he could understand it. For years he'd had to restrict his flight to visits to secluded cove in an island about eight miles off the coast. Those visits happened three or four times a year and there he'd been allowed to fly. Those times on the island were the only times he felt real, the only times he felt whole. The movement, the constant sense that the destination was less important than the journey—God! He'd once stayed aloft for almost four days in a row, traveling over the ocean and then back until finally landing in the cove at the last possible moment where his parents waited fretfully to get in the boat that would take them back to their mundane, boring existence.

He leaned against the wall and stared at the chain link fence again. The storage center lay right behind it, the abandoned storage center. He looked at the garage doors: one, two, three, four, five, six... There had to be a hundred units there. He didn't know why it had been abandoned. His parents said something about property tax or something along those lines. It didn't matter. They'd bought it up. They tended to buy up real estate. A year back he'd heard them talking about putting condominiums on the lot. He didn't know; he didn't care. The center was two stories tall, and its horseshoe building formed a sort of a courtyard. He knew there were no cameras. He'd taken them all down when they bought the property and sold them for eleven-hundred dollars and a bottle of vodka to a man who owned a chain of liquor stores. He'd given his parents the eleven-hundred and kept the vodka for himself. The point was that the courtyard offered some privacy as long as nobody was on the third or fourth floor of the office building. He could do whatever he wanted and he could be whomever he wanted. No, not who he wanted to be. He could be who he was.

Including the barbed wire, the fence was probably about nine and a half feet tall. This would be the most dangerous part. He could easily clear the fence, but if there was a risk of discovery, it would be right then. The freeway curved here so there was no part of the fence completely hidden. It was unlikely he'd be seen in the dark but it was possible. He'd already decided on a spot that hid him completely from north bound traffic but exposed him to south but the riskiness of it all hit him hard. Nonetheless, the idea of even five more minutes or, for that matter, even five more seconds without release was too much for him. Alec took a deep breath, ran the four or five yards to the fence and leapt into the air. It was torment not to transform right then, not to continue his upward movement by a quick shifting of himself so that his wings would take control.

It was torment but he managed and a moment later he landed lightly on the crumbling gravel surrounding the unit. His heart beat terribly fast now. He didn't wait to see if anyone had seen him, but instead rushed to the left. He found the alley behind the first set of garage doors and made his way through it to the second story building. At the second story building, it was simply a matter of making his way down to the gate. He heard noise ahead and almost cried out in disappointment. He knew occasional squatters would use the tiny shelter provided by the courtyard until his parents noticed and made him run them out.

He took a deep breath. He wasn't afraid, certainly not afraid of them, but the idea that he wouldn't be able to complete his transformation was horrible. Worse, it was very late. There was a chance the squatters would panic because of the late hour and fight with him. He didn't know if he could control his strength as desperately as he wanted to change. He leaned against the gate and tried not to breath.

And then he heard the shuffling again. Right as his feet a plastic shopping bag blown by the wind had hooked onto the wrought iron gate scraped against the ground. He laughed. He'd forgotten how his senses grew even more heightened when he was close to transforming. He lifted the latch on the gate and stepped inside.

This was it. It had been almost two months. He'd been stuck at his new job and missed the trip to the island. Two months, and he hadn't been able to do this. Frankly, he was proud of himself for waiting, especially since he'd realized how ideal the storage center was for the transformation, how often he'd sat in his office on the fourth floor of the building and stared at the key to having what he couldn't have and desperately wanted. He did a quick look around though he knew he was alone. He couldn't see anyone. He couldn't hear anything other than the cars.

It was time.

He took a deep breath and started the transformation but then stopped. There was someone else there. He was hidden in the shadows, but his voice was not. It came from behind.

"Stop."

Alec didn't know what to say. He started to stammer an excuse, but it was too late. He felt a sharp pain in his shoulder and looked down. It was impossible. A high powered handgun maybe but not an arrow. But there it was: the head glistening red and the shaft protruding sickly from a wound that seemed too small to cause him such pain. He turned around. Whoever had spoken was gone. Maybe. He couldn't tell. He broke the tip from the shaft and then reached behind his back to yank the arrow out. The pain was breathtaking and he fell to his knees.

Dra'acheck.

He'd heal faster in dragon form.

He took a deep breath and began the transformation. It took concentration now, though, and almost immediately another bout of searing pain hit him as another arrowhead exploded through his other shoulder and then from the center of his chest. Another hit, he thought, before he fell to the ground. He groaned in pain.

Pain.

He realized he'd spent most of his life never experiencing real pain. To be dra'acheck among humans meant a life of almost no physical pain.

He felt a foot nudging his shoulder and then flipping him over. He felt the arrows splintering, and the pain was almost blinding. He stared up at his attacker. He couldn't be a random killer and those couldn't be normal arrows. "Why?" he asked. "How?"

He had other questions but the pain kept him from asking them. It didn't matter. His only answer was the sound of the bowstring stretching and the burn of another diamond tipped arrow.

Petros

Petros didn't know what the hell he was either. He stepped back, just one step. It didn't do any good. His reflection in the little side mirror didn't show him enough. He looked down. His skin was thick, grayish. No. It wasn't even skin. What the hell? Scales. He had scales, thick scales like an alligator not smooth scales like a snake. Damn it all. It was like a manga artist drew him. He had a body that would fit right at home in some Japanese anime, and he'd be the villain the heroes had to beat. He looked like some strange superhero combination of the Hulk and... who was that guy? Who was the one that turned himself into a lizard, fought Spiderman? The Lizard. That was it.

That was Petros.

He looked like a combination between the Hulk and the Lizard, except the gray Hulk, not the green Hulk, and except his hands were like claws and his face... His face... Jesus. It was like some kind of a twisted geek's nightmare. It was vaguely human, but only human in the way that animals seem human when personified. It wasn't...

"Well I don't know what the hell I am either," he said.

Daniel chuckled and Petros almost laughed along with him. If Philip had laughed or if his father had laughed, it probably would have brought rage but there was something about Daniel laughing that, even if it didn't mean everything was going to be okay at least gave Petros the chance of a glimmer of a spark of hope that okay wasn't out of the realm of possibility.

The spark faded when he realized he was naked and felt a sudden moment of panic. He rushed to the dumpster. His clothes lay at the bottom or rather the shreds of his clothes lay at the bottom. It made sense. He figured his body was at least twice as large as before the change and the change hadn't been gradual but had exploded over him with enough force that cheap jeans and a polo shirt never had a chance. He looked back at Philip and Daniel and Justinian.

"How can you not know what I am?"

His father sighed heavily. "For some time I thought you'd be...well, I thought you were turning into a dra'acheck. Well, I thought you were a dra'acheck and you were going to transform for the first time, like maybe things were different but this isn't..." He shrugged and looked desperately to Philip and Daniel but they just shrugged in return. "Petros," he said. "It...I don't understand. I just don't know."

"Well, I don't understand either," Petros said. "I'm twenty-one years old. I mean, fuck, Dad! You couldn't have told me about this when I was twelve? I can be the youngest winner of the Harton Prize for Mathematical Achievement but I can't hear this?"

"There was never a reason, Petros. It never came up."

"Dad! You interrupt a conversation to tell someone he's not human!"

Philip stepped forward and put his hand on Petros's shoulder. It felt so strange. Philip, was an enormous man, tall and strong, and for years Petros had to look up to meet his gaze. He was almost two feet taller than him now. "Petros," he said, "until a few weeks ago, we thought you were human."

"That just doesn't make any sense."

"Listen," Justinian said. He crossed over and Petros caught the look in his eyes. He'd be listening and not talking for a while. "We didn't think you'd change. You didn't for twenty-one years. We wondered about it in the beginning but we assumed it would never happen. Your mother is not dra'acheck."

"Mom's human." The words came out softly, almost a whisper, and he turned and looked at the men in front of him. "But you aren't."

"Yes."

"I'm not."

"Yes."

It seemed odd to Petros that he should so easily distinguish himself from humans already. Odd? It seemed insane. It had only been seconds, right? He should have been freaking out and at least throwing some kind of tantrum. Instead, he found himself accepting it and the curious thing about it was the most profound feeling he had was one of relief, relief that he wasn't crazy, relief that the voices he'd heard were real voices (just voices he shouldn't have been able to hear), relief that he wasn't losing his mind, relief that he wasn't in fact suffering from some late-onset schizophrenia, and relief that he was normal.

Normal? How the heck could he come to that conclusion?

He stared silently at his uncles and his father and then a horrible thought hit him. "You're really my father, right?" Justinian smiled warily and nodded. "God," Petros said, "I think I finally understand what Percy meant." The three men looked blankly at him and he smiled. "Fourth grade, except I was younger than everyone else. Percy Talon was one of the kids that didn't stay away from me. He was adopted. He said that meant that no matter how much you loved the people around you in the back of your mind, there were always these thoughts of a prince or a king who was your father, or a queen or a princess who was your mother who spent their entire lives wishing they knew where you had gone to and would someday come and take you away."

"Is that what you want, Pete?" Daniel asked quietly. "You want someone to take you away?"

"Oh, Jesus!" Petros groaned. "Does Mom even know about this?"

"Of course she does." Justinian replied. "Of course she does."

"Of course? No," he said. Everyone stared at him, and Petros felt anger building up again. "There's nothing about this situation that… Of course? You think that just because this is something that—that—that I have to live with that—I mean, this just doesn't make any sense!"

They didn't get it. They looked at him like he was crazy. What in the world was he supposed to do, just blindly accept this thing? "Do you think I'm being unreasonable?" he realized the question was weird primarily because the tone of his voice was so damned even. They just continued to stare at him, complete shock on their faces.

"What? You think that I have to just accept this as though it—it—it isn't the strangest and most bizarre damn thing that's ever happened in my life?" Why did they look confused? What right did they have to be confused?

Justinian didn't say anything. He simply stepped up and grabbed Petros's arm, lifting it in the air. It was human again. It was human again! Petros stared in shock at the pale, pink flesh. It was so strange, too, because he'd always been athletic, never had any trouble whatsoever holding his own in any kind of athletic endeavor and had even avoided sports, afraid he would hurt people because of his suddenly explainable superior strength. Now, looking at that arm, he didn't think he had ever seen anything punier.

"But…wait…how did I…this really happened, right? I mean, I'm not crazy…I…" Suddenly, he realized, this time with a great deal of embarrassment and shame, that he was naked. He was naked, and it wasn't some strange lizard-body naked. It was his body, his human body. He dove toward the town car, crouching behind it. "Dad! Get me some clothes!"

It seemed that Uncle Phil chuckled a little bit, but, thankfully, he reached into his backpack, a backpack Petros hadn't even noticed yet and pulled out a pair of sweatpants and a sweatshirt. He tossed them to him. Hurriedly, he put them on and then walked out. "I just don't understand what is going on," he said. "So I am something you've never seen before, and you're all Dra…Dra'acheck. And…this just makes no sense. What makes me different than you?"

"Take your clothes off again," Justinian said.

He stared in shock at his father. "Why the hell would I do——?"

His father gave him a look that made it impossible, even now, to refuse the request. Then his expression softened. "It takes young dra'acheck a very long time to manage transitions between human and dra'acheck. A very long time. You just turned back without any effort, Pete. Just take your clothes off. Go behind the car if you want do. I want to see if you can change back without being tossed around the alley. I mean, if you prefer, I could toss you around the alley again."

Petros rolled his eyes as he walked around the car. He didn't say what he somehow knew, that at this point he probably had the ability and the strength to toss his father around the alley. It wasn't bravado, and it wasn't rebellion. There was no belligerence. He just knew it. He just knew despite the tremendous and almost remarkable strength his father had shown earlier when he'd somehow forced this change to the surface. He just knew with absolute certainty that he had more strength than Justinian now and for that matter, he knew he was stronger than Uncle Phil and Uncle Daniel.

Perhaps that was why he complied. He'd spent a good deal of his life careful not to let his strength impact those around him, careful to be cognizant of the differences between him and his peers and… He shook his head. It was mental masturbation, a delaying tactic.

He did manage a petty rebellion. He didn't bother getting behind the car but took off the sweatshirt and the sweatpants and though it felt strange and embarrassing to stand there naked in the alleyway, he put them there on the hood of the car and turned defiantly toward his father.

Justinian nodded. "I want you to——"

Petros ignored him and simply changed. He wasn't entirely certain how he did it. It seemed to come instinctively. It seemed to come in the same way that breathing comes. He didn't have to understand that his diaphragm moved, creating a vacuum or compressing the lungs. He didn't have to know any of that in order to accomplish inhalations and exhalations. He didn't need to know how to change either.

He transformed and almost instantly, after a strange and shimmering kind of blurring blue heat, he stood again in grayish scales. Somehow, it felt more comfortable the second time. He switched back, shook his head. "It takes years for people... I mean, for dra'acheck to learn how to do this?"

Justinian just nodded.

"I can't believe this is my new reality." He wanted to add that it sucked but he realized right before the words came out that he actually felt pretty damned badass about it. "If I wake up tomorrow morning and you guys don't remember any of this, I'm going to be so damned pissed."

Uncle Phil laughed. Justinian gave a half-smile. Petros said, "So do we have a secret lair? Do we beat up bad guys and fight supervillains and all that?"

More laughter. Finally Justinian said, "We wait until humanity can handle our existence. That's all."

"God, Dad. What a wasted opportunity. We could be freakin' superheroes." When he saw the look of consternation of Justinian's face he said, "I'm only kidding," even though he really wasn't. Finally, he sighed and said, "Okay. So I'm something different, but what the are you? Change."

"We didn't bring clothes to change into," Phil said.

"That's a cop out," Petros said.

Justinian laughed. Petros watched as he stripped. A moment later, the alleyway seemed bathed in that same blue light, the shimmering and the heat. When it stopped, Justinian no longer stood there, or more accurately Justinian the human no longer stood there. Instead, in the alleyway, looking at Petros with the eyes of his father was a dragon, a real honest-to-goodness Thomas Mallory, Brothers Grimm, J.R.R. Tolkien, Terry Brooks, Gary Gygax, pull out the Monster Manual and the polyhedral dice dragon.

Phineas

Phineas stared down at the scene in the alley. He wasn't sure what that human had become, and he certainly didn't understand what Justinian and Philip and Daniel were doing talking to it but it confirmed suspicions nonetheless. He reached into his pocket and swiped his cell phone but then stopped. He'd need to be much farther away. He'd need to reach the confusion of a crowd before he communicated anything, at least if he wanted any confidence at all that none of the dra'acheck in the alley would know about the communication.

Quickly, he put the phone in his pocket and made his way across the rooftops. It was strange because, on the ground, the city was certainly dark and quiet, but from the height, he could see the cars moving on the freeway, and even without the freeway certain streets were always full. It seemed on a night like this, at least in this country, the city would never sleep. Instead, the cars traveled along the streets until one or two in the morning and then, after a brief lull, more cars would arrive beginning at four or four-thirty as groups of humans went to work. He never understood the constant movement, but, on the other hand, humans lived for such a short time that he supposed it made sense that they should be always moving, always getting to their next destination, always making their way to whatever came after, after, after.

There were no afters for far too many dra'acheck. Yara. His son. Others. It wasn't easy to determine exactly whom to blame for a great many of the deaths but the death of Yara's son at Dorylaeum was easy to determine. That weight belonged directly on Philip's shoulders and for almost ten centuries, Phineas traveled to Eskişehir to place a single stone on the site of Calipha's death and to renew his vow to avenge his adopted brother. He paused and watched the line of bright white dots traveling from the west and bright red dots traveling away. Movement. Constant movement. Movement had decided the battle at Dorylaeum as well. Phineas smiled bitterly as he recalled the terror the flames rising up from the camp had caused. He remembered Yara staring in shock as the Turkish humans fled from the Norman humans. Phineas would likely have been punished that very day if the chaos hadn't taken over. They'd manage to avoid the rest of the Crusades, though. It was easier than expected, really, since Yara had arranged the pride with little contact with the neighbors.

And then Yara had brought them to France and tried to kill Philip.

Phineas shook his head and got moving. He had no difficulty at all leaping across the small street, but the roof of the building on which he landed gave way beneath him. He felt it crashing around him and landed among a series of beds. The entire place smelled of humanity and alcohol. He got up, almost retching. A person lifted his eyes and looked at him through bleary eyes, then turned. He didn't know what it was that made humans destroy themselves the way they did. The reek of alcohol was strong, too strong, but he made his way forward, doing his best not to smell or see or think about any of the sights he saw. And then, quickly, he found a window. It was an easy thing to pry the window open, and an even easier thing to climb outside and lightly land on the street below.

He was too close to the alley. If Justinian and his group became slightly less distracted, they'd be certain to sense him. He began to run, and even that was hobbled because he had to balance the desire to move quickly with the certain knowledge that if he ran too fast, he would draw attention to himself, and any attention was bad attention tonight. Nonetheless, he ran, avoiding all of the lit places, staying to small side streets and running as well as he could but frustrated because he wasn't fully aware of his surroundings and not familiar with the layout of the city. He ran nonetheless, making his way up and down streets, over buildings, until finally he reached mountains. And, at the mountains, he began his climb upward until the lights of the city seemed far away beneath him, and only there at the top did he pull out his phone and dial the number.

It rang twice before someone answered, and Phineas said, "We were right."

And then, with a great leap, he threw himself from the mountain, transforming almost instantly, spreading his wings and flying quickly toward the north.

CHAPTER SEVEN

THEN

Yara

Bethusula.

Images of his rival filled Yara's head.

Counting.

Bethu always did that.

Yara wondered why he didn't think to count how many humans should die in response.

Even though Yara found his excitable manner distasteful and his tendency to caprice unbecoming the thought that he was gone was almost unbearable, and Yara supposed if rage hadn't supplanted grief so perfectly he might have simply collapsed to the ground and wept. Rage did supplant the grief, though, and it filled him, empowered him, and made the beating of his wings sound to him of vengeance and hate.

The hunters were near to their village, and Yara wondered if any knew he pursued them. They didn't appear to know but he wasn't sure if his anger clouded his abilities to sense such things at a distance. He thought of Bethu's body. Their weapons were crude, only just able to pierce the hide so he hadn't been killed cleanly but chopped and pierced with weapons that might have cleaved human bodies with little effort but hacked at Bethu with blunt, tearing force. It hadn't been an easy death. Yara regretted he was unsure how to make a human's death anything other than quick.

He was almost upon them now. They were only a mile away or so. The anger was lovely, and it rose up and filled him, changing even how he saw the tops of the broad-leafed trees from a deep, reflective green to a sickly, shadowed red. He felt the fire warming in his belly but fought back the urge to release it. Fire would be too fast, too simple, and there was something inherently unsatisfying in quick vengeance. Timely vengeance was fine, even desirable. Not quick. Bethu was hacked to death. Hacked! The humans didn't deserve instant incineration. He could feel his blood rushing through his body as his heart beat more and more rapidly.

One more rise.

One more rise and he'd be there.

Damn it all! He crested the ridge and then dove, realizing as he did he'd arrived ahead of the hunters. He'd envisioned tearing them apart while the denizens of the village watched and waited for justice to reach them. A young human looked up and pointed, and a female's eyes opened wide with terror as she threw her arms around the young boy and rushed to a small hut, carrying him in his arms. The terror thrilled the dra'acheck, and though he felt a strange stab of guilt in the back of his mind the thought of hatchlings hacked like Bethusula was far more powerful than any regret. The fire was uncomfortably urgent now anyway, and he let it go, spraying red and yellow death down against the hut as he swooped toward the Earth. When he completed the arc and turned as he ascended, he saw the entire village was in chaos.

It would have been easier to simply release the fire again but again he found himself desperate for a more fitting violence. A half dozen villagers ran toward the tree line, and Yara changed course and headed toward them, landing on the human in front, a thin man in ragged goat skins. Yara heard the crack of the man's spine as the dragon's weight fell upon him and though it gave him a small measure of satisfaction, he was again dissatisfied with the speed of the man's demise. He felt the soft impact of a human at his side and turned his head. The woman hadn't time to stop her forward motion and had simply run into him. He turned his head and closed his jaws around her leg and then snapped his head in the other direction as he bit down hard.

The woman landed several yards away.

Her leg remained in Yara's mouth.

He spat the appendage onto the grass in front of another human who stared at the bloody stump in terror. The woman yards away screamed and Yara finally felt the satisfaction he sought. He roared and swiped at the staring man, his claws ripping into flesh and only slightly disappointing Yara because their sharpness made the cuts clean rather than jagged. A leap crushed the chest of another human and his jaws made quick work of the last. The woman missing a leg still screamed as he leapt into the air and dove again at the village. This time, he didn't hesitate but released his fire in a wide arc, watching joyfully as huts ignited and the screams of the murderers filled the air.

Humans scattered toward the edges of the forest, four or five groups. There was simply no way to reach them all before some would reach the tree line. He dove at the closest group let his fire go, sending a stream though the middle that killed half a dozen and knocked the remaining two to the ground. He landed on one, tearing at him with his claws and then snapped at the other, crushing her in his jaws. He spat her out and lifted up his head in an angry roar that seemed to echo across the burning landscape before he rose again. Instantly two other roars responded, and he headed for another group of runners as he saw Phineas dive at the edges of the trees, his golden scales glistening as he arrived and began a flurry of motion that sent blood and gore spraying in all directions.

Hotilla dove but didn't join in the tearing violence, choosing instead to release her fire and destroy runners from a distance. Yara reached another fleeing group and left the last for the other two as his claws, teeth, and tail danced a composition of death that left another eight humans dead. When he lifted his head, there were only a few humans remaining, perhaps a dozen. One hid in a well, and Yara flew toward it, opening his mouth above the hole in the ground and letting loose with fire that sent screams and steam up over his face. The rest hid in the village, and he took to the air again, joining Hotilla and Phineas there and raining down fire with them until the huts were reduced to flame and smoldering cinders and all sense of life was gone. Only then did Yara return to the ground. The hunters, about twenty of them, were still a few minutes away.

"They must see the smoke," Phineas said. Yara nodded. The young dragon had grown powerful and perceptive since his sheep-stealing days.

"I have killed enough for today," Hotilla said. Yara watched as she lifted her body high on her hind legs, and then leaping into the air. She never killed with her claws or her teeth, and sometimes Yara wondered if she resisted just out of memory, if the thought of any blood of her amber scales was too hard to bear. He watched her rise high into the sky, circle once or twice, and then dart away. It would take her a day or two to reach their home by the gorge.

"How long have we done this, Yara?" Phineas asked.

"Almost three centuries now."

"It still isn't enough."

Yara turned to look at him, hiding a smile. Phineas shared his understanding of the responsibility of dra'acheck to dra'acheck. He understood the effrontery of this puny race that had somehow convinced itself dragons held treasures and wealth, that had somehow turned the death of hatchlings into stories of bravery. It was difficult to avoid pride in the hatchling who'd become a son to him, even when the situation warranted no levity. "No," Yara said. "It is not. But there is more for today."

Phineas lifted his head and closed his eyes. A moment later he said, "They are close. Very close."

A sudden buzzing sound interrupted him and Phineas flinched as one of the human arrows bounced against his cheek and fell harmlessly to the ground. "Remember," Yara warned as he leapt into the air, "Those can pierce if you're too close." Phineas didn't respond but leapt into the air as well. The hunters remained in the trees, and Yara said, "Be patient. Burn behind them and force them into the open."

And then the smell hit him.

Through the smoke and the human blood he smelled it and realized the human hunters had been successful. He roared, and his roar was loud enough that Phineas turned and hovered in the air to stare at him. Yara saw more arrows sailing through the air, bouncing harmlessly from Phineas except for one, which pierced the young dragon's wing. It was a minor wound but it put Phineas off balance, and he spiraled toward the ground. Yara only noted the circumstances in the back of his mind because in the forefront of his mind was nothing but murder, the murder the cowards in the trees had accomplished. He dove toward them, crashing against the top of an Oak tree as fire sprayed before him, the branches splintering and the leaves burning in his path. The hunters, still focused on the smaller dragon, screamed as he reached them, panicking and running from the suddenly unsafe forest. He caught two, throwing one thirty or forty yards to where he crumbled against an old oak and swinging the other against a smaller tree, cracking its trunk, and then against the ground over and over until the man's body was lifeless.

He heard roaring and leapt back toward the village. Phineas was surrounded but already four of the hunters were dead while a dozen others jabbed at the younger dragon with swords and spears. A dive and a swipe sent four of the men flying through the air and all but one scrambling for cover. Phineas dispatched of the foolhardy one with a quick bite down over his head. Yara breathed deeply and sent fire in a wide arc streaming after them. A second later Phineas joined him until the inferno of death melted flesh, metal, and bone into black spots on the ground. Phineas roared in triumph but Yara was silent. Phineas stopped and stared at him. "Are there more?"

"No."

"Shall we leave?"

"There is a hatchling in the forest. They killed her."

Phineas nodded solemnly. "I'll carry her." He headed for the trees but turned and said, "And we'll avenge her."

Again, Yara withheld a smile of pride.

Phineas

He swooped in like a god.

God. That was the perfect term to describe it. Yara, the one who'd fought so constantly with his father swooped in like a god the moment his father was dead. Took over. Took control. The dragon came in and in seconds made it clear he intended to utterly replace Bethuselah, to take over as though Phineas's real father never existed, as though Phineas had sprung from the mind of Yara, that the powerful and always correct Yara had somehow generated Phineas just by thought and was therefore entitled to all of the love and respect Phineas had for Bethuselah, was entitled to be respected, revered, and loved.

And Phineas didn't hesitate to give him all of those things.

Bethuselah wasn't principled. He was good. He loved the dra'acheck and he loved his mate and he loved his son. He did all of those things, though, not based on a moral code or a moral principle but instead based only on his emotions, on his feelings for other dra'acheck.

Yara wasn't like that at all.

There was right.

There was wrong.

There was nothing else.

Impotent. That described Phineas perfectly. Impotent. He'd impotently failed to save his father and impotently allowed his mother's endangerment. Impotence defined him and smothered him and overwhelmed him. It surrounded him just as definitely as the walls of their cave surrounded them. Not all of them, of course. Nothing surrounded him until Bethuselah died and immediately afterward nothing surrounded him except for impotence. It was all.

And then came Yara.

And Phineas felt no impotence again. Oh, in the beginning he felt eagerness, almost painful desire to join Yara on his quests for vengeance, and the waiting forced inaction but not impotence. Power. Yara's power first and then power of his own as Phineas joined him to find the killers, to punish them, and to keep them from killing again.

And the feel of fire! The feel of it erupting from within him and bursting out to consume them as they fled. These creatures were weak, only strong in groups and only, really, when they preyed on dra'acheck who slept or hatchlings caught unaware. The fire was beautiful.

The fire was beautiful but it wasn't nearly as satisfying as the feel of one of them breaking, rending apart from his claws or his jaws. It wasn't quite as satisfying as snatching one up in a hasty dive and then ascending as it tried to free itself and then stopped because freedom so far above the ground meant death. It wasn't quite as satisfying as the panic on its face when he let it go and not quite as satisfying as the scream as it fell.

There were so many wonderful ways to kill them, these creatures that dared to hunt perfect hunters.

So many wonderful ways to do away with them, and probably more for Phineas to learn. He could be patient about that. Yara was a perfect instructor.

Agathon

Atheni was gone, and countless others. Justinian was somber but though Atheni had taken it upon himself to take the role of father to the younger dragon, Agathon had truly performed those duties and although it was unspoken between them, he knew Justinian felt a measure of relief over which of his companions was killed.

Killed.

The idea was almost unthinkable. Humans had killed Atheni, and from what Agathon understood, Atheni was one of many. He was also the exception. Evidently, the humans killed the younger dragons rather than mature dra'acheck. It made sense. The hatchlings were easy prey. Just a few centuries before, a simple rock blade would have pierced Justinian's hide. Now, sharp steel would do very little damage, and if steel were struck against Agathon's scales, it would simply dull the blade. Agathon moved to the ledge and let himself fall forward, spreading his wings and catching the air as he opened his senses. The snow covered land seemed barren but in fact held great herds of huge deer, any one of which would provide a meal for Agathon that would keep him fueled for three or four weeks. A single deer would do the same for both Justinian and Linara.

The two were likely on the way back from the mountain of awakening, the mountain the dra'acheck had come to call Tatra, calling the range the Tatra Mountains. They left shortly after Agathon's return, and he'd learned they'd travelled to the mountains with increasing regularity so that now they traveled there once or twice a year. It seemed so strange. Just a short time ago, humans were mere curiosity but now they were terror, and Agathon couldn't reconcile his experiences with them to the stories.

Evidently, the race had progressed dramatically over the last five or six hundred years and while tents and huts still represented the bulk of humanity, others had gathered in great civilizations and wood and stone dwellings were built in great cities where men ruled other men, some with words and some with violence. Evidently, the cultures were different. There was no race of men, per se. Two of these cities not a day's flight away might consider themselves bitter enemies and war with one another. Great empires grew as well so that a city far to the south on the edge of the sea might rule vast tracts of land even far to the north.

He paused in his thinking when he caught sense of the herd. They were startled, on edge. He realized there were men there, men hunting. He realized with an amused smile they could very well be men from that first village, the one he'd studied for a few decades before rushing home to Tynboleth to share what he'd learned. Surely, those men wouldn't kill a hatchling. The dragons understood that men had different cultures. They had to understand that all men were not enemies, that not all men perceived dragons to be enemies. He sighed as he turned and headed toward the herd. None of this made any sense.

According to Justinian, the Dra'acheck had taken to calling the situations with humans the Hunt.

Hunt.

He didn't care for the name. A hunt was a discreet act. Agathon was on a hunt right now. He was on a hunt and he would get his deer and the hunt would be done. Surely to call it that was to suggest humans did nothing but murder dragons at all times. Justinian said it was if one day the humans hunted their game and gathered herbs and fruit and in the next they worked their fields and built their homes of stone. Then, they sent hordes of men into the mountains and forests, murdering new hatchlings in their sleep. Nobody, not even the elders, had anticipated the level of destruction. They'd anticipated there would be trouble at some point and even recognized humanity as dangerous but none expected this. After all, a human was no match for a dragon.

Human, singular.

When they grouped together, though, the situation was entirely different. Any human foolish enough to venture into the forest alone to fight a dragon was unlikely to return, even if he came upon a hatchling. The newest hatchling was as large as a human and though it might be wounded or even killed, it wouldn't die before dispatching the human that killed it. Naturally, it didn't take the men long to hunt the dragons in war parties. Of course it didn't. Agathon had lived among men who hunted, and though the young would hunt birds and rabbits and other small forest creatures alone, they always hunted larger game in parties. Game? Did they think of dragons as game? When he lived on the steppes, he'd joined groups of hunters who left their settlements to reserved cheers and returned weeks later to shouts of exaltation as they presented the people with antelope, sheep, and more. Those animals were always used completely, from the skins to the meat to the sinews. There were

81

no humans with tools strong enough to use a grown dragon in that manner, at least Agathon didn't believe there were.

Did they kill for sport? There were certainly humans who took joy in the hunt, joy that went beyond the simple need for food and skins. Agathon had hunted next to them, and Agathon found joy in hunting, joy in the moment when his prey was cornered and joy in the moment of the kill. He'd taken the joy as one of the wonderful aspects of life, one of the wondrous things about being dra'acheck. He'd killed often, and rarely did the hunting lack joy. He'd never killed without need, though. Did the humans find joy in killing? Agathon found most men to be like the dra'acheck. They wanted to live their lives, to find their mates, and to rear their children.

The herd was very close, and Agathon slowed, making his way down into the forest where he could study the herd and the men hunting it before hunting his own meal. There were seven of the men hiding in the trees, holding spears at the ready. They cooperated, making simple hand gestures to communicate with the others. He saw one gesture to another, and the second man nodded. The man surely believed he was moving soundlessly and Agathon almost laughed. The herd immediately began moving as the man gingerly stepped forward and then ran to cast his spear. As the heard parted and stampeded off several yards, his spear struck home, felling a young deer as the other men rushed out. One other man got a deer and the others stopped running. Agathon watched as the men efficiently went to work, tying the animals to sleds and pulling them away.

They were done.

Their village needed two, and they'd killed two. Any excitement the men felt was incidental. These men didn't kill for sport. So why did men kill dragons?

According to Justinian, the men killed for profit. It was absurd. Dragons kept no possessions or so few possessions that to kill for them made no sense. Evidently, the killings began as sport or even from fear. A group had descended upon an older dragon, which had easily dispatched them. Later, a group had attacked the same dragon and found the outside of his cave littered with the belongings of the first group. Somehow, that had been embellished and retold so many times that men believed dragons hoarded treasure. That made sense to Agathon. While the dra'acheck were blunt and honest in all ways, he'd noticed humans could never resist embellishing a story. Around the campfires after a successful hunt, he'd heard men tell in glorious detail of the stalking and killing of bears or rams or wolves. He'd seen men turn thirty seconds of action into thirty minutes of storytelling. So now, men hunted dragons believing a prize kill would indeed yield a prize.

His time with men had certainly taught Agathon that they valued possessions but on the other hand nearly all of their leaders treated too much love for possessions as weakness.

Agathon shook his head in wonder. This wasn't a simple situation. Men weren't monsters. They weren't evil. No. That wasn't it. There were monsters among men and there were men who weren't monsters. All men couldn't be classified in the way all dragons could. Despite personalities and differing thought processes, all dragons shared a love for quiet and peace. All dragons shared a tendency to solitude, and all dragons tended to be ponderous in thought and careful in action. He smiled sadly when he thought of Bethusula. He'd been impulsive, rash even. Compared to the average human, though, he was like a village elder who spoke slowly and dispensed wisdom at a glacial pace.

Agathon determined there were no answers available immediately so he took a deep breath and let his senses roam freely for a moment. The men were gone, well into the forest with their game. He crept from the trees and then quickly downed a young deer. He ate as the herd scattered skittishly but he ate quickly, the nervousness of the herd almost overpowering. When he finished he took to the air, a little sluggishly but not too tired. He flew quickly, eager to rest and to think. There had to be an answer to humanity. There had to be.

In short order, he reached the cave, and he knew by scent Justinian and Linara were back. He smiled as he entered and said, "I would have brought you a deer if I'd known you'd be back."

"We must leave again, Agathon," Justinian said.

"Where are you going?"

Linara shook her head. "He means the two of you must leave."

Justinian nodded. "Godon has passed from this world. The elders have chosen you to replace him."

Agathon

Yara might have become the elder. It was strange for Agathon to feel that way, especially strange given the way he and the hot-tempered Yara often found themselves on opposite sides of the issue. Of course, nobody could doubt Yara's commitment to the dra'acheck or his love for his fellow dragons. The story of Bethusula still dazed him. Naturally, that had a great deal to do with learning his friend had been killed but Yara's response was unexpected as well. He and Bethu had seemed bitter rivals, and on more than one occasion Agathon worried one or the other would be the first to die at another dragon's hands. Instead, Yara had taken responsibility for Bethu's mate and son. Hotheaded or not, there was no denying Yara's very consistent perspective on honor.

An elder.

An elder, and not only an elder but the elder who replaced Godon.

In some ways, the burden seemed far too much to bear. He flew silently and actually fantasized that Justinian had misunderstood, that he was traveling back to the Tatra Mountains not to become an elder but instead to pay homage to a new elder, an elder other than himself. "It should have been Yara," he muttered.

"How could you say that? You're what the council needs. You're what all of us needs."

He turned his head and looked at Justinian. "I didn't mean to say that out loud, and I was actually..." He let the words trail off. He wondered if it was ego that he didn't want Justinian know of any insecurities he felt. "If the council wants me, than I will do all I can."

Justinian laughed. "You always do everything you can. It can't be Yara. Yara would have us all at war."

"What do you mean?"

"When Bethusula was killed, Yara went on a rampage. He killed the men that killed Yara but that wasn't enough and for centuries he's been killing humans, destroying whole villages, at every opportunity."

"Even unprovoked?" Justinian didn't reply and Agathon flew around, hovering in the air in front of the younger dragon. "Even unprovoked?"

"I heard you," Justinian said. "I heard you but I had to think. I think about half of the dra'acheck would say his actions are unprovoked while half would probably believe he was justified."

"Because of Bethu?"

"Are you going to turn around or are we going to stay in the air here?"

"Because of Bethu?"

Justinian shook his head. "No. That was a few hundred years ago. Can we please keep moving? I'm no good at floating in the air like this."

Reluctantly, Agathon turned his body around and then fell back so he was even with Justinian as they flew forward. "Then why?"

"Yara kills villages when hunting parties leave them. Sometimes he follows hunting parties home sometimes he destroys them just when they leave. There are at least two instances where the men left to hunt normal game, not dragons."

"How many has he killed?"

"Many hundreds. Maybe thousands. I don't know, Agathon. Maybe many thousands."

"No wonder they hunt us." Justinian didn't respond but Agathon wasn't particularly expecting a response anyway. They passed over the enormous plains that would soon give way to the hills and then the valley and then the mountains. They'd arrive within a day.

After several minutes, Justinian said, "You're not the only one that believes that. A number of dragons believe as Yara does, and a number of them have attacked humans with only slight provocation, even attacking travelers just crossing a forest or traversing a mountain pass, killing them just in case they could be dragon hunters. You know there are humans who believe we demand their female virgins? To the south and west, a group of people tell stories of a kingdom where virgins are chosen by lottery ever year to deliver to a dragon as tribute. Thieves and killers flock to that kingdom promising to rid it of dragons."

"Is it true?"

"It's true that the stories are told. I suppose there could be a dragon who lost a daughter, a young hatchling, and I suppose this could be her revenge but I don't think so. I think humans are convinced we're vicious, dangerous." He paused a moment and then added, "It's easy to imagine something powerful

85

is also evil." He paused again, this time for a longer time before he added quietly, "I think Yara and his followers have contributed to that, at least reinforced it."

"Vicious and dangerous..." Oddly, Agathon had always anticipated awe were a human to see him. Perhaps it was ego. Perhaps it all hearkened back to that first sight of himself reflected on the surface of the water of the basin in the mountain, that first picture of majesty that represented his first exploration, his first discovery. Ego, certainly. It had to be ego. Still, fear and hatred weren't right, weren't natural. "We need to stop this, Justinian."

"Do you mean we as in me and you or—"

"I mean the dra'acheck. We need to stop this."

Justinian nodded. "Of course none of the elders said this to me but almost everyone believes they chose you because everyone believes you can protect us from the Hunt."

"Me?" He shook his head in disbelief.

"Do you really not understand how loved you are, how respected?"

Agathon didn't respond but flew in silence. He wasn't sure if he wanted Justinian to know he hadn't meant stopping the hunt so much as he meant stopping the wholesale killing of humans, presenting to them an image of the dra'acheck that just wasn't accurate by recklessly attacking. If the only interactions humans had with dragons were showered with blood, how could anyone expect there to be anything other than slaughter in response?

Images of Bethusula rose in his mind and terrible sadness weighed on him as he and Justinian continued their journey. Justinian didn't press for conversation, and Agathon was grateful. He was no stranger to leadership among the dra'acheck. He'd taken it upon himself to teach the young almost from the awakening itself. He'd settled territory disputes, helped teach others to understand how to rotate hunting routes so game populations replenished, and he'd even offered advice to dragons seeking mates. Still, the thought of taking leadership at a time like this was daunting. Worse, it was clear to him the council of elders wasn't interested in him being one of the elders so much as they wanted him to be the primary elder, the elder who would somehow find the light in the dark situation, find it and make it brighter.

"I want to speak with Tynboleth before I see anyone else, Justinian," he said. "When we arrive, will you keep the others for a while? They'll want to see me but..."

"Agathon…" Justinian paused and then said, "There is no other dragon who could lead at a time like this, and no other dragon I… I'm trying to say that nobody else could do it and I wouldn't wish this upon you or anyone else but as much as I hate the weight you'll carry I feel hope only because it's you carrying it."

Agathon paused. Justinian was always so serious. He wasn't serious like Yara was serious but he was serious nonetheless. After a moment he said, "Will you ensure me time with Tynboleth?"

"She's not there," the younger dragon said. "She's a half day's flight south of the mountain. She travelled with her daughter and her mate. She's supposed to return tomorrow. Do you want me to take you there?"

Agathon shook his head. "No. Let's get this over with. We'll fly to her tonight and return with her in the morning." He paused for a moment and then said, "Godon is dead. It seems impossible. He was the most powerful creature on this earth. And now, Godon is dead."

Justinian didn't speak for a short while, and when he did it he spoke softly, "But you are alive, Agathon. You are alive and we need an elder with life."

CHAPTER EIGHT

NOW

Justinian

"Of course I know he was there." The words came out a bit more harshly than he intended but if Philip or Daniel took offense to it, they said nothing. Daniel did, however, pause in the midst of pouring drinks for the three of them until Justinian nodded slightly and the liquid began to flow again. He took a deep breath and said, "There was nobody else, though."

"What if he was just in town visiting and came across us by accident?" It was possible. A hundred years ago, the idea would be unthinkable but it wasn't beyond reason at all. Integrating with humanity meant blending in, not to mention supporting himself and his pride. He'd been careful and built a large fortune over centuries but not all stewards ended up in areas with the same opportunities. So, even today many might need to keep real jobs to make ends meet. Perhaps Phineas was in town for a human job. If Justinian traveled overseas and happened upon members of another pride, he'd certainly observe them.

It didn't matter, though. "Even if he came upon us by accident, we need to be wary. Discovering us might be the opportunity he's waited for."

"Opportunity for what?" Petros asked, and all heads turned toward the doorway. Justinian glanced at Daniel, who shook his head slightly and shrugged. He got the same response from Philip. None of the three had heard, smelled, or even sensed him.

Justinian sighed. There was no protecting him. "Revenge."

"Revenge for what?"

"That, son, is a long story."

Petros shrugged. "Well, then," he said. "I guess you'll want to pour a fourth drink." Justinian stared at his son. The boy had always been exceptional but there was something different now. He wasn't dra'acheck. If he were, he'd be fumbling now, trying to make sense of the world. Hell, if he were dra'acheck he likely wouldn't be able to go anywhere unaccompanied. Now, within hours of his first transformation, if the change in him could be called that, he was already confident and already likely better and already powerful in disquieting ways.

"No," Justinian said. "There is much to discuss but there are higher priorities for you. You feel your strength and you feel the empowering of your senses but you need to learn how to control all of them. There will be plenty of time to talk of dragon politics, son. Now is not that time."

Petros hesitated, and Justinian realized he was trying to decide whether to argue. An argument wouldn't be good at all. Though Petros could certainly be excused for knowing nothing of dra'acheck decorum, an argument would require a harsh response from the steward. He didn't relish the thought. Fortunately, Petros didn't argue. He gave a slight nod and said, "Okay. When do I start learning control?"

"As soon as I can arrange it." Again, there was hesitation but again Petros didn't argue. Justinian wondered if he'd ever loved his son more than he did right there. He stared at him for a few moments but then Petros nodded again and stepped out of the door, closing it behind him. A moment later, Justinian lifted a tumbler to his lips and let the alcohol warm its way down his throat. He sighed and turned back to Daniel and Philip.

"Of course I know he was there." The words came out harshly again so he took a deep breath and said, "I didn't mean to snap. I knew he was there but I couldn't find a way to send you after him without opening up a whole new can of worms with Petros."

"Your boy is strong. He's handling this quite well," Philip said.

Daniel nodded. "This must be impossible for him, really, but he's not wallowing in the craziness of the situation."

"He's always been smart, too smart. This solution, though unimaginable, filled in all the questions. His mind likes when the questions are filled in." Justinian sighed and drained his glass.

Daniel rose to refill Justinian's drink. "That may be true for now but there are a great many new questions that will come. God, Justinian, we don't even know what the hell he is."

Justinian sighed. "We know he's Petros. That's enough."

Daniel turned around. "You're not a hatchling. Stop behaving like..." He took a deep breath. "Steward, I... I'm worried about him. Forgive me."

Justinian dismissed the apology with a wave of his hand. "Fill the glasses, Daniel. I would trust you with my life. I suppose I would trust everyone in the pride with my life. Only you and Philip, though, would I trust with the lives of my family. I understand the fear and the worry but for centuries we've been dra'acheck and human. Now, there's something else." Daniel handed him a full glass and he took a deep sip, wishing for what might have been the thousandth time that alcohol affected him the way it affected humans. "Centuries of memories and experience and not any frame of reference for this at all."

"What about Phineas?"

Justinian turned to look at Philip. "How much do you think he saw?"

Philip shrugged. "The alley was filled with shadows and we blocked a great deal of the view. Still, he wasn't a human spying on us. He saw enough. He won't have any idea what it means, though."

Daniel said, "We don't know that he was spying."

Justinian held up a hand. "You're right, Daniel. It doesn't matter, though. The effect is the same. He saw Petros transform and even if he doesn't understand anything about what the transformation was, he saw it."

"Do you think he's here for Philip?"

"I hope so," Philip said but Justinian shot him a look the instantly made him backtrack. "I'm sorry, Steward."

"They came to kill you, Philip." Justinian said. "But that has already cost enough blood. There will be no more shed for a war ten centuries past."

It appeared for a moment that Philip would argue but the defiance melted away, he sighed, and he drained his glass. He set the glass down and said, "I will take no action unless I'm attacked, Steward." Justinian stared at him still so he added, "And I won't seek to be attacked."

Justinian nodded. "We don't know for sure Phineas was here because of anything having to do with us. We'll be careful. In the meantime, I want you and Daniel to head to the mountains with Petros. The need for him to train is no greater, perhaps, but it's certainly more urgent now."

Daniel asked, "What do we tell him?"

"That he needs to control his abilities."

"I don't mean that, Justinian. I mean what do we tell him when he starts asking questions about Philip and about you and Cheryl and—"

"Just use your judgment. If you wonder if it's a good idea, say nothing and send him to me."

The three stood for a while, looking at empty highball glasses. Justinian didn't really want another drink but he stood and walked to pour himself one just to do something. He stared at the liquid and realized they were drinking whisky. He didn't much like it. He hadn't noticed, or had he? The situation with Phineas was bad. Very bad.

Petros

The impact of the tree was astounding, and Petros stumbled back, stunned completely. He shook his head until his vision cleared and then looked. The trunk was splintered. Already, the top of the tree was leaning downward toward the ground. He figured if he left it exactly as it was, by the next day or with the first rainfall, certainly, it would end up broken completely.

Damn. The thing was forty feet tall. He'd just broken the trunk of a tree that was forty feet tall.

"Eventually, you'll learn to control it."

When Philip said it, Petros thought he noted in his voice something oddly disbelieving in the comment. He groaned and rolled his eyes. At least, he thought he rolled his eyes. He wondered if his eyes rolled in this body. "We've been at it for almost a week. I don't feel like I'm getting anywhere."

"We can see the progress, Pete," Daniel said. "I know it's hard for you to see it but we can."

Petros smiled, or at least he thought he smiled. It was funny to be able to see better than he ever could before, smell better, hear better, and even taste better but nonetheless to feel absolutely unskilled at everything he did. "If a tree falls in the woods and nobody is around to hear it, will it still make a noise?"

Daniel looked at him. "What?"

Petros shrugged. "It doesn't matter. I'll hear it now."

Daniel smiled a half smile. It wasn't difficult to see even though Daniel wasn't a human at the moment. He wondered why he found it so easy to see Daniel or, for that matter, Philip or even his father in their dragon form and yet still distinguish them one from the other. It wasn't just the color either. The mannerisms that they had in normal conversations as humans seemed to somehow translate into mannerisms that made no sense for them to have when they were dragons.

Dragons.

Jesus.

There were still times when he thought he'd wake up and see a nurse smiling down at him, a nurse looking at him with a sympathetic expression, and then her eyes opening wide in surprise when she realized he was awake. He still expected that he would find himself the newest newspaper sensation, the young man who fell into a coma and then woke up three years later. It was the craziest situation, but he knew he wasn't dreaming. He knew it couldn't be that. He knew it was real. There was nothing dream-like about it and there was nothing about the knowledge that confused him.

It made no sense. It was strange enough to think his father was a dragon, crazy enough to think that his mother had married his father knowing that. That was crazy enough but the idea that he was some combination of dragon and human was almost impossible to consider. It was like some roleplaying teenager had come up with the perfect thing to be and he was really just an avatar in a video game. It was impossible but he had no trouble believing it, and he didn't understand why.

He almost didn't see Philip strike at him. He had to jump back to avoid the tail. The tail crashed right into the tree and finished the job Petros's headlong run had started.

"Stop daydreaming. Pay attention."

He groaned, tried to roll his eyes again, and then nodded.

"You don't need to be so hard on him," Daniel said.

"He doesn't need your coddling," Philip replied. Then the tail swung again.

The reality was Petros had no problem avoiding attacks like these. The problem wasn't avoidance. The problem was his mind couldn't yet comprehend the speed of his reflexes, so in his mind, he thought he should be a foot away but he ended up four feet away. He would duck just a little bit, trying to avoid a blow but he would end up on the ground. It was impossible to control. He'd run into the tree simply because he'd thought he'd only run a few feet, not yards. On the other hand, his strength was extraordinary, and there was something remarkable about that.

He was supposed to practice controlled dodging and such but the next time Philip's tail shot out toward him, he grabbed it in his hands. Philip grunted as the momentum of his tail swipe instantly ended in Petros's fist. Immediately, the rest of his body twisted around from the aftershock. He yanked his tail away, turned around, and glared at Petros. "Do you think this is some kind of a joke? Do you think this is something just for fun? Do you think for a second that if you don't learn to control this that you're going to be okay, that the people around you are going to be okay?"

"Come on, Phil, give him a break."

Phil glared at Daniel now. "Give him a break? Let me tell you something. The next time he goes to hug that girl he loves, he could break her in half. He could break Cheryl in half. I'm not giving him a break. He's gonna learn how to control this, and both of you better goddam well get on board with that."

Petros immediately straightened up. The chuckle that had been forming in his throat at the trick he'd played disappeared instantly. "You're right, Uncle Phil. I'm sorry. It's a lot to take in but you're right. Let's get to it," he said.

Philip turned, and again his tail lashed out.

And again.

And again.

It lashed out dozens of times, the exact same swing, and finally Petros felt like he was beginning to adequately deal with the reflexes and his ability to control their aftermath. Philip kept it up, though. He couldn't quite understand why he thought he was jumping aside in a jump that might carry him two or three feet, and yet end up four or five yards from the spot in which he stood. He couldn't understand why he couldn't stop quickly, how running twenty or thirty yards somehow took him seventy-five yards into the trunk of a tree. If all of his senses were heightened, shouldn't they adjust for his speed and power?

The tail continued to shoot toward him.

He continued to go through sprints and jumps and dodges until he couldn't even guess at the number of attacks he avoided. Gradually he gained confidence but only about his ability to dodge the tail. Ultimately, he was far less concerned about what he could do in this body, this strange reptilian crazy body than he was about the way some of his abilities seemed to cross over so that even in his normal form he was far stronger than he should have been, far faster than he should have been. It was terrifying, really. The next time he goes to hug that girl he loves, he could break her in half.

On the other hand, he'd learned to instantly control the changing. There was no longer any pain. The light didn't bother him, the headaches didn't bother him, and he could transform easily and efficiently. He'd also overheard his uncles talking with his father, explaining that there was something utterly different about him. He already knew that. It was weird enough that his father was a dragon, but that he was some…well, he didn't know what the he was. But, evidently, he was stronger than he should have been, stronger than the average dragon. He was faster than the average dragon. Actually, if what he'd heard was correct, he was stronger and faster than exemplary dragons. It was an interesting situation. He would've imagined that a dragon and a human would have created the exact opposite, a weaker version of the dragon. Stronger than a human, certainly, but as strong as a dragon? It made no sense at all.

But, evidently, it was utterly unprecedented.

A whole different world, whole different opportunities.

Eventually, they stopped for the night, and only then did Petros realize it was almost pitch black. They started up in the morning again as though nothing had happened. The days ran by until, finally, they became a week. A second week. Though he wasn't fully confident of controlling his reflexes while he was in dragon form, he at least had a basis by which to do it. He was much better, much better in human form, able to keep his strength and speed under control. He supposed it was the innate desire to conceal what he was and the innate need to in some way keep himself from giving himself away. He certainly wouldn't be able to pretend the second door was faulty workmanship, wouldn't be able to shake hands with someone, break their hand, and pretend it was an accident.

On a cold morning, as he ran the newest obstacle course created by his increasingly sadistic uncles, his phone rang. He paused and saw it was Patricia on the line. He smiled, lifted the phone to his ear, and answered.

"Hey, honey, I'm here."

"Here? At the airport?"

He couldn't believe he'd forgotten the day she was arriving. "Not at the airport, silly, your mom picked me up. I'm at your house."

He looked at his uncles. Philip rolled his eyes and looked angry. Daniel didn't. He said, "Tell her you'll be home in an hour."

That, of course, made Philip angrier, but Petros spoke as instructed, and all of them headed toward the cars.

CHAPTER NINE

THEN

Agathon

It had been painless, relatively painless anyway, though Agathon knew most of his trepidation had nothing to do with the initial meeting, this first moment when the elders would make plain their wishes. In reality, any real nervousness about that moment disappeared when he learned Tynboleth had flown south with Jaelene and Jaelene's mate. That meant the matter was already decided, and it meant the council truly did hope that Agathon could be a savior to his kind, a leader to somehow take the dra'acheck from this time of darkness into safety and security.

Already, an idea or at least the seed of an idea formed in his mind but he couldn't grasp it, couldn't hold it firmly enough to let it sprout into something that might work or even might form the basis for real consideration. Justinian could tell he was lost in thought but misunderstood, eagerly seeking to hear Agathon's ideas for change but misinterpreting his recalcitrance as a desire to keep his ideas close rather than reluctance to verbalize only half-formed thoughts. It didn't discourage Justinian at all, though, and the younger dragon persisted until Agathon finally lied and said, "There are some things I can't share with you now, part of being an elder. I regret that but all elders must decide certain things together before they are shared."

It had the desired effect. Justinian still wanted the information, still believed it existed, but instead of resentment his face displayed wonder and respect. Agathon wondered why he'd found it so hard to just admit he had no ideas yet, why he didn't want Justinian to know solutions hadn't come to him yet but instead flitted around on the outside of his consciousness. There were likely only two or three dra'acheck with whom Agathon could share such thoughts without fear, and Justinian was one of them. Of course, he could share such things with Tynboleth as well, though she'd likely know of them just by looking at him.

Oddly, he could probably share his indecision with Yara, who was probably more like Agathon than any other dra'acheck though only Yara and Agathon really understood that. Perhaps Tynboleth did as well. He trusted those three dra'acheck beyond all others, though there were scores of dragons he liked a great deal more than Yara. He trusted him, though. No dra'acheck was more committed to the safety of the race, misguided as his actions could be. Agathon shook his head. Even now, he wanted to share his thoughts with Justinian but couldn't do it. Was this to be an elder or was it just to be Agathon? He sighed heavily and prepared for another cycle of unformed near-thoughts but Justinian's head suddenly snapped up.

"Agathon!"

They were still several miles away, and if he hadn't been lost in thought Agathon was certain he would have seen them before Justinian. He didn't see them first but he saw them now. Humans. Dozens of them. They rushed single-file up a game trail on the side of a peak. He looked as Justinian and said, "We're too far away. They don't even see us yet."

"I'm not worried about us," Justinian said. "That's where Tynboleth is."

Strangely, it was only then that Agathon realized the humans held swords and spears, wicked looking implements that he might have dismissed in other circumstances. He wondered why he hadn't seen them before and then the significance of the circumstances hit him. They were running up to attack. It seemed strange. He'd been led to believe they only attacked the weak or the young.

Or the sleeping.

He screamed a warning. To the humans it would be distant and perhaps indistinguishable from other sounds in the forest but Tynboleth, her daughter and her daughter's mate would hear it. He screamed again, and this time his voice echoed from the rocks around him. The humans didn't pause at all but he hadn't expected it. Finally, he took heart when he saw the shadow of a dragon near the top of the peak. A moment later, Tynboleth came into view and Agathon smiled. She could easily flee or simply breathe down an inferno against them. He hoped she'd flee. There'd been enough bloodshed.

She didn't flee, though. She didn't flee and she didn't rain fire upon the humans. Instead, she lifted her head and her eyes met Agathon's. He watched in horror as she smiled in recognition and lifted her head to roar back a greeting.

Justinian and Agathon both screamed again, and she looked confused for a moment and then looked down the pathway.

It was too late.

A spear sailed through the air and bounced harmlessly from her shoulder but the surprise of the attack put her off balance, and a stone on which a foreleg rested fell away, making Tynboleth stumble. It exposed her, and more spears shot through the air, most bouncing off like the first but one piercing under her foreleg. Her scream of pain shot through Agathon and brought as much agony or probably more than she felt from the actual wound. Justinian roared and shot forward but Agathon watched helplessly. There was no way for Justinian to reach her in time. Where were Jaelene and her mate? Where the hell were—

More spears sailed through the air and arrows, too. Most bounced but several stuck, one arrow piercing Tynboleth's eye and making her roar and thrash about. It was fruitless, he knew, but Agathon still shot forward, beating his wings as quickly as he could as cold fear gradually grew to blind anger. She was dead. She still moved and struggled but the outcome of the battle was already determined. He roared, and this time the humans heard, several turning to look and a number of them readying arrows to attack the approaching dragons, dragons that were surely just specks in the sky to the men.

A piercing, terribly nauseating wail exploded through the rocks, and Agathon turned. He saw her. She saw him. Her one good eye stared directly at him as the wail disappeared into silence. It shone brightly at him, filled with every moment of council, reproof, and love she'd ever shown him.

Then it dulled.

It dulled into lifelessness and grief rose up but Agathon dismissed it and allowed his anger to drive it back. He screamed but his screams held no warning, only rage. Justinian had shot forward several seconds before him but Agathon easily overtook him and then outdistanced him. The men began releasing arrows while he was still too far away for them to reach him, and he opened his mouth to spew out flame, diving to catch the stragglers at the foot of the path and then shooting up, spraying death from his belly as he moved. He shot up and turned around in the air. The first arrows and a spear hit him but bounced away as he let loose another burst of fire.

He'd already killed a half dozen men, and the others scattered, two falling from the side of the mountain, screaming as they hurtled downward to death on the rocks below. He landed on top of two others and released his fire in all directions, burning flesh and leather and armor as the humans screamed. Justinian joined him a moment later, and his fire joined Agathon's until the men lay dead at the mouth of her cave, the smell of death sickening and made more sickening by the acidic smell of the fire.

Agathon paused, breathing heavily. Justinian landed next to him and Agathon said, "Find Jaelene. They have to return to Mt. Tatras." Justinian nodded and took flight. Agathon looked at Tynboleth for only a moment. It wasn't her any longer. She was gone and the body on the peak was just a husk. He lifted his head and howled an anguished cry of rage and now, finally, the grief the rage had supplanted.

He finally stopped and turned his head, shaking his head in wonder. Death. So much death. Why? What purpose?

He felt the spear bounce from his back and turned to see a man staring at him in wonder and terror. It made no sense. None at all. The man seemed paralyzed.

Awed.

Agathon stared for a few breaths and then shook his head. "Why did you kill her?" he asked. The man's eyes opened widely. He said nothing and Agathon asked again, this time angrily. "Tell me why!"

The man shook, staring in what looked far more like shock than awe or wonder now. "Y-you can speak?"

Agathon tilted his head and then turned to look at Tynboleth. No. Not Tynboleth. What Tynboleth had been. He turned his face back to the man on the ledge. "My mother will never speak again," he said. He opened his mouth and released his fire, screaming in rage but taking comfort in the screams of a murderer.

Agathon

"We should just kill them all, Agathon," the words weren't really unexpected but it was still strange to hear the voice of a dra'acheck forming them.

Agathon said, "What if that's not the only way, Yara?" He realized his voice had none of the conviction in it he wanted it to have, realized he wasn't fully certain that Yara was wrong. What he knew for certain was that only Yara could speak with him on such issues as an equal and not a subordinate whether or not Agathon was now an elder.

Yara snorted. "It is the best way. As long as a single human walks the earth, the dra'acheck will never live in peace."

Agathon didn't say anything but continued walking. Yara walked in silence as well, and Agathon turned to him. Even with a human body, he looked like Yara, his face perpetually scowling and his eyes dark with hurt. It was difficult to hold him accountable for his feelings. His hatred of humanity was born of pain and death. He'd been an elder for almost a century now, and Agathon often wished it had been Yara. He was certain the dragon would think more rationally when the entirety of the race depended upon him. He looked at Yara, sighed softly, and said, "In a war with them, the last dragon will die long before the last human."

Yara opened his mouth to respond but closed it without speaking. Agathon turned his face back to the front and walked. He wanted to add to his statement but to do so too soon would undo the ground gained with the last comment. He waited and finally Yara said, "There must be a way."

He couldn't have hoped for a better response. "I think there is, Yara."

He didn't share it right away. To do so would be to invite contradiction, and it seemed better to Agathon to show Yara humanity's differences, to illustrate somehow that they weren't all dragon-hunting opportunists. The walls loomed large ahead, and Agathon noticed Yara slowing. He wondered if there were any fear involved of if perhaps his level of disdain for the humans was so strong that the thought of interacting with them was just that distasteful. He remained silent. To comment on either possibility could only bring conflict.

He could almost feel Yara's anger growing as they approached the gate. It was open at midday but a guard stood on either side. Each wore a thick leather tunic and each held a wicked looking sword of dull metal. Agathon whispered, "Just keep walking," and Yara did but it seemed at any moment he would transform. He hated human weapons almost as much as he hated humans. They walked through the gate without incident and almost immediately a woman and her child ended up walking next to them. She carried a basket filled with bread.

"Are you going to market with that bread or have you bought it?" Agathon asked.

"I go to sell it, sir," she said.

"It's the best bread in the city," the little boy added, and he was quickly shushed by his mother.

"Well," Agathon said. "If it's the best bread in the city I must buy a few loaves." He reached for his pouch and pulled out a few coins. "Will this suffice?"

The woman's eyes grew wide. "That's enough for the entire basket."

He smiled. "Well, then. One for me. One for my friend. You find others who need it but can't afford it and give the loaves to them."

She nodded, "Yes sir."

The young boy gave Agathon two loaves and then hurried away with his mother. Agathon gave one to Yara and said, "Do those two look dangerous?"

"She'll still go to market and sell the bread."

Agathon smiled, "So what?" He took a bite. The bread was very good. "Take a bite."

Yara rolled his eyes and reluctantly bit into the brown, crusty loaf. His eyes betrayed his surprise before he could get his scowl back in place. He chewed his bit and swallowed, trying and failing to hide his satisfaction. Finally, he said, "How do they eat this stuff?" His voice lacked conviction, though.

Agathon laughed. "Usually with something else. Come with me." He led Yara through an alleyway to another street until they arrived at a door under a sign that said, "The Branded Iron." Again, Yara rolled his eyes. "It's just a place where humans eat and drink, Yara."

Yara sighed and Agathon opened the door for him. There was a little bit of risk bringing him there, sure, but if Agathon's plan had any hope of succeeding, Yara would have to be on board or at least he'd have to comply. For a moment, it seemed he wouldn't step forward but evidently his respect for the station of elder was greater than his desire not to go in because he finally stepped forward. Agathon took his arm and led him inside. There were ten or twelve customers in the tavern along with the owner, who stood behind the bar and the owner's daughter, who delivered food and drinks. She saw Agathon and smiled.

He smiled back. This was his ninth or tenth visit, he thought, over the last year. He led Yara to a table along the far wall and motioned for him to sit. "Have you eaten the food of humans?"

"You just saw me eat a bite of bread," Yara growled back.

Agathon put what was left of his bread on the table and Yara did the same. "Just experience this, Yara. They are not all what you think they are. In fact, those who would hurt us are few. Just be open."

Yara looked like he wanted to reply but at that moment, the tavern owner's daughter arrived with a mug for each of them. "Are you hungry?" she asked. Agathon nodded, she said she'd be right back, and she left.

"What is this?" Yara asked, pointing at the mug.

"It's ale. It's made from fermented grain. It has a slightly intoxicating effect on humans. Some drink a great deal and become incapacitated. It doesn't do that to us. At least, it doesn't do that to me." He took a sip and, thinking it strange as he always did how it seemed to both cool and burn his throat at the same time. Yara shook his head slightly and then reached for his mug, taking a similar sip and then taking on a surprised expression as he drank.

"It's not bad but it has to be this damned body you made me wear."

Agathon laughed. "Wait until you see how good meat tastes when it's cooked. It's like the difference…" His voice trailed off as the sudden darkening of Yara's eyes drew his attention to the door.

Damn it all.

One of the hunters.

He'd come across them before in his various journeys into the human world, and that darkening in Yara's expression was his reaction as well. In fact, there had been occasions he'd indulged his anger but those occasions were rare, and he always felt weak after giving in. The hunter walked in, beaming because he knew all eyes would be on him, and all eyes would show respect and even a bit of awe.

"You need to hold back," he said.

"How can you say that, Agathon? Are you dra'acheck or are you human now?"

He understood the immediate repulsion. When he'd first seen the practice, he'd come back to the forest disgusted at the sight of dragon bodies used as trophies. The hunter was one of the worst. His necklace of dragon teeth had been highlighted with colorful paint that made the teeth seem bloody. He had scales interwoven in the breast of his tunic and gloves turned into weapons by the addition of dragon claws. The worst was a helmet designed from a dragon skull. All of the parts were from a hatchling, an infant hatchling. The symbols of the hunter's power came from killing the weakest of the dragons.

"You must control yourself, Yara."

"These are your humans? They slaughter hatchlings and brag about it?"

It angered Agathon. Of course it did. That wasn't the point, though. There had to be six or seven thousand people in this city, and they'd seen one, one that represented anything about the horrible hunt the humans waged. He stared at Yara. He was boiling. The anger was evident enough on his face that when the tavern keeper's daughter stepped toward them with the food, she turned away and Agathon had to coax her to drop it off with an extra coin. "Yara, you're drawing attention."

"How can you see what that creature is wearing and just sit here?"

"But you don't understand, Yara. They don't realize we can think, at least most of them don't. They either think we're just beasts like a wolf or a sheep. They think they're just killing an animal. Most of them who don't think that way think we're evil." He didn't add, though he wanted to, that Yara's regular unprovoked attacks on human settlements did nothing to alter that perception.

"They are—"

"Get out, Rangorn!" It was the voice of the tavern keeper. The man stood at the side of the bar, holding a cudgel. "I told you before. You won't recruit men from here, and you won't have my daughter either."

The man laughed. "Are you a coward, Gregor? Are you afraid of the dragons? Maybe the men here aren't so fearful."

"You take a hundred men into the woods and twenty come back. Nobody ever sees the treasure you promise and whole villages are destroyed because of how you provoke the beasts. Get out of my Tavern. You're not welcome."

"And what if I refuse?" The man smiled.

Agathon breathed in sharply as Yara stood. He got to his own feet quickly. "You're disturbing our meal." Yara seemed perturbed that Agathon interfered. It didn't matter. The risks of letting him deal with the situation on his own were too high.

The tavern keeper stepped forward, cudgel in hand and said, "Get out of here, Rangorn."

Rangorn ignored Gregor and turned to Agathon. "I've slain dragons. You think you can scare me?"

Yara said, "By the look of your helmet, you killed a dragon smaller than yourself, coward." Agathon sighed. It was too late. Yara moved swiftly and the man sailed through the air, crashing into and then through the doorway, leaving splinters where the door had been. Everyone stared and Agathon turned to the tavern keeper, reaching into his purse.

"I'm afraid my friend really enjoys silence during a meal." He pulled out several coins and tossed them onto the table. "I think this should get you a new door and compensate you for the disturbance." The innkeeper said nothing but stared at the coins and then the door. His daughter rushed to the table and scooped up the coins. "More than enough, sir, but Rangorn has many friends. I fear if he returns you and your friend will be hurt."

Agathon nodded and headed to the door. Rangorn could bring many friends but the risk to Agathon and Yara was small. It was irrelevant anyway. Rangorn wouldn't return, of course. Yara had probably already killed him, and if he hadn't he was already on the way out of the city to do so away from human eyes.

He stepped from the Inn and saw the man's broken body. Yara was several yards down the alley, heading out. At least he hadn't transformed. Agathon took the body and slung it over his shoulder. It wasn't the smartest thing to do but if the man were already dead at least he could take the terrible trophies from him.

An hour later, the two flew in silence. Yara was angry but Agathon was angrier. There was another city among the humans Agathon couldn't visit. "There is a way we can live in peace," he finally said.

"Agathon," Yara said slowly. "There is no dra'acheck I love more than you. Still, your thoughts are wrong. We don't need to live in peace. We need to decide to win this war."

Agathon

It was likely he would miss his friends. Of course he would. Perhaps more than his friends, though, he would miss the freedom of adventure, the certain knowledge that he had no knowledge of where he might be or what he might do a decade into the future. In truth, his plan meant the liberation of the dra'acheck.

But it meant the imprisonment of Agathon.

He fought back the idea as melodrama but it wasn't easy to do. The dra'acheck would be limited in the new paradigm but they would remain with their friends and their families. It would not be so for Agathon or the other elders. They would remain on Tatras, separated from the rest of their race.

Separated.

Agathon had spent centuries at a time with no contact with other dra'acheck but the opportunity always existed. A few days journey put him in front of Justinian. A few days more brought him to the mountains where he could always count on seeing a dozen or more hatchlings and small groups preparing to leave. His plan would end all of that. He would stay on the mountain. His days of exploration were at an end. Again, he wished the elders had chosen Yara. Then he'd be free, as Yara was, to take his family, take his friends, and start a new life. Jealousy filled him but just as soon as it did he dismissed it. Had Yara been elder, this plan would not be. Had Yara become elder, there would be war, all-out war.

He realized wistfully that he was likely as far away from Mount Tatras as he would be for many hundreds or even thousands of years. If he leapt into the air and flew with all speed, he would reach the mountain range in about two and a half days. He took a deep breath. Four more days. Four more days to exile.

A twig snapped, and the familiar sound along with heavy footfalls brought disappointment. His solitude was broken, and broken by humans. They were about a mile away, perhaps a mile and a half. He closed his eyes and listened.

"It's still too bloody muddy."

"Oh, then I suppose we should just stop for the night."

"Ah, much obliged to you, I—"

"Shut up. I wasn't serious. Quit your complaining and pull harder. If we don't get past this by the next rain, it'll take us a month to get home. Right now, we can make it in a week."

"But it's impossible!" another man complained. "We should wait for it to dry up a little."

"Are you a fool? These are dragon woods."

Agathon was pleased to hear that the humans were simply passing through and on their way home but his next thought was that it wasn't going to be that simple. In only a few days this forest would be filled with dra'acheck on their way to the council, the meeting already dubbed the Great Counsel by some. They wouldn't be out of the forest in time. It had rained the night before, and the path was filled with mud. He extended his senses. The fat human in the rear, the one who spoke like the leader, sank deeper and deeper as he struggled to push the cart through, and it would only get worse. They were unaware the rains had turned a depression a mile or so ahead into a waist-deep pond. The votes were already too close for comfort. If he left the interaction to chance, violence could result, and that risked everything.

He turned to leave, worry deep in his mind but he stopped. He knew a way for the humans to traverse the forest quickly. He could share it with them.

As a dragon.

It was a dangerous gamble. All of his interactions with humans were performed as a human, excepting of course his defense… Well, his vengeance, he supposed. Except for the encounter immediately after the death of Tynboleth, all of his interactions had come in human guise.

He wasn't entirely sure why he didn't just become human now but he leapt into the air and spread his wings with a loud roar. He figured it made more sense to give the humans warning than to just show up. It would scare them but that ought to give him time to talk before they acted.

Agathon was right. The panic on the faces of the men was evident when he crashed through the trees and landed only fifty or sixty feet from them. Two of them screeched like newborn hatchlings, and they all fumbled for their swords. The fat man fled to take cover behind the wagon. He extended his wings again, hoping the sight of his red body, the majesty of it, would keep them still for a moment.

"I told you there were more!" the leader said, his voice dripping with fear almost as palpable to Agathon as the fear he smelled coming from their bodies.

The others responded with a fearful babbling, each trying to speak over the rest. Agathon watched them patiently, waiting for them to calm their fear, but finally realized that they weren't going to do any such thing. Worse, they were likely to take action that would result in the opposite of what he desired. He had to keep from chuckling. They'd probably never seen a dragon before, and even if hunters had brought bodies home for display, Agathon was certainly larger than any they'd seen. He'd inspired terror, and it was amusing but it was no way to start a civilized conversation.

"Gentlemen," he said, "You need not fear my kind, for we have left these lands. I am the only one left in this forest." It was a lie but it wasn't too big of a lie. The dragons would indeed leave this land. Unless Agathon failed miserably at the council, his words would be true within a week. He paused, wondering if they would believe him, and hoping that they would. They all stared in shock. He took a deep breath and said, "You are far from home, and are weary with your travels. This path is not a good one and in a mile it becomes completely impassable but I'd like to help. Shall I show you a new path?" They still stared in shock. More pleasantries were needed. "Why are you here so far from home?"

"I told you they speak! I told you my uncle was right!" The man speaking was a small, mousy kind of human, and Agathon smiled.

"Of course we speak. We're like you."

"I know they speak!" the leader said roughly. Agathon smiled again. He hadn't known, just as he couldn't know the tone of his voice told Agathon he hadn't known.

A few moments passed, and silence reigned. Finally, the mousey one said, "W-we're just heading home. We've traveled far. The storm, the rain last night, it made it impossible to see and we ended up in the forest, driven into the the trees for some protection and now we're trying to get home. We should have left the forest and left you in peace but... But the roads are terrible, and we thought we would save several weeks. I... please don't kill us."

There was something in his voice indicating deception. Agathon imagined the roads outside of the forest were perfectly passable. He didn't mind. He wasn't interested in punishing a territorial infraction. "I don't want to kill you," Agathon said as gently as he could. He tried to speak quietly but from the cringes, he realized even speaking quietly had to be shouting for them. He smiled and then wondered if a smile on a dragon would appear threatening. There was no helping it. "No harm will come to you from me. Still, these lands are dangerous after the storms, and this path is impassable. Even if you could somehow make progress, rising waters and mudslides could surely harm you." He turned his head north and gestured in that direction. "Go that way for two miles, and then turn back toward your original direction for a short while. You'll come to a small gorge where the water collects. The north face of the gorge has a wide ledge, almost entirely rock. You will be safer there and your cart won't get stuck.

There were a few moments of hushed but frantic muttering behind the cart. Then the mousey man stuck his head out again. "Y-you're going to let us live?"

Agathon chuckled. "Of course I am. Have you harmed me? Have I come to your land to harm you?" He thought of Yara and changed course. "You have come into my lands seeking only to go home, and I'll not stop you, or harm you. I wish you only well."

The fat leader stood, emboldened now, a sword in hand. He was formidable looking for a human, taller than most and combined with his weight it made him appear imposing. "I'm warning you, dragon, if this is a trick we'll cut you down."

"I tremble at the thought," Agathon mocked, despite himself. He shook his head. "I bear you no animosity, and I wish you no harm. There is no trick."

The leader didn't speak for a while but he finally said, "If this is a trick, we won't be easy to dispatch of."

Agathon kept from laughing. "This is no trick."

The other men hesitantly started to rise. When they all stood, they stared at him, and Agathon stretched down toward the ground, allowing them a better look and admitting to himself that he enjoyed the looks of dumfounded awe. He knew the break he formed in the trees when he crashed down allowed sunlight to filter in and his scales, still wet from the rain, glistened in crimson beauty.

"This isn't, isn't some kind of dragon trap?" The mousey man spoke, and this time Agathon couldn't keep his chuckle to himself.

"If I meant to kill you, wouldn't this be the place for it? The mud would hinder you but cause me no trouble at all. Go in peace and be safe."

The fat man slowly lowered his sword and then motioned to his men to do the same, not realizing only one of them had the courage to draw a weapon in the first place. "I'm going to trust you. Don't try anything, though. We'll let you live if you honor your word."

Agathon was about to laugh again but when he considered the words, he realized they indeed could kill him. He had an absolute advantage with his size and with the terrain but they were all close enough to him to cause damage before he could release his fire and though he could easily kill one or even two at a time, five armed men was another story altogether. He'd risked his life to speak with them and hadn't really considered it.

He nodded and said, "You have nothing to fear from me. I wish you safety on your journey home and hope we meet again in peace." He turned around, a terrible idea if the humans decided to attack but somehow necessary if he were to prove no ill intent. He walked slowly away, only slightly sad he didn't get to awe them again with a leap into the sky.

It could work.

It wouldn't be easy. Not at all.

But it could work.

CHAPTER TEN

NOW

Cheryl

She hadn't seen him yet, hadn't actually seen his new form, anyway. She wondered how she felt about it. Strangely, Cheryl couldn't really remember an internal battle over Justinian. Perhaps that was because she knew him first and really thought of him first as a man. It didn't hurt that he'd been a knight in shining armor for her.

Of course, Patricia didn't have the benefit of eternal gratitude to Petros, at least not in that particular way. She wanted desperately to lay everything bare, to simply tell her or trick one of the pride into transforming in her sight. She wouldn't do it. It was unthinkable. After nearly twenty-five years she couldn't imagine violating such a simple and basic precept of their existence.

She wanted to. God, did she want to.

Had Justinian talked to Petros about her? Had he discussed what level of disclosure was appropriate? He couldn't let Petros marry her without telling her, could he? No. Not on Cheryl's watch he couldn't. Cheryl took a deep breath and let it out slowly and then gasped.

"Oh, God, Honey! You must think I'm horrible!"

Patricia jumped from the outburst and nearly spilled her iced tea. She smiled and said, "It is kind of awkward, isn't it?"

Cheryl shook her head. "Nope. I'm just thinking about Petros and imagining ways to torment him if he mistreats you."

That got a laugh from Patricia. She said, "I've got the torment covered I think but you're going to come in handy if I'm sick or pregnant or something."

Cheryl joined in on the laughter and looked up, catching the eye of Cimmran, a younger member of the pride who appeared about thirty but was really centuries old. He was the butler, officially, and Cheryl's bodyguard unofficially. She certainly tormented the hell out of Cimmran, teasing him unmercifully and even trying to lose him in department stores and while grocery shopping. He took it all in stride and certainly showed no resentment at her nod to summon him.

"I had no idea you guys were so rich," Patricia said. Almost immediately, her face colored painfully red.

Cheryl laughed. "Honey. It's good you fell in love with Petros before you knew that. Really, we don't think about it much."

"But this estate!" Cheryl shrugged. They sat on one of the patios, and there was no way to pretend the estate wasn't gorgeous. Acres of sculptured gardens. Fountains. Gazebos. A man-made lake. A colonial style mansion. Patricia lifted up her glass. "I'm drinking iced tea, and this is probably Waterford Crystal and probably costs more than all of my pots, pans, plates, and glasses put together."

Cheryl giggled and said, "I don't know. There's some pretty expensive Tupperware out there." It wasn't Waterford. It was Baccarat, and if Patricia was like the college students of Cheryl's youth, the glass probably did cost more than everything in her cabinets. "Don't hold it against us," she said. She noticed Cimmran and decided not to make a smartass remark. "Cimmran, would you be so kind as to see if Carl could put together a snack for us. Tell him Petros will be back soon so make enough for him, too. I don't know if Daniel and Philip will be staying but they might."

"Are they really his uncles?" Patricia asked as Cimmran walked away. "He talks about Daniel all the time and sometimes he calls him his uncle and sometimes he calls him his dad's friend."

"They've been friends long enough that they're family. They live here. Eleven others live on the estate, too. We have nine guest houses behind those trees." She pointed over the wrought iron of the patio fence past an ornate marble fountain and into a line of oaks. "Justin's family came from France, and there were a great many who came with them. That was in the 1800s, and this estate was built so the whole community could stay together. All of the buildings except this one were completely rebuilt over the years. This one's been remodeled a bit, re-plumbed and re-wired mostly. Other than the central air, it pretty much looks like it did in the 19th Century."

"So this estate was all inherited?"

Cheryl laughed. "I guess so. You think you're marrying a man of leisure?"

Again, Patricia colored with embarrassment. "That's one thing Petros will never be." Cheryl nodded and Patricia added. "Even though everything is easy for him, he still puts in effort. It's like he's not even human sometimes." Cheryl took a deep breath at the statement and Patricia immediately backtracked. "I didn't mean that as an insult!" she said. "I just mean he's dedicated. He's so serious and ambitious and…" She let her voice trail off miserably.

"Relax," Cheryl said. "I've been trying to get him to relax a little so if I looked surprised at what you said, I wasn't irritated at you but at Mr. Superman."

"Superman," Patricia said. "I guess I wouldn't be all that surprised if he suddenly started leaping tall buildings or… or whatever else Superman does. Faster than a locomotive?"

"Speeding bullet," Cheryl laughed. "More powerful than a locomotive." She wondered how accurate any of it was in relation to Petros. Justinian could leap the buildings, and he was fast. She didn't know just how strong he was."

Cimmran arrived carrying a tray of canapes and Patricia's eyes grew wide. "Oh my God," she said. "Is that how you guys eat? I'm gonna seem like—"

Cheryl laughed again. "This is company food. I cook most of the time for Petros and his father and maybe one or two others. Once or twice a week the cooks make us dinner. It's like going to a restaurant, kind of, I suppose. They keep busy handling meals for everyone, though."

"I thought I'd have to go to culinary school." Cheryl chuckled a little and then pointed out a water cracker, bleu cheese, fig combination and told Patricia to try it. She wondered why she was surprised that she liked Patricia so much. She'd met her before a few times when they'd flown out to see Petros. She imagined it was probably the girl's wonder, her nervousness over the wealth instead of desire, that currently impressed her. The girl took a bite of the indicated appetizer and paused with a surprised and very happy look on her face.

That look, though, was nothing compared to the expression that came over her when Petros's voice sounded from just inside the patio door. "There she is!" Patricia leapt up, banging the table in the process and overturning both glasses of tea. One rolled off, and almost two-hundred dollars of lead crystal shattered on the polished stone floor. She stared in horror but the horror was short lived as Petros threw her arms around her and twirled her in the air.

Cheryl motioned to Cammrin to deal with the spills and then stood and stared. God. Her boy was a man now. He was a man, and it seemed absolutely appropriate that he should hold a young lady in his arms and... Well, and now they were kissing. That part wasn't as easy to take, and she looked away and pretended to pay attention to how Cammrin brushed the broken glass into a dustpan.

"Give it a rest, Pete. She needs to breathe you know." Cheryl held back a laugh and turned to look at Daniel. He grinned widely. Philip stepped in behind him, not as happy but then, again, he never was.

"I told the cook he might expect you to join us for our meal. Justin won't be back until tomorrow morning but we'd be enchanted if you ate with us."

"Who's in the kitchen today?" Daniel asked.

"Carl."

"I'm in, then."

She laughed. Daniel was in no matter who cooked. She looked at Philip but he shook his head. "I need to get to Nevada and prepare some things." He didn't say exactly what he needed to prepare but imagined it was more of the training for Petros.

"Aw, come on, Uncle Phil." She turned and saw her son again. Patricia was flushed, a little embarrassed for the very public display of affection. She kept getting better. "You can eat first."

Philip shook his head. "Not this time, Pete. I'll book tickets, though, and you and Daniel will come see me after your visit."

"I'll fly up in a few days," Daniel said.

The two men turned to leave and Cheryl cleared her throat. Daniel looked confused but Philip said, "Miss... Um, Patricia. It's very nice to see you again. I'm sorry I won't be able to see you this trip."

Patricia smiled, again just slightly embarrassed. "I... I look forward to another time, then."

Philip nodded, and Cheryl nodded in his direction. He left the patio and Daniel stepped forward. He enveloped the poor girl in a bear hug. The nervousness melted and Patricia said, "Nice to see you, too, Uncle... um..."

Just as Cheryl, Petros, and Daniel started to tell her, her eyes lit up and she said, "Daniel. Uncle Daniel."

Yes. She was a good find. Cheryl liked her.

Philip

Philip reached for the handle of the door and then paused. He realized with a bit of shock that he'd now been alive after the dispersal for longer than he'd been alive prior to the dispersal. The shock wasn't really the realization so much as that it had been that way for at least a hundred and fifty years and he didn't know why it just occurred to him then. But he'd spent more time as a human than as a dra'acheck, at least more of his life in the human form.

So why did simple things still impress him? Why did they still seem odd? Like the doorknob. Was it the fascination with privacy that humans had? Was it their holding onto possessions as though those possessions defined them? Was it their belief that a door offered security? He didn't know. It was interesting nonetheless.

Okay, he did know. He admired them, admired the way they grew and changed. He wasn't exactly a young dragon but he was by no means old and it seemed countless lifetimes had passed in human terms. They'd progressed as a race. They'd changed dramatically and even though they were capable of great violence, they were also remarkably capable of tremendous kindness. As far as he knew, the only change the dra'acheck had ever accomplished was the change Agathon drove, the Great Plan. Even now, though, the dra'acheck held tightly to their identities, held tightly to what made them dragons.

No dra'acheck would have invented a door knob. Of course, no dra'acheck would ever see the need for a door knob. It was a bad example. No dra'acheck would ever have invented a computer or a train or an airplane. While some dragons felt the need to explore almost constantly and while Agathon had certainly revolutionized the way the dra'acheck cooperated to avoid over-hunting and too many territorial disputes, the race was essentially content. Not the humans. He could do without the constant improvement in weaponry but really, even something as simple as pneumatic tires showed a level of brilliance he found fascinating.

He opened the door and stepped in. Immediately, the cool air from the swamp cooler washed over him, and he breathed out a sigh of relief. That was another interesting thing. In human form, he noticed the weather. In dragon form, he only noticed the weather because of how it impacted the ability to fly or how it impacted visibility. Wind and snow had nothing to do with comfort but everything to do with freedom of movement. Humans weren't so fortunate but they adapted, developing ways if not to harness the weather and bend it to their will then at least to make its impact on them irrelevant.

He crossed the living room and stretched. He would have rather been training Petros but ultimately the boy was doing a fabulous job. He'd have to work a little bit harder after his fiancé left, but until then, there was just no purpose. His mind wouldn't be in it and his heart was with the girl. As for Philip, he really didn't enjoy staying in California anyway. There was something about watching Petros with that girl, something about realizing that it hadn't yet occurred to Petros just how dramatically his life had changed. It had been the hardest thing for Justinian to comprehend, that a relationship with Cheryl ultimately put Cheryl in danger. Justinian had been blinded by his feelings and Justinian wasn't just a dra'acheck but a mature dra'acheck, one of the finest. There was no way to stop the relationship. At the time, Philip had not been happy with that at all, but ultimately time had shown that Cheryl could be a resource for the pride, and not only a resource for the pride, but a remarkable resource. Even better, she understood discretion. He certainly didn't look forward to the day she realized she was old and Justinian was still young.

Philip wondered if Petros would discover on his own the risks associated with the relationship, or if they'd have to be pointed out to him. He wasn't looking forward to that day no matter how it came. On the other hand, there was some definitely troubling things about Petros that had nothing to do with Patricia. Perhaps "troubling" was the wrong word, but the boy was fast. He was fast by dragon standards, and he wasn't even dra'acheck. Not only that, he was strong. In his human form, he was stronger than any of the pride's dra'acheck human forms, and in that strange half-dragon kind of form he had, he also appeared far stronger. Philip just didn't know how that strength could be mastered, how he could deal with yet another area of extreme exceptionalism, this one exceptionalism that came with potential tragedy.

Philip looked over to the hutch where he held his alcohol and considered pouring himself a drink but changed his mind. Instead he made his way into the kitchen, walked to the refrigerator, opened it, and pulled out a beer. A moment later, he wiped his mouth and let the cool liquid settle. The one thing strange about being human was how the sense of taste seemed extraordinary. As Dra'acheck, all of the senses were powerful, but taste had never been such a tremendous and powerful motivator before. He reached into the refrigerator and pulled out a peach. He took a bite, and the tanginess and the sweetness of it seemed overwhelming. In some ways there was still nothing at all that could compare to the satisfaction of a meal that had been running from him moments before, and the idea of cooking meat as a dragon seemed utterly foreign. But then again, he never would've tasted the incredible flavors associated with fruit, bananas, apples, peaches, he never would have thought about consuming vegetation. And now all of those things enriched his life. Human taste, though, had so many options. He knew of holdouts in the dragon world, holdouts who couldn't comprehend acceptance of life in human guise, much less celebration. He wondered if they tasted the same food he did.

He finished the peach, downed the rest of the beer, and closed the refrigerator. Then he went and sat at the table. He wasn't sure what to do, wasn't sure what the next steps with Petros should be. He felt fairly certain Petros could control himself now, that he wouldn't accidentally run into someone or break someone's arm trying to shake it. That wasn't the same as learning to function, especially if Petros still had aspirations of being a doctor. To be a doctor, and to know that at any moment you might intend a millimeter cut only to create a long gash in someone, well, that was more than a little bit terrifying.

On the other hand, Petros was in many ways beyond training. The boy didn't know it, but if he and Philip were to wrestle, Petros would most likely win. Philip was certain of that. In fact, he thought it might even be possible that Petros would beat Justinian. Hell, it was even possible he could stand a chance against Agathon himself. The boy was strong, beyond strong. At some point, the elders would have to know.

Was this dire circumstances?

Was the boy's existence an exception to the no contact rule?

It was all so impossible. Utterly impossible. How did you go about dealing with someone when you had no idea what that someone was?

"Are you gonna offer me a drink?"

The voice was startling. Philip looked up and then smiled warily. "Welcome."

"It's good to see you too. How about that drink?"

Philip got up and made his way toward the living room, heading to the hutch, where he pulled out two high-ball glasses, and then began to pour. He didn't realize something was wrong for a moment. It didn't make any sense at all. But when he looked down, he saw it. The glittering edge of the sword was obviously studded with something: diamonds, sapphires. He turned around, his face a contortion of pain but more than anything else, confusion.

"Why? You could have..." He heard his voice garble away as he fell to the floor. Strangely, Philip's last thought wasn't about his attacker, but instead about the pride. His spent his final moments wishing he could warn them, even more than wishing he could survive this attack.

Petros

So sex was different.

Patricia lay with her head on his shoulder, her soft breathing sending calm but almost exhilarating waves of sensation over his chest as she slept. He didn't know if heightened senses made her breathing so damned erotic or if somehow the whole situation had his mind reeling. He had no idea how he could figure it out either. Hey dad, remember when we had the birds and the bees talk and I already knew about the mechanics because I was already studying college biology courses? Well, I've been sexually active for a long time now and slept with a great many girls before Patricia and I've slept with Patricia a lot but this week every time we did it was like the first time and is that normal when you're really a dragon?

He laughed softly as he imagined Justinian's expression, and Patricia stirred. He stroked her back softly until she was still again. Yes, the sex was different. It was more than better, though. It was also terrifying. He kept hearing Daniel's voice warning him he'd break her spine or something like that, and the whole act consisted of trying to be gentle while simultaneously having a difficult time controlling animalistic desire. She certainly seemed to enjoy it, alternately calling him sweet and ravaging. They'd slept together every night for her visit, twice on a few days. He imagined they were making up for lost time but there was also enough masculinity within him that he imagined it was just that good for her.

And then felt stupid for imagining it.

Really, did life ever change? She was there with him, her head on his shoulder, and for him the sex had been wonderful despite the fear and the need to maintain control. Still, he lay in bed feeling that same strange sense of wonder and accomplishment he'd felt the first time when Keri Lawless told him she needed a chemistry paper and would be very grateful for his help. He'd arrived at her house and typed it on her laptop in about an hour. His hour in service resulted in fifteen minutes of service from her, and when he returned home he lay in his bed and stared at the ceiling no longer a virgin and suddenly aware of the possibilities in front of him. He was sixteen. Now, all of the same feelings flooded him but he was older and had almost lost count of the term papers and resulting rewards. Sure, there had been something different about Patricia, and he'd been overwhelmed by the first experience with sex that wasn't transactional. It didn't have that wondrous uncertainty, though, the uncertainty and wonder that filled him now.

He let his hand run over her shoulders and down to the small of her back. He could feel his thoughts growing dark. He'd avoided the issue for the entire week, and if he could make it through the next day, he'd be able to avoid it a while longer. It wasn't fair, though. Patricia deserved better, and if he didn't end things now it only meant greater pain later.

A sudden loud knocking at the door made him bolt upright on the bed, and that sent Patricia to the edge. She would have fallen off if he hadn't grabbed her quickly to steady her. The knocking continued and she quickly gathered sheets to cover up. Petros didn't bother as he rolled from the bed and walked to the door. "Who is it?" he asked.

"Daniel. Open up."

"It's not gonna happen, Uncle Dan."

"Petros, open up." Petros rolled his eyes and found where his jeans lay on the floor. He pulled them on quickly and then opened the door.

"Yeah, I'm not a kid anymore, Uncle Dan, I'm allowed to have girls in—"

"You had girls in your room when you were a kid?" Petros turned and rolled his eyes at her. She giggled but she stopped giggling when Daniel walked in and she saw the expression on his face. She pulled the sheets more closely around her, and Petros turned around.

"Phil is dead," Daniel said.

CHAPTER ELEVEN

THEN

Agathon

It could work. That thought was foremost in his mind and suddenly the forest seemed greener, the light streaming though the canopy more beautiful, and the sound of rain dripping from the leaves melodic and lovely. Agathon inhaled deeply as he stepped into the trees.

And he stopped

He tried desperately to believe he was wrong, that there was some strange twist in the air that altered his senses but there was no mistaking it. He'd come across that smell before, far too many times. He felt a root tear and break in his talons and looked down. He'd clenched them and dug almost two feet into the ground.

He'd offered to let them go in peace.

He'd advised them of a route to make their journey easier.

They'd accepted his help.

They'd accepted his help and all the while they'd known what they'd done, what he hadn't discovered until the wind changed and he caught the scent. They'd known. They knew now.

He knew, too, and the knowledge sent flames dancing behind his eyes.

His body trembled as the rage grew, and part of him wanted to let them go still, to let them go and then spend the next century convincing himself he was wrong about what he smelled. He'd seen Yara convince himself time after time that everything positive about humankind was actually negative. He'd done it despite his inability to argue that Agathon's perspective wasn't better for the dra'acheck. He'd believed in the evil of man even though the benefit of the doubt could end the Hunt and save the dra'acheck. Surely, Agathon could be like Yara. Surely he could believe in the goodness of men despite the evidence.

No.

He could believe that most men were not these men but he couldn't believe there was good in this party. He whirled around, wings spread, and branches cracked and fell as he brushed against them. "Wait!" he roared. He realized the word was louder than the first roar, and as he stared at the men, clear malice in his eyes, he also realized the birds and the rest of the noises in the forest were gone.

The mousey human fell to his knees. The leader drew his sword and a few of the others followed suit.

It would do them no good.

"It occurs to me," Agathon said, "That I haven't been as kind as I should. Surely the cart is a burden slowing you down. I, on the other hand, could easily carry it ahead to the rock path for you. It will save you a day of travel."

"Um... We couldn't impose," the fat leader said.

Agathon smiled, baring his fangs as he did. "Surely it would be no imposition. I could even carry all of you."

"I'm afraid your... um, your claws would frighten us. They seem far too sharp, good dragon, Sir."

"You have reason to fear them," Agathon said. "Pray, tell me what you carry in that cart."

The others instantly froze but the leader chose belligerence, puffing himself up as he said, "That's no concern of yours, wyrm. You've already tried my patience. Now be on your way. I let you leave before because it amused me. I don't need to talk about the cart or anything else."

"Of course you don't," Agathon said icily. "I already know what's in the cart."

The fat man' followers didn't see Agathon move, so fast did his leap carry him to their leader. The force of his wing beats knocked three back just from the wind. For his size, the leader was far faster than Agathon would have anticipated, and he swung his blade in a high arc, hitting with a great, clanging blow right at Agathon's elbow. It stung, but the limbs were the most heavily armored areas of a dra'acheck's body, and as the blade rang out its frustration

123

from simply bouncing against the scales, Agathon swiped, his talons, tearing into the man's leg. A second swipe severed it as the man screamed and blood sprayed from the stump.

He stared at the fat man, whose face went from flushed with exertion to pale with blood loss almost immediately. "You'll find that only our infants have skin you can pierce so easily, murderer," he said.

He caught movement and turned his head. Two men headed toward him with swords drawn. The other two, seeing their leader flailing on the ground, fled, the mud suddenly not an impediment to fast movement. He watched the mousey one run and felt a strange and almost sympathetic pang. He shook his head and growled at the two attackers.

One hesitated.

And died.

Agathon whipped his tail around, connecting with the man's neck and severing his head. It hit the ground and bounced, landing on the screaming leader's chest before rolling off. Of course, that did nothing to quiet the man's screams.

The second attacker was far more skilled than the others but he misunderstood the brownish color of the scales on Agathon's underside to suggest they were softer. They were actually only muddy from the ground. His struck a savage blow but shook as the impact traveled over his arms and shoulders. Agathon snapped his head forward and closed his jaws at the man's waist. He swung down but his sword never made it to the dragon's neck as his torso detached from him and the weapon fell uselessly to the ground along with his legs. Agathon spit out the man's upper body, and it landed next to the leader.

The man screamed again but Agathon ignored him and walked to the cart. A thick fabric covered the contents, and he yanked it away. His anger disappeared in sadness. The hatchling had been no more than fifteen years old, the son of Yanos, a well-respected younger dragon Agathon had plans for. He'd shown an interest in the stories about the river and the predators and the grazers, and Agathon intended to let him observe it himself. He'd mentioned just a week ago the hatchling had wandered off. It wasn't unusual for hatchlings to disappear for weeks at a time among the dra'acheck. It was something in their makeup, and even with the Hunt in full swing, it was something that just couldn't be helped.

For this hatchling it was tragic.

Hatchling.

Agathon felt horrible guilt rise up as he realized he couldn't recall the little one's name. He couldn't recall his name, and with the Hunt and the danger, Agathon should have searched for him as soon as he learned he was away from his parents. He hadn't, though! He hadn't. He'd been too wrapped up in his plan to think about it and now the poor thing was dead, murdered. Mutilated. There were deep gouges in his neck, and the little body was filled with wounds. He'd been pierced dozens of times.

He fought back the sadness and the screams of the man on the ground gave him anger as a good alternative. He walked to him and placed his talons on the man's chest. The man flailed his arms but he was losing blood fast. Already, he couldn't move the leg he had left. "Tell me," Agathon said. "Do you have children?"

The man's eyes narrowed. "You will never harm them." Agathon tilted his head. The man was trying to shout but too weak.

"Ah," he said. "So you know what it's like to love your offspring. So do I. So did the father and the mother of the dragon you murdered, a dragon only as old to them as a baby just delivered would be to you." He dug his nails into the man's chest, easily piercing though skin and splintering bone. "I would sprinkle his body with your blood so he goes into eternity knowing he was avenged."

The man tried to speak. His eyes told Agathon he wanted to beg for his life. It wouldn't have mattered but the dra'acheck elder was still glad the man couldn't find his voice. A moment later the gasping for air turned to gurgling and then replaced with silence.

Agathon

The sun shone brightly in the sky, brightly enough to illuminate the tops of the trees in a lovely way that made them seem almost like ground cover, like Agathon could somehow walk atop the pillowed green surface without falling though, without breaking even the stem of a leaf. The sight did nothing to cheer him, though. The sun warmed him as he basked at the edge a tall cliff overlooking the forest.

The forest. Home in the Tatras Mountains.

Miles away from the cart in the mud.

He'd left the humans on the forest floor and carried the son of Yanos some distance away, where he felled a tree and used it as a pyre. He didn't really believe it would offer the hatchling any comfort but he still shook his claws over the body to sprinkle him with the blood of his murderers. Then, he called his fire. It was the standard form of burial but it was the first time he'd ever unleashed his fire on another dra'acheck. He'd lacked the heart for it with Tynboleth and Justinian had ignited her pyre.

It felt wrong.

It felt wrong, and it wasn't just the untimely passing of a hatchling. It felt wrong that flames should leave his belly and burn dra'acheck flesh. He sighed as he watched the smoke rise and he stayed with the fire until nothing remained of the body but ash. It was curious, really, how fire had little or no effect on a living dragon but a dead dragon seemed to burn with intensity beyond any other combustible.

He still hadn't decided what he would tell Yanos.

He still hadn't decided if he would tell Yanos.

No. He had decided. He wouldn't tell Yanos until after the council voted. He'd tell him in a few weeks and do all he could to lessen the blow, all he could to ensure Yanos wouldn't seek vengeance, all he could to somehow make the father understand.

Understand? His son was murdered. How could he understand?

Agathon lifted up his head and roared angrily. He cursed the elders who had made him elder instead of Yara. Yara was so certain of his course of action. War. Kill humans. Kill them on sight. It was so much easier, so much more satisfying to take action.

But it was wrong. Agathon was certain of that. The echoes of his roar came back to him and he sighed. The roar had done nothing to relieve his confusion, his sadness, or his frustration.

"Are you really going to do this?" Agathon looked up as Yara landed next to him.

He was more disturbed than he'd imagined. He felt wet, as though the water from the pond still clung to him. He'd rolled in in, covered himself with the mud and then taken flight in the rain to wash it away along with the blood and the death. He'd succeeded in washing away the blood and mud. "Yes," he said quietly. "Will you speak against me?"

"Only now. Only here." Yara seemed to sigh. "There is only one dra'acheck who loves the dra'acheck as much as I do. I don't understand why he protects those who would murder us cruelly."

Agathon didn't answer right away. Perhaps Yara was right. Perhaps they were cruel. Perhaps war, and death, was better than peace and death. No. It was not the way. "You were at the inn, Yara. Not all humans are hungry for our blood."

"But those that are kill hatchlings!"

Hatchlings. The word was like a blow to Agathon. He closed his eyes and saw the flames rising, smelled the blood of the fat man. "How many of their children, their hatchlings, have you killed?"

It was Yara's turn to pause. Agathon opened his eyes and looked at him. "Yara," he said. "If I had a son." He thought again of the hatchling's body burning. "Or a daughter, I suppose. Whatever hatchling came to me. If I had one and I died, with my dying breath I would beg you to take him in and protect him."

"You wouldn't have to beg. If you couldn't find any breath at all I would still take them in."

Agathon nodded. "I know. I would trust you above all others. This isn't about my hatchlings, though. It's about all hatchlings—"

Yara snorted. "I would take any orphan in! I took in Phineas and his mother, and—"

"That isn't what I mean." Agathon sighed heavily and looked out at the canopy of the forest again. "There is no dra'acheck I would trust more to protect a dragon." He looked back at Yara. "But none I would trust less to protect dragon kind."

He braced himself for the argument but it didn't come. Instead, Yara grew quiet. "Do you really believe your plan will work?"

"It will."

Yara shook his head. "It won't, Agathon. It may delay things for a while but one way or another we're doomed against them. One way or another they'll destroy us all. I'd rather fall while attacking than while hiding but I will do whatever the council says."

"Do you think the council will vote my way?"

"I hope not," Yara said. "But I won't speak against it." He rose into the air just as Justinian approached. He smiled. "He's a lot like Phineas. He follows you blindly."

Agathon smiled. "Phineas follows you blindly?"

Dragons didn't shrug, not exactly, but Agathon noticed Yara's gesture and pictures of Nallal making gestures suggesting a noncommittal response while smiling knowingly came immediately to his mind. Nallal. She'd been dead for at least two centuries now.

Justinian arrived and said in a voice laden with concern. "Was he trying to convince you not to go through with it?

"Not exactly," Agathon said. "I think we're both just hoping one of us can see." He didn't really want to explain that so he asked, "What have you learned?"

"I think your support is solid."

"What of you, Justinian?"

He looked hurt at Agathon's words and he said softly, "Of course I will support you."

"Calm down. I didn't mean that," Agathon said. "Do you think my plan is right? Do you think I'm doing the right thing? Do you think there's any chance Yara is right?"

Justinian took a deep breath. "I was angry with you when Tynboleth died. I—"

"I couldn't have saved her! I tried but—"

"Now it's your turn to calm down. I was angry because you killed the men so that by the time I got there, I was really only cleaning up after you. You got vengeance, I got... well, I got to send her on to the next world." He paused and took a deep breath. "There are times when I want to gather all of us up and travel from one city to the next, destroying all evidence that humans ever existed. I understand Yara's hate."

"So I'm doing the wrong thing, then."

"No. There are times I feel that way but I'm wrong. Even if it were justified we would fail. We would fail and we would die. That in itself is justification for your plan. Without your plan the Hunt continues and eventually, all dragons will believe as Yara does, all dragons will raid as he does, and all dragons will die."

"So you do think it's right."

"That's not the only reason, Agathon," Justinian said. "I've heard your stories of time among them. They aren't evil. They're like us. I'm not Yara and Bethu wasn't Yara and Godon wasn't Tynboleth and you're Agathon. Even if we could succeed, we would do so becoming the very thing Yara hates. How could we not? How could it not turn into another Hunt, and how could we face ourselves if we succeeded? I am behind you, Agathon. I will stand with you no matter the cost."

Agathon sighed. "Is everyone here?"

Justinian nodded. "Tennark from the East arrived with his family this morning. He doesn't understand the fuss at all. Evidently, the humans there worship dragons."

"Worship them?"

"Venerate them, like your tent nomads worshipped the rain clouds and—"

"No. I know what worship is. I'm just surprised. In less than a hundred years, they've got the humans to worship them?" The idea was almost unthinkable.

Justinian shook his head. "No. There were already sculptures and carvings of dragons. They've been worshipped for a long time. Tennark named his son Kwing Long. It's one of the dragon gods' names."

"You think there were dra'acheck there before the awakening? You think…" He paused. It was a worthy question but not yet. "Will Tenmark support us?"

"Oh yes. He already walks among the humans a great deal. He's certainly not interested in warring with them." He took the air, "We have to go, Agathon." Agathon remained and Justinian turned around and said, "They will go along. You're asking for the right thing."

Right.

Maybe.

Probably.

That didn't change that he was asking the dra'acheck to give up being dra'acheck.

Agathon

He felt as though his life had been inexorably building up to this moment and then immediately felt foolish for the overly-dramatic perspective. What had happened to the days of hunting with the young dra'acheck and hatchlings? What had happened to the thrill of discovery and adventure, to the sudden and remarkable burst of development, to breathing fire for the first time and to—

He sighed. Young or not, he certainly thought like an elder now. He glanced at Justinian. He wondered if the younger dragon knew just how much his strength mattered, how much Agathon relied on it. He let his eyes scan the others, and there was something unsettling but wonderful in the sight. Dra'acheck by nature were solitary or close to it, living in small groups. A gathering of this size hadn't really happened since the years following the Awakening. Now, they were all here, all here against their nature. In moments, he would call upon them to act against their nature even more profoundly. The number of dra'acheck was surprising, definitely more than a thousand, and perhaps as many as fifteen hundred.

He told himself once again that his plan was correct, the great hope for all of them. The Elders had waited far too long for a gathering like this, far too long to address the issue. It was understandable given the nature of the dra'acheck but it was long overdue. He took a breath, thought of the hatchling murdered and the many others who'd suffered and leapt into the air. He spread his wings and noticed a gasp from the assembled dra'acheck. It made him realize just how imposing of a dragon he was. Any dragon his age was impressive but Agathon was impressive beyond what was normal. He thought back to those moments of near-terror looking at the ancients, especially Godon. He wondered if they felt the same kind of detached wonder at the reaction.

"Dra'acheck!" He didn't intend to roar but that didn't stop the echo of his voice. He alighted on a perch jutting out from the rock face and looked out at the assembly. Again, he was struck by the majesty of the gathering. All eyes turned expectantly toward him and he paused again, realizing just how much power he possessed and somewhat impressed with the way he'd just commanded everyone's attention. It gave him confidence he desperately needed. He'd never before addressed such a large crowd, and it felt odd to expect this group, many of whom he had never properly met, to listen respectfully to his plan.

A plan with which many of them would disagree.

Many of them would speak out against him. It was only natural. There was no matter among the dra'achek that raised such emotions, and his response was unemotional and based purely on a logical assumption many might question. For now, though, the group was silent, waiting respectfully for him to speak. Reverence. That was the term other elders used when they described how the others felt about him. He believed it now. The dragons would listen and they would expect him to fix their problems, to do great things. The burden of his people, a burden almost intangible before suddenly weighed on him in a real and visceral way.

Would his words disappoint them?

Of course they would. His words would disappoint most, if not all, of them and infuriate some of them. There was a more important question. Was he right?

After a moment, he took a deep breath and began. "Humans..." He hadn't intended to pause after the word but the reactions on the faces of the assembled were profound. A few immediately filled with disgust. Other's showed fear and sadness at just the word. Some displayed anger but the vast majority displayed hope. They had hope that Agathon would save them all from the Hunt. "Humans have done terrible things to us, and many of us here have done terrible things to humans in return." Here he paused and shot a pointed glare in Yara's direction. "There is satisfaction in fighting back, in refusing to watch our hatchlings die." Murmurs of approval grew with his words.

"However I would ask you to remember our ways. We are honorable, peaceful. We are not warriors. We are not killers." He expected the first shouts, the first bouts of resistance but they didn't come. He continued. "Centuries have passed since I woke on the shores of the basin." The words were calculated to remind all of those present he was there in the beginning. "In that time, we've learned a great deal, and one thing we know is that humans were here before us. We all have hoped they would lose interest in us, that we could live with them in peace or that they would just leave us alone. I too, hoped they would tire of their Hunt and learn to live peaceably with us." He paused and noted nodding heads and fewer expressions of wariness.

"Those hopes are lost. The humans were here before us but even still they are a younger race. The elders have spent too long ignoring this situation and we've come to the conclusion it is time to act. The humans will not change. They will continue their hunt, fueled by their wild imaginings. It will not change. How many of you have seen a human this season? Can you recall a time when most of us had never seen one? Those times are gone. The humans will not change, and so we must act out of reality and not out of hope."

Agathon stopped and let his eyes travel slowly around the gathering, making eye contact occasionally, focusing on allies but also the occasional dragon he knew would be resistant to what he said. Well, none would like what he was about to say. Some, though, were of a nature to hear it and accept it. Some were not. "The humans are expanding in number across these lands. They breed far faster than we do, and they are ready to take up arms only a few decades after birth while our hatchlings are still helpless for far longer." He shook his head. "They mean to spread over the world. I've walked among them, and I've heard them talk. They mean to take this land for themselves. They want to cut down our trees, hunt our game, and live in the shadow of our mountains. Already, villages grow just outside of the forest."

A younger dragon roared. "Let us destroy those villages! We will rain down fire upon them and pour the suffering of the dra'acheck upon their heads!" Agathon sighed but he'd anticipated the outburst.

"Don't be blind!" Justinian called out from among the crowd. "It is against our nature. Why must we stoop to their level? They kill dragons for sport. We don't. Even the great Yara attacks only those villages that serve as starting points for their hunters. We cannot be murderers."

"And it will not work," another, older dragon added. Agathon noted with surprise it was Hallentia, a dra'achek distantly related to Yara. He'd expected her to oppose him. "Agathon has already spoken truth. They are more in number. They outnumber us ten to one, or more and by the time my son is ready to leave my perch they will outnumber us twelve to one or more. Do you think it's just the humans from the villages around us? They will come from everywhere. They journey to find us, to these very mountains simply to fight us. We must flee to another land, somewhere without humans, where we can live in peace! It's the only way."

Immediately, others began shouting and arguing, raising their voices to be heard above everyone else. No one listened but Agathon realized it didn't matter. None cared what the others might say. The meeting rapidly approached total chaos. He realized there had been no discussions on the subject, at least no group discussions. In front of him, some shouted for war and others for peace. Most seemed to want to move, to find somewhere safe. He searched for familiar faces. Neither Yara nor Justinian participated in the yelling. Justinian stared expectantly at Agathon and Yara seemed to have the strangest combination of smugness and sadness.

"Silence!"

Immediately, the gathering grew quiet. It took Agathon a moment to realize he'd shouted the word, and there was a moment of strangeness as the earth itself seemed to shake and the trees rippled in the aftermath of that single word. The crowd of dra'acheck fell silent in shock, wonder, and perhaps fear. Agathon was getting to the point of awe himself. He wondered at the strength and power in his voice. He remembered that moment long ago when he'd seen his reflection on the surface of the lake and realized who he was. The moment had come again. The dra'acheck needed more than an elder. They needed a leader. They needed him.

"All of us agree the humans are dangerous. All of us agree the humans will not stop. Some of you shout for peace. That's foolhardy. The humans have no stomach for peace. Some of you shout for war. This, too is foolhardy. We have no stomach for war, and even if we could live with ourselves we would not live. They would destroy us." He paused. "To call for peace is foolishness driven by hubris. To call for war is foolishness driven by anger." All still stared at him and he sighed. "And we cannot find a place of safety. There is no place of safety."

Confusion etched itself over the faces of those assembled. He'd accurately described the situation but offered no solution.

Yet.

"Dra'acheck," he said. "We will yet still survive. We will live on this world with the humans. With them. As them." To punctuate the point, he took human form.

134

CHAPTER TWELVE

NOW AND THEN

Justinian

The evening was cool, wonderfully cool. Justinian stood on the roof, looked out over the valley. It was strange, really. What had been his home for almost a hundred years was so different than it had been at first. It was all right, though. He loved the way the skyline had grown, the way the city had become so powerfully bustling and so much movement and…it was lovely. Of course, the smog could be frustrating, but it didn't affect him, or, for that matter, any of the dra'acheck the way it seemed to affect the humans.

He stretched and looked at the sky. He'd already sensed her, but he hadn't seen her yet. He kept his eyes trained in the direction from which he knew she'd come, and finally he saw her, the form beautiful, almost heavenly, though such a thought was more human than dra'acheck. He wondered if he was now more human than dra'acheck. She was beautiful in flight. That was certain. Everything about her movements showed impossible power that had no right to simultaneous grace but somehow displayed that grace even more than the strength. He watched as her wings moved slowly and gracefully until, finally, she was there. Only then did he transform because it seemed somehow wrong to meet her in human form when she was still dragon. She lighted down, her lustrous green scales almost glowing in the moonlight.

"Justinian. You are well?" It took a moment for him to speak as the power of her voice flooded him. She saw him every five to ten years, and for him that should have been nothing, a blink. Nonetheless, to hear the voice of an ancient was always so damned overpowering and he resolved as he had countless times before not to lose that memory, not to allow the awe to seep out from him in all of his quotidian responsibilities. She was beautiful, too, and beautiful in a way humans could never understand.

"Quite well, Katya," he said. He recognized the tone of ancients in his voice as well and wondered when that had come. He didn't recognize the same power but he imagined Katya wouldn't hear her own power either. "How are the mountains?"

She leveled her gaze on him and smiled. Niceties in conversation meant more to dra'acheck than they did to humans. She nodded in a way that seemed surprised and Justinian wondered if she'd noticed the different tone in his voice or if other stewards in their long years among humans had grown impolite. He waited patiently and she finally said, "We are well."

There was something in her voice that sounded off. Of course, for almost a hundred years she seemed to hide something during her visits. It wasn't surprising. The entire foundation of the plan for dispersal relied on no contact between prides. If she were worried about a group in Australia or Sweden or Gabon, she wouldn't be able to say anything. Still… "And how are the dra'acheck?"

"They are as they always are," she said softly. She leaned close and said, "Some thrive and some struggle." He smiled as she chuckled slightly. That answer hadn't changed in hundreds of years.

"And what about the mighty Katya?"

"Katya is old, Justinian. Katya is not as mighty as she once was."

"Perhaps not," Justinian said. "But she manages to speak of herself in the third person nonetheless."

The green dragon laughed, a long hearty laugh that set a lot of Justinian's unease to rest. Finally, she brought her gaze back to him and said, "I thrive, Justinian."

They perched on the roof for a few minutes, not speaking. Finally, he asked, "Are there instructions for me?"

She lifted up her head and inhaled deeply. "You are growing." He nodded. "Four hatchlings were added this year. Is it time for Philip to become a steward, to lead his own pride?"

He shook his head. "Philip refuses. He wishes to keep this pride intact." He left out the angry disbelief Philip displayed when he first suggested it. "Daniel as well, and we have no others who would do the title justice." She inclined her head and looked narrowly at him and he added, "We've acquired more land. We have a compound nearby, well a state away. Nevada."

She nodded and her gaze grew softer. "That is wise. Others have done as you have done, expanding slightly but close enough to maintain control and to ensure that the—" Her words trailed off and he nodded. It was hard to say the words, even harder for some of the ancients.

"To ensure the plan stays in place."

She smiled and lifted her head to the sky. He wondered if there was something about all the time he'd spent in human form that made the sight magnificent. He realized with more than a little surprise that he'd never noticed the way a dra'acheck's head attached. As he watched Katya's serpentine neck grow almost rigid and straight, he realized it seemed impossible that the neck could support the head's weight. He wondered again if his time in human form influenced the wonder.

She lifted up her head again. "There are humans here."

He nodded. "We've taken on some servants," he said. "Every now and then, new servants so we blend in with others in this area. The wealth gives us a degree of eccentricity and humans are growing more distant from each other but for an estate this size, servants are expected and the idea that a maid or a gardener would remain in our employ for decades is unthinkable in this area."

She nodded again. "Blending in is important. It's the whole point." She sighed. "There is never enough time, Justinian. I'll leave now."

"Wait!" he cried out and then realized he'd almost panicked. He calmed himself and asked softly, "How is Agathon?"

She smiled sadly. "Agathon is Agathon. His back remains strong though he carries the weight of both worlds."

He nodded. The tone of her voice meant he'd get nothing else from her. He hadn't seen Agathon since that terrible day with Yara. He missed him. "Please convey my respects," he said.

Katya smiled warmly. "Perhaps there is no other dra'acheck entitled to convey more than respects. He speaks often of you and of your adventures from the beginning."

"Then please convey my love."

She nodded.

He smiled. "Can you stay for a while? May I bring you something? Food? Drink?" He realized how foolish the question was. She could still hunt, could still dive down among a herd of elk and snap one up, could still hear the heart beating as the blood filled her mouth. There was nothing for her in his home.

"I have a long journey."

That was it. She leapt into the air and extended her wings. He watched her disappear into the night sky and sighed. He'd have to visit the new compound to ensure things were as they should be. He had to do a great many things. Still, he spent a long time just staring at the sky before he finally returned to human from and climbed from the roof.

Justinian

All in all, Justinian thought, wealth made things a lot easier. Nearly a thousand years to build the wealth, and though they'd started out with twenty-seven Dra'acheck, they had forty-six now, and none new. None had been born in four decades despite some couples actively trying. It was strange and troubling, but unless the elders of Mount Tatras had something to say about it there was certainly nothing he could say about it.

But wealth made a lot of things easier.

Above all, it allowed for a much more insular lifestyle, and insular was important when you didn't age. In France, he'd had to deal with the occasional questioning look until he finally moved the entire pride away into Italy for almost a hundred years before returning home, this time as "The Descendants" of himself.

He felt a quick burst of pain as thoughts of Linara struck him. He wondered if the pain ever went away. How long had it been?

Almost nine hundred years.

Nine hundred years, and he still missed her. He'd been without her for longer than he'd been with her, and still her absence was felt every day, at every moment of every day, every time he woke just to find the bed next to him empty. He chuckled at that. The bed. Had he lived so long among humans that the bed was the natural place to wake?

Probably.

Nonetheless, there was something exciting and wonderful to leave the compound, what humans called "an estate" but in truth primarily kept the world away from them and to some extent them away from the world. He walked along the streets, enjoying the feel and fighting back the urge to run. What was that movie he'd just watched? The one about the hero who could fly?

He couldn't remember the movie, and of course for him "just watched" was a relative term. It was probably two decades prior that he'd seen it. But he remembered the boy running, running alongside train tracks and then leaping across them. As he watched, he thought of how slow the man had run. He was thankful that these spells, these little desires to use his real abilities came only rarely so that the risk to himself and his pride was minimal but it didn't change the almost desperate need every now and then to just flex the muscles of who he truly was. He managed to resist, though, as he always did, and he made his way down the narrow street to the main highway.

He knew he should have taken one of the cars but he didn't enjoy the thought of adding to the time of his journey that would be spent inside walls or on top of wheels or in a tube flying through the sky. At the edge of the highway, though, in the external garage they kept, he unlatched the padlock, opened the door, stepped in, and chose one of the non-descript white sedans. A quick turn of the key later, he was on his way to the airport.

It seemed that Philip had chosen a good location in buying the land through a series of companies and subsidiaries and subsidiaries of subsidiaries. He'd placed it squarely within their ownership but it was impossible to trace. He wasn't all that excited to be located so close to Las Vegas, but on the other hand Philip assured him that while Vegas itself was highly developed, only a few miles outside of Vegas was nothing but desert. He drove along the streets and then went through the irritation of the airport, from parking to boarding until at takeoff he felt the strange contradiction of flying through the air and not feeling free. An hour and a few minutes later, he touched down in Vegas. As promised, Philip was at the airport, a bright smile on his face.

"Nice journey?"

Justinian rolled his eyes. "Did you really just ask me that?"

Philip laughed. "I'm a slow learner."

"Where are we going?"

"We're going directly to the compound," Daniel said as he stepped into view, holding car keys up.

Justinian smiled. Daniel was always no-nonsense. Always. "All right." The three of them walked toward the exit, bypassing baggage claim and making their way toward the short-term parking. He raised an eyebrow as they approached a bright red van.

"I told you time and time again we drive white cars. Didn't I tell you about those studies that—"

Philip held up a hand. "Our car's behind this one." His tone of voice made it clear he found Justinian's lack of faith surprising.

Justinian nodded an apology but didn't speak. Behind the van was a non-descript sedan almost identical to the one Justinian left at the airport back in Los Angeles. The three got in and hours later arrived in the middle of the desert at the small structure that looked almost like a house and almost like a warehouse.

"We can transform here," Justinian said.

"Naturally."

Daniel raised an eyebrow at the thought. "Would that be all right?"

Justinian tilted his head and considered. "The prohibition is against transforming in front of humans. I don't think there are any humans anywhere near here."

"But what about airplanes traveling overhead?"

"This is the opposite direction from how I flew in. Is this in the flight path from the East?" Philip shrugged. Daniel shrugged as well. "Well, let's keep our eyes and ears open and see if any come through."

They nodded. Philip smiled a little bit. Justinian knew that smile. It was the smile that came from hope. They made their way into the compound, and Justinian explored for a while before finally returning and saying, "What are your plans for the evening?"

Philip said that he'd hoped to finish the security system, and after that, he was up for anything.

Justinian said, "I'm not really interested in us doing something together, but I am going to go back to Vegas to explore."

Philip laughed. "You love watching them, don't you?"

"Maybe I just love to gamble."

Cheryl

Cheryl sighed.

One more year.

Only one more year.

It was hard, though, walking along the streets with the light assaulting her from every direction. It was so strange. People came here all of the time, enamored with it, overwhelmed with the excitement of it and somehow believing there was magic behind all of the lights, that they'd somehow step into town poor or just barely making it or even just comfortable, and walk away multi-millionaires. It weighed on her.

It weighed on her in ways that she couldn't completely understand but she knew it weighed heavily because of those times when a man sat at the table, all hope gone from his eyes so that his actions were almost entirely automatic, gesturing for her to deal another card. It was terrible. Oftentimes, she found herself desperately hoping that his card would come. And it did, sometimes. But even that joy was always short-lived because, thirty minutes later, his last chip would find its way into the circle and he'd stand at seventeen and she'd make nineteen, take his chips, and try not to see the moment of utter hopelessness and try to will the frozen time to move faster until he mumbled some kind of thanks or some kind of exclamation of disgust before getting up and walking away.

How many times had she seen that? How many cards had she placed face up on the table to control the emotions of countless people? For Pete's sake, she studied statistics and she had straight A's. She ought to be able to figure out exactly how many cards she'd dealt. Supporting herself as a dealer had been thousands of times more emotionally draining than the school itself was. She had a friend who kept up with bills and tuition stripping in one of the clubs. Cheryl had the body for it but not the heart. Evenings like tonight, though, almost convinced her to take her friend up on the offer of an introduction.

She lived in two worlds.

No, not two. Really, it was like she lived in three different worlds. She had the world of the casino, a world of hopes constantly dashed but somehow kept alive in a bizarre cycle of… of hopes and dashed hopes. God, was everything in her life circular reasoning? She almost stumbled as her foot hit something, would have stumbled if the something didn't roll out of the way. She squinted and couldn't make it out but it rolled far enough that it caught the dim glow of a streetlight. A roller skate.

A roller skate.

Just off the Strip. How the hell did a...?

Well, that was Vegas. Her casino world was nestled inside the world of Las Vegas, a world that was built on flash and entertainment and all you can eat buffets designed to make you forget all about the damned casino world and the hopelessness it really represented.

Three?

Hell. She had more.

There was the world of college, its own little island completely detached from the real world, but detached in different ways, detached in protests against Apartheid in South Africa by young middle-class Whites who'd never traveled to South Africa and couldn't even name anyone other than Botha (and when thy did they pronounced his name incorrectly) and Nelson Mandela. They'd have their protests and then go to the pub to drink and pretend that they'd done their civic duty well enough that they had no further obligation to be human.

You got a brand new key.

How did that get in her head?

Oh yeah, she'd kicked a roller skate.

I've got a brand new pair of roller skates, you got a brand new key.

She smiled in spite of herself. Congratulations, Mom. I'm officially singing your music, now. The song was so oddly out of sync with her emotions, and it felt strange and wonderful and silly all at once.

I rode my bicycle past your window last night.

I rollerskated to your door at daylight.

It almost seems like you're avoiding me.

I'm okay alone but you've got something I need.

Yeah. She needed to get out of Vegas. She needed to get finished with school and just get away. She needed to see people smile with real smiles and not these silly smiles of false hope or desperation and—

And what the hell was she going to do with a degree in statistics anyway?

She shook her head violently, trying to get rid of the thoughts. She didn't like herself very much when she finished a shift. People she considered friends suddenly seemed shallow and useless. People she already felt little of became despicable. It was stupid, and she knew it.

On the bright side, she had her paycheck and her tips.

Ride my bike, I rollerskate, don't drive no car

Don't go too fast, but I go pretty far

For somebody who don't drive, I been all around the world

Some people say I done all right for a girl.

This particular combination of tips and paycheck meant she'd be able to pick up her books, only two weeks into the semester. This time. Still, after a shift nothing seemed nice. Beauty seemed ugly and ugly seemed unbearable. She walked along, cursing herself for parking so far away, for needing the walk to steel herself for her shift earlier. It was one thing to walk a few blocks at three o'clock in the afternoon; it was another thing altogether to walk away from the strip at one forty-five in the morning.

She heard footsteps and didn't react at first. It wasn't all that atypical to hear footsteps at any time in Vegas. People said New York was the city that never slept. That was bullshit. Vegas made New York look like a toddler who needed a nap. She walked toward her car and tried not to feel disdain for another group of suckers heading to another casino to lose another sum of money. She reached her car, exhaled heavily, and put her key in the lock.

"Hand over your purse. Now!"

They weren't locals. Locals would never bother to rob her. It made absolutely no sense to try to rob a dealer. Dealers, at most, had a couple hundred dollars and when they had more they got a check, not cash. The locals, those particular criminals who preyed on people at night outside of casinos, they were after the gamblers. They'd never go after someone wearing a stupid dealer tux.

I've got a brand new pair of rollerskates.

She turned around, hoping they were locals and they'd see the bow tie. There were three men. One tall and lanky, one that looked like he'd be perfectly at home on a football field, and one thin and wiry. The third had a sick look about him that made her think he had to be addicted to some kind of a drug. It was the sickly-looking one that shouted, again, "Hand over your purse!"

She shook her head. "I don't have any money." It was a lie, of course. She didn't know why she said it but everything felt unreal anyway.

He smiled, "You got a lot we can use."

It took a moment for her to realize what he meant and then she turned again to grab at her car door. She was far too slow. Football Guy grabbed her and as she kicked he lifted her up from behind. She heard her keys hit the ground and then felt a jerk on her wrist as her purse fell from her shoulder and the strap caught.

You got a brand new key.

She screamed and kicked, but the sinking realization that she wasn't going to get away hit her, and hit her hard. It was a moment of absolute clarity, and never in her life had she wanted more desperately to be confused. She still struggled but now the struggle was just to give her something to do other than wait for the inevitable as Football Guy handed her over to the wiry one and the sickly one. They slammed her down to the ground, and she stared in confusion at the sky before the wiry one put his face in front of hers and said, "Quiet!"

Maybe we should get together and try them on to see.

She could smell alcohol on his breath, and not for the first time she noted the difference between the cheap booze people bought for a dollar a pint at the liquor stores and the cheap booze somehow disguised with sweet and sour, bitters, and soda in the casinos. She closed her mouth as much to get away from his breath as to obey. She screamed again, though, when she felt the sickly one's lips against her neck.

They all froze, and she saw a man standing a few feet away, staring at them. "Help!" she shouted. The man hesitated for just a minute but then looked away and hurried on.

I been looking around awhile, you got something for me.

She screamed and felt tears on her temples as she heard laughter from the three men. She stared blindly at the sky as she felt hands at her shirt yanking, sending buttons flying across the parking lot. She realized she'd given up struggling, given up hope.

And then the sickly one screamed.

She didn't understand at first what was happening, but she turned her head. He was there on the asphalt right next to her, but something was wrong. His arm was bent in the wrong way. Something different, something strange. It was only when she caught the wet glint of white in the dim light of the streetlight that she realized the man had a broken arm, broken hard enough that the bone had pierced the skin.

Nobody was holding her down anymore.

She turned and looked for the wiry guy just as he landed next to her and rolled to a stop against the wheels of her car. She looked. The man was there, and he moved with speed and ferocity. It was insane. Wiry Guy got back up and he and Football Guy lunged at him. They threw punches in a blur of motion but he moved as though they were somehow dancing in slow motion. It was like all of them were campfire songs and he was some Norwegian death metal band.

Oh, I got a brand new pair of roller skates.

He moved with speed and power and strength, and even though she could hear the voices of her parents screaming at her to get up and run, she stared in shock. It made no sense. He didn't just outclass them, he made them seem impotent. Finally, football player jumped at him and he easily stepped to the side and landed a crushing blow right on the barrel chest. Football Guy gasped, and she thought she heard his bones crunching. She didn't even know that was possible. Could someone punch someone so hard that his ribs would break? Whether or not that happened, Football Guy wheezed and fell to the ground. Cheryl got a good look at the man.

It wasn't the one who'd stopped earlier. That man had brown hair and looked like a businessman. This one had a shocking mane of blonde curls and looked like… He looked like… Well, like a god.

The wiry man didn't learn from his friends' misfortunes because he tried a final attack on the stranger. A second later he sailed through the air, this time not rolling and stopping but instead landing on an old Japanese import. The little coupe almost crumpled from the force of the throw, and the back window shattered, exploding in different directions so that Cheryl turned and covered her face.

You got a brand new key.

And that was when she saw the man she'd cried out to, the man she'd wanted to help. He was in a car, rushing headlong out of the parking lot. He was studiously avoiding looking at her, doing his best to pretend he didn't see what he assumed the three men were still doing to her. She turned and tried to warn the hero but he was approaching, his face the picture of concern for her. He crouched down, and she found herself unable to form words.

"Are you o—"

She stared in terror and confusion as the car hit him, and sent him sailing through the air to crash against the back of another car, crumpling it like aluminum foil with a loud cracking sound. She stared back at the car that hit him. The front was devastated as well, and the driver was trying desperately to get the gears to engage. She managed to stumble to her feet just as the driver got his car to lurch forward and tore off. She tried to get the license plate number but had no luck.

She turned back to her hero. He was on the ground, flat on the ground. She rushed forward but stopped when she saw a shimmering blue blur, and felt heat filling the area, making her light-headed and taking from her all pretense of sanity. He was a man and then a dinosaur and then a man and not a dinosaur but some kind of lizard or demon and then a man again. She felt her breath catch in her throat and forced herself to breathe in and out slowly and evenly.

She looked on the ground again. He was a man. A perfect man, maybe. He wasn't a monster. He was a knight. She went to her car and found her key and her purse and got inside. It took a great deal of effort to get him into the backseat, and she stared in indecision at the wiry man still screaming on the asphalt. Finally, she shook her head. "Screw him. He can make his own damned way to the hospital."

She turned the key and that new group from Seattle was screaming out lyrics to a heavy base line. It was just what she needed, and she felt some energy coming back.

"No!"

The voice came from the back and she pressed the button on the radio. "Okay! Okay! You don't like them? It's Nirvana. They're playing everywhere."

"No hospital." The voice was hoarse and he let out a long sigh after he said it. She turned to look. His eyes were closed again.

Great.

So some mobster or something had saved her.

She sighed as she put the car in gear.

CHAPTER THIRTEEN

THEN

Justinian

Naturally, Justinian didn't want to go. Who the hell would? Nobody wanted to go. These were the affairs of humans, not the affairs of dra'acheck. It didn't matter. The conflict was imminent and the day approached. Participation was inevitable. Justinian noticed the looks he and his pride received. They had to go fight infidels or at least pretend to go fight infidels. There was no other choice.

There was no way around it.

If they remained in France, they'd be outcasts. Worse, humans might start asking questions. Their antisocial quirks might instead make them outsiders instead of gentry. He desperately wished he could somehow get a message to Tatras and get guidance but there was no way. In the end, he pulled his group together and simply did it, and now, here he was in a hot desert, in a climate utterly different than France, and all that he'd learned to adapt himself to over the last two hundred and fifty years was now gone. Instead, heat, sweltering heat, lay like some kind of a twisted and horrible blanket over him. It was terrible, absolutely terrible, and the worst part about it was he had no idea how to determine just what should still be done and what should not.

Two hundred and fifty years. That was how long they'd lived among humans. It had been shocking, obviously, to the dra'acheck when Agathon finished the Council in human form. Justinian had a good idea about the plan prior to the council but even so, to hear the words spoken aloud by no less that Agathon himself still sent a moment of terrible trepidation through him. They would disperse. They would disperse and live among humans, several prides separated from each other and only able to return to their natural forms under particular conditions that would keep discovery from humanity.

In short, dragons would disappear from the Earth.

It came down to faith, really, Agathon's faith in humanity, his certainty that if dragons became relegated to the realm of legends, humanity would progress and grow to a point at which dragons could reveal themselves and do so with no fear of a return to the days of the Hunt, with no fear of a return to the death and the violence. On the whole, Justinian was pretty sure the plan, the Great Dispersal, was working. Humans had indeed grown, some gathering toward cities and some travelling great distances to bring goods back but, for the most part, farmers fed their families and traded for what was missing.

Progress.

They seemed to change and to move so quickly. They created countries and then redrew boundaries and then married to change the boundaries again. Everything seemed constantly in motion, and Justinian believed Agathon was right. Humanity changed. Perhaps that was their primary quality. They changed.

But Agathon couldn't have anticipated that living among humans would make them subject to human governance. He couldn't have anticipated the likelihood dra'acheck would be expected to participate in human conflicts.

Philip stood next to him. "I have an idea," he said. He hastily added, "Sir," as a human walked by. Justinian nodded, and when Philip didn't immediately respond, he looked around and then raised a hand a nodded again. "Here's my thought," Philip said softly. "What if we just don't involve ourselves in the fighting?"

"So we're here with a giant contingent of humans screaming about all of the hatred they have for these Moors and Saracens and camel lovers and dogs and whatever else they call them, and you expect that somehow we're going to be able to be a part of this campaign to reclaim their holy land, but not actually fight?" His tone was harsher than he'd intended, frustration boiling over but he didn't apologize.

"Well, that's not exactly what I meant. What I meant was, what if we find some way to be the ones that handle the supplies? You know, make sure that the food gets where it needs to go, make sure that the weapons get where they need to go. One of the concerns we built in France involves shipping of goods. You could claim experience."

Justinian didn't respond right away and evidently Philip believed he disagreed with the idea. "Obviously it's not as good as if we were able to just stay home, but at least that would give us some opportunity to avoid some of what's happening here." Justinian still didn't respond but Philip didn't add any more to his thoughts but waited.

Justinian considered it. In more than two thousand years, not one dra'acheck had killed. Not one had killed without a damned good reason. This idea had merit. "Gather the others together," he said.

It didn't take much persuading to get the commander to allow Justinian to handle the logistics, and while the commander had no idea that at least some subtle tricks of the mind were used to make it happen, he was nonetheless very satisfied with the way that supplies seemed to get where they belonged, that typical graft was no longer typical, and that appropriations of livestock from locals were handled far more efficiently with far less destruction.

And so the campaign wore on.

Justinian had to suppress a laugh when the commander told him that he might be the most Christian man in the entire crusade, and not just because of his zeal to drive back the infidels but also because of his clear and obvious concern that the crusade be handled in the least painful way possible. Justinian suppressed the external laughter but couldn't keep from laughing inwardly at the thoughts. He didn't give a damn about any infidels and the only pain he wanted to avoid was the pain that would result from discovery.

Things might have gone on like that.

Things might have continued with no problems whatsoever.

Things might have simply gone their course.

For Justinian and for his followers, two hundred years was no time at all. Waiting out the war seemed like it might be a perfect opportunity to continue to disguise their place in French society while simultaneously participating (but not participating) in violence.

It might have worked.

It might have worked, but it didn't.

It took one day with a new commander before it all changed. He had a different philosophy, a philosophy that said forage from the locals which Justinian knew to mean, Kill the locals as you move along and take their supplies and food to feed your army. He didn't believe in taking one person, a quarter-master, to be in charge of the weaponry. He didn't believe in that at all. Instead, he expected each soldier and each knight to manage their own weaponry and, if something were to happen to it the efficiency of the army was far less relevant than the need for every man to brandish a weapon.

So Justinian found himself with no alternatives. Though he still had limited duties in regards to storage and disbursement of supplies, his soldiers had none. Philip was required to join the fray first, and Justinian marched along with him although the commander hadn't specifically insisted that he go. As they walked, he told Philip to avoid areas of clear combat but if he could not, to stand back, to parry blows and pummel, to knock people to the ground but do his best not to kill.

It was useless advice when it came right down to it.

Their very first battle, both Philip and Justinian killed three men.

That made things worse. Their reflexes, so superior to their human counterparts, made it impossible for them to only deal minor damage. Naturally, that brought a great deal of attention. They'd walked into the campaign utterly reluctant, and in the course of one sixty-second battle, they were heroes. Heroes!

They didn't want to be. Trapped, they marched along, casting glances at each other that betrayed their desperate desire to be anywhere else. There was no hope. They were stuck. To Justinian's great shame, they killed their way from battle to battle until finally they reached a small settlement with a huge stone mosque. It appeared abandoned, and the men began to scatter, to search, to plunder.

Justinian was about fifty yards from Philip when the ambush came. The strange and violent screams of the Moors were everywhere, and suddenly scimitars flashed, arrows loosed, and the entire area was overrun with enemies.

Philip became a blur of motion. As long as Justinian could see him, it seemed that, with every movement, every step, every slight dancing move, another foe died on his sword. For all of the violence and the horror that it represented, Justinian thought it was the most elegant and beautiful thing he had ever seen. And then, he dealt with his own enemies, his sword moving quickly, deftly knocking one foe away, entering through the ribcage of a second foe, and slicing across the neck of another.

It seemed like the battle would last forever. The enemy kept coming and then, suddenly, Philip let out a piercing wail. Cold fear pulled him, and Justinian kicked the man in front of him and sent him flying almost thirty feet.

Justinian didn't wait to see if anyone had seen him. Instead, he rushed to Philip's side.

Philip wasn't hurt.

He wasn't hurt at all.

In fact, though his hand and his sword were covered with blood, he looked like he might've just started marching. But the expression on his face was terrible, horrible.

"What is it?" Justinian asked.

Philip didn't answer. He simply lifted his sword and let it fall to the ground. With his now-free hand, he pointed. Justinian stared, confused, but then his confusion turned to horror and shock. There was a man, a dead man.

Only it wasn't a man.

It was dra'acheck.

It wasn't just a dra'acheck. It was the son of the great Yara.

Justinian

Justinian looked at Linara and wondered if the other dra'acheck found the situation quite as peculiar as he did. Even after four hundred and seventy-eight years, he stilled looked at her human face and saw her dragon form. It was wonderful but at the same time somewhat...

He didn't know the word.

Disturbing?

No, there was nothing about Linara that ever disturbed him. It was curious. That was it. Curious and strange. It was strange to see that mouth forming words that belonged to her, strange to see eyes that were not Linara's but without question were.

She smiled sadly and asked softly, "Do you think he'll be here? Do you really think he'll come?"

Justinian shrugged. "I hope not. This is all overkill, really. He's probably the most respected of all dra'acheck, except for Agathon. He's angry. Sure he's angry, and I suppose any of us would be. Still, there's no reason to believe he'll take this any farther. We shouldn't really have prepared so hard, and we can probably go back to the city tomorrow."

He was lying. He was lying, and he knew that Linara could tell he was lying, but added another sentence anyway. "Maybe, if it were someone else, some other pride, Yara might act rashly but he and I go back longer than most." She could tell he was lying but she acted relieved anyway, for his sake he knew. Once again he was struck by how perfect of a mate she really was for him. "Do you remember when you first met Agathon?"

She nodded and smiled a little less sadly. "He wanted to celebrate but you had to tell him Artemi was killed in the Hunt."

Justinian closed his eyes. He'd forgotten about Artemi or at least driven the thought from his mind. "Even back then, I think Agathon knew dra'acheck and humans shared the same future. Did you know he'd lived among them before he came back to the cave?"

"Of course I did," she said. She said it indulgently, though. "You talked about it almost every day. You even tried spying on villages to find him."

"He and Yara were very close. They argued all the time but I think Agathon respects none more than Yara and I think Yara respects none more than Agathon. In many ways, Yara will think of me as Agathon's son. He won't come."

It was a lie because there was no way as long as breath remained within him he would let this matter go. Yara was not the type to let even the slightest issue remain unaddressed, and this wasn't a slight issue. The council had ruled. The council had ruled, and they'd ruled that this event, while tragic, was obviously accidental but Yara hadn't even attended, and if he'd arrived earlier and tricked the council into revealing the presence of the pride, he was coming. He'd already given up on anything resembling procedures."

Obviously accidental.

There was no justice to be had but Yara never saw nuances. Everything was black and white, and he'd be here. Justinian shook his head sadly and wondered what in the world had possessed him to feel happiness and even fulfillment when he'd been made a steward. Now the responsibility weighed on him in ways that he'd never imagined his position would. He looked at Philip. Philip nodded. He was ready for whatever came. He looked over at Daniel, Tyrus, and Arthur. They were all ready, every one of them. A dozen men stood by him. No, not a dozen men, a dozen dra'acheck. Some were young, not as powerful as some others but all of them were loyal. They stood, weapons at the ready, which seemed pretty useless given that whatever was to happen would not happen in human form.

"Remember," he said. "Let me speak with him. If we can make this happen without violence, we want to." He looked at each in turn and then Linara. She smiled slyly at him, and he realized he'd just destroyed the illusion afforded by their shared deception. "You should wait inside now," he said.

"My place is here."

"Linara," he said, "Please. If I have to deal with Yara and I fear for you I don't know what will happen."

"I will stay out of the way but I won't leave."

He wanted to argue more but he couldn't because Yara was close, and he'd brought warriors. He looked up at the sky. He couldn't see anyone, but he could sense them. At least a dozen, maybe a few more. A dozen dra'acheck in France, a dozen in France who didn't belong to him. They didn't belong to him, and they were coming. He tried to sense Yara, to see if he could, but he couldn't. Didn't matter. There was no other reason for a delegation.

For a moment, hope rose up within him because he thought he sensed Agathon, but any hope that brought was immediately dismissed when the sense disappeared. He sighed. He'd have to deal with this on his own. Agathon was in the Tatras Mountains, and Justinian was here in the French countryside, and while Agathon would certainly get involved he wouldn't get involved any time soon, at least not in time to prevent whatever was to come. It was up to Justinian and he'd never wished so much for someone else to be in charge.

He thought he felt Yara's roar before he heard it. They landed in the courtyard and Justinian considered how smart Linara had been to suggest he take everyone to the estate. Out here, the likelihood of a human seeing them was all but nonexistent. Even if someone did, it would be containable.

Yara wasted no time on pleasantries. "You must hand him over."

Justinian sighed. "We visited the council, Yara. Kalleta arrived right as it ended and told us of your visit. The council made its ruling, Yara, and the ruling was one of innocence."

Yara transformed suddenly and stood in front of him, and Justinian thought there was no possible way he could look more appropriate as a human. He was a tall man with a swarthy complexion and dark eyes. He had bushy eyebrows and a thick mustache. Dragons didn't really have black hair but his hair was dark, very deep brown. He stared defiantly at Justinian. "Innocence? One of your men killed my son."

"It was him." Justinian turned. Another dra'acheck had transformed and pointed at Philip. Justinian was pretty sure it was Phineas, the adopted son of Yara. With lifespans in the thousands of years, death for a young dra'acheck was especially tragic.

"I grieve for you, Yara, but it was an accident."

"Give him to me!"

"Yara, will you be the first dragon to defy the council? Will you be the first dragon to deliberately harm another?"

Yara looked at him angrily. It was strange. The old intimidation returned, the kind of intimidation that Justinian hadn't felt since he was a hatchling looking at the older dragons. Of course, Yara was one of the oldest.

In fact, he couldn't imagine a worse dragon to have this kind of a conflict with. He sighed loudly. "Yara, I will not hand him over."

"Then we will fight," Yara said. "We will fight and all of you will die instead of just one."

"Justinian—" Philip began but Justinian held up his hand.

"I don't wish to fight you Yara," he said. "And I can tell only you and Phineas desire this fight among your own. It's not too late to leave. If you're unhappy with the ruling, you can appeal to the council but don't do this." Yara scowled and Justinian knew there would be no reasoning with him.

Already, Philip and Daniel were changed, but he felt the heat and saw the blue reflection of lights playing off the others' faces. His whole group was changing. He groaned miserably and then transformed himself. It was strange. In the history of the Dra'acheck, as far as he knew, none had ever killed another except for that moment in the Crusades, and that had been accident.

Never before.

Not once.

Yet there were two dozen dra'acheck in his estate in the French countryside transforming to their natural forms and waiting for the first blow that would spark the battle.

"Yara," he said. "Think. Let this go. Go home."

Yara didn't respond. Instead, he simply leapt into action. As the voice of his roar boomed across the courtyard, dragons sprang into action everywhere. Justinian didn't find himself in front of Yara, but instead in front of a younger dragon. The dragon lashed out, and Justinian moved easily. The younger dragon wasn't trying. His heart wasn't in it any more than Justinian's. He lashed out and the young dra'acheck parried. Really, they fought the way hatchlings fought and played. It wasn't real.

No. He knew Yara and Phineas wouldn't fight like hatchlings. He sidestepped a swipe from the young dra'acheck's tail and then leapt into the air. He saw Yara trying to make his way to Philip and saw Daniel defending him. He dove, and the force of his dive pushed the ancient dragon away but only a few yards away. He roared and grabbed Justinian at his shoulders and then threw him, actually threw him. The strength was remarkable, almost impossible, and Justinian realized suddenly there was little hope. If all of his pride fought only Yara alone, perhaps they would have a chance. But Yara wasn't alone. He had Phineas and warriors from his pride. The prospects for survival were bleak.

Yara threw him as if he weighed nothing. He sailed across the courtyard, crashing into the fence. He heard Linara cry out, but he shook himself and lied. "I'm fine," he said. He wasn't fine. He wasn't fine at all. He leapt at Yara again but dove away when the courtyard suddenly filled with a terrible roar, a roar that seemed to call on the energy from the sky and the trees, a cry that had most of the dra'acheck in the courtyard on their knees trembling. Justinian would have fallen to his knees if he weren't tumbling through the air. He knew the voice of the dragon who roared.

The battle was done. Agathon was there.

CHAPTER FOURTEEN

NOW AND THEN

Justinian

The man was sick. Justinian could tell. Worse, the smell of heroin was strong, very strong. It was strong but stale, old. He didn't understand why humans did it to themselves. Philip always said he was too judgmental, that dra'acheck had their own idiosyncrasies and if a dragon could spend almost a decade sunning himself on the same rock, a human could use chemicals to change his outlook. Of course, only the elders had the luxury of a decade in dra'acheck from now. This man, though, the heroin addict, had no luxuries left. Even as he ran to the scene he hadn't fully made up his mind to interfere. The sight of the man with his lips and tongue running over the girl's neck and cheek, though settled it. He could smell the man's lust, the man's rising excitement. At the same time, the girl's shock and horror was almost overwhelming.

He shook his head, tried to clear himself of the smells. It was impossible and he leapt forward, realizing the others probably wouldn't even be able to see him or if they did that he'd appear to them as a blur. He became tangible quickly for the addict, though. Justinian reached down, grabbed his neck and lifted him into the air. Immediately, the man flailed his arms and legs. He connected a few times with his legs, his feet bouncing harmlessly against Justinian's thighs and stomach, and he connected with one wildly moving hand, a solid hit to Justinian's nose that didn't really cause pain but was irritating enough that he quickly grabbed the man by his wrist and yanked him around before slamming him onto the ground.

Justinian heard the sickly crush of bone as he moved and winced. It had been a long time since he'd failed to manage his strength in relation to humans, and he'd hoped he wouldn't do any real damage. Suddenly, the weight of another man was upon him, and he reached up and swatted him from his back. He got to his feet and the first man stared up at him in shock, and then his screams filled the air. He felt the weight on his back again and again swatted the man away, trying his best not to damage this second human as he had the

158

first. The man hit the ground next to the girl and rolled a few times before hitting a car.

He shouldn't have been interfering in the affairs of humans. He wondered just how many rules he was breaking to be there in the first place. Perhaps it was his thoughts of Linara of late. Perhaps Daniel with his talk of humans was finally getting to him. Perhaps it was the idea that someone was being victimized. He didn't know his motivations and realized he was only trying to figure them out in the most cursory of ways. He was angry. He was angry at the men and something in him kept him from stopping.

The biggest of them, a man who probably represented a brute among his kind but was no more than a child to Justinian, stepped up and lunged at him. He easily side-stepped the man's first blow and shot a fist out to catch him on the jaw, again holding back. Even holding back, the man seemed stunned at the force of the blow, and along with an expression of pain came an expression of disbelief. He lunged forward again. This time, Justinian didn't hold back. A quick left-hook caught the man on his face, and this time the sounds of cracking bones wasn't quite so sickening. A hard right to the chest followed, and the crunch of bones was loud. He felt sadistic and even a little guilty as he wondered how many ribs, in addition to the sternum, had been broken.

The man stepped back, stared in horror at Justinian, and then looked down as though having to convince himself the pain that he felt was real. He gave a startled, wheezing kind of a cough and fell to his knees. For a moment, Justinian worried he might have killed the man but then he saw buttons on the pavement and looked at the girl. Her shirt was pulled open, her midriff exposed. Her eyes were wide with terror, and anger took over again. He shot another fist at the wheezing man, catching him on the side of the head and sending him to the ground.

Justinian started to head to the girl, but before he could, the man he's casually thrown was at him, leaping onto his back from the top of a car. Justinian felt fury rise up. It felt like every frustration he'd ever felt about living among humans crashed down upon him. It felt like every desire to transform and spend weeks in the air descended onto him at the same time. He reached back and grabbed the man's leg, whipping him around effortlessly. The man's head crashed into the front of a car, smashing the headlight. Justinian reared back and threw the man, sending him several yards away in a cartwheeling spin that ended half on and half off the roof of another car. The impact sent shattering glass everywhere.

He turned around and was disappointed to realize he'd get no fight from the big man, who lay on the ground moaning weakly or from the addict, who still screamed and stared in horror at the bone protruding from his forearm. Almost instantly his anger disappeared, replaced immediately by a sudden sense of foolishness. It was stupid. The whole situation was stupid, and Justinian took a deep breath. It was insane. He needed self-control, not this kind of crap. He moved forward. The girl lay on the ground, staring at him. He had to comfort her, had to say something.

She spoke first. "Are you finally awake?"

He stared at her, not comprehending. She hadn't spoken, at least her mouth hadn't moved. He made his way the last few feet over, walking as slowly as he could, letting the adrenaline and the anger fade from him until he knelt in front of her.

"I think you're still dazed."

He could see her still shaken and then her face seemed to take on a look of absolute terror. It made sense. He'd just shown a display of power she couldn't possibly understand. She was beautiful for a human, and perhaps there was something about the damsel in distress aspect that appealed to him. "Are you…"

"Are you awake?"

No. Not that. "Are you…" He'd intended to say, "Are you okay", but for some reason, he never got the words out. He felt something on his forehead, a cool hand. It was comforting, and only then did he realize his head hurt. It hurt badly.

The man was sick. Justinian could tell. Worse, the smell of heroin was strong, very strong. It was strong but stale, old. He didn't understand why humans did it to themselves. Philip always said he was too judgmental, that dra'acheck had their own idiosyncrasies and if a dragon could spend almost a decade sunning himself on the same rock, a human could use chemicals—

Wait.

That man already had a broken arm. Why was he still there with his body weight holding the girl to the ground and his lips and tongue making tracks on her neck and her cheek? He shook his head to clear his mind, and that only sent shockwaves of pain through his neck and his eyes. He leapt forward, lifting the man into the air.

Immediately, the man flailed his arms and legs. He connected a few times with his legs, his feet bouncing harmlessly against Justinian's thighs and stomach, and he connected with one wildly moving hand, a solid hit to Justinian's nose that didn't really cause pain but was irritating enough that he quickly grabbed the man by his wrist and yanked him around before slamming him onto the ground. Justinian heard the sickly crush of bone as he moved and winced.

No! That already happened damn it. He broke the man's wrist. He felt guilty about it. He threw one of the men into a car and hit the other man so hard in his chest he'd probably killed him.

"You need to stop moving around! Calm down."

The hand was back, and it felt wonderful on his head but he looked around wildly. There parking lot was as he left it, the girl lying there with a look of terror on her face. The addict screamed and looked at his broken arm. The big one wheezed and the third one, the one on the wrecked car, was silent. He moved toward the girl, "Are you..."

Darkness came then, beautiful darkness made even more beautiful by the feel of cool fingers on his forehead.

Justin(ian)

Justinian opened his eyes and saw clouds, just clouds and that was it. His head hurt, hurt very, very badly. He wanted to shake or nod or do anything to try to get rid of the fog in his vision, but he couldn't. He squeezed his eyes shut tightly and reopened them.

Still just clouds.

He did it again.

Still just clouds.

"Well, looks like you're finally awake."

The voice was lilting and soft. He tried to speak but when he felt a cool hand on his forehead, the effect was one of sudden and wonderful relief, and he just sighed instead. There was something in the touch that drove the clouds away. He blinked twice and, in front of him, he saw a picture of absolute beauty. The woman stared back at him. Her eyes were wide and almond-shaped and blue. No. Blue-green maybe? They weren't quite blue. They weren't quite green. Kind of a steel color with flecks of...flecks of something.

She didn't respond to his stare but just looked back at him with a half-smile. He studied her face. It was oval. Her cheekbones were high and her lips came together in an interesting way, almost as though her face would never show anything other than a smile. Her hair was straight and long and silky and lovely and deep, deep jet black. Jet black.

He sat up straight, sending nauseating pain through his eyes, his temples, and his neck. He ended up falling right back down and thanked whatever gods decreed a pillow would be there still when his head reached its previous location. Even still, the impact was horrible, and he winced.

"You're going to want to rest, unless you enjoy being stupid."

That was how Linara talked. Linara.

He tried to shake his head and got another helping of agony for his effort. There was no way the woman t was dra'acheck. It was a curious thing. Dra'achecks in human form almost always had some distinguishing characteristic that linked them to their dragon nature. For nearly all dra'acheck the biggest commonality was hair. A red dragon had red hair. A yellow dragon was blonde. Green dragons usually had hair the color of their eyes. The point was there was only one color of hair no dra'acheck in human form ever had. Black.

There was brown. There was even very dark brown. There just wasn't black. Those very rare dragons that had black scales almost always appeared in their human form with pure white hair. It was a strange anomaly that made no sense to anyone, but it was a fact. As it was, black dragons were few and far between. Often, Justinian wondered if black-scaled dragons were something like the dragon equivalent to albinos. He didn't know about any of that but he knew it was impossible that the woman in front of him was dra'acheck. That meant he was in a human hospital.

"I need to go," he managed hoarsely. Even speaking felt like torture, like he'd somehow swallowed a glacier and had to learn to move his throat while frozen.

He felt hands at his shoulders. "You're not going anywhere."

He found it hard to form words and even harder to lack the strength to fight against very human hands. He eventually managed, or at least he thought he managed, to say, "No. I can't see a doctor," or something along those lines.

And then everything went black.

Thankfully, the darkness seemed to pulse into place and then pulse out, only lasting a second of so. He opened his eyes again, and this time there were no clouds. She sat at the foot of a bed. He looked around. He'd never been inside of a human hospital, but it certainly didn't look like the human hospitals he'd seen on television.

"Ah, you're awake again!" she said.

"You're very observant," he said. Then he blinked his eyes. "Again?"

She smiled. "You were awake for a second or two and complained about not wanting a doctor. Then you lost it again. I made you lunch but that was hours ago."

He stared at her and said, "Who are you?"

"My name is Cheryl."

"I-I need to get out of here. I can't—I can't be in a hospital."

She laughed, and Justinian found it strange that her laugh should be so pleasant, that her voice should fill him with comfort. He hadn't felt that way in a long time. "You're not in a hospital, and I'm not a doctor," she said. "I think you need to go to a hospital, though, and you need to get over whatever stupid macho thing tells you that you shouldn't."

"N-no," he said. "It's not...it's not macho, it's just..."

"Macho, Macho, Man!" He smiled as she started singing. He tried not to but he smiled nonetheless.

"No. It's not that. I..." How the hell was he supposed to tell a human why he couldn't go to a hospital? He shook his head and pain burst through his senses again. "God," he groaned. "What happened to me?"

"You mean, what happened to you before you came to my rescue like some kind of a knight in shining armor? Or do you mean what happened to you while you were rescuing me, or what happened to you after you rescued me?"

He would've rolled his eyes if he could have. Instead he just stared evenly at her.

"Uh oh," she said. "Is macho man getting angry?"

"I'm not being macho! I just—"

"Oh yes you are. You're totally a Village Person. There's the construction guy, the Indian, the Sailor, and the knight in shining armor."

He groaned. "You don't expect me to start dancing, do you?" She giggled and the sound was musical, wonderful.

"So what do you want to know, um... uh... You might want to tell me your name unless you want me to keep calling you Macho Man."

He paused, realizing that for some stupid reason the idea she would keep calling him by a nickname appealed to him. Finally, he said, "Justinian."

She raised an eyebrow. "Figures."

"What?"

"A guy like you doesn't have a name like Bobby or Chuck. What do you want to know?"

"Well, how about all of it?"

She smiled, and he realized her smile was beautiful. It was so strange. He'd been hundreds of years without Linara, and the idea that he should feel anything for any other female was off-putting. The idea that his first romantic stirrings should come because of a human female—well, that was insane. Still, that smile, that laugh... He couldn't help it. He found himself focused on her, and he wondered if there was something about her that was different. Maybe she was dra'acheck. He couldn't smell it but maybe whatever happened to him impacted his senses. Women dyed their hair these days. Maybe she was really blonde. Just in case, he inhaled deeply. She smelled human. On the other hand, whatever injury that had been done to his head could have just as easily damaged his sense of smell, couldn't it?

"What are you doing?" she asked. "Your eyes just glazed over and you start sniffing the air like you're crazy."

"I'm trying to figure out what you are," he said and then realized he'd said it. "God," he muttered. "I must be worse off than I thought. What happened?"

She smiled, "You're trying to figure me out? That's rich." She said pretty matter-of-factly, "Well, I have no idea what you were doing before you came to my rescue. What I was doing was screaming and struggling and seeing my life flash before my eyes."

He remembered it now. He'd arrived, he'd fought off her attackers, and then, suddenly, he'd been in a great deal of pain. "What happened to me?" he said.

"Right before you showed up, another guy was there and he ran away, just left me to deal with things on my own. After you saved me, he was still scrambling to get away and he ran into you with his car while you were checking on me."

"A car?"

She nodded.

"Clumsy weapon," he muttered.

She laughed again. "It looked a lot clumsier after it hit you."

"How did you get away?"

"You really don't remember?" In response to his blank stare, she said, "I was scared, and I think I'll rub my neck and my cheek raw over the next six months trying to wash off that assholes lips but other than that I wasn't hurt at all. I mean, a piece of glass cut my hand when you… when a car window exploded. Other than that I was fine. I got you in my car, and you weigh a hell of the lot by the way, and I took you home."

"Home?"

"Yeah. You told me no hospital."

"I did?" He couldn't remember that at all, couldn't remember anything after the car. Hell, he couldn't even remember the car.

She nodded again. "And then I took you here, because the only words you could manage were 'no hospital' and I figured if you were hiding from the law, you'd done me a big enough favor that I could keep the law out of your hair."

He started to shake his head, remembered the pain, and said, "No, I'm not hiding from anyone."

"Well, then let's get you to a hospital."

"I can't do that," he said.

"Really? Why?" She asked the question as if she already knew.

"It's...complicated."

She smiled. "Would it have anything to do with the way you keep changing into a monster for a few seconds and then changing back into yourself?"

He sat bolt upright, and the movement immediately brought lightheadedness. He groaned and fell back down, pain shooting through him in the process. "At first, I thought you were, like, a yellow Swamp Thing or something," she said. "Now, I'm wondering if you're going to destroy villages and wait for St. George to show up.

"We don't do that," he said. She raised an eyebrow. "Um... I mean," he added lamely. "I don't know what you're talking about."

She smiled. "Fine, Justin—I like that. I'm calling you Justin. Fine, Justin. Let's pretend you're not a person who can change into a..." She tilted her head. "Or are you a monster that can change into a person?" When he was silent, she rolled her eyes and said, "Look, I've got you hidden in my dorm room, and my roommate is coming home. She'll be here any minute and she's going to ask me about the strange guy in my bed. Under ordinary circumstances I'd talk about how I seduced you and played you like a violin but you're obviously injured and I don't want her think I have to almost kill a man to get any attention so how about you tell me something to say to her?"

"What?" He realized he'd been lost in thought. She started to respond but he held up a hand. He'd seen dragons transforming at times of great pain or injury, transforming involuntarily. It took a great deal of adjusting at the start of the Great Dispersal, and dragons unused to their human forms had suffered a great many injuries. If she'd seem him doing that, it meant he'd been close to death. He shook his head. "At least it took a car," he mumbled.

"Macho, Macho Man."

"Okay," he said, and he couldn't avoid a smile. "Can't you just tell her you were attacked and I fought them off?"

She rolled her eyes, "She'll never let me go work a shift again. Besides, who are you trying to impress?"

"How about you?"

"I don't know," she said. "Guys who are sick are all like little boys."

"What, knocking out four guys wasn't impressing you enough?" It would have been a lot funnier if pain hadn't exploded over him and turned the last words into a pitiful groan. Finally, he managed to day, "You could just tell her." He realized he hadn't finished but he couldn't. Blackness took him again but this time his only visions were visions of her face.

CHAPTER FIFTEEN

NOW

Petros

"I don't understand why you're telling me this now," Petros said. "Twenty-one years of lying to me about everything was just fine but damned if you'll make it to twenty-one and a half?" Cheryl frowned and Petros desperately wanted to backtrack but the frustration was greater than the guilt. "I should be with them," he said.

"There's nothing you could do," she said softly. "Your father and your uncle will—"

"Is Daniel really my uncle?"

"Do you want to pout like a child, Petros?" Petros. She called him that a great deal more than his father did but when she used that tone it took him directly back to weekday afternoons where she'd stand with her finger pointed at the door until he put down his latest book and sulked in that direction. Of course, she was always right back then and seconds into the open air the sun would fill him with excitement and playfulness and he'd find a friend or just explore on his own. He wasn't a child, though. Not now.

"I'm not trying to pout, mom. You don't think this is a big deal? I haven't even had a chance to come to terms with being… with being whatever I am and now Philip is dead. He's dead!" He could feel tears threatening to burst forth, and his mother moved closer. There was nothing he could imagine that would be worse than crying while she comforted him. He swallowed hard and held up a hand. "Why was he killed? Does it…" He lifted up his hands and shook his head. "I mean, is it because of what we are?"

"I don't know. Your father doesn't know. Uncle Daniel thinks maybe it is."

Petros couldn't keep a tear from traveling down his cheek. "He should have lived to be an old man."

168

Cheryl smiled and said. "He did, Sweetheart. He was alive before your great, great, great grandfather was born. He was alive before his great, great grandfather was born. He was alive before the Mayflower, before the Magna Carta. He was alive before the Crusades, before… Honey, he might have been alive before recorded history. I don't know."

Petros stared at her for a while and said, "Will I live long like that?"

"I don't know. I don't think anyone knows."

He stood up. "I have to say goodbye to Patricia."

Cheryl stood and put her hand on his chest. "Did she move her flight forward because of Uncle Philip?"

"Mom," he said softly, stoically. "I don't mean goodbye and I'll see you for the wedding. I mean goodbye, goodbye."

"Oh, Pete," she said. "Honey, that's why I told you about your father and me. You don't have to say goodbye. He didn't. I didn't want him to."

Peter turned away and walked to the window overlooking one of the numerous fountains on the property. The sun shone down and the light glinted off the water. "He saved your life, Mom. He saved your life and you only found out about him because he couldn't hide it."

"He would have told me if—"

He whirled back around. "That's not the point, anyway! What if I'm going to live like Uncle Philip? Has Dad? Has Dad lived that long?"

She nodded slowly. "He's older."

He threw up his hands. "So I watch her grow old and die? All the while I stay young forever? What kind of life is that for her? What kind of life is that for me? Jesus, Mom! What am I going to say to my grandchildren on our fiftieth wedding anniversary?"

Cheryl walked to him and put her hand on his cheek. "Honey, the fact that you're talking about grandchildren is exactly why you can't let this girl go."

Petros stared at her. She seemed so damned sure. She always seemed so damned sure but usually her confidence, her surety changed his perspective and offered him some comfort. Not this time. This time, he felt worse. He'd taken some comfort in the nobility of his sacrifice but now he thought of children and grandchildren. "I have to let her go, Mom."

Cheryl shook her head. "Not yet. Send her home and give it thought."

"I don't see any other way!" he shouted and then recoiled in horror. "Oh, God. Mom... I'm sorry. I just..." he crossed the room and opened the cabinet where Justin kept the booze.

"Petros—"

"I'm twenty-one, Mom, and if there was ever a reason to have a drink, I've got one."

"That isn't what I was going to say." He turned around. She smiled softly. "Give it time, just a little time. Let her decide."

"But how could she decide to be with me? Why would I put that on her? I could break things off without all that and it would hurt now but she'd be able to get past it and never feel like she disappointed me or even the opposite, like she made the wrong choice when she starts getting wrinkles and I'm still..." He turned back around and poured something clear into a glass.

"What is this?" he asked. "It has no label."

"I don't know." She raised an eyebrow. "But be careful. It's probably some Sumatran date liquor with ninety-five percent alcohol or some Burundi amaranth vodka aged in wildebeest bladders."

Petros laughed. "Amaranth is Mexican, mom."

"Hey," she said. "Drink it at your own risk. Just promise me you'll wait a while before you say anything to Patricia."

He wanted to stubbornly hold to his decision but at the same time he didn't want the conflict with his mother. Also, he didn't look forward to the conversation when it came. He took a deep breath and let it out slowly. "Okay. I'll wait to tell her."

Cheryl smiled. "Things will work out. You'll see." He didn't respond but instead lifted the glass to his lips and took a sip. He had to fight back coughing because the stuff burned like hell. His mother laughed. "I told you to be careful."

"Those guys in Burundi make a mean drink," he wheezed.

"I want you to do something else for me," she said. "I want you to change."

"Change what?"

"No, Petros. Change. I want to see you."

He stared at her for a moment. "You see me right now."

170

She shook her head. "I see part of you. I want to see the rest of you. Change for me."

He didn't want to do it, and that made it strange to obey without thinking. Without thinking. That meant without removing any of his clothes and without considering what he held in his hand. He felt his body heat and then explode with the transformation, and his mother backed up as his newly massive hands shattered the highball glass and his clothing fell away in shreds. She backed up but she didn't recoil. Instead, she stepped forward and put her hand on his scaly cheek. "You're not like your father, not like the rest," she whispered. "You're all yourself."

The touch was tender and Petros sighed. "Sorry about the glass."

Cheryl smiled. "It's probably some insanely expensive crystal made during the reign of Louis IV. Who the hell cares about the glass? You didn't hurt your hand, did you?"

He shook his head. "I don't know if I even can."

Cheryl walked around him and ran her hands over his back. If the ridges, plates, and scales disturbed her, she didn't let on at all. "You don't have wings."

He shrugged. "No but I can run fast. Really, really fast."

"Quickly. Not fast. You run quickly."

He turned around with a smile. "My grammar? Do you think now is really the appropriate..." His voice trailed off as he looked at the expression of horror on his mother's face. Her voice... It had... Dear God.

"If you're going to talk to patients, you want to make sure you use the..." He turned, his newly massive heart beating crazily in his chest. Patricia stared back at him. "...the right words," she said before she crumpled to the floor.

Justinian

He wondered if Katya would allow him to travel to Tatras and if she wouldn't he hoped she'd at least relay the message for him. It had been years since he saw her last and this would be a most unhappy meeting. He stood on the roof of the compound, emotions fighting to wrest all control from him. Philip, one of the most loyal and most cherished of the pride was dead. The worst thought was that he died alone. Philip wasn't just taken from him, he was taken from the pride. Rage was strong, and more than that, it felt good. It was a hell of a lot easier to take than the grief. He fought to keep it down, though. There would be a place for rage but this was not the place. There would be a time for rage as well.

He hoped.

No. There would be neither a place nor time. The best he could hope for was a herd of javelinas somewhere near the compound he could hunt and kill with no desire to eat but when it came right down to it, killing pigs wouldn't even begin to satisfy any of the anger that flooded him. Wait. Did javelinas gather in herds? Were they even called javelinas in plural? Was is javelini or something like that? They were peccaries, weren't they? Did peccaries travel in herds? Peccaries were South America and javelinas were North American, right? How in the hell could he have been alive since before man even discovered the world was round but not know if javelinas traveled in herds. It was settled. He was going hunting and he was going to kill every damned four-hooved New World pig he could—

He sensed him before he saw him and thoughts of rage disappeared, giving way to awe and elation. Katya wasn't coming. For the first time in hundreds of years Katya wasn't making the visit. It was Agathon. He could feel him about two hundred and fifty miles away and he hadn't seen him in years. Centuries. This was the first time since the second council. Should that be Second Council? Did that need to be capitalized? It had to be, right? It was a proper noun, wasn't it?

What the hell? First the pigs and now this?

He knew. Deflection. The anger was there. The anger was there and it was so powerful it threatened to steal all rationality from him, even in the face of a meeting with Agathon, a meeting only about a half hour away.

Agathon?

Why not Katya?

The rage almost immediately disappeared with the sudden onset of terrible trepidation. Dragons didn't change. They didn't change suddenly, and though there hadn't been a visit in a decade or so, the only possible reason Agathon was here was because of a crisis that called Katya away. Perhaps other elders visited other prides even now. Perhaps—

Perhaps he knew about Petros. Perhaps Katya wasn't here because of that. No. It couldn't be that. He could sense Petros's presence but the others couldn't. He didn't sense him as dra'acheck but as his son. That was part of the whole mystery, the entire problem with trying to figure out what he and Cheryl had created between them.

All of the speculation was academic. Agathon would be there in only a few minutes. He stood straight in surprise. A few minutes was right. He could sense him only ten or fifteen miles away. He'd always been the strongest but now he was the fastest. Ordinarily, age would slow a dragon down, perhaps not physically but emotionally. The ancients wanted to bask and think not to move. Perhaps all of them could move at this speed but never became motivated to do so. He was at least twice as fast as Justinian, maybe three times as fast.

He stared at the sky and waited, and when he saw him, he held back a gasp. Agathon was magnificent. There was no other word to describe him. There were times when dra'acheck flew that the sight appeared inelegant but there was nothing inelegant about the dragon flying toward the rooftop. Despite his massive size he moved with impossible grace, even at the blistering speed. It was magical.

Magnificent.

He stared as Agathon approached and then held his breath because he seemed to dive too quickly but at the last moment, the great red dragon reared back, beating massive wings twice as his rear claws touched the roof and then transformed until a massive red-haired Saxon god stood just a few feet away. Justinian stared for a moment and realized he was awestruck as much as the sight of Agathon in human form as he ordinarily found himself in the presence of Katya's dragon form. He stared for a moment and then Agathon smiled sadly.

The smile broke the spell and without thinking, Justinian rushed forward and threw his arms around him. He realized what he'd done as his head reached Agathon's chest and would have recoiled in horror at his behavior if Agathon's arms didn't encircle him and hold him tightly. "It has been too long,

173

my old friend," he said and Justinian felt tears threaten to fall. Agathon held him and made no move to push him away as the fear and stress and worry seemed to fade until finally, Justinian could push himself away. Agathon took a deep, long breath and said, "Katya told me about your second home, the one here. It is secluded. Safe. It's safer than your home in California."

"Oh, this is secluded but the home in California is safe."

"Perhaps," Agathon said. "It is certainly beautiful."

"Katya told you about it?"

Agathon smiled again. "It's been far too long."

"Yes, old lizard," he said. "Far too long." Agathon smiled again and the smile had as much warmth as sadness. "I wish there were a better time for a reunion, though. I find myself grateful it's you this time and not Katya. Why isn't she—"

"Why?" Agathon stared at him and Justinian stared back. "Why are you grateful, I mean?"

"Well, I would be grateful to see you under any circumstances, and—"

"Justinian. It's me. It's not the leader, not the ruler or king or whatever it is they call me. It's me. Talk to me and not the elder elder."

"Philip is dead, killed right here in the compound by someone who understood dragon physiology. Diamond weapons or something like that. Phineas finally got his revenge, and I want permission to—"

"It wasn't Phineas."

"He wanted revenge for the hatchling and revenge for Yara, and—"

"It wasn't Phineas."

Justinian opened his mouth to speak but Agathon held up a hand. "Others have been killed as well. I thought at first it was only those being reckless. One died in the mountains where she transformed for hunting every few months. Summer. You don't know her. She was hatched long after the dispersal. Another, almost a hatchling, transformed at every opportunity like some kind of an addict. Others, too, and almost all of them were reckless but there have been some, some who were not." He leveled his gaze on Justinian. "Forget your allegiance to Philip for a moment. Was he reckless?"

Justinian's eyes widened. "No. Never. He was light-hearted sometimes but never reckless."

"Then there are three. Three killed who took all of the precautions that should have kept them safe." He turned away from Justinian for a moment that seemed to last for an eternity. Finally Justinian sensed as much as heard, "It is time."

"Time for what?"

Agathon leapt into the air, transforming instantly into his glorious form. "Time for another gathering in Tatras," he said. "I'll send word." Agathon's wings beat twice and sent him into the clouds and out of sight.

Harlan

The shoes felt clunky on his feet but he didn't mind. He was about to be free of them and it was about damned time. How long had it been? He couldn't remember time much anymore. It either moved at an agonizingly slow pace or at speeds that rivaled the fastest of his kind diving after prey. They were wrong. They were all wrong. It wasn't right to robe all of this power in the flesh of mankind. It wasn't right and it wasn't healthy. For centuries he held hope that Agathon was right and that one day they'd throw off the false bodies and be free but the world changed and now humans took to the skies and warred over oil and water and not just ideology. There were computers that talked to other computers and all of it came from their minds, from innovation that said rationality achieved it all.

There would be no revealing.

The primitive men who thought epilepsy was demon possession or those who thought the world was flat or those who thought a train moving at faster than forty-five miles an hour—those were the humans who could handle the existence of dragons among them but not mankind of today. Not the mankind who actually fought over whether or not the word should be womankind or humankind. Their world of advancement and information and horrible bigotry masked by false tolerance could never handle the existence.

God how he hated shoes!

The only way the world would change would be with violence and that violence was inevitable. Eventually everyone would see it. The steward would see it, and that meant all the stewards would see it. Everyone would see it and shoes would be a thing of the past, a hated thing of the past.

He walked past the chain link fence disgusted by the sound of his soles on the concrete. He stopped at the gate, disgusted with the need for a key in the padlock and for that matter the need for a padlock in the first place. The door creaked open and he resisted the urge to tear the damned thing from the hinges.

They weren't humans.

They weren't humans, damn it.

Why the hell did they have to walk around like they were?

One hundred years. That was it. That was all he got before the damned plan. He'd had almost no chance to flex his wings, no opportunity to really be dra'acheck. How many others? How many dra'acheck lived now who thought they were humans with strange abilities? How many had never known real freedom but instead were stuck wearing work shoes with non-stick soles and orthopedic inserts to comply with the rules of a sixteen dollar per hour job with benefits designed to ensure a secure twenty-two and a half years of retirement. That was, at last look, less than one third of one third of one third of one percent of the amount of time he'd need.

He smiled despite his sour mood. He had no idea, actually. He was unaware of dragons dying of old age. There had been a few who died peacefully but he wasn't convinced it was age so much as giving up a reason to live, a reason like the skies and the clouds and soaring through them. There were times he was tempted, times he wanted to just roll out of bed and leap from his eleventh story room to soar right in the middle of the city. To hell with the Great Plan. To hell with the humans. To hell with all of it. Three days every few months in the wilderness somewhere, three days that was really only two because he couldn't even travel there by flying but had to travel the way humans travelled—it wasn't enough, damn it.

But he was a coward.

He wouldn't do it.

He'd bitch to himself about it and walk around angrily and when he got up enough energy, he might even complain to the steward about it and then back down when all the stupid platitudes about Agathon's wisdom and the lasting peace and the end to the hunt and all of the rest was tossed at him. He backed down but he did so because he was afraid and not because he agreed, not even because he deferred to any authority. He was a coward. It was that simple. He got to the end of the pathway and put another key into another lock he resented on another door he resented with more hinges he wished he could tear off the jamb.

Why? Why contain all this power in a body like this?

The lock stuck and he cursed and tried to force it, succeeding only in sheering the damned thing, leaving the lock filled with no way to turn it. He felt anger boiling over and pulled his arm back but stopped before striking the blow that would have shattered the lock and a good portion of the door. Then, of course, he cursed again, disgusted with his inability to act like a dragon and not like a man.

He sighed and stepped away. He'd have to enter through the multi-purpose room and find a way to squeeze fixing the lock into an already filled

Thursday. All of the sports teams practiced on Thursdays and combined with the after school intervention programs, that meant four locations to clean between the end of school at two fifteen and the start of all the damned activities at three. He was a damned dragon. Why the hell was he cleaning up after human hatchlings?

He stomped toward the multipurpose room and then stopped. Someone was there. He couldn't see them but he could sense them or at least he thought he could sense them. Them? No. It was one.

No. Two.

Aw hell. He hadn't needed to sense anything in so long he wasn't even sure what it was he sensed. It could be high school brats here an hour early to make out where Mommy and Daddy wouldn't see them. Who the knew? Maybe, if he were lucky, it would be a serial killer or a mugger and he'd have no choice but to transform.

He chuckled as he realized he actually hoped for the violence and then sighed as he realized with just as much certainty he'd likely not transform even under those circumstances. Was he broken? Was he really that broken?

Probably.

"You're useless, Harlan. Completely useless." He didn't know why it felt better to say the words out loud.

"No. You're not."

He whirled around at the sound and then gasped at the sight of the crossbow or whatever it was. It was medieval but high tech at the same time. It was out of place and really not that intimidating. Even before the dispersal his skin had grown tough enough to repel an arrow. It was curious, though, because he knew that and anyone had to know that, didn't they?

He realized his thoughts made no sense and he looked down at wet, red oblong… What the hell was it? Whatever it was attached to a nylon shaft and it was facing away from him. The wet… wet and red. It was his blood. His blood was on the arrowhead but arrowheads couldn't pierce his skin.

He reached for it and ran his thumb over the blood. The blood smeared only a little but beneath it, the arrowhead was white, opaque and white. It looked like a rock, like a moonstone or something like that. Rocks didn't pierce dra'acheck, though.

The impact of the second arrow on his chest surprised him, and he turned to look at his attacker. Nothing made sense. The arrow shouldn't have hurt. He needed to fight back. He needed to fly. He needed to roar. He needed to do all of those things.

But he didn't.

He was a coward.

Another arrow hit and he watched the sky move overhead, unaware of how he'd ended up on his back. He felt the arrows coming out. No, just two of them. Why only two? Why were the clouds so far away?

"You're not useless at all. You are the most glorious of creatures in all of creation. You are a god among insects. Die in the knowledge that your passing serves a greater purpose."

Why would he say that to a coward?

It didn't matter. He realized as the clouds got farther away that the voice was sincere.

CHAPTER SIXTEEN

NOW AND THEN

Cheryl

"You're putting every one of us at risk."

Cheryl was pretty sure that the voice belonged to the man they called Philip, the one Justinian had introduced her to.

Justinian. She was going to have to start calling him Justin because he sounded like some kind of Roman soldier. She was pretty sure, in fact, the Roman Justinian was the man...

Wait.

He wasn't a man.

He was one of the Dra—Dra— One of the dragons. He was one of the dragons.

It was so bizarre. The whole idea, the whole thought, that her life was real made no sense. Wasn't it just a few weeks ago that she was complaining about her stupid job dealing blackjack? Wasn't she trying to figure out if she'd made the right or wrong decision majoring in statistics? None of this made sense, none of it at all.

No, that wasn't true.

Justinian.

Justin.

He made a lot of sense. He not only had the body of a god, but he had the mind of everything she could possibly want. She didn't know how much of it was the hero effect and how much of it was the Nightingale effect but he was everything she'd ever imagined wanting. She shook her head and walked away from the door. If they were going to yell at each other, she didn't have to hear it.

Everything was so strange. The land, for example. He had thousands, thousands of acres out here in the middle of nowhere. As if those thousands of acres weren't enough, there was a city here or at least almost a city here. There were normal buildings but also very large buildings. At first she'd worried that she'd stumbled into some kind of a secret cult or something along those lines, but it was nothing like that. He was their leader. There was a group of them, and evidently there were groups of them everywhere, not just in Las Vegas. In fact, he wasn't even from Nevada but instead had expanded because his group kept growing.

Growing.

It was crazy.

He transformed for her. Completely. Not just the blurring flashes. He'd transformed and suddenly she was confronted with the picture of every dragon she'd ever seen in any movie except, somehow, better. Somehow, less fantastic and more real. She didn't understand it entirely. He looked a lot like what she'd pictured dragons to be, what she'd seen in art and movies and video games. On the other hand, there was none of the stylized roleplaying game art cover crap she dealt with on a regular basis among the college students who seemed to flock to the sciences while spending their evenings locked in combat with polyhedral dice.

She giggled suddenly as she recalled a picture of a dragon with a nearly naked (and completely topless) warrior woman holding onto a scaly spike on the dragon's head as she rode his back through the skies. She could be Justin's topless warrior woman. She blushed as she thought about sleeping with him, wondered if there would be sexual things to do if he was in his normal form. Hell, she didn't even know if the dragon was the normal form. One strange thing about it was she could recognize him. She could see his eyes were the same, the same burning green. She had no idea how green could burn, but that was how they looked.

She walked further away from the door and couldn't hear those voices anymore, but she heard others. She turned the corner and saw the man he'd introduced as Daniel. She stepped back away before he noticed her and listened to his conversation, feeling slightly guilty about it, but the topic of conversation was her. So she listened.

"No," he said. "You're wrong. She saved his life. She deserves our care. She deserves our attention."

"It doesn't matter." She didn't know who he was talking to. But the next lines struck her and stuck with her. "No. She's not here out of repayment. She's not here out of gratitude. She's here because he loves her."

He loves her. He loves me?

The thought was overwhelming and wonderful and terrible all at once. Evidently, the wonderful was a little bit better than the rest of it, because she turned and, as she walked away, she almost had to keep herself from skipping.

God, Cheryl, what are you, some kind of schoolgirl?

The self-reproof didn't do a thing. She couldn't help but feel giggly anyway as she made her way through the vaulted ceilings and large hallways, finally arriving back at the enormous suite he'd presented to her when they'd arrived. There were a lot of things to get straight in her mind, and most of them were simply far too enormous to consider. So instead she focused on the smallest things, the things with the least impact. When was she going back to school? Was she going to quit her job? Even those were confused. She needed answers beyond any that could be given at the moment.

A dragon.

A dragon who was a human...or was it a human that was a dragon?

None of it made sense. She wondered if she was making a better or worse gamble than all of the blackjack fiends who held out hope that they'd somehow magically get their card the next time she flipped one over. She opened the door and stepped inside. It was still amazing to think what an incredibly furnished room it was. Nothing else was so lavishly appointed, and she wondered if Justinian—Justin—had done it all for her.

Dammit. There's just no way I'm going to be able to think of him as Justin no matter how hard I try. She headed over to the bed, sat down and then almost jumped up in shock because he was right beside her.

"I'm sorry. I didn't mean to startle you."

"Oh, the hell you didn't," she said. "How—that I don't know. I would ask you how the hell you appeared so quickly, because that I don't know. I know the why and the what though. I know exactly what—you did that on purpose."

He smiled. "Does it make you uncomfortable?"

"No! It infuriates me!" She said it, but as she did, she couldn't stop from laughing. He laughed along with her.

"Would you stay here? Would you stay here with me?"

She sighed. "Look, Justinian, I've only known you for two weeks."

He nodded. "I know."

"Well, how am I supposed to make a life choice when it's only been two weeks?"

He smiled. "The last time I felt about someone the way I feel about you was...well...if you traced your ancestry back as far as you could, whoever you traced it to probably hadn't been born yet. My guess is there's just...God, Cheryl, I have no way to tell you this. I don't understand how. But let me say that you've brought something back to me that was lost, that was lost almost a thousand years ago. You've brought it back. You've done that, and I need you."

She looked at him, and then tilted her head to one side. She raised an eyebrow. "You don't need me to agree to this to keep me here, do you?" She already knew the answer but she said it to cover the way her heart raced, to cover the fact that she was almost breathless from his words. A damned schoolgirl.

He looked uncomprehendingly at her for a moment before he said, "Of course I do. If you'd like to leave, I'll take you back to your dorm room now."

She stared. He was nothing like he should be. He had so much power. He could take anything. And instead of taking it, he...he just...what the hell was going on? "You'd let me go?"

Again he looked at her uncomprehendingly. "If you're asking if I'm capable of forcing you to stay, the answer is no. Oh, if you were an enemy or something along those lines I could physically do it but the only thing worse than losing you would be keeping you anywhere against your will."

She swallowed hard. "Are you the strongest of your kind?"

He laughed. "Oh, no. My goodness, no. I'm strong; I'm very strong. I'm one of the oldest of my kind. But, oh, no. No." He stood up. "I suppose I'm... blackjack, that's what you play, right?"

"I deal it."

"Okay, well I don't know the rules. Do you know poker?"

"Yes."

"Okay. I'm like a face card. I don't know how many are higher. When our kind split up I was probably a ten or a jack. Now, I'm probably a queen or a king. There are a few aces, though." He shrugged. "That didn't explain a damned thing, did it?"

"Do you all have gold scales and green eyes?"

"No," he laughed. "The greatest among us is red."

"One of the aces?" He nodded and then frowned.

"I can read everyone in my pride, my group, the ones I lead. I can't read you. I have no idea if it's because you're human or just because you're impossible."

"A red dragon?" she asked.

"Red. Agathon, yes." He rolled his eyes. "Didn't you hear me?"

"Does he wear his grandmother's dentures and bite reporters' lips off?"

"What?"

"Does he... oh never mind. I'll buy you the book. So, there are...there are...how many of you are out there?"

He sighed. "I just don't know. We...we all split up. It was called the Great Dispersal, and..."

"Oh my God! The Great Council, the Great Plan, the Great Dispersal...is there anything you dra'acheck—that's what it is! Dra'acheck! Is there anything you dra'acheck do that isn't great?"

Justinian laughed. "All right. All right. Evidently we do a poor job of sweeping fair maidens off their feet." She looked at him expectantly and he said, "We were down to just a few thousand of us, and then things got really bad, and we were somewhere in the neighborhood of eleven or twelve hundred, and then the dispersal happened. We all split up, and I had eighteen with me when we started. Maybe nineteen. Nineteen with me when we started. Now I have forty-two. So, if everyone worked the way I did and things worked out that way, there might be three or four thousand, maybe a few more or less of us on Earth."

"On Earth. So you're not just in the United States?"

"Everywhere. I was in France before we came here."

"France?"

"We started in Paris, and then moved out toward Normandy, and then we—well, it doesn't matter. I was in France, and I stayed in France for most of the time with a short jaunt in the Netherlands, and...then we...well, it doesn't matter. We've been in the United States, in L.A., since the late eighteen hundreds."

She nodded. "And where is everyone else?"

"Throughout the world."

"This is crazy," she said.

"I know. I shouldn't have asked you to stay." He wasn't sincere when he said it but insincere was cute on him.

"But then you wouldn't have heard me tell you, 'Yes.'"

"You'll stay?"

"Of course I will. No way some other bimbo gets to be your topless warrior."

Phineas

"Something is different."

"Of course something is different. What do you expect? They've only been gone for seven or eight months and evidently constant prayers toward Mecca aren't enough to give victory over the Great Satan."

"What the hell are you talking about?" Phineas lifted his hand and a servant brought him two steaming cups.

"You're not talking about Iraq? It has the whole region a little less defiant and everyone is afraid Israel will use it as an excuse to attack Iran."

"Khaled," Phineas said and the other man winced. Phineas sighed and said softly, "Kronhiss, there are humans in the building."

"It isn't my name."

"And Annz isn't Mahmoud, and Harkoor isn't Ali. Anlana isn't Bahiyyah. Fostelleff isn't—"

Khroniss lifted his hand. "Forgive me, Steward." He sighed and took a sip of his drink. "Anyway, it's understandable. There's a bit of unrest because the entire region has been spanked, put it in its place. I don't see how it matters to us."

Phineas laughed. "Of course it doesn't matter to us. I'm not talking about humans and their idiotic conflicts. I'm talking about the dra'acheck. Something has changed. I can feel it." He took a sip of his coffee and waited. About half of his pride trusted in the feelings that came to him a few times per century. Khroniss was not one of them. Oh, Khroniss would never defy him or speak poorly of him. He simply chose to believe Phineas arrived at decisions intellectually or even subconsciously through an intellectual process. Phineas wasn't sure if he believed the intuition was an act designed to inspire awe or if Khroniss believed Phineas didn't see the workings of his own subconscious. It didn't matter. The dra'acheck, who'd been his second from the day he took the pride, was loyal beyond question.

"There are already so many…" Khroniss took a deep breath. "For almost a millennium we've hidden the truth from Tatras. Couldn't your feeling be simple fear of discovery?"

Phineas laughed. "There is too much hubris, too much ego in Agathon. He couldn't comprehend such defiance, even petty defiance."

186

Phineas could tell his second chose the next words carefully. "Your father respected nobody, nobody but Agathon." Khroniss seemed to cringe in anticipation of an outburst but though Phineas felt the anger rise within him, he didn't lash out as he might ordinarily have. He was right. He was right and he'd been careful to refer to Yara as his father, something important to Phineas. Khroniss still cringed, and though Phineas felt for a moment he ought to give him some amount of reassurance, he didn't.

"Yes. Yara respected Agathon but Agathon was wrong. He was wrong to separate us, he was wrong to make us join the humans and he was wrong to judge against us."

"Yara said he would kill him."

Phineas nodded slowly. "Yes. He knew the attack would mean his death. He knew that when we left for France." He took a sip and added, "And that was one thing Agathon was right to do."

"Will he kill you if he finds out what you've done?"

Phineas shrugged. "Probably. Gryflin too. Maybe all of us. He'd be right to do so." He took another sip and then leveled his gaze on Khroniss. "Do you regret what I've done?"

Khroniss shook his head. "We have the right to make our own decisions about our lives. We are dra'acheck, and it's not right that we should be ruled."

Phineas nodded slowly. "Agathon awoke. He didn't hatch. Tara too. Agathon was at the awakening. Yara was as well. Nobody knows why, though I've heard rumors a few of the ancients now gone had memories they didn't share. You, me. We're the hatched, born into this world. Not Agathon. There aren't many left."

"Many awakened?"

Phineas shook his head. "Many gods."

There was silence for a moment and Phineas took another sip. The tea was bitter, strong and bitter. He waited patiently for Khroniss to respond. Finally, he heard the deep breath and then the pause. He turned and looked at him. Khroniss spoke slowly. "So... We're seeking revenge on a god."

"You weren't there in France, were you?" He already knew the answer and didn't wait for a response. "You weren't there when one god descended and made another god seem feeble."

Khroniss took a deep breath and again said, "We're seeking revenge on a god."

"Oh no," Phineas said as he drained his cup. "We're not seeking revenge. This has never been about revenge. This has never been about Yara."

"Then what are we after?"

Phineas attempted to drink from his cup again but it was empty. He sighed and put it down. "A reckoning. We seek a reckoning, Khaled."

This time, Khroniss didn't wince at the sound of his assumed name.

Cheryl

"You're what?"

Cheryl smiled brightly. "I'm pregnant."

"But...how could you..." Justinian stood, walked to the liquor cabinet and poured himself a tall glass of Pernod. "Are you...are you sure it's mine?"

He turned around and knew instantly it was the wrong thing to say. He'd seen her upset before. Her face got a little flushed, her eyes got a little narrow, and her mouth, remarkably, always looked like it was on the verge of smiling and not snarling. All of those previous experiences were nothing compared to what he saw now. She wasn't flushed; she was scarlet. Her eyes weren't narrow; they were pinpricks. And she was right on the verge of what had to be a snarl. He lifted up his hands.

"I'm sorry. I know how that sounded. You don't understand, though. There's never been... Cheryl. I'm not questioning you. It's never happened. A dra'acheck and a human, I mean. A human and a dragon child. I-I didn't even know it could happen. I'm not..."

That wasn't enough for her. She turned around and immediately walked from the room, slamming the door hard behind her. He took a long drink of the licorice liquid and let it burn its way down his throat. Then he took another long drink. Finally, he sighed in resignation. It was better to take his lumps now than to wait. He walked through the door after her.

She wasn't interested in listening, but he took her arm and turned her around. "Listen. You caught me off-guard. I'm sorry for how it sounded. I'm— I'm happy, I really am. I'm just completely shocked. I mean, dragons don't usually have relationships with humans, at least, not any long-term, and while I know that there have been some times that dragons have been with humans, I've never...this just doesn't happen. It's...it's unprecedented. It's incredible."

She softened a little bit. "Well, who was the last dragon to marry a human?"

"You really don't know, do you?" He shook his head with a smile. "We're the only ones. At least, I think we're the only ones. The dispersal means we don't contact others much at all but... It's a safe bet you and I are the only married... Aw, hell, Cheryl. I'm really sorry." She didn't completely warm up to him, so he added, "Yeah, we're the only ones. Of course, no other dragons had a chance to meet you."

She rolled her eyes. "All right. You're off the hook."

He smiled and took her into his arms. "Now, are you sure you're pregnant?"

She nodded. "I'm not just late. It feels different. I'll go to the doctor tomorrow and—"

"No!" He didn't realize he'd spoke it so loudly.

She didn't respond to his tone but asked calmly, "I can't go to the doctor?"

"There are doctors among us. We can have someone look at you here."

She shook her head. "If you think for one second that any one of the people that live with us are going to be taking care of this, you're wrong. I'm going to the doctor."

"But…but what if…?" He didn't know what to say. How was he going to say What if the baby inside you gives us all away? Finally, he asked, "Can we at least have a sonogram done here first?"

She smiled. "These first visits are just going to confirm I'm pregnant. There's nothing for them to see, at least nothing that will show up on a sonogram. And it's an ultrasound, dummy. The picture is the sonogram. You have the ultrasound done."

"Great," he said. "That'll come in handy for the next human wife I get pregnant." Cheryl laughed and Justinian said. "Okay. We'll used regular doctors but, how can I say this? We're rich, Cheryl. We're very rich. The money is in three continents and dozens of countries and it was all obtained legally but how do you explain deductions from nine hundred years ago? I… Damn it. I don't know why the hell I brought any of that up. I just—"

"So my big strong dragon is going to make sure I get the best medical care available? Is that your point, Mr. Steward, Sir?"

He intended an angry retort at her cavalier attitude but he ended up laughing instead. She smiled triumphantly and he pulled her to him, kissing her briefly and then just holding her. "Is there anything I can do?"

"Well, you can start coming up with names," she whispered softly.

"Petros," he said.

"You already had a name?" He smiled and then shrugged. Cheryl smiled back. "What if it's a girl."

"Petra."

"Okay but I'm probably calling him Peter or her Penelope."

"Penelope?"

"Shut up. They're my kids and I'll call them whatever the hell I want to, Mister Man."

He got up and kissed her cheek and then walked out of the room back to his study, where he immediately sat and began work on a second glass of Pernod. Nothing made sense. He wondered if it was time to alert the council. It was forbidden to communicate with the council except in cases of dire emergency, and the last time a dire emergency had occurred was Yara complaining about an accidental death in war-time. This time, if he were to…

He shook his head. No. He'd have to just deal with whatever the situation was.

A father. Ages before, he and Linara had anticipated hatchlings of their own. He wondered, briefly, if he loved Linara more than he loved Cheryl. He decided he didn't. He wondered if he loved Cheryl more, and he couldn't quite decide on that. He knew for certain, though, that there was no way for him to truly comprehend the thought of a son, a son that was…well, what would he be? He knew the name. Even though he was pretty sure it was some kind of stupid blind confidence to believe so, he was also sure the hatchling would be a son.

He hoped he was human.

For Cheryl's sake.

Almost. He wanted to hope he was human for Cheryl's sake.

Justinian hoped he was dragon.

CHAPTER SEVENTEEN

THEN

Justinian

Agathon was larger, far larger than Justinian remembered. At first, he thought it was just the years. There had been stretches of time, even centuries, where he hadn't seen him before the dispersal, though. It had to do, he was sure, with the mountains and not just the passage of time. There was something different about living in the Tatras Mountains, something different to the physiology than living among the humans.

Perhaps.

Perhaps it was simply the leadership, simply that his body responded to the need to be more than what it was before he became an elder. An elder? Before he became an elder of elders, before he became the leader and the great hope for all of dragonkind. Agathon wasn't just dra'acheck. He was all that dra'acheck could hope to be. He was all dra'acheck could aspire to be. He was... was...

Perfect.

Agathon had aged and grown and become an ancient of his kind, while the rest, though powerful and though growing, were simply incomparable. He wasn't just ancient, he was (as he was elder of elders) an ancient of ancients. Automatic and nearly overwhelming awe, almost paralysis, fell over him as he saw his old friend.

His father.

Yes. His father. Of course, the term had nothing to do with biology and everything to do with the dragon that had raised him from a hatchling after his parents perished.

He stared, shock and the overwhelming intensity of admiration and fear keeping him from moving at all. Agathon stood silently and, finally, turned his head, surveying all of the Dra'acheck in the courtyard. He pause when his eyes made contact with Justinian and though Justinian doubted any others saw it, there was a moment of shared regret, pity, and deep compassion. There was none of the doubt Justinian had seen during the Great Council, doubt that required resolve to overcome. There was resolve, though. There was resolve and Justinian realized Agathon needed it not to overcome doubt but to carry through on a course of action that brought the regret, the pity, and the compassion.

Finally, Agathon's eyes came to rest on Yara. The dra'acheck's bluster was gone. The bravado he'd shown and the complete disregard for the council seemed almost nonexistent. Agathon loved Justinian. He knew that. He loved all dra'acheck but Justinian held a special place. Justinian knew that as definitely as he knew the cost to Agathon of implementing his plan, as much as he knew the terror of the day Tynboleth fell. Justinian knew that but he also knew only one other dra'acheck mattered as much to Agathon, and that dragon had forced his hand. Agathon spoke, and though his words were harsh and uncompromising, his voice held nothing but sadness.

"Yara, you've deceived the council. You have defied the elders. Worse, you have plotted the death, the death of another dra'acheck. I thought I would never see the day when dragon fought dragon, but you have sought it out. You've called mankind your enemy while becoming far worse than the worst of men." He paused. It seemed that everyone cowered and yet Justinian did not. He felt a terrible and horrible foreboding but that look in Agathon's eyes took the awe away. Instead, Justinian felt deep sadness, deep sympathy for his friend, his mentor, his father.

Of the rest, Yara alone wasn't scuttling backward. Justinian didn't move backward either, and he was certain the relationship each of them held with Agathon kept both of them still. One glance told him his relationship with Agathon still meant something but what of Yara? He didn't know if that relationship meant anything anymore; at least, he didn't understand how it could. It meant pain. It meant pain for Agathon and perhaps that was all. Agathon was so vastly superior to him now. He'd always been stronger, always been wiser, always been faster, and always been more respected. But he was still dra'acheck and not the dragon god-thing that stood before him.

Wasn't he?

"Yara, I've known you for more than fifteen hundred years, and for fifteen hundred years, we've been friends. We've disagreed at every turn about what was best for the dra'acheck but never once did I doubt that what was best for the dragons motivated you, that your heart was filled with love for our kind." Justinian thought he saw a tear fall but it couldn't be. "Never once did I doubt that until today. The council has made a decision, and I..."

He paused. Dragons shed no tears in their natural form, but Justinian imagined if Agathon were in human form, tears would flow down his cheeks. As if hearing him, Agathon changed. He stepped forward and, where the tall and beautiful red-scaled dragon had been stood a man with a shocking mane of fiery red hair and eyes that burned brightly. He stepped forward. Yara transformed instantly as well.

Agathon reached forward, took one of Yara's shoulders in one hand and the other shoulder in the other. "I'm sorry, old friend," he said. "The decision has been made."

Justinian realized what was happening just as it began. "No!" he cried as Agathon's hands closed. He watched the man-dragon's muscles ripple, and Agathon gave out a loud scream as he tore. He lifted Yara, his ancient friend, off the ground and in a single motion ripped him clean in half almost without a fraction of effort.

Terrifying.

It was a terrifying sight. Yara simply came apart. Holding onto his shoulders, Agathon pulled the man apart so that his neck tore from his body, his ribcage was split down the breastbone. Justinian felt tears flowing down his cheeks and realized he'd transformed. He wondered if the need for a physical expression of emotion forced the change. Yara was dead. Yara was dead and it had happened, impossibly, in seconds. He didn't have a chance to defend himself with word or action and, instead, was reduced in seconds to two parts. The half of his body that still held the head seemed to roll to the side so that his eyes, though unseeing, seemed to stare at Justinian, and Justinian stared back, overwrought at the thought of what had occurred.

Agathon stared down at his body for some time. No one else dared to move or to speak although Justinian continued to openly weep. Finally, Agathon took a deep breath. He looked from one Dra'acheck to another in the courtyard, and then finally said, "In four weeks, the council will meet again. Four weeks, every pride is to be at Tatras." He turned so that he stared directly at Justinian. Only then did he allow himself tears and Justinian saw them through the blurry wave that obscured his vision. Again, they shared an unspoken look.

Justinian had spent centuries with Agathon but that look seemed to convey more than decade long conversations ever could. He loved Justinian.

Justinian knew that. He knew something else, something he'd never spoken but knew nonetheless. He loved Yara more. He loved Justinian the way a father loves a son, the way a superior loves an inferior. It was powerful love. It was wonderful love, remarkable love. His love for Yara was greater. He loved Yara as an equal and among the dra'acheck, equals to Agathon were rare. The blood covered Agathon's body as horribly as the grief covered his face. Agathon breathed out, "Yara," in a sound so soft it sounded like a sigh.

And then he left.

When he leapt into the air, he was still human, but he transformed as he leapt and soon the sight of the magnificent body of Agathon the Red shot upward, his wings tucked beneath him as he rose into the sky. Justinian watched after, wondering what would become of Agathon, what would become of the dra'acheck, and what would become of him.

That was when he saw it. Somehow at some point in the battle, Linara was wounded. Wounded badly. In the terror of what was transpiring between Agathon and Yara, Justinian hadn't even noticed his mate, his wife, dying. His eyes locked with her and dread swept over him as he rushed to her side and called the others for help.

Phineas

So Yara was right.

Yara was right and there was strange comfort in that. Phineas sighed as he sat and tried his best to accept the decision. There was a council, and that, too, Yara predicted. But would the rest of Yara's grand plan work? Phineas hoped so, hoped he and his pride and all of the prides could return to Tatras where they belonged and be free of the damned humans any dra'acheck not blinded by hubris would understand represented the end of their kind.

Yara was right, and it was little comfort.

God, he wanted to hate Agathon!

But he couldn't. He couldn't hate Agathon for killing Yara any more than he could hate Yara for traveling to France, traveling to his death.

He could hate the damned humans, though. All they did was kill. They killed in an endless sea of blood. They killed animals and not just for food but to sacrifice to their gods or for the sport of hunting them. They killed dra'acheck for sport, or they had. They killed dra'acheck for money. They killed. They killed and they killed indiscriminately and the only good in that situation was that they killed each other by the thousands.

And their wars killed dra'acheck pretending to be human.

"Khaled! Ali!" His voice rang out louder than he intended so he scowled to make sure when they stepped into the room they'd see an angry face and assume he was upset rather than out of control. He added, "And bring something to drink, damn it!" even though he wasn't thirsty. He yelled for food, too, though he wanted that less than drink.

This was it.

If Yara's calculations were correct, in just over three weeks they would travel to Tatras and stay there. They would, again, fly over the forests at the foot of the Great Awakening and hunt as they were intended to hunt. They would celebrate there in the mountains for some time, perhaps a century or perhaps two. Then, they would split up again but not as humans but dra'acheck. They would travel to the North and to the South. They would travel to the West. Some would return to the East where the humans treated them like celestial gods and held parades in their honor. They would once again be dra'acheck, and Yara's sacrifice would be valid, justified.

Khroniss arrived a moment later and behind him came Ashkaram with a tray in each hand. Khroniss pulled a table toward Phineas and Ashkaram put the trays on the table. The two stood and Phineas said, "Sit with me."

Khroniss nodded and walked to the corner for a cushion for himself and for Ashkaram. He returned and the two sat. Ashkaram reached for the silver tea service and set three cups in line on the table. He poured the tea and it steamed upward. Phineas stared at the steam rising and he wondered if the steam portended anything. Was there something, anything, there that represented an omen?

Omens.

Phineas took a cup and sipped. Omens were for humans, not dra'acheck.

He took another sip of the tea and enjoyed the bitterness of the flavor, wondering why in the world the humans here drank something so beautiful but ruined it. They ruined it with cloying sweetness. Yet another failure of humanity. Another damned failure in a race that had no right to the world they overran. He took another sip and realized he was hungry after all. On the tray were dates and cheeses. He took a handful and put one in his mouth.

He realized abruptly that the other two still waited for him. He gestured to the table. "Drink. Eat." They weren't hungry. They weren't thirsty. He could tell. Nonetheless, they reached for their cups and took a handful of dates. Yara was right about that. They already showed him the deference due a steward. He smiled before he got control of his expression and flattened it. It felt good to be a steward even though he wasn't.

Even though he never would be.

It felt good nonetheless but he sighed and said, "Is there anything here we want?"

Ashkaram said, "What do you mean?"

Phineas smiled. "Is there anything here we want?"

Khroniss took a breath. "Do you mean for us to leave?"

Phineas nodded. "When we travel to Tatras for the gathering, I believe we will stay there."

There was silence for a long span and Phineas didn't break it. Finally, Khroniss said, "That was why." Ashkaram looked lost. Khroniss didn't elaborate but Phineas knew he understood. "There is nothing here, Phineas. There is nothing at all we can't leave here. The war still rages so should we be missed the people will assume we've been killed. A few weeks after we've left, the estate will be looted anyway, and it will complete the picture.

Phineas nodded.

Ashkaram said, "You think he will punish us all. You think he will take us away from our home."

It took a great effort of will to keep from laughing. Away from their home? Away from home?

No.

They were going home.

Justinian

Justinian wouldn't have expected the emotions that suddenly flooded him to have come. It was overwhelming, beyond overwhelming. The sight of so many dra'acheck in the same place after so many years astounded him, overpowered all other thoughts and senses. There were reds and blues and greens and golds and...

Beyond what he had expected. Beyond anything he could have expected.

Their numbers had grown. Their numbers had grown dramatically, and in that respect, Agathon's plan had worked and worked well. He realized he shouldn't have been surprised. After all, his numbered thirty now.

Twenty-nine. Not thirty. He paused and let the pain wash over him.

A population of Dra'acheck that numbered in the thousands rather than the hundreds made a great deal of sense given the growth of his own pride. To see them all in the familiar home, there at the basin lake and at the foot of the mountain, though stunned him. It was breathtaking, beyond breathtaking. He led his pride, seeking somewhere to land where they could remain together, but there was nowhere. So, instead, he landed at the beach, at the shore of the lake and simply signaled to the rest to find space where they could.

The mood was somber but something curious made the somber mood irrelevant. An energy beyond any energy he'd felt before filled the place and he didn't know if he should fear it or embrace it. Of course, it was arrogant to believe he had a choice. The gathering was remarkable and he felt almost a renewal of purpose, a renewal of strength. Above all, he felt better. Any doubts that had come to him over Agathon's plan, the doubts that had come to him entirely because of the episode with Yara and the tragedy—no, the two tragedies—it produced were gone. It had worked. It had worked, and Agathon had saved the species, and if it took another thousand years or two thousand or five thousand before they could reveal themselves, they were here now. They were here now together, and they were alive.

He looked at the reflection in the pool. It was beautiful. It had been probably two hundred years since he'd seen his reflection as dra'acheck. It was majestic, and it wasn't conceit that made him think it was majestic other than conceit, perhaps, for his race as a whole. He was powerful, too. He'd developed as had Agathon. Certainly Agathon was more powerful but even if Justinian wasn't a god among them, he was certainly powerful in mythic ways. He glanced around. There were so many he didn't recognize but he recognized some of those who awakened. Compared to later generations, they were all superior.

Superior.

Superior. What a strange and almost horrible thought.

He looked around. Almost half or even more of the faces at the lake were unknown to him. He looked up. High in the rocks he could see only a few elders, elders he rarely spoke with in his youth and never spoke with in his adulthood. And there was Agathon. Even among the elders, he was bigger, he was stronger. There was an aura about him, a strength and a power that seemed to call the very air itself to him. Justinian looked. Was this the same dragon, the same that had taught him to hunt? Was this the same dragon that had taught him not to think of humans as threats or as prey but as creatures deserving of respect, creatures not entirely unlike the dra'acheck?

It couldn't be the same Agathon, because that Agathon was at least mortal, and this Agathon looked as eternal as the mountains. On the other hand, he hoped at least part of this Agathon were the same, the part that strove with all of his might to keep the humans and the dragons from war with one another. He knew the situation with Yara had profoundly impacted him.

It was strange. In his youth, time and time again he'd wondered why Agathon showed any toleration for Yara. He understood a little better now. Agathon had defended Yara, explained that love for the dra'acheck had motivated everything he did. There, at the top of the rocks, Agathon looked down at what most likely represented the entirety of the dragons. If Yara loved the dra'acheck, he loved them no more than Agathon, and probably quite a bit less.

He wasn't sure if there was protocol, but he didn't care. He'd spent more of his life with Agathon before the dispersal than with any other dragons and, for him, Agathon was father, teacher, mentor…everything. He stretched his wings and took to flight, making his way up to the rocks, expecting at least in some way to be stopped with every beat of his wings.

It wasn't stopped. It seemed, though, that all of the dra'acheck on the shores of the lake and those sunning themselves on the outcroppings and along the sides of the mountain seemed to stop their conversations and just stare at him. Even a few of the elders looked at him with absolute incomprehension. Still, he wasn't stopped despite the stares.

Agathon didn't stare, at least not in surprise.

He recognized Agathon's smile long before he reached him, and when he did, Agathon stepped forward and said, "Well, old friend, what terrible circumstances bring us here today."

Justinian nodded. "We didn't know what to do, but to be among humans is to be among wars."

Agathon nodded. "What happened to Yara's son was a terrible, terrible tragedy. But the only wrongdoing was Yara's. Tell me, how is Linara?"

Justinian bowed his head suddenly. "She is hurt, hurt very badly, and won't be here."

"Hurt? How did this happen?"

"In...in the fight with Yara." Justinian took a breath. "She is not hurt, Agathon. She is gone."

Agathon's eyes suddenly seemed to grow dark. He leapt to the sky suddenly. "Dra'acheck!" he bellowed. Instantly, all eyes were upon him. Hovering in the sky with his great wings beating, he said, "This, the second council, is necessary because life among the humans, while it has protected us, and while it has kept us and kept us what we are, nonetheless brought new challenges, new ideas, new fears, new thoughts, and new rules. It is a terrible thing that humans war among themselves."

Justinian stared at him, Awe creeping over him. He looked out among the gathered dragons. Only a few didn't cower. "No dragon will ever participate again in a war with men!" Agathon said more but Justinian heard none of it, caught instead in a wave of sadness and thoughts of Linara.

Agathon

The eyes of all dragons were upon him, and he fought to keep the anger from his voice. Linara was dead. Yara's stubborn foolishness had cost more than one life. Agathon looked to the sky, primarily to keep from making eye contact with any of the others for at least a moment. The roar of his words still seemed to echo but he knew a great deal of that had nothing to do with his volume. He blinked twice and then brought his head back down, beating his wings slowly to hover above the thousands gathered. Phineas looked up at him, anticipation etched on his face as plainly as grief plastered Justinian's.

The air felt thick and strange but he hovered and stared at all those below, strangely nervous despite his resolve. Announcing no participation in human wars was the easy part. He turned his head slowly and the sea of blues and yellows and greens stared back up at him expectantly. "We called you to Tatras. We called you to another Great Council," he began. "But we didn't call because we wanted to see you, although we did. We didn't call because every day on Tatras without you feels like a part of us is lost forever, although it does. We didn't call because the elders miss our race, although we do."

Below, Georgio's pride stared nervously up at him. They had more hatchlings than any other pride. Most of those hatchlings had never been to the mountain. Some of those hatchlings would never be on the mountain again. "Things have changed," he continued. He turned and flew to an outcropping about fifty feet above the basin. He wasn't certain if he chose the outcropping for intimacy, for an opportunity to perch and not fly like some kind of king above them. King. That's what he was now, wasn't it? That's at least what this new council would make him, wasn't it. He fought back a roar of anger. "We elders have been troubled by the changes. We've come to realize the plan, and the dispersal, has not gone as we hoped." He took a deep, heaving breath, and noticed Justinian staring at him.

Justinian.

He would have given anything to hunt with him, to arrive at the rocky slopes and dive to the opening of the cave and to regale him with stories of his adventures with the human tribes. He would have given anything to spend eight or nine decades hunting elk and speaking of life and the world and dragonkind. He would have given anything to see Linara again. He knew Justinian saw someone different now. Arriving to dispense justice on Yara, Justinian had seen power. Now, Agathon felt certain, he saw something entirely different. Was he tired? Was he overwhelmed? Was he sad?

He sure as hell felt overwhelmingly tired and sad.

"We began the great dispersal to protect our race, to keep ourselves alive." The crowd was already hushed. Now, they were hushed and expectant. "Someday we would reveal ourselves to a mature race, a race that could understand and accept..." He let his voice trail off but then added softly, "This was our purpose, our hope." He realized how powerfully that word, was, impacted them. Already, some tensed in anticipation that he would dismiss the plan. He understood. There was great pain in the separation.

"But things are changing. I doubt any of you are unaware of the recent tragedy. One dra'acheck. One dra'acheck I have loved has fallen and he fell because of pride, anger, and hatred. He fell because he set aside love for his kind and replaced it with deception and anger. He fell because for him, revenge was sweeter than life. He fell because he allowed hurt to rule his heart." Agathon paused. "And so plans must change."

He thought he caught the faintest hint of a smile from Phineas but for the most part he noticed anticipation and even a bit of fear among the rest. "Most of the prides will be moved to new locations, and only Katya will know their locations."

Silence.

Stunned silence.

He looked at Justinian. He probably seemed impassive to the rest but Agathon saw the hurt in his eyes. He'd let him stay in France. He'd let him stay and keep his memories of Linara. Agathon lifted himself up and said, "Yara came to Tatras as a friend. He gathered information from an elder who could not know there was murder in his heart. He came to Tatras and gathered information and used that information for evil. We cannot allow this to happen again." He paused again. For the most part the reactions among the crowd were neutral. That wasn't surprising, really. So far, the council had to be fairly anticlimactic.

Yara.

He was gone and for the briefest moment, Agathon would have traded all of the assembled dragons for Yara. He felt tears threatening and to stop it he lifted his head and roared. He hoped none would know he covered his grief and would instead assume he was punctuating his point. He looked down again and repeated, "We cannot allow this to happen again."

"Only Katya will know where you are. She may move you occasionally. Only Katya will know and she won't share the information." He stopped for a moment. He didn't want to share the next decision of the council of elders. "And no one is to come to Tatras unless summoned. Never."

Naturally, the words travelled through the assembly in a shock wave of disbelief and even horror. He'd anticipated that. It didn't make things any easier but he'd anticipated it and now that it arrived, he realized the pain of his next statement would be far worse than he'd imagined. So, he delayed it. He offered explanation first. The final, horrible pronouncement would come soon enough. "My friends," he said. He realized in the context of the situation friends sounded a hell of a lot like subjects. He hoped there were at least some of them there who didn't feel that way. "My friends, please know this decision wasn't made lightly. We didn't arrive at this in a haphazard way and we didn't set out to keep anyone from the home we all love." He scanned the crowd. Most looked at him with disbelief, even Justinian. Of course, Justinian and his pride also looked at him with faith, faith he felt he didn't deserve but nonetheless coveted greatly.

"You must understand," he said, and though he felt terrible for using his body to manipulate the crowd, he reared back and spread his wings. Awe settled over the assembly. "We enacted the plan to protect the dra'acheck from humanity but the threat comes now not from humans but from other dra'acheck. Yara came to Tatras with deception, with murder in his heart. We can't risk that happening again. Further, we can't risk someone without such deception coming to Tatras only to be followed home by another intent on hurting their pride." He remained reared back with his wings outspread. He didn't know how much of the assent he sensed came from his words or from the imposition of his presence. He wasn't certain he cared.

The next words, though... they were too important. He pulled his wings back and assumed an easier stance. The next words would need to act without the benefit of his personality. "To violate any of the new edicts is to play a hand in the death of dra'acheck. Therefore, violation is punishable by death."

Phineas

Death.

A pronouncement of death for violation of the rules. Absurd. Utterly absurd. Phineas had a great deal of difficulty restraining himself and only thoughts of Yara and his death kept him from creating more problems.

Yara was dead. He was dead just as he'd predicted he would be and instead of his death ending the Great Plan, it had only entrenched it. Instead of separating the dra'acheck from the humans Yara's death only ensured further integration and, worse, even greater distance from Tatras. It was utterly unthinkable. No, it was worse than unthinkable because he couldn't keep his mind from it. All he could do was think about it, and all of the thinking was terrible. "It's not enough to live among humans, Yara," he whispered softly. "Now we've become them."

"Agathon!" he cried and silence descended over the assembled group. The great red dragon Yara loved so much turned to fix his gaze upon Phineas and Phineas fought back the urge to flee. "There is still a matter left undiscussed," he said with far less power than he'd hoped. Agathon simply stared at him and Phineas felt his resolve weakening. He knew nothing would come of what he said but he knew his pride demanded it.

"I understand the decisions announced here today, and I understand why they were made," he began. He thought it was obvious he was showboating. He hoped it wasn't obvious to Agathon. "I understand these things but there is still the matter of my dead brother. It was his death that drove Yara to his behavior, his death that started all of this." He paused. His pride looked on him with... with pride. The rest of the dragons appeared shocked. "We demand justice for my brother. We demand the life of Philip, the dra'acheck who took his life."

Agathon said calmly. "The elders have already ruled on this matter, Phineas. They have already ruled on this matter. Yara could not accept our decision. Will you?"

"You expect my brother to be unavenged?"

Agathon looked at him sadly. "Your brother's death was an accident, an accident—"

"He was murdered!"

205

"An accident!" Agathon roared, and the power of his voice sent most of the dragons in the assembly cowering. Only by a supreme effort of rule could Phineas remain upright. Agathon's tone softened. "A tragedy, Phineas. A terrible tragedy that can't be helped. We must grow, we must adapt, and we must suffer a little. We all feel for your loss. I feel for it." Phineas hated that he believed Agathon to be sincere. "Yara has left a void that may never be filled but Haaman will now be your steward. Can he count on you to accept the decision of the elders?"

Phineas took a deep breath and let it out softly. "I accept the council's decision. I many never forgive Philip but he will suffer no harm from me."

There was a long moment of silence that seemed to last centuries before Agathon said, "Stay for as long as you'd like, everyone. Stay but for no longer than a month. Katya will meet with all of you and let you know where you must go." It took a long while for the assembled dragons to begin moving. Phineas stood and watched Justinian's pride. He watched the others. All of Yara's foresight amounted to nothing at all.

No. Not nothing. Haaman appeared before him. "There is no steward but you, Phineas," he said before he spread his wings and leapt into the sky.

CHAPTER EIGHTEEN

NOW

Phineas

He didn't appear to be dra'acheck but he obviously was. Something was wrong with him, some kind of defect or some kind of... Well, there were dra'acheck who were so small as to never grow imposing in any way, shape or form. In fact, they grew only slightly larger than a human. There were some whose wings couldn't support them for any extended length of time. There were those injured in one way or another who never healed the way they should have. Still, what was wrong with the dragon he saw with Justinian and Philip and Daniel, the one Justinian called Petros, the one Justinian called his son?

There were some hatchlings who grew confused as they grew in the human world. Sometimes their transformations weren't successful right away. Had something like that happened to Justinian's son? It was clearly a transformation attempt. There was no other explanation for the way Justinian threw his son around that Alley. What would it mean, though?

Of course, it was good he had a son in the first place. Phineas hadn't seen a new hatchling in years. He often wondered if that had to do with the cursed humans, the dispersal that did wonders for their numbers in the beginning but then gradually resulted in fewer and fewer new dra'acheck. He sighed. There would be a confrontation eventually. With the upcoming council there would be a confrontation, and there was no doubt a great deal of his actions, actions directly in opposition to the elders, would come to light if not there then shortly thereafter. How would he react when he faced that inevitability?

He knew how Yara would react in circumstances such as these. Yara would state his case and then accept the consequences. Of course, he'd done that in France and made an entirely inaccurate prediction that his death would end the damned plan and everyone would return to freedom. Would he follow in Yara's noble but ultimately misguided path?

It still hurt. It still hurt like hell that he'd given himself for nothing. He'd given himself in what was probably the most significant sacrifice any dragon had ever made, more significant than any likely would. Yara was gone for his love of the dra'acheck and now more than ever the dra'acheck were at risk and in need of another sacrifice.

Many sacrifices, perhaps.

There were no Yara's left to perform them. Well, there was one. There was Agathon. Instead of sacrificing himself, though, he'd chosen to sacrifice the dra'acheck.

God, he wanted to hate the red dragon. He wanted to hate him more than he wanted anything he could imagine wanting. He wanted to hate him but Agathon was like Yara in more than his love for dragons and more than his power. He was like Yara in his propensity for misguided attempts at dra'acheck salvation. It cost Yara his life in his misguided attempt to preserve all that the dra'acheck were. As for Agathon, he still lived. His misguided attempt had cost the dra'acheck all that they were.

Misguided. That was it. Two misguided giants had acted with noble intentions and now perhaps there was no fixing any of it. Could Phineas even call himself dra'acheck, though, if he didn't try?

"Steward. We're ready."

He turned from where he stood at the summit of the mountain and smiled sadly at Haaman. "My friend," he said softly but then paused as he felt the wind blowing over him. "It's come to this now, hasn't it."

Haaman didn't respond right away but just stared at Phineas. Finally after the long pause he said softly, "It came to this centuries ago." Phineas nodded slowly. "Do you think they know?" Haaman asked.

"Justinian? He certainly sensed me when I saw them."

"That's not what I mean." Phineas already knew that but didn't respond. "Is this council because they've found out? Is that what this is about?"

"No. We've been careful. They may have discovered the consequences but not the actions. This council... who knows?"

Haaman said, "Are you sure you only want to bring four of us?"

Phineas shook his head. "If all is at an end, four hundred wouldn't make a difference. He took a deep breath. "Four, yes. You won't be coming, though. As far as Tatras knows, you're still steward." He turned around and stared out at the sky. "If something goes wrong, you can deny you were aware of anything I've done." He knew the words were hurtful. He knew Haaman would suffer a thousand deaths on his behalf and so he added, "So that you can keep our hopes alive if I am taken from you."

Petros

"Can we talk?"

She was still groggy, at least Petros thought she was but she sat up straight and said, "I'm unfamiliar with the proper etiquette in this particular situation." It was classic Patricia. Classic. "I mean, am I supposed to be angry because you lied to me, afraid because you're like the incredible hulk but not as cute, or disgusted because... okay, I made that one up on the fly so I guess angry and afraid win. Mostly angry."

Petros said. "I never lied to you."

"There are some omissions that jump right past the forgot to tell you thing and dive headlong into the complete and utter liar thing." Something was wrong. More accurately, something was right. She wasn't freaked out. She wasn't even all that angry. Shock, maybe? "You know I never made love to anyone else?" He stared. She was lying. Why would she do that? "I had sex, sure, but I never loved while I did. You were the first. You were the first and there were a million reasons for it." She paused and he opened his mouth to say something but then shut it again. "But your honesty was the most important one."

"I was—"

"And I was wrong about that." She'd lied earlier. She wasn't angry. She was sad. She was very sad. How the hell did she see something like what she saw and go right to regret instead of shock or fear or, for that matter, insanity?

"You weren't wrong," he said. She tilted her head and stared at him. It was her How in the can you be so smart and say something so utterly stupid? look. "I found out about it just a few weeks ago. I was trying to figure out how to tell you, if to tell you. I mean, I don't even understand any of this crap myself." Her look softened a bit but she still stared at him. Unnerving. Damn she was unnerving. "Why the aren't you freaking out?"

She smiled thinly. "Because I believe you. I expect in the future you'll tell me the moment you discover something so significant but I suppose the whole situation was pretty damned unprecedented. I'm okay. You weren't lying to me."

He stared at her and then sprang to his feet. "Mom!" he yelled. He heard footsteps from below but before they reached the stairs he heard Patricia laughing. She'd thrown the blankets off and was getting off the bed. "Wait!" he cried. "Wait! I'm afraid you're in shock, you can't get up!" She laughed some more, which didn't do a thing to offer Petros a bit of comfort.

"What's wrong?"

He turned to his mother. "She's... she's cracking up."

That made Patricia laugh louder as Cheryl rushed to her side and put her hand over Patricia's. "What happened?" she asked.

"She's not mad. She's not freaking out. She just wanted to make sure I wasn't lying and now she's..." He didn't know how the hell to finish the thought. His mother looked at him for a moment and then back at Patricia.

"Are you okay, Patty?"

Patricia stopped laughing. "As long as you promise to stop calling me Patty." Cheryl smiled at that and Petros stood and wondered how in the hell his mom could be sucked into whatever delusion his girlfriend had.

"Fiancé," he whispered. God, why did it still feel good to say that when he didn't even know if they were still—

Smiling. Why the hell were they both okay?

"Are we still..." He couldn't bring himself to actually ask the words.

And they weren't smiling any more. They were just staring at him.

Staring.

Patricia sighed. "I don't know. I need to think. I mean, your mom did it with your dad, I guess but I don't know."

"But—"

"I'll help you pack, Sweetie," Cheryl said.

"But—"

"Out!" He backed away. His mother's tone allowed for no discussion.

He shook his head and stepped from the room. Cheryl closed the door behind him with a smile. He got to the stairs before he heard her say, "He was different than I expected."

"Me, too," Patricia said.

"No, I mean when I saw Justin after he'd changed, I though there would be something about him that wasn't the man anymore."

"I know." Petros waited, trying to wrap his head around it. "That's what I mean, too. It was still Petros." He could almost hear Patricia take a deep breath. "But there's so much to think about... I mean, he was already so complex and brilliant and... Oh, God."

"That was real," Patricia said. "I thought I was prepared. I mean, you'd convinced me and then when your husband changed for me but I still..."

"Why not just talk to me?" he whispered as he started down the stairs.

"To protect your ego, Pete." He almost tripped at the sound of his father's voice. Justinian stood at the foot of the stairs.

"Mom told her? You changed for her?"

"Yes she did. Yes I did. It was your mother's call. I told her it was out of the question but she made the case that with everything going on, with Philip, with everything, we needed to stabilize. She was worried you were going to break things off with Patricia without any explanation and that could have made the situation even more complicated. I talked to Daniel and a few others in the pride and we all agreed."

Petrol just stood there dumbfounded for a moment. On the one hand he felt incredible relief that Patricia knew and he could stop his worrying about how to tell her, or if to tell her for that matter. On the other hand his father, uncle Daniel and uncle Phil had been drilling into him the whole principle of the great plan. To stay hidden. To not reveal themselves to the human world. How were those principles thrown out the window so suddenly?

Almost as if his father were reading his thoughts, wait, can dragons do that? Justinian continued speaking after a pause. "It's because we trust you Pete. We trust you the way the pride trusted me when I brought your mother in. Give her space. You'll never have enough power to understand women. Let it go." Petros remained still about halfway down the stairs and Justinian said, "Let it go and let's go."

"Go? Where are we going?"

"To something that hasn't happened in almost a thousand years. We're going to the Third Great Council of the dra'acheck. And you should have sensed me before I arrived. You can't afford mistakes like that now. None of us can."

Justinian

"Are you sure it's wise, Steward?" So, it was a steward issue.

"Of course I'm not sure," Justinian said. How could he be sure? He looked at Daniel and missed Philip terribly. "But Agathon said everyone was to be there and therefore everyone must go." He took a deep breath and looked out of the window. He didn't like the Nevada property as much as the property in California and he liked it even less now after Philip. Of course, there was nothing to be done about it. They'd keep it and use it and wait for their long, long memories to fade enough to allow at least some measure of comfort and forgetfulness.

Petros sat quietly but Justinian could tell he was nervous. That made a great deal of sense. If anyone other than Agathon were the leader he wouldn't take his son but if there were one thing about which he had utter confidence it was in Agathon's love and protection. Still, he'd bring his son and keep him distant, keep him somewhere apart from the gathering but close by. He'd wait until he could speak with Agathon alone and then tell him about Petros.

"How can we even get him there?"

The question hung in the room for five or ten seconds. Justinian hadn't even considered it. Damn. They could get within twenty or thirty miles with human transportation but after that he'd have to walk. Of course, they could put him in a hotel about eighty miles away. That wasn't really any distance at all for a dragon.

Or he could just stay in the United States.

There had been times when decisions in regards to his pride cost Justinian a night or two of sleep but for the most part those decisions were made in the first few seconds and the sleeplessness had everything to do with the consequences of what he knew to be necessary. This was different. He was lost. He didn't particularly want Petros there. At the same time, he couldn't imagine not taking him. He supposed at least to some extent he expected to deal with something along these lines, had expected it for years. Now that the time had arrived, though, the decision not only didn't come easy but evidently didn't come at all.

"What do you think is going to happen?" Petros asked, and the sound of his voice startled Justinian enough that he had to control his reaction and hope Daniel wouldn't notice.

"Each of our councils in the past had to do with the dispersal," Daniel said. "The first announced the great plan and then the second added new restrictions, restrictions because a dra'acheck attempted to murder another dra'acheck." Thoughts of Yara came to Justinian with Daniel's words and, of course, lingering concern about Phineas and the spying in the alleyway.

"Do you think there will be more restrictions?"

It was a fair question for Petros to ask. Justinian said, "You don't know enough about us, yet, Pete. We're already restricted and restricted almost beyond our nature. Philip is gone." The statement hurt more than he thought it would and Justinian had to take a breath to steady himself. "And there are others. Two others, maybe more."

Daniel sat up straight. "Agathon said more than three were killed?"

"He said there were three that were dead who took proper precautions. He asked me if Philip was careful before he told me that. It could mean more are dead, some who didn't take the right precautions."

"What precautions are you talking about?" Petros asked.

Justinian smiled. It was tinged with at least a little bit of bitterness but it still felt good to smile. "You lived for more than twenty-one years in my house, Pete. You lived in my house and spent almost every summer and plenty of holidays here in Nevada. Even now, you have no idea how many of the men and women you grew up around are dra'acheck."

"Forty-eight."

"Close. Forty-nine. Still, that was..." He paused. "Why did you say forty-eight?"

Petros was quiet for a moment. "I'm sorry. I forgot about Uncle Philip. I mean, I should have added one to the rest when I—"

"It's okay," Justinian said quickly. "But how did you know? Only a dozen or so have revealed themselves and—"

"You can't sense them all?"

Daniel stood up. "We can sense them but... you sense forty-eight distinct dra'acheck right now?"

Petros shook his head. "No. Not now. There were thirty-two in Los Angeles and I sense seventeen now but since Dad was one of them in LA, I subtracted but..."

"You can sense seventeen here?"

"Sure. You can't? Isn't this normal?" He turned to Justinian. "You said I should have sensed you this morning back at the house before we left for the airport. I assumed that meant everyone could sense other dra'acheck. There are nineteen people at the house in L.A., too. I don't—Is this another test, like more training?"

Justinian shook his head. "We can sense others but not so specifically, not dra'acheck. I could estimate a herd of cows and get within three or four. I can get within five or six hundred if I tried to sense the number of humans at a baseball game. Dra'acheck, though... I can sense if there's a group and I can sense individuals to whom I'm close but counting the presences if there are more than four or five is almost impossible. Each presence is too..." he turned to Daniel. "I don't know the right word."

"Powerful? Imposing?" Daniel turned to Petros. "You shouldn't be able to sense them that precisely. Can you tell me more about who's here?"

Justinian stared at his son. He had the same look on his face he'd had at eleven years old when a teacher called his parents into the office to explain how he'd, in one week, completed a college calculus textbook the teacher had on her shelf, a textbook from her days at the university. Petros couldn't understand why anyone found it remarkable. It took a long while for them to convince him he wasn't in trouble. The idea the accomplishment itself was remarkable was lost on him.

"There's dad and you. Bernard, the man who visited last Thanksgiving. Well, I guess he's not a man. Jorge and Hanna evidently aren't just gardeners. Kaitlin, Ian, Paul and Paulie, Sean, Jean, and six more I don't know. The six I don't know are stronger than everyone but you and dad though Bernard is a hell of a lot smarter."

"Petros," Justinian began.

"Heck, sorry dad. All of them are on edge, and Bernard is very angry about Philip."

Justinian held up a hand. "That's not what I meant. Bernard is in charge of our security. The six you don't know work for him. It's because they're stronger. How can you tell all of this?"

"You can't?"

"Some of it in some ways but not all of it in all ways."

215

"Is it from his mother?" Daniel asked.

Justinian chuckled. "She has irritatingly good intuition." He sighed. "It could be the combination or it could just be that damned brain of his. He processes everything else so easily."

Daniel nodded slowly. "I think—"

"I know," Justinian said. "You're right."

Petros nodded. "Can I fly home first and see Patricia to the airport?"

Justinian looked at his son. "What did you just sense?"

Petros smiled. "That was the damned brain, Dad. I'm going to the council now. There's too much I can learn from you there to miss the opportunity."

CHAPTER NINETEEN

NOW AND THEN

Justinian

"You're disappointed," Philip said softly. Justinian turned to look at him. Philip looked sympathetic and Justinian raised an eyebrow. "It's okay to be disappointed," Philip said.

"Why would I be disappointed?" he asked. "He's perfect."

Philip gestured past the glass to the bed where Cheryl lay holding her newborn son. She slept and so did the boy. "But not dra'acheck."

Justinian smiled. "How exactly could I have expected a hatchling from a wife who doesn't have the anatomy required to lay an egg?" Philip shrugged but kept the same expression. He didn't believe him but that was fine. "This situation is unprecedented, Philip," Justinian said. "We don't know what he is." He paused and then put his hand on Philip's shoulder. "But we know who he is. That's enough."

"I was wrong," Philip said.

"It's understandable you would think me disappointed."

Philip took Justinian's shoulder and turned him so that he faced him. Under other circumstances, the familiarity might have been effrontery. He stared at him and Philip said, "I was wrong to question your marriage. I was wrong to question your wisdom. I was wrong to question any of that."

Justinian smiled. "No. You weren't. You and Daniel are important to me and that matters. You're also important to the Pride. You had then and still have now permission to make me consider my decisions."

Philip nodded. "Then I was wrong to have the concerns. Right to question but proven wrong." He smiled at Justinian. "You lost yourself for a while, if you'll forgive me mentioning it. You lost yourself for a while after Linara, and though you had all of us to care for nobody was there to care for you. Now, you have someone who cares for you as Linara did, and she's given you a son."

The statements were accurate. They were also bittersweet, and Justinian realized at least part of what added the bitterness was that he didn't hurt. "I still miss her, Philip," he said. That was true but he didn't hurt anymore.

"You'll miss her always, and you'll miss Cheryl someday, too." Before Justinian could react to that, Philip added, "But Linara taught you to find joy in now, and not in the certainty of tomorrow."

That wasn't entirely accurate. Linara didn't teach him that at all. Her death didn't teach him that either, though it should have. Cheryl taught him that. He turned back to look at his son. The sight was strange. He'd seen dozens of human infants in the flesh and perhaps hundreds in the last century with photographs, television, and film. They always seemed so weak, so helpless. Hatchlings were weak compared to dra'acheck adults but that weakness wasn't as profound as the absolute helplessness of a human child. He felt an urge—no, not an urge, an absolute need to protect Petros.

He wondered if he would have felt the same way if a hatchling had arrived with Linara. Oh, he'd love the hatchling. He knew that. He'd love the hatchling as much as he loved the infant. Would he believe it needed such protection, though? He watched as Cheryl's eyes opened and then watched her roll them. He nodded to Philip, who quickly walked away and he stepped into the room. She smiled at him but said wryly, "When I said I wanted a nursery, I didn't think you'd build one like the hospital nurseries."

"What else would I do?"

She smiled. "What are you, a dragon or something?"

"I don't understand," he said. "I had Daniel look and make sure everything was right. The medical equipment arrived this morning."

She smiled again and shook her head. "I'll fix it. I'll get started tomorrow. I kind of like the window, though. It will make it easier to look in on him."

He slumped his shoulders a bit and asked, "Are you feeling okay?" She nodded. "I should have told you I was making it. I guess I—"

"Stop talking, Justin," she said. "I would have changed it no matter what you did."

"You can design one from scratch for the home in Los Angeles."

"Are we still moving there in two years?" He nodded. "Then it doesn't matter. He'll need a real room then. I'll take care of the room there and tomorrow I'll start on the nursery here."

He'd probably gotten the other surprise wrong, he realized. Nonetheless, he said, "I... I did something else for you, if you're able to walk."

She rolled her eyes again. "You made me stay in the hospital for a week. Of course I can walk."

He smiled, reached for Petros, and held him. She stood up and he noticed she wasn't shaky at all. She smiled as he handed the baby back. "I didn't just do this for you. I mean, I've been working on this for, well since you told me you'd stay."

She smiled and said, "What have you done?"

"Come with me," he said. He walked slowly from the room and she walked beside him as he led her out of the house. She had to tell him to pick up the pace twice but he still walked slowly.

"You know, human women have been giving birth for as long as there have been human women."

Justinian shrugged. "And I imagine human men have walked slowly next to them."

They walked along the hedge of ocotillos until the break and then around it. From there, they walked past the false barn, the oversized building really set aside for transformations, one of five. That led them to the real barn filled with real barn animals. She'd loved that about the place and he hoped he was right about how she'd like what he was about to show her. "Did you get more of those prized Spanish goats you like so much?"

"No," he laughed. "Well, yes. Another dozen ewes and a ram came in but that's not the surprise. They're not here anyway. They're in a ten acre field about a mile away."

"New boars? New breed of chicken that lays fifty eggs a week? New—"

"It's not an animal," he said. He stared at her and reached down to lift the blanket from Petros just enough to see his face. "Maybe I should show you later. Is it too cold for him?"

She laughed. "It's in the nineties."

"Are you sure?"

"Just a guess but it seems right."

"No, I mean are you sure he's not…Oh." He smiled. "Come with me." He walked along the outside wall of the barn and then to the tree line about fifty yards distant. "Are you sure it's okay for him to be outside like this?"

"The pediatrician said he was the healthiest baby he'd ever seen."

"I'd like him to stay that way."

Cheryl smiled. "My grandmother raised my mother in a little hut with a dirt floor along the banks of the Mississippi. She was there until she was twelve and my grandfather found a coin on the banks that turned out to be something rare and special. They sold it and bought a house with a real floor. You know, my mom said she missed the hut."

"Okay," he said. He led her to the trees and stopped her at the beginning of a path. "I made you a garden," he said.

"Out here?"

He shrugged. "Our people know the way of the earth. We imported the soil, of course but the weather, the lack of water, doesn't matter as much when plants are grown by our hand."

"You're so full of crap," she said. "I know what wells are, and you have nine here. One would be enough for all the buildings. I always thought you had lake somewhere on the property."

He smiled. "Can't I try for a little dra'acheck mystique?"

"Yeah, dragons. The creatures with the greenest thumbs on the planet and their thumbs are claws."

He led her down the path until they reached a high hedge and the path ended in a gate. "We don't really have to shop. We grow almost everything here ourselves, enough for here and for Los Angeles," he said. "But it's all been functional. Crops. I wanted to make something nice for you, he said." He took a deep breath. "Go ahead. Step inside."

She started to make a smartass comment but as she stepped through the gate, she instead drew in a deep breath. "Oh, Justin," she said. "It's beautiful." He stepped close and put his arm around her. He'd build her something out here, a little building with a sitting room and a bathroom, maybe a refrigerator for drinks. Something that would allow her to spend as much time as she wanted. "This is paradise," she said.

Justinian squeezed her shoulder. "With you here, it is."

Phineas

Centuries.

It had been centuries since the damned council and then the second damned council, and though his plan began in earnest immediately upon the conclusion of Yara's failed efforts… "Ali!" His shout was louder than it should have been but Phineas spent too much time in his head lately. The volume at least gave him a break from the noise.

Khroniss arrived in only a second or two. "Steward?"

Phineas glared at him. "Not today. Today Katya comes. Address me as Phineas."

"Of course. Sorry, St—Phineas."

He sighed. He was taking out his frustration on Khroniss and it was wrong. Damn. He was growing careless. The frustration was too powerful. He made sure his voice was softer as he asked, "Where is Ali?"

"His flight arrived about hour ago. He should be here shortly."

He nodded. "Do we have any of the bourbon left, the bourbon from America?" It wasn't easy to get alcohol into the country anymore. The world grew smaller every day because of the damned humans and though twenty glasses of the alcohol had little chance of influencing dra'acheck biology it was one of the few things that helped make the human form tolerable.

"I believe so. We brought back twice as much last time. I'm sure Ali will bring more as well."

"A bottle, please."

Khroniss nodded and disappeared. They'd begun traveling to America in the early nineteen hundreds, seeking a potential place to move but when Hamaan broached the subject with Katya, she'd informed him there were no areas available in North America. He asked about South America and was told she'd look into it. On her next visit she offered South Africa. There wasn't anywhere else, evidently, where the pride would blend in because of skin tone, at least not until another pride moved. Again, the humans constrained the dra'acheck.

Khroniss returned with a bottle and a glass. "You didn't bring a glass for yourself?" Khroniss looked like he wasn't sure how to answer. Phineas sighed.

He ruled too absolutely. Far too absolutely. "Get yourself a glass," he said softly. "Let us sit together."

Khroniss nodded but he still looked a bit unsure. He'd misjudged, things, tried too hard to carry on the legacy of Yara. He'd done well in many regards. He'd certainly modeled his life correctly, modeled it with a very clear understanding of right, wrong, and nothing between. Yara, though, never had trouble also expressing his love for the dra'acheck, also expressing his love for his pride. Phineas had become what Yara appeared to be but not what Yara actually was. The dra'acheck in the pride were loyal to Phineas but did they love him as well as respect him? He tried to determine if he cared and decided he did. He tried to determine if he only cared because Yara would have and decided it didn't matter.

While he thought, Khroniss set down the bottle and the glass. He walked from the room and Phineas filled it. He returned with another glass and Phineas gestured to a cushion next to the table. "Sit, please." Khroniss sat and reached for the bottle but Phineas waved him away and poured the drink for him. "You are a…" What were the right words? "You are a fine dragon." Khroniss looked at him in surprise and there was still a bit of nervousness but Phineas noticed he also sat up a bit, his back was straighter. Was such a small encouragement so effective?

It would have been from Yara. For Phineas, it would have been. It was. It had been. So, they did see him as Yara, after all. "I haven't told you that before," he said softly.

"Your responsibilities weigh on you, St-Phineas." Khroniss said. Phineas nodded in half agreement and brought his glass to his lips. He took a sip and loved the way it burned his lips, his tongue, and his throat even if there'd be no effect from the alcohol. Khroniss took a sip of his own drink and said, "Things are not pleasant, and perhaps there is no time for pleasantries."

"Perhaps," Phineas said. "But perhaps they are needed precisely because the world is unpleasant."

"You may be right," Khroniss replied. "Thank you. You are the finest of the dra'acheck. I would follow you to hell and be grateful for the chance."

Phineas smiled, put down his glass, and put his hand on the other's shoulder. "Let us hope it doesn't come to that."

He heard the car about a mile off. Khroniss did as well. "Ali is coming," Khroniss said. Phineas nodded. That was good. It wouldn't do for him to arrive when Katya was on the roof. As it was, he had to ensure there was a great deal of activity just to avoid others showing him too much deference. He wasn't sure if Katya could sense that but it had worked through nearly a dozen visits and he didn't want to risk changing anything.

He stood. "Is Hamaan on the roof yet?"

Khroniss stood as well and then shook his head. "It's still early."

Phineas nodded and drained his glass. He put it on the table. He could hear the car in the driveway now. "Sit down. Finish your drink," he said. He walked to the window and glanced down. Ali was already out of the car. He had others getting bags from the trunk but he walked toward the house. Phineas turned around. Khroniss still stood. "Please," he said. "It's fine. Drink." Khroniss still seemed reluctant but he sat and reached for his glass. Phineas didn't want to sit but he did, intent on making the other more comfortable. He reached for the bottle and filled his glass again.

A moment later, Alinada walked in. "Ali," he said. "Welcome home."

It was a testament to how distant he'd become from his pride that his greeting caused Ali to pause. "Thank you Steward, I—"

"Katya comes today."

"Apologies. Thank you, Phineas. I've just returned from America."

Phineas nodded. "I know. Did you bring more bourbon?"

Ali nodded absently. "Yes, two cases, but..." He swallowed hard and said, "We found them. They're in Los Angeles."

That was welcome news. Very welcome.

"Then I suppose it's time Arctel Global opened an office in California," Phineas said softly.

Petros

The party really wasn't all that impressive but Petros didn't find that surprising. He had friends, the kinds of friends that always followed the popular kids even when the popular kids were younger. Of course, he was younger but appeared older so it all worked out in a superficial way. Still, he'd never gotten into the drinking or even the whole desperate quest for sex. He didn't need to. He could drink any of his friends under the table and it was a chore to even get buzzed. As for the sex, he'd been active for two years before the party, active from the moment he realized there were cheerleaders willing to trade favors for his abilities to help with their academics.

He didn't know why thoughts of the party came to him now, two years later. He imagined it was the return to school. Sure, he'd done some tutoring (both for special rewards and just to keep busy) since he graduated but his mother wouldn't let him actually head to college until now.

Finally.

He'd finished his father's library, almost seven hundred books, six months before. He hoped like hell there'd be something in college that challenged him or at least interested him. If he couldn't find anything, though, at least he wouldn't be utterly bored. His mother refused to allow him to move as quickly as he wanted but she'd relented on his triple major, and that was a start. He thought about that for a moment and wondered why he wasn't particularly excited to be free of his mother and her rules.

No. It wasn't that. It was the same thing that made him think of the party. He was looking forward to friends again, shallow as the relationships might be. There were always plenty of people at home and there was always plenty of activity but everyone either gave him respect he didn't deserve or overprotectiveness he didn't want. Nobody just hung out with him. Nobody just talked about girls or music or the latest television shows.

Okay, outside of the girls, he wasn't really interested in a conversation and he'd never found himself as frustrated as his friends in that regard anyway. Maybe he just wanted companionship his own age. He wasn't sure about that. What he knew for sure, though, was that he wanted to be somewhere. He wanted to spend some amount of time out of the house, away from everyone who knew him intimately, away from everyone who knew he was some kid genius and treated him like that trick of genetics made him something more than he was.

Mom and Dad were proud. Sure they were. Of course, they'd spent most of his childhood proud, and pride from them was nothing more than the norm. That was fine, he supposed. On the other hand, he didn't like the times his mind went to dark places, the times when he realized he was smarter than both of them. He felt that differently than he felt it with others. He was used to being smarter than those around him. He realized he was smarter than his teacher when he was in second grade and by fourth grade he realized he always would be smarter than his teachers. He didn't look down on them, at least not consciously, but he knew they had nothing to offer him.

And that was the fear.

It was only a few months ago that the thought struck him and struck him like a blow to the face. He was smarter than his mother. He was smarter than his father. Had they nothing to offer him as well? He shook his head hard, not negating the thought so much as trying to drive it away. As he did he realized he was being foolish. They'd never tried to instruct him in math or science or language. They provided him with education he couldn't learn from books or in institutions. It didn't matter than he'd finished a library his father took years to build in less time than many would have taken just to read the first three volumes from Gibbon. He could rattle off the stats for the games but his father still picked the winners far more effectively.

He laughed for a moment. That was it, though. That was still why he was eager to leave. He didn't like knowing he was smarter. He didn't like feeling— no matter how hard he fought against the feeling—that same sense of superiority about his parents that he felt about everyone else. It wasn't haughty. It wasn't driven by some egotistical self-analysis. It didn't even really impact his day to day life. It was simple fact. It was fine to have that sense in regards to his peers, and he supposed it was even fine for some who weren't his peers.

Not his parents.

But then it struck him. He knew the stats because he was smarter, but Justin, his father, actually picked the winners because... because... he was wiser. That was it. That's what separated his parents from everyone else in his world. That's what they offered him that no one else seemed to be able to. His parents were wise, maybe wiser then he'd ever be and he loved that about them.

"Pete!"

His father's voice startled him and he called out, "Coming!" He grabbed his backpack, slung it over his shoulder, and rushed down the stairs. His mother looked like she was going to cry so he avoided her gaze as he walked to where they stood by the car and then got into the back seat. A moment later, she got into the front passenger seat. His father said he'd be right back and disappeared into the house before returning to take the wheel.

"Take a good look, Pete," his father said. "Don't want to forget where you came from."

Petros laughed. "You know most people who say that are talking about remembering you were poor once. You'll telling me to look around an estate only a couple dozen people in the state could afford. Don't forget you're rich!"

His father chuckled. "You're not rich, Pete. Your mom and I are rich."

He smiled. "Good point. I suppose I'll only be rich if you don't decide to give my inheritance to charity."

"Oh, you'd end up rich anyway, Pete," his father said. "If you wanted to. Rich is nice. It gives you choices. On the other hand, if you find out in college that what makes you happy is library science, that's what you should do. There are far too many unhappy millionaires."

"I don't even know if universities offer library science anymore, dad."

"Don't be a smartass. You know what I mean. You're intelligent, Petros. Make sure you're smart enough to choose real happiness over fake."

His mother looked like she wanted to add something but he could tell she was afraid she'd cry if she spoke. "I will, Dad," he promised. He added, "And I'm going to miss your cooking, mom." He added it for her benefit but he realized as he said it how true the comment was.

They rode in silence for a little while and then a terrible thought hit him. He reached for his backpack, opened it, and frantically began rummaging through the contents. About halfway through, he knew the search was fruitless but he still kept it up. Finally, he said, "Um, we need to turn around."

His mother looked at him with surprise but his father chuckled. "Forget something? Like maybe on your nightstand? Your nightstand next to the wall, for example? A ticket maybe?" He watched as his father passed it to his mother.

Oh yeah, superior. Absolutely superior.

CHAPTER TWENTY

NOW

Phineas

The the third great council began and Phineas watched as Agathon and the other elders descended from the side of Mount Tatras and landed before the basin lake in an area kept clear of dra'acheck. There were a great many there. Phineas had estimated there would be about five thousand. If other prides were like his, there hadn't been hatchlings in hundreds of years. He looked around. He saw no hatchlings, saw none in fact likely younger than four hundred years old. Justinian and his pride were together at the side of a basin but he didn't notice one young enough to be the son he'd seen in the alley. Perhaps he'd not figured out his transformation yet. Perhaps Justinian was ashamed of his son. No. That wasn't really possible. Justinian, like Agathon and Yara, was an honorable dra'acheck. Something else was at play.

He looked back at the elders. Where was Katya? She wasn't there but there was one dragon he didn't recognize. He was young, perhaps half a century old. His scales gleamed purple against the morning light, a purple closer to red than blue but shimmering and almost metallic. The color, unique among dra'acheck as far as Phineas knew, seemed to reflect over the water and draw attention even from Agathon's imposing frame.

He looked back at Justinian. He, too, studied the new dra'acheck and Phineas stared at him in the hopes of getting his attention. If this council went badly, and Phineas felt certain it would, his hope lay oddly with the dragon who most likely considered himself an enemy. It was a fair consideration. If they weren't exactly enemies they certainly weren't allies. Still, barring Agathon, Phineas believed only two dra'acheck loved their kind as Yara had. Two.

Two dragons and both raised by the giants of dra'acheck history.

Phineas could be convinced of the wisdom in the approach Justinian had taken, the way he led his pride. He certainly hadn't complied with the letter of the Great Plan. Well, he hadn't complied with the spirit. Nonetheless, there was only one dragon of substance he had any hope to convince. Agathon was far too committed to his plan, far too committed to finding new ways to restrict the dra'acheck to coddle to humanity's frailties. Justinian, though... he had a son. He had a son and for hundreds of years he'd had to contemplate what that meant for a future among a race that wasn't his.

Justinian had to listen.

If he didn't...

"Dra'acheck!" Phineas almost jumped at the sound of Agathon's voice. Had it been so many centuries? His voice was unthinkably powerful, far more powerful than it had been at the second council. The other elders appeared different. They were old, certainly. They were old and powerful but they'd reached that point where their will, their motivation, and their power began decline. Certainly they'd remain more powerful than most dra'acheck for several centuries longer but Agathon, too, should have shown some of the almost lackadaisical luster to his eyes. He showed none. His eyes gleamed with power as he waited for the assembly to grow silent and still.

Silence descended and Agathon reared back, still on his hind legs but wings extended. Awe rushed through the gathering like an ocean wave and even as Phineas felt it and fought back the urge to cower, he realized the movement was intentional. In fact, he realized the imposing nature of Agathon's presence at the previous council was intentional. It was smart, actually. The power of Agathon's personality drove the first council. The power of Agathon's will drove the second and here, at the third, it was just his power. Phineas felt a moment of panic. How could he possibly hope to bring other dra'acheck to his point of view? How could any measures he took, even desperate measures, overcome the almost omnipotent strength of Agathon the Red?

"My friends," Agathon said softly but even speaking softly his voice pummeled Phineas, almost drove him to his knees. He chanced a look around. Some dragons cowered. Some dragons, perhaps smarter than the rest, began the assembly already seated. Justinian stood tall. There was hope there, only a glimmer of hope but hope nonetheless. "Humans murder dragons again."

Phineas still looked at Justinian when Agathon made the announcement, and Phineas noted that Justinian showed no surprise. What did that mean? If Justinian knew of murdered dra'acheck convincing him could be much easier.

Or harder.

"No fewer than twenty." Agathon paused and then roared, "Twenty!" Again, his voice exploded over the assembly like a blast and more than one dragon reared before controlling their involuntary reaction. "No fewer than twenty dragons have been killed in the last four months." Phineas stared at Agathon's face. He saw, or at least he thought he saw, a tear. "Katya is among the dead."

Perhaps no other words could have broken through the dullness of the awe among the gathered dragons. Phineas felt the shock profoundly. Katya? Dead? She couldn't be dead. The others, certainly, but Katya? Sure, the death of a number of dra'acheck was inevitable for Phineas' plan to work but Katya? It made no sense at all. He stared at Agathon, not comprehending or perhaps simply refusing to comprehend.

"There is more," Agathon said. "She was mine. Katya." Agathon's eyes closed for a moment and then slowly opened. "Shortly after the tragedy of Yara's death and the death of his son, I realized Katya alone held me to the standards I hold myself—I mean." He paused again. "Katya alone had the power to tell me when she believed I was wrong. It was for that reason she was chosen to hold the knowledge of the pride's location. It was for that reason she was my most trusted advisor, and…" again he paused and he seemed on the brink of tears, again. "And it was for that reason she and I became mates."

The gasps were audible and Phineas felt the strange but familiar longing that affected him from time to time. He'd found no mate. He enjoyed pretending that his love for the dra'acheck as a whole was too great to love any single dra'acheck completely. But Agathon found Katya.

"And Katya is dead." It took Phineas a moment to realize the words were Agathon's and not a continuation of his own thoughts. "I saw her killed by a group of men." Saw her? Perhaps the only thing more unthinkable than the death of Katya was that Agathon and Katya together could not have prevented it. "So did my son."

His son? Agathon had a son? Elders didn't have children or, at least it happened so rarely that the very idea was almost unthinkable.

The purple dragon.

Phineas stared at him. It was very possible he was more powerful than any dragon at the assembly except for Agathon. There were, at most, one or two children of elders in the history of the dra'acheck. One sat among the elders now and one, Katya, was dead. Agathon was at the Awakening but Phineas always assumed sometime before the Awakening he was sired by two ancients.

"We often spent time in the jungles of Africa," Agathon continued. "Katya enjoyed the solitude and there are wide areas free of both dra'acheck and humans. My son and I met her after a decade and came upon... a group of men." He paused. "They killed her. We arrived and drove them away but they killed her." He paused and said softly, "Son."

The purple dragon stood. His voice held the power of Agathon as he said, "I am Dimitri."

Justinian

Dimitri.

Agathon had a son.

Justinian felt foolish because his first reaction was jealousy. Justinian was Agathon's son, not this upstart. It was strange and even a little pathetic to allow those thoughts ground given the far more important revelations of the day. He'd been right. The three dra'acheck who took precautions weren't the only dragons killed.

Killed by humans.

Dimitri finished talking. He spoke with Agathon's voice but with none of the compassion that was impossible to separate from anything the great red dragon said. He'd made a case and the case was shocking. He'd made a case for war.

War!

His head seemed to swim. War? Almost two thousand years of the Great Plan designed just to prevent such a thing and the final consequence war?

He looked at Agathon. It was impossible to read his expression. He made no move to rise but another elder, Marius, stood. "Twenty dra'acheck have died. Seventeen prides including the pride of the elders have lost a loved one. We have found notes, signs. Unnatural beasts. Monsters. This is how the humans see us, and there is a concerted effort to kill. The humans know the locations of our prides. They hunt us again. We can no longer wait for them to grow, for them to become what they must be to accept us. I concur with Dimitri. We must have war."

Another silence followed. A long silence. Justinian imagined that, like him, the dragons processed the extraordinary turn of events. He thought back to the First Council and the almost incomprehensible idea of the dispersal. It had shocked all, and it had shocked Justinian even though he'd been privy to the plan ahead of most of the rest. War? The idea of war was even more unthinkable than the idea of the dispersal had been. He looked among the dra'acheck in the crowd. A great many of them were simply confused. Of those who remained, if he read their faces correctly, there was an almost even split between those who showed revulsion as Justinian did and those who showed Angry eagerness.

"The council is at peace with the recommendation," Agathon said softly.

Recommendation? This wasn't decided?

Agathon stood again as Marius sat. "The council of elders favors the terrible and sad decision to defend ourselves by attacking those who persecute us. However, such a decision does more than protect. It also puts you at risk. So, we ask for ratification. If you agree with me, there will be war. If you do not, we will create another plan."

Disagree with Agathon?

There was no question of the vote.

He scanned the crowd again. Those repulsed before were still repulsed but a number of those who'd shown confusion no longer did. In fact, the majority of them seemed resolved. They weren't angry. They weren't ready for war. They were just ready to follow.

"We'll ask for those in favor of the elders' recommendation to take to the air. If the vote isn't clear, we'll count those who remain on the ground."

Justinian watched as the angry took the air almost immediately. The others, those who had been undecided, began to follow their lead. It was decided. The only real question left was whether Justinian would take to the air to protect his pride from any resentment or if he would hold to his morals and trust his relationship with Agathon to smooth things over.

"Wait!" The voice came as a shock, and Justinian turned in wonder as he saw the speaker. He almost didn't recognize him. He stood, unwavering, and stared at the council. Agathon slowly lowered his head from where he stared at the flying crowd and fixed his gaze on Daniel. "Agathon, please," Daniel said. "We have lived among the humans for longer than most of those here had been alive. To vote without first hearing alternatives…" Daniel's voice trailed off, and Justinian knew why. To speak against Agathon's gaze was all but impossible even for Justinian.

There was a pause and Agathon said, "You're right Daniel. In my grief I didn't consider the fairness of the vote. Will you speak against war? Will you provide alternatives?"

"I will," Daniel said.

Then he began.

The words didn't matter, not really. Justinian stared at Daniel and realized for perhaps the first time how much he'd underestimated a dra'acheck he'd considered one of his closest friends for longer than most at the assembly had lived. Daniel spoke with passion about the rise of the human race, about the conditions of superstition and hatred that motivated humanity at the time of the First Council and about the progression of cultures and the war of cultures that led to the Second. He spoke of a history of violence that, with each horrible evil, nonetheless gave way to a better race, a growing race where a majority steadily grew in favor of peace and enlightenment. He spoke of art and music and hope and he spoke of the nature of a lifespan so short that life was experienced individually at a pace that seemed erratic but collectively at glacial speed.

Justinian noticed dragons returning to the ground as he spoke.

And then Daniel said words that sent all but a few back to the Earth.

"If today we announced that dragons were real, humanity wouldn't believe us. Short of the war itself, humanity would choose not to believe. They portray us in their literature and their films and even that has progressed. Centuries ago, dragons were almost always evil, except perhaps in Asia. Now, a dragon in a book or a film is just as likely to be good and noble. There are films about human children championing the cause of dragons. To them, we are fantasy, a dream. To humanity, we are not nightmares. Whatever group of them seeks to harm us is the minority. Whatever group of them seeks our doom is no more misguided than those of us who once hunted humans for fear or revenge. But war... that will turn all of humanity against us, and all of humanity will be right."

Silence filled the assembly, and to Justinian the silence was as powerful as when Agathon first spoke.

And as profound.

The silence was almost unbearable until Agathon stood. "Daniel," he began. "You are one of the finest of the dra'acheck. I recall your hatching and I recall your joy when you discovered your fire. Thank you for speaking." Justinian stared as Agathon continued. "I'm not sure I can agree with you in this matter any longer, though." The silence remained until finally sparse mumbling broke out and then grew to cacophony as the dragons spoke among themselves. "My friends!" Agathon shouted over the din. Silence returned and he said, "My friends, Daniel has spoken as have others. Return to your prides. We will gather again in a month. Consider carefully what you've heard. Our next vote will determine the fate of the dra'acheck." He paused but didn't say what Justinian thought he would. He didn't add, "…and humanity."

Petros

"Nice speech, Uncle Daniel," Petros said. "It was almost enough to make me wish I'd majored in history. Oh yeah, history and humanities. Um, literature, too. Oh, let's not forget art and comparative religion." Justinian stared at him, as did Daniel and a few others. He smiled. "I mean it, Uncle Daniel. Your speech gave me confidence that maybe a liberal arts degree isn't a stupid waste of time."

"Who told you about it?"

He looked at his father and shook his head. "Nobody. You and I came home together and the rest flew back."

"I've had enough riddles, Petros," Daniel said. "Just tell us."

"I was there." Naturally, everyone stared at him.

"I couldn't sense you," Justinian said. "I couldn't see you and I couldn't sense you."

"I hid in the trees around the lake. I hid and watched."

His father looked like he intended to say something else but the phone rang. That was unusual. They sat in the study at the Nevada compound and the phone in that study was almost never used. When it was used, Cheryl used it. His mother was only a few rooms away, though. Justinian stared at the ringing phone for a moment or two and then picked up the receiver.

Almost immediately, his father's face grew enraged. Petros stood suddenly as Justinian all but screamed, "How did you find this number?" Daniel stood immediately afterward but Petros headed for the door. Daniel grabbed his arm. He considered pulling free but a glance at Daniel's face stopped him. Justinian was listening now, not speaking but his face was just as angry. Daniel stood still as Justinian hung up the phone and stood. "That was Phineas," he said. "He wants to meet. Get Bernard and join me downstairs."

Petros and Daniel nodded but Justinian shook his head. "Daniel, get Bernard. Petros, you stay here."

"But-"

"Stay here!"

The tone of his father's voice was shocking, and Petros imagined that was why his immediate inclination was to obey rather than to argue any more.

Justinian filed past him and Petros remained in the room. There were three of them. Justinian, Daniel and Bernard made three. Phineas wanted to talk.

He listened and then sensed their progress, though he already knew where they went. They were meeting at Mother's garden.

And there was no way Petros was staying put.

The decision was easier than putting it in motion. Petros could think of no time when he'd directly disobeyed his father. He hadn't at the gathering of the dra'acheck. His father had assumed it was obvious he should stay out of sight and not forbidden his attendance.

"We need to talk." He assumed that was Phineas.

Damn. No talking. His father had already transformed and attacked.

Petros rushed from the room and down the stairs. From there he rushed past the barns and to the tree line and waited. Three dragons against three dragons, all shouting about honor and all accusing the others. He stepped through the tree line and then leapt silently over the hedge, landing as he expected behind the little cabana he remembered from his youth.

"This is the second time your pride has arrived to do harm at my home, Phineas," Justinian roared. "There will not be a third!"

"We need to talk!"

Petros glanced around the corner. Even now it was difficult to keep from a romantic fascination about the realities of dragons. It was also hard to keep from feeling pride because his father's pride was clearly superior in battle. Phineas might have been a match for Daniel or Bernard but was in no way a match for Justinian. As for the two that attended him, they were far inferior. The other two his father didn't yet know about were the problem.

"You have to understand why I've done what I've done!" Phineas cried. A moments later the two dragons Petros sensed, the ones who'd hovered far above the ground, swooped down and joined the battle.

"What you've done?" Justinian's face clouded with disbelief and then anger again. "You gave humans our locations?"

Phineas shook his head but Justinian was already in motion. "You found my pride. You found the others and dra'acheck are dead!"

Justinian fought with fury but the odds had changed. He would kill Phineas but already the extra two dragons changed the course of the battle. Bernard and Daniel each faced one, and Petros realized they'd fall.

One lashed out at Daniel and Petros roared. One leap and a blur of motion sent a dragon hurtling through the air against the far hedge and a second leap repeated the process. Only one dragon kept fighting, one still fighting Daniel but Daniel was wounded. It was a slight wound but it affected his speed and balance. Petros prepared to leap again but Phinaes cried out suddenly, "Khroniss, stop! You'll harm him!" The dragon backed away immediately as Daniel collapsed to the ground. Immediately Petros rushed to him. He was hurt. He was hurt badly.

He'd survive.

Phineas said quietly, "We have to talk."

Petros stared at his father. Justinian stared back and for a moment Petros thought he was angry. He realized after a moment, though, that his father was still reeling from the sight of his son easily dispatching two enemies. "Can I suggest we meet somewhere other than Mom's garden?" he asked. "She's already going to be angry about her gardenias."

His father didn't react immediately but then he nodded and suddenly he wasn't Justinian the dragon but instead Justinian the man. Petros watched the rest of the transformations and then transformed himself. He walked to Daniel and said, "I'll carry you."

"The hell you will," Daniel said. Daniel allowed him to pull an arm so that he was supported by his shoulder, though.

A few minutes later, seven dragons and Petros sat in the now crowded study. The eighth dragon, Bernard, poured drinks from the cabinet. He poured one for Petros.

"I've known of your pride's location for years," Phineas said.

"And now Philip is dead," Justinian said bitterly. "How could you share information with those who would harm us?"

"I didn't," Phineas said. "I wouldn't"

"Ah," Justinian said. "So your plan was to discover the location of the prides and not give it to humans. It's all so clear now."

"That wasn't my plan!" Phineas snapped. Almost immediately, all in the room tensed, ready to strike. Phineas held up his hands. "Please. I mean you no harm. Yara meant Philip no harm. He knew he would fail and he knew he'd be killed. He believed his death would mean the end of the dispersal, the end of trying to live among those who warred." He paused and added, "We grieved for my brother but we knew there was no vengeance to be had."

"Steward," one of the others said. "If I may." Phineas nodded and the other turned to Justinian. "He speaks the truth. Our plan is not a plan of war but separation. For almost a millennium we've proven it works."

Justinian stared for a moment and then said, "Why do you call him steward when he owes his allegiance to you, Hamaan?"

"We have no steward but the son of Yara." Hamaan stood. "Our plan is simple. We've lived as dra'acheck. We never joined the dispersal." Silence descended on the room. "We hired humans to run our estates and returned for a few weeks every year. Of course, we also returned for Katya's visits. That is the plan, and it's worked."

His father seemed to consider this for a moment and then said, "That doesn't change the situation. We still face a threat to dragons."

"But don't you see. If we all did this. We could return to Tatras. We could hide from humans. Daniel was right. We live in an age where we won't be sought out. We simply disappear and the humans against us eventually die out. Do you really think their children will believe their stories?"

"Enough!" Petros shouted. Everyone turned to look at him, and Petros stood. . "I don't understand why you find something so obvious so hard to see." They looked at him blankly and Petros shook his head. "You really don't see it?" Nobody said anything.

"Look, how can you believe that humans killed Philip, even if they somehow understood that dragons were back in the world? Why would they kill Philip? He was the biggest advocate for humanity of anyone that I'd ever known. I didn't even understand it. I just thought it was a peculiar quirk, something strange about him. When I first learned about all this, you and Daniel went on and on about dra'acheck culture and history. Philip talked about people the way Daniel spoke at the council." Justinian and Daniel nodded but they still didn't understand.

Petros sighed. "But who else? You told me this woman Katya was an advocate for humanity. In fact, one of the things you keep saying about almost every one of the murdered dragons was that they were somehow in favor of humans, how the humans had to be stupid to kill off their own allies. What makes you so sure it's a human doing the killing?"

Justinian stared and then grew pale as he understood what Petros meant. He dismissed it, though. "Petros, if you understood the Dra'acheck, you'd know what you're suggesting is impossible."

"Why is it impossible? You told me the story of Yara. Yara was a dragon. He killed other dragons, or at least he tried to. Agathon killed a dragon. It's about time you stop thinking your whole race—my whole race I guess—is spawned from some kind of sainted perfection, that it's impossible for them to do something that could possibly be considered irrational and human. For God's sake, Agathon even said he found Katya killed by human weapons. What the hell is a human weapon? Is there anything that's a human weapon anymore? What is going to keep a dragon from holding a sword too?"

The words were harsh, he imagined, and it took some doing before Justinian finally shook his head and said, "No. I can't believe that. It just makes absolutely no sense. Everything I know about the dra'acheck says it doesn't."

Petros sighed heavily, but he found an unlikely ally in Daniel. "But wait. Justinian what if someone hated humans?" He took a breath, "And what do we know of the dra'acheck that we can still claim to be true?"

"Go on," Justinian said. He didn't appear like he really gave a damn whether or not Daniel went on.

"Well, if the council is going to invoke a vote on revealing ourselves and going to war, who would benefit from it? It would be those dragons in favor of the war. So who would benefit from getting rid of all the dragons who opposed it?"

"If we were human, maybe but…but who?"

"I think that answer's obvious, Dad," Petros said. "He's never had to live among humans, and he saw his mother killed."

Justinian shook his head. "You don't understand. If what you're saying is true, he would have had to kill his mother. He didn't see his mother killed."

Petros paused at that thought. That was something he hadn't considered. Finally, he said slowly as the thought occurred to him, "How do we know…"

"How do we know what?"

"Well, how do we know that her death wasn't real? That she hadn't been careless and some humans found her and panicked, and she ended up dead? Katya never lived among humans. Africa is pristine wilderness and perhaps she was foolish. The humans behaved as any might if they came upon a monster and that spurred Dimitri into the actions he's taken since then?"

Justinian sighed heavily. "It's unthinkable." Then, he sat bolt upright. "We couldn't reach her." Nobody spoke. "We couldn't reach her and I wanted to kill them all. Only Agathon stopped me." He turned to Petros. "What Dimitri said at the counsel, it doesn't add up. If you're right, this is the most urgent danger our race has ever faced. Only one thing can stop this."

Petros nodded. "And that puts this one thing in danger."

Phineas lifted his hands. "What one thing?"

Together, Petros and Justinian said, "Daniel."

CHAPTER TWENTY-ONE

THEN

Justinian

There was something about fire.

It felt strange to reflect on the nature of fire and the beauty of it. It felt strange to consider the truth of it. Fire cleansed. It consumed. It destroyed but even in destroying it renewed. Forests burned and the burning gave way to new growth and healthier forests. Fire took—and fire gave.

Justinian shook his head. He was dra'acheck and to be dra'acheck was as close to being living fire as was possible. These thoughts, wondrous perhaps for a human, were silly and emotional crutches to a dragon.

A dragon saying a final goodbye.

Linara.

He couldn't say her name. He hadn't been able to say it all day. She was "her" or "my mate" or "my wife" and he found himself amazed at how often the need to refer to her occurred. He looked at the ashes on the stone slab. They were weeks old now. Fire had done its job.

"The stone is so small," he said. He didn't intend to speak aloud, at least not those words. He intended to tell her about the meeting, about the decisions made in the wake of Yara's attack, in the wake of her death. Her death. Would the thought ever come without pain? He'd settle for the pain simply dulling, growing dim. Of course everyone said it would.

They were wrong.

He grieved for Tynboleth for centuries. He grieved for her and he didn't love her. At the least, he didn't love her more than he loved any given dragon. Perhaps he loved her a bit more because of her relationship with Agathon but certainly not the way he loved Linara.

His wife.

Damn it.

The Great Dispersal required he lead his pride in a time of upheaval beyond any the dra'acheck had ever experienced and now this. Now, he would have to lead at a time when conditions were added to the dispersal that made it more than upheaval. It was a sea change, a paradigm shift imposed upon them unlike any they'd experienced before, unlike even the dispersal that sent them from Tatras in the first place.

And Linara was dead.

What could he do to lead at a time like this? What could he do?

He stared at the ashes and thought of her. She'd been killed in her human form. Her body burned in human form. He felt his mouth curl up in a smile, a sad smile but a smile nonetheless. Dra'acheck and human—fire took away their differences. He tried to stop smiling at the thought but only succeeded in adding tears to the smile.

It was his fault.

Of course it was.

It wasn't.

That was the problem. It wasn't his fault. He knew it wasn't his fault. He knew that with absolute certainty but what his mind told him with certainty his emotions nonetheless clouded into nothing more than an obscured parade of guilt and self-loathing. It didn't matter that he couldn't find the logical reasons. It didn't matter that he couldn't find a way to follow the series of events, couldn't somehow move from point A to point B to point C and so on. He couldn't determine what he could have done differently. He searched for the point D or F or J where he could point to an error, anything that would allow him to find concrete blame anywhere.

It couldn't be meaningless.

But it was.

Linara was there on a stone slab. Her scales didn't gleam in a soft rose glimmer of beauty. Her hair didn't shine and hang in waves to just past her shoulders. She had neither the shape of a dra'acheck nor the shape of a human. She had no shape at all but ash. A very soft breeze blew and agitated the pile but not enough to send any into the air and not enough to scatter them at all. Even the wind wouldn't let her go.

Justinian lifted his head and screamed into the sky. He didn't know why exactly. He screamed for the loss or maybe for anger. He tried to hate Yara and couldn't. He tried to hate Phineas and couldn't. He tried to hate Philip for killing Yara's son but had even less success. He even tried to hate Yara's son. He couldn't hate. He tried and failed.

He could scream, though. He screamed at the sky and then found his human voice too weak, too ineffectual for the scream and without really deciding to do it felt his transformation so that instead of screaming at the sky he roared from above, beating his wings about thirty feet above the damned slab, the wind from them buffeting the ground and sending the ashes away in a grey cloud that dispersed far too quickly to offer much satisfaction at all.

Still he roared. He stared at the blackened stone slab and roared. She was gone. She was gone and she was gone even though he'd done everything he was supposed to do. He roared again and felt his fire growing within him. He stared at the slab and let his fire flow forth in a blast that engulfed the slab and sprayed back toward him but he kept it up, a stream of heat and red and orange. The fire felt better than the roar and he sent it toward the slab until no more came but still he stared with his mouth open willing more fire but failing.

The smoke cleared and he closed his eyes as he saw the slab, not black now but glassy. Glassy and broken. A jagged scar ran through the middle in a diagonal path of destruction. He stared, transfixed, and found himself nonetheless unable to focus. There were shadows, and he saw Philip step into view, human Philip. Human Daniel was there, too. Human Bernard, human… what did it matter?

Dra'acheck Linara was dead. Human Linara was dead.

He tried to roar again, found he had no voice left, and turned to fly toward the clouds.

Agathon

What had he done?

What, for the love of all that was good, had he done?

They were gone now, and he missed them terribly. Once again, he'd convinced them to do something against their nature, convinced them to—

Convinced?

No. He'd browbeat them. He convinced the elders, certainly, but for all intents and purposes the elders did what he said simply because he said it. He hadn't convinced at all. He'd simply decreed, and though he knew without any doubt that the majority of the dra'acheck were repulsed by the idea of any rule at all with a consequence like death they didn't argue with him. He'd banished them from their home and they didn't argue. Even Phineas didn't argue but given the perspective of Yara and his pride, he might have believed his life was in danger from the outset.

He made his way to the basin and thought back to the first time he saw himself in the lake. His reflection now was different from then. He almost laughed at the obviousness of the thought. Oh, that first glance at himself as he hovered above the lake had been glorious, beautiful. It had filled him with wonder and revealed to him his name. He'd always intended to ask Tynboleth about that moment but never could before she was murdered.

He was different now.

Everything before had been joy, joy and expectation. That moment as he saw himself for the first time was so filled with that joy, joy that came simply from existing. Then, the expectation. He'd come into his identity and known immediately that exploration and adventure waited for him.

Hope? Gone. Expectation? Gone. Now, there was only holding on to the plan as the only chance for survival.

Yara was gone.

That single truth overshadowed all others. For so long Yara provided the other argument, the other side of the equation that allowed Agathon to think clearly, to weigh options and come to decisions for the good of the dra'acheck. Yara was the check. Yara was the balance. What the hell was Yara supposed to do now?

What could he do to lead at a time like this? What could he do?

"Shall we mate, Agathon?" He turned his head and stared at Katya. The question was unexpected. It wasn't entirely unwelcome though Agathon had long ago accepted there was no real likelihood he would love as other dragon's loved. Katya was beautiful, though, completely beautiful. Her green scales showed luster even in the dim light of the sunset. She said only those words, no more, and he stared at her for a while before nodding.

An hour later, she left him but returned the next day. This time, she announced she'd leave to handle the new dispersal and he instructed her to allow Justinian to remain in France, should he choose. She nodded and repeated the question. "Shall we mate, Agathon?" He nodded and then watched her as she left an hour later.

She returned weeks later and asked the question before reporting on the prides. He nodded and a few hours later she told him the prides all had their assignments and she anticipated the new dispersal to be complete within a year. He wanted to thank her but not for her help with the dispersal. He wanted to thank her for that question, the one that helped. It didn't provide the check and it didn't provide the balance but it certainly provided comfort. He wanted to thank her but he didn't. She left and returned the next day.

"Shall we mate, Agathon?"

The days passed, a series of questions and nods and no conversation about them. His thoughts grew clearer in regards to the dra'acheck but cloudy in reference to Katya. That was good. It was very good. The confusion and insecurity could be limited to one portion of his life and those areas requiring leadership moved with crystal clarity.

The year passed and Katya announced that all prides were in new locations save for Justinian, who remained in France.

"Shall we mate, Agathon?"

A decade passed with no incidents, though Phineas led a deception. It was minor. His pride considered him steward and Agathon elected to let them. He'd been concerned about vengeance when he named Hamaan anyway.

"Shall we mate, Agathon?"

Did he love her? A century passed and the question was asked thousands of times but he didn't know. He needed her. That he knew. He needed her and when she asked the question the cloudiness came and relieved him of the clarity of the rest of his thoughts.

"Shall we mate, Agathon?"

One-hundred and seventy-three years after the Second Council, Katya arrived and didn't ask the question but instead smiled softly up at him and said, "You shall have a hatchling. A son, maybe. Perhaps a daughter." She paused as he tried to process what she'd said. He opened his mouth to speak but she added, "No. Not a daughter. You shall have a son."

He stared at Katya and the clouds parted. A son. A son who could replace the son he lost, the friend he lost. A son who could learn to be dra'acheck unhindered by the hunt or the world of danger around him. He could raise him and teach him of Yara's fierce attachment to his kind. He could teach him to challenge his decisions and together they could lead the dra'acheck in a way that would drive off the danger.

Even as he thought it, he knew he deceived himself. He didn't need another to help him drive away the danger. He needed another to help him drive away the loneliness, the solitude of leadership.

Katya drew closer and said softly, "What do you say to that, Agathon the Red? Agathon the Hope of the dra'acheck? What do you say to that, Agathon the Great?" He didn't know if she mocked him. If so, she mocked him mildly. He didn't mind. He knew exactly what to say.

"Shall we mate, Katya?"

Justinian

"We're leaving," he said. He said it far more confidently than he'd expected to say it, far more confidently than he'd felt. Daniel and Philip both turned to look at him and Justinian said, "As soon as we can manage it."

"Katya is moving us?" Philip asked.

"I'm moving us," he said. "With Katya's blessing. Agathon made some sort of special dispensation for me. We could remain in France for as long as we want. He wants to make sure I don't have to leave the home I shared with Linara. She told me when I told her I wanted to move."

"We can stay and yet you want to move?" Daniel stood and looked carefully at him. "Is there something you know, something you're not telling us?"

"What do you mean?"

"More violence? More unrest?"

Justinian smiled and shook his head. "No. As far as I know, the guillotine is gone from France forever." It was a fair concern. Perhaps no conflict among humans had brought the pride to the brink of another situation like the Crusades like the revolution had. Daniel and Philip stared at him, clearly expecting more. "Are you so attached to France?" he asked.

"We go where you go, Justinian," Philip said.

Daniel nodded but asked, "Is it wrong that we ask not to go blindly?"

He hadn't wanted to explain, though now that the explanation was requested he didn't feel the terror he'd felt at expressing the words he'd anticipated. He looked at the two of them and smiled sadly. "The pride lives and dies by me," he said. "And I have been dead for centuries."

Philip and Daniel stared at him but said nothing for a moment. Then Philip stepped forward and embraced him. It wasn't really appropriate but Justinian recognized that only intellectually. Emotionally, he felt Philip's arms around him and it offered comfort beyond what he might have expected. Philip backed away and Daniel seemed unsure but then awkwardly hugged him as well. Justinian smiled a bit less sadly and said, "With such friends, how can I regret?"

"The pride lives," Daniel said.

"And so do you," Philip added.

Justinian nodded. "We go to America, the United States."

"But what of the war?" Daniel asked.

"The rebellion is in its last legs. The war will be over within a year or slightly after. Nonetheless, we're heading to the West. It's untamed, mostly. We'll keep most of our interests in Europe. We'll arrive as aristocracy, such as it is over there."

"Kentucky?"

"No, farther west. California."

"You don't think Spain will reclaim it?"

"Daniel, it's Mexico. They're independent of Spain now, and no. It's already a state." He took a breath. "Everyone there is a stranger to everyone else. It will be easy, and we'll be the only pride in the United States." He paused and looked at the two of them. "I know this is unexpected."

He turned and looked away for a moment. They stood in the courtyard and the glint from glassy sheen of the broken stone caught his eye. "We'll keep our property here. I don't want anyone to own this place, ever. We'll keep it and employ a staff to manage the estate."

"Of course," Philip said.

He turned around. "I can't be here. I can't. I see her in the garden. I see her in the trees. I see her in the damned dinner plates. I can't do it." He saw nothing in their faces other than compassion and for some reason compassion was worse than anything else they could have expressed. "I can't!" he yelled. He took a breath and willed his heart to beat more slowly. "I'm sorry. We've spent centuries stagnant."

"Stagnant? We own half of Paris and a pretty good portion of London." Daniel lifted up his hands and his face looked almost comical in his disbelief.

Justinian sighed. "Yes. That's still stagnant, though. The wealth hides us, it gives us excuses to avoid contact. Wealth matters in the world of men, and we've acquired it. It would be hard not to acquire it when they're born and die in a span of time not long enough for us that we'd let a hatchling that old…" His voice trailed off and he fought back tears. Finally, he said softly, "Linara and I hoped for hatchlings."

Philip looked like he would hug him again but thankfully that didn't happen. Daniel said, "I think a move will be good for us. We won't be comfortable and sometimes comfort is the most dangerous thing of all."

Justinian nodded. "Tell me. What can I do to lead at a time like this?" The two looked at him curiously. "I want to know," he said. "What can I do?"

CHAPTER TWENTY-TWO

NOW

Cheryl

She probably didn't need to be there and she imagined Petros would have liked to be alone with Patricia but Cheryl thought it was safest if she were available to smooth any rough edges over, should they come. She watched as the luggage disappeared through the access door and rolled away on the track and then turned to Patricia and Petros. "When I was your age, Petros and I would be able to wait with you right at the gate. Not now, though."

Patricia smiled. "I'm going to miss you."

Cheryl nodded. "I'll miss you, too."

Patricia turned to Petros. "Whatever happens, I'll miss you also." Petros sighed and Cheryl noticed the sigh tormented Patricia. She wondered if it would have been as easy to marry Justin if he hadn't shown up and rescued her. Patricia said, "I love you, Pete. I do."

"Well then—"

"That might not be enough," she said and there was no doubt she was right on the brink of tears. Cheryl wanted to spare both of them from it.

"Listen," Cheryl said. "How about we don't talk about this now. You're going home and Petros has some things he needs to get done before next semester." She didn't point out that those things involved continuing to learn how to use his new body. "How about both of you agree not to talk to each other for a week but instead spend the time coming up with all of the questions and thoughts you have. No decisions yet, just the things you have to talk about. When you talk, you guys can do it with some of the emotion a little less sharp."

Patricia nodded. "It's a deal." She leaned forward and hugged her. Cheryl wondered briefly if Patricia was as troubled as she seemed. Perhaps it was more like Cheryl's experience. She'd been certain she should have been repulsed. She'd been certain she should have been afraid. She'd been certain she should have run away at full speed. All of that certainty about how she should have felt

251

created emotions that almost felt like guilt, guilt because she didn't feel any of those things. Of course, then, her response was fear because if there was guilt she had to be making a mistake. It took an almost cold, unemotional decision to be free of all of that baggage. Was Patricia going through that?

Was she honest about the anger when she thought Petros had kept the secret from the beginning of their relationship? Was she honest about anything? Well, of course she was honest with Cheryl and Petros but was she honest with herself? The girl was remarkable, though, and Cheryl imagined things would be much easier on her than they'd been on Cheryl. Petros was still going to medical school. He was still going to be a doctor. He wouldn't be confined to a compound like a cult member for the rest of his life.

But would Patricia let it get that far? She broke off the hug and said, "I'll let you two say your goodbyes."

Petros smiled a sad thanks to her and she watched as the two stepped toward the gate. Twenty-one years old. Twenty-one years old and the boy had everything going for him. She hoped he had Patricia, too. Cheryl wondered if he knew just how fortunate he was even if Patricia couldn't marry him Her phone chimed. She looked down. A text from Justin. The GPS coordinates for the camp so Petros could meet them for training.

Training.

She was pretty sure they didn't know how to train him. They wanted to learn what he could do. That was fine. They couldn't admit it to the boy, though. That was one thing about dra'acheck. They all seemed oblivious to easy solutions and held tightly to the most complicated schemes. She remembered when a well in Nevada went dry and Daniel and two others spent days talking about the engineering necessary to create a pipeline that would stretch for thirty-seven miles to the White River with some kind of regulator that would ensure the water level of the river wouldn't change. She listened to them argue about the way to do it for almost a week and then Justinian announced he needed all of them back in California for three days. They left and she stayed. She called the contractors who'd dug the well in the first place and they returned to drill another twenty feet. After almost a decade, the well still produced water.

She watched her son kiss Patricia goodbye, a good sign. The kiss was tense but as their lips met, Cheryl felt certain Patricia's body relaxed with relief. Petros backed away uncertainly and watched Patricia walk into the queue.

How could she help Patricia understand? Really, life with the dragons was, for the most part, actually pretty boring.

Daniel

"That speech you gave was impressive, Daniel."

Daniel sighed. Petros was right. He turned around. "Dimitri. I only said how I felt."

"And you said it quite eloquently." Now that he had a close look at him, he realized Dimitri was indeed powerful looking. He'd never seen the son of an elder before, at least not in such a long time. Dimitri's color was dark, very deep, very red, much like Agathon but even darker, so dark it appeared purple. His eyes seemed to burn with clarity and purpose. "I think that there would have been a unanimous vote. Or, at least, there wouldn't have been a second vote scheduled if you hadn't spoken. I think everyone would've been ready to turn on these insects that you seem determined to protect."

"Insects? Tell me, Dimitri, what happens when dragons disagree with something else you want? Are you going to kill them too?"

"You are part of the problem, Daniel. You're part of the reason we've been kept in bondage."

"Bondage? You're insane, Dimitri. We're not in bondage. If anything, we control more wealth than most humans. Bondage? There's nothing close to bondage about our lives. Besides, this plan, this dispersal, it was your father who came up with the idea, and it very likely saved our race."

Dimitri smiled, and there was something wicked in the expression. "I think I'll save it again," he said, and he leapt. Daniel realized with a sickening feeling as the younger dragon leapt at him that he had no chance of winning the battle. He turned and immediately flew, sending branches splintering in his wake. He hoped his familiarity with the area would allow him to out-distance Dimitri and said a silent thanks to Justinian for bringing everyone back to Los Angeles where he was more familiar with the terrain. He moved quickly, headlong, doing everything he could to get away. It wasn't easy. A rising and mounting sense of urgency filled him as he dodged around tree trunks and made his way over the familiar valleys and gorges and hills. He saw a herd of cattle up ahead and dove into it, scattering them, hoping the distraction would keep Dimitri at bay at least to some extent, as he made his way toward the camp and the safety in numbers he knew would wait there.

Camp. That was Justinian, too. Smart.

Dimitri roared. Daniel heard a whooshing sound as the younger dragon released his fire and veered to the left, missing the stab of flame by only a few feet. There was an advantage. Dimitri was young. The thought that his flames could harm another Dra'acheck only displayed his youth. Daniel dove, almost touching the ground before rising back up again and speeding in a different direction.

As he slid along the ground, he used his hind legs to push himself up into the air and shot straight up, breaking through the canopy of the trees and almost immediately reaching clouds. He dove among them, hoping to lose his pursuer, and then flew above the cloud line for a while before diving back down. He figured they were four or five miles away from where they'd started, maybe farther. He descended with as much speed as he could manage, and then dove back underneath the trees. Dimitri waited for him. It was almost supernatural how he'd anticipated his move. As he crashed through the trees, Dimitri lashed, hitting him hard with his tail and then swiping with a foreleg and sending Daniel sprawling against the tree. Daniel turned and snapped at him. His jaws locked onto one of Dimitri's wings, and Dimitri began beating it, knocking Daniel back until Daniel crashed into another tree.

Damn it.

Where was he? The camp couldn't be far. By now, Justinian and the others had to know he was fighting. Dimitri was powerful. Daniel felt like a piece of crepe paper, so little did his jaws on Dimitri's wing slow the dra'acheck's beats. It didn't take long for Dimitri to tire of moving Daniel's body like a rag doll. Time seemed to slow as his tail came around and lashed across his chest. Daniel felt his grip grow slack and the force of the blow pushed him backward against a black walnut tree, destroying it completely. Black walnut. That was good. That meant they'd reached the valley, and the valley meant Justinian and the others had to know and would have to arrive soon.

They needed to arrive soon. If they didn't, Daniel would die.

He realized in a sad but still detached sort of way that he hadn't said goodbye to Petros. He'd lifted his hand in a half wave as Petros started his car to bring that girl to the airport. That was it. He'd assumed he see him at the camp. Of course, he had. Now... Now it was far more likely he'd never see him again.

Dimitri laughed. "Are all of you so weak? Humans. You spend all of your time shaped like the enemy and you've lost everything that makes you what you are." He lifted himself up higher, and Daniel prepared for his next strike. "No. Not what you are. What you were." The purple dragon sped forward and Daniel dove to the left, uprooting another walnut tree in the process but realizing with sickening clarity that he had no dodges left. Dimitri laughed again. "Your precious humans have made you pathetic."

Daniel groaned and got up as well as he could. "They're no more mine than they are yours, Dimitri. But if we go to war with them, we will lose. They will destroy us all and not because they're evil but because you will force them to it."

Dimitri smiled and said, "I'm afraid you won't be around to see if your theory holds." He reared and Daniel sighed. Justinian would have to say goodbye to Petros for him. Dimitri roared and Daniel wondered why he didn't find the roar intimidating since is meant his end. The purple dragon dove at him and Daniel closed his eyes.

He sensed the impact of Justinian's body against Dimitri's before he heard it, and opened his eyes. Justinian and Bernard. He felt weak but he lifted his head and roared. He had a little fight left, and he liked the odds a great deal more now. Phineas and two others from his pride arrived at the same time and he welcomed them. He imagined Justinian was a match for Dimitri by himself but the others would help.

And then tragedy happened.

Phineas and his men weren't used to fighting with Justinian's pride. Bernard leapt into the fray just as Phineas and one of the others did. They were all headed for Dimitri and at top speed but instead they ended up colliding not only with each other but with Justinian as well. They all fell to the ground and Daniel rose to try to help. Justinian got to his feet but he was wobbly. Dimitri laughed and a blow from his tail sent Justinian through the air.

By himself and at full strength Justinian might have been able to match Dimitri. Now, though, the son of elders was facing uncoordinated and wounded dragons. Daniel roared but his heart wasn't in it. They were going to lose.

Petros

Petros could hear the sounds of the battle. He lifted his head, breathed in deeply. He could hear it. He could even sense it. He couldn't figure out exactly from where it came. He tried the deep breathing that Philip had suggested, but thoughts of Philip only filled him with sadness so that he got distracted too easily. He parked the car next to the tents at the campsite. He almost checked the tents but shook his head. He would have sensed them.

He determined that there was a bear, a bear walking through the forest about a mile and a half away, and sensing it would have been cause for tremendous celebration just weeks before. But now the urgency of the situation weighed heavily upon him. He nearly screamed in anger. He sat down, leaning against the rough bark of the oak tree, leaning and breathing deeply. He let his mind move outward in circles, imagined his consciousness radiating outward in waves. He could still hear the crashes, the sounds of the blows landing, the grunts and the labored breathing. He heard a sound that almost seemed like a yelp of pain, and he tried to fight back the sickening realization it was his father's voice.

He passed under a flock of geese seeking out a watering hole, moved through a small family of sheep, feral sheep and not the bighorn variety, a ram leading three ewes and several lambs. Finally, he did his best to forget of the existence of the noises, did his best to simply think. And then he found them. Eight miles to the south. Eight damned miles to the south of the camp.

He leapt to his feet and began running. Almost instantly, the transformation was upon him. It was strange to transform and to become cognizant of the fact that his clothes were tattered somewhere behind him but not to in any way be encumbered by their destruction. He ran, feeling each of his feet hit the ground in a strange explosion of sound. He didn't mind. The hardest part was the still unsure way that he managed his body. He rushed forward and it reminded him of video games, driving a car and avoiding obstacles.

As he ran, things got easier. It seemed like every few steps, a tree would jump into the way, and he'd have to dodge. He also found himself strangely aware of which obstacles meant nothing, crashing right through brush as though it were air. He even found himself running directly over a wild pig, not even considering the damage it might have done to it and in no way slowing down.

It was crazy, but far crazier was the thought that his father, that Daniel, and maybe others would die if he didn't reach them. He ran and came across an obstacle he hadn't anticipated. He ended up running along a gorge, and then suddenly the gorge was blocked. He considered leaping over it, but the thought that he might not make it kept him from that course, and instead, he leapt for a break in the rocks, far too small for his body, and instantly transformed. Suddenly, he was human, climbing through the rocks as quickly as he could and then bursting out the other side and instantly transforming back into whatever the hell it was that he was.

He ran, his senses still on high alert, the battle still raging. The raging of the battle gave him hope. It meant, at least for the time being, his father was still alive. At least, for now, there wouldn't be death. Still, there was no question that Dimitri was beating the shit out of everyone else. His breathing wasn't even labored. It was like he was toying with them, enjoying how far superior he was to them. It was everything the Dra'acheck were supposed to not be. It made no sense at all. He could almost feel the pride, the anger, the haughtiness in Dimitri's manner.

He could also sense that his father was losing hope, and that was perhaps the scariest part of the whole situation. In all of the years of his upbringing, he couldn't remember a single time when his father didn't display a level of confidence, a level of surety, and a level of understanding that things were going to turn out okay. He supposed it had a lot to do with the lifespan. As he ran, he wondered if his lifespan would be like his father's. It was still almost impossible to comprehend that his father was more than two thousand years old. It was even more impossible to comprehend that he would likely live for decades or even centuries longer than his mother.

He tried to force the thoughts away from his mind, tried to think only in terms of getting to the battle. He couldn't sense necessarily how close he was, but he imagined he'd already crossed half the distance. He'd already run four miles, probably a minute a mile. It seemed strange and wrong that it should take him even this long, but he rushed along, treating obstacles in his path as though they weren't there, jumping distances that made no sense to jump, scaling hills and debris as though it were nothing.

Faster.

Every single step was maddening because it didn't bring him to his destination fast enough.

And then he was there, bursting through the trees and joining a battle of deities.

"Petros, no!" Justinian called. Petros ignored him, not that he could have done much, already leaping in the air toward Dimitri. Dimitri turned his head and looked almost happy. He didn't even bother to try to dodge.

"You have a hatchling?" His expression lost its smug satisfaction a second later as Petros crashed into him, though. The whole body of Dimitri, in dragon form, was pushed back four or five yards. Petros didn't hesitate, but grabbed Dimitri's foreleg and pulled hard, making the dragon stumble.

Dimitri roared, as much pain as anger in his voice. Petros was pretty sure he heard Daniel say, "Holy shit!"

Dimitri immediately swiped hard with his other leg. It caught Petros on the shoulder and sent him careening through the forest to land smashed against a tree. He got back up immediately. The shock on Dimitri's face was priceless. He rushed at him again, and this time, the dragon was far more careful. As Petros rushed, he sidestepped it, but Petros changed direction quickly.

He didn't hit Dimitri full-on like the first time, but instead turned his body and grabbed hold of where Dimitri's wings met his shoulders, yanking hard and causing the dragon to howl in pain. Immediately, Dimitri's tail came around, striking Petros on the side of the head and sending him spinning away again. Justinian shouted again, but his shouts were weak, and Petros worried he had to be injured, horribly injured. As for himself, Petros didn't feel any pain at all. There'd been a brief moment when the tail had hit his head, but other than that, he was fine.

He roared, and then found it strange that he would roar. He found it even stranger that his roar was just as loud as Dimitri's had been. He rushed forward, and again, Dimitri's tail struck, but the training with Philip paid off. He moved. The tail struck again; he dodged it again. Twice more, the tail came out, and twice more, Petros avoided it easily. And when it came the third time, he grabbed ahold of the dragon's tail and yanked. He had to imagine it looked crazy. Justinian and Philip were looking at him and he imagined the sight was insane. Pertros, there in the battle with a body a fifth the size of the dragon in front of him.

But he yanked the tail, and Dimitri howled as he unwillingly turned around. Petros pulled hard, and then tried to flip the dragon over. He couldn't manage it, but he did manage to find himself underneath the dragon. Naturally,

Dimitri took advantage of it, digging the claws of his hind legs into Petros's back.

For the first time, Petros felt real pain, but it was oddly not debilitating. Instead, it almost empowered him, filling him with anger and additional strength somehow. He put his hands under his body and pushed himself up, crying out as he did. It hurt like hell but he managed to reach his hands and his knees. Dimitri took his foot off of Petros's back and instead kicked as hard as he could. The blow caught Petros on the head and sent him spinning and tumbling backwards. Instantly, he got to his feet and leapt, this time landing on the dragon's back.

He managed to get his arms around Dimitri's neck and held tight as the dragon thrashed. It wasn't easy. The dragon moved its head back and forth, and every time he did, the spikes behind Dimitri's head, the spikes that would ordinarily protect his neck, slammed against Petros's face. He still held on. He could feel the blows now, and he could feel himself weakening, but he clasped his hands together and pulled. It was strange. He realized he'd never really had to exert himself. Even the training, which had been horrible and had been extraordinarily taxing, hadn't been physically exerting so much as it had been mundane and overwhelming, and it had been frustrating as he tried to control his newfound strength and his newfound speed. Now, it wasn't about the frustration; it was just pain.

He felt repeated blows against his back, and he realized that Dimitri was whipping his tail upward and against him. Over and over as Dimitri's wings buffeted the air, as he bucked and tried his best to dislodge him, he was almost thrown.

Petros held on. He held on tightly, and he thought of Philip. He thought of all the times Philip had talked to him, all the times Philip had trained him, all the times Philip had offered him a shoulder, a word of encouragement, a word of warning.

And he thought of what it meant for Philip to die.

Philip.

Dimitri had killed him.

Dimitri had killed him.

"You killed him!" Petros screamed, holding tightly. He didn't quite hear the crack of bones or anything along those lines, but the reaction from Dimitri was nonetheless satisfying. The dragon began moving more spasmodically, clearly panicking in his attempts to get Petros off his back. Petros held tightly. He held tightly as the dragon's movements became more panicked but simultaneously more feeble. The blows from the tail weren't landing on Petros's back anymore. Desperate to breathe, Dimitri's head was leaning at an awkward angle, meaning the spikes didn't strike Petros's face anymore.

Petros held tightly.

Dimitri tried a roll, flipping over so that he rolled atop Petros. Even as the ground crushed against his back, Petros held on. Even as the dragon wiggled, grinding him against the earth, he held on. "You killed him!" he shouted again. "You killed him, you son of a bitch, you killed him!"

He held tightly. He held, and he squeezed, and he imagined the dragon's neck breaking. He imagined the bones snapping. He imagined the damn thing dying a thousand deaths as he held. He didn't know how long he held. He felt like he lost himself somewhere in the middle of the battle, but gradually, he became aware that Dimitri was no longer moving. Still, he held tightly, and it wasn't until he felt hands on his wrists and he heard his father say, "It's over. It's over Petros," did he let go.

There was a shuffling and a movement, and a moment later, the weight was off his body, but he lay there, still staring at the sky. He saw his father's face and then Daniel's face staring down at him with concern, and he realized that he'd transformed back; he was human. He saw Phineas step into view. He was human now. They all were. He could feel wetness on his cheeks. For a moment, he thought perhaps it was raining. But when he breathed out one last time, "You killed him, you son of a bitch", he understood it wasn't rain making his cheeks wet.

"It's okay, son," Justinian said. "It's over."

Petros sighed and got himself to his knees. They were all hurt, every one of them. His father looked like he'd been hit by a truck. "What do we do now?" he asked.

"We get Dimitri to Nevada and dispose of the body." Justinian seemed on the verge of tears. "I don't look forward to telling Agathon his son is dead."

CHAPTER TWENTY-THREE

THEN

Justinian

"Welcome. Surprised you came in this way instead of through San Francisco." Justinian smiled at the man and wondered why he'd been warned the man would be dirty. He wore a suit, in fact, and while Justinian favored a more natural facial hair, the man's slick hair and waxed mustache displayed the exact opposite of what he'd been led to believe he'd find in America.

Justinian extended his hand and the man took it. "Are you Mr. Denton?"

"I am," the man said. "Pleased to meet you, Mr. Renault."

The man pronounced it Rennalt. Justinian decided not to correct him. "We were led to believe if we went to San Francisco we wouldn't be able to get a steamboat to take us here, something about the government firing on the boats."

Denton shook his head. "That's only if you're going past Alcatraz Island, and none of them do anymore. Anyway, happy you're here. I believe everything is ready for you."

"So you got my letters?" A whistle startled him and Justinian looked back.

"The railroad just arrived. You're part of history right here."

Justinian watched as several members of his pride stood with luggage.

"Did you send more than two?"

"No, two."

"Then I got your letters. I've rented a house for you with five rooms. You're committed for two months there but that ought to give you enough time to search for somewhere permanent, and I can also show you around to different lots for sale. I'm afraid…" The man paused. "Well, four years ago everything would have been a great deal less expensive. Now, with the railroad, prices have really gone up."

Justinian smiled. "I trust you'll help me see if anyone tries to take advantage of me."

He took a deep breath. The air didn't seem much different than the air in France but his senses were all but overwhelmed by the constant activity around him. There was excitement and unending movement, and he could tell the others in his pride felt the same way.

"Your crates arrived yesterday and they've been delivered to your temporary home. I have some men available to get them unpacked for you if you'd like. "

"We'll manage," he said.

Five rooms. That would be comfortable. He'd already sent a dozen ahead and they had various hotel rooms and he believed Bernard was in a boarding house.

"Shall I show you to your house, then?"

Justinian nodded. "And perhaps you could then show my…" He paused because he had no idea how to describe the members of the pride. He finally settled on the deception of employment. "I mean later. Perhaps you can show my servants where they can buy supplies and groceries and the like."

The man nodded. "The house you're renting is furnished, so whatever furniture is in your crates can be kept in the crates until you find a new place. If you want anything moved out, I can do that, too. If you want to store your crates, I can help you with that, too. You need it, I'll help you with it."

"Do you have a bank?"

"You mean to store gold?"

Justinian shrugged. "Gold and currency."

"There's talk of one opening but most people just use the Wells, Fargo and Company offices."

"Okay," he said. "We'll work that out later. Can we go to the house now?"

"Yes sir."

The man raised his hand and a carriage of some sort arrived. It was large, larger than any Justinian had seen before. He waited as Denton opened the door and gestured for him to enter. "How many can sit in this?"

Denton said, "Six comfortably or eight a bit squeezed. We can have the driver come back if you need two trips."

"We'll need three."

The man seemed a little surprised and Justinian said, "I'm afraid I've grown accustomed to my house staff. I took them all with me, and their families, of course."

The man nodded and said, "Well, then. We'll put the ladies on this first coach and I'll have Frank let them into the house before he comes back."

"The ladies?" The man seemed confused by the question and Justinian felt a hand on his arm. He turned to see Philip.

Philip said, "You'll have to forgive my brother. He's unfamiliar with America. To him, a lady means a member of the aristocracy, a noble." Of course, that wasn't what Justinian meant at all. He'd forgotten that humans treated their females as frail and in need of coddling. He had to fight back a laugh at the thought of any humans here treating one of his pride like she couldn't take care of herself.

Denton smiled at him and Justinian noted a look of wonder in the man's face. "Are you... I mean, are you a duke or something?"

"Something like that," Justinian said. "But in the United States we're all equal, right?"

Denton nodded. "I suppose we are." There was genuine warmth in his face as he said it and Justinian wondered for a moment about this new country. In France, the revolution rightly addressed injustices but only replaced them with more. This place had actually gone to war to end the slavery of a group of humans with different skin color. Perhaps humanity was growing along with the remarkable advances in technology. Humans had always done well with improvements in their methods of killing but of late their advances had impacted commerce rather than war. Denton waited for a while and then said, "Let me take you to your place, sir."

Justinian nodded and said, "No need to call me sir. Mr. Renault is fine." He hoped the comment suggested he wasn't hung up on the issue of nobility or some kind of an aristocratic dandy. He wasn't sure, though. They'd lived among humans for a long while but in reality rarely interacted with them. Perhaps it was time to change that.

Philip gathered together the female members of the pride and Justinian watched them enter the coach. A moment later, the human with the reins clucked his tongue and the carriage left. Mr. Denton grew distracted by an obvious friend and while they were engaged, Philip said in soft tones, "You pronounced your name the way he did."

With the t sound. Justinian hadn't realized he'd done it. He shrugged. "We'll fit in better," he said. Philip smiled slyly at him but Justinian pretended not to notice. "How much gold do we have here?"

"Enough to support us for a decade or so in France. Here, I don't know. There's chaos in the north with humans mining gold and in some of those camps, costs are extraordinary. I don't know what it's like here but we should be careful."

"Should we send someone back to withdraw from the banks?"

"No. We still have the deposits in New York City and in... What is the other city?"

"Chicago."

"No, then. In six months, a year maybe, you'll go back and sell off a few of our interests and we'll use the funds to buy more here." He turned and looked at the steam coming from the wheels of the locomotive. "We own a stake in all of these, right?"

"The railroads? Yes." Philip paused for a moment and then said, "You hate money, don't you, Justinian?"

Justinian laughed softly and said, "Humans certainly seem to love it. I want us self-sufficient, Philip. I want us to grow our own food, all of it. I want..." He paused and then sighed. "I want to be back in France."

Philip's hand on his shoulder was welcome. "Steward," he said. "There is no France. There is no America. There is no California or Los Angeles. There is only the pride."

Justinian

"Are you saying the key to keeping anonymous is to be more visible?"

Daniel shook his head and said, "When you put it that way it seems pretty stupid but I'm not just saying this." He looked surprised, like the idea was simple and Justinian smiled and looked at Philip. Philip shrugged and made a face. Daniel shook his head and asked, "Didn't you pay attention at all to what was happening in France?"

"You mean the theocracy? The monarchy? The rise and fall of absinthe? The revolution? The kicking and screaming way they were dragged into the enlightenment? The war with Great Britain?" Philip laughed but Daniel rolled his eyes.

"Listen. We've been her almost forty years, and we've jumped through some hoops to make sure everyone thinks were the second or even third generation but this world is different now. It's filled with newspapers and society pages. Now, with the pictures and the newsreels for films, there's even more. We're richer than the Rockefellers and the Vanderbilts and they're in the news every day. "

"You want us to be in the papers?"

Daniel shook his head. "That's not what I'm saying. I just mean that the more the nobles in France tried to be secretive, the more they attracted attention."

"But nobody knows we're richer than those other families."

Daniel laughed. "You think we can build an estate this size and people won't know? You're insane."

"Steward?" Justinian turned and saw Bernard. He nodded and Bernard continued. "We might have a problem." He paused and when Justinian didn't respond he said, "The President was just assassinated. I've heightened security and we have some contingencies in place for when the conflicts start but—"

Daniel shook his head. "This isn't Europe. There won't be conflicts."

He said it with a great deal of confidence, and Justinian couldn't help but smile. There was a long running dispute, albeit a mild one, between Bernard and Daniel. Bernard saw humans with pitchforks, torches, and broadswords around every corner. Daniel saw walking give way to horseback riding and then carts and then bicycles and trains and now there was even talk of motorized carriages individuals could use. Philip had them invested in a number of enterprises but until someone created a vehicle accessible to the merchant classes, those investments wouldn't pay off. Merchant classes? Was that even a real term in the United States? Was it a term at all now that they were in the Twentieth Century?

Twenty centuries. For humanity, that represented an extensive history. For the dra'acheck it certainly didn't feel that way, though he'd now lived among humans for far longer than he'd lived away from them. They were fascinating, really. Here, in Los Angeles, there was so much hope and excitement and the changes in their world seemed so revolutionary to them. Their memories were so short, though, and he wondered if they realized just how remarkable it was for them to create ships capable of crossing the Atlantic reliably, to create the explosives they used to blow portions of the mountains from the paths of their railroad tracks.

"Still," Bernard said, noting Justinian's smile. "I would prefer if I could increase our security efforts to be safe."

Justinian nodded. "Of course you can, my friend. Keep us safe, as you always do."

Bernard seemed satisfied with the answer and left the room filled with purpose. Daniel took a seat, and Philip stepped close to Justinian. "It worked," he said.

Justinian raised an eyebrow. He was close to Philip, closer to Philip and Daniel than the rest of them but it was utterly inappropriate for Philip to comment on an interaction between him and another member of the pride. "How do you mean?"

"You've come alive again, here in America."

The words hit Justinian almost like a blow and he sat down abruptly. He took a deep breath. "It's easier when I don't see her in every blade of grass, in every paving stone." He paused for a moment. "I feel guilty about it, about not being...what's the word? Grieving? Grief struck? I don't know what it is but I feel guilty sometimes. Last week when we finished the northern wing and I knew everyone had a room, now—I remembered how there was space in France and I thought about how we have more here, how we can take a small journey and transform and fly for a while and come back. I thought about how wonderful this place is but how there was nothing in France and then I felt horrible, like I betrayed her memory."

"You should take another mate, Justinian."

He turned to look at Daniel. "There's nobody here int—"

"Any of them would be glad to have you."

Justinian rolled his eyes. "Pour us all a drink. Maybe I'll go pick one from the harem later."

"I mean it, Justinian! You're entitled to a measure of happiness, and you should take another mate. It's not a betrayal of Linara, and it's not something you'll have to—"

He stopped talking at Justinian's upturned hand. "Pour us all a drink." He knew Daniel had his best interests in mind, knew Philip and Daniel had likely discussed this and perhaps even drawn straws to see which of them would suggest it. He smiled at the thought. "If you're done planning my life for me, perhaps you can explain what you meant by being visibly invisible."

Daniel rolled his eyes. "Let me get the damned drinks."

Philip laughed and Justinian laughed as well.

Real laughter.

Good laughter.

Philip

"Do you really think they'll do it?" Daniel stared at Philip and Philip shook his head.

"Something's changing. That's all. They love their politics, and they buy esteem and votes with strong words but do you really think they believe any of it?"

Daniel nodded. "I think some of them do. I think Reagan believes it's really an evil empire and I think there are plenty of communists who believe in their theories. Sure, there are plenty of people in leadership positions who are there to take advantage, just get what they can but the world is changing so it's really hard to get away with that now."

"So we are going to die in a nuclear holocaust?"

"No. That's not what I'm saying. Things are changing, though."

Daniel shook his head and Philip almost laughed. Sure, he was bating him but it was fun to do so. Even after all of these years, most of the dra'acheck in the Pride thought of humans almost like pets.

Not Daniel.

To him they weren't just fascinating creatures to be seen at a distance. To Daniel they were... Well, what the hell were they to Daniel?

Equals.

That was it. They were equals. Philip wondered why he hadn't thought that before, hadn't really considered that. Sure, the whole point of the great dispersal was to hide among the humans for the sake of survival. Only Philip never actually thought of the humans as anything other than...

Well, what in the world did he think of them?

"Well what does this have to do with whether or not atom bombs are going to be dropped?"

"Some of the futurists—"

"What's a futurist?"

Daniel shook his head. "You don't remember anything I ever tell you. Alvin Toffler. I told you all about his book."

"What was that? Twenty years ago?"

"Fifteen or sixteen but that's not the point. Don't pretend you don't remember. The point is there's an information age coming, and it means leadership is going to have a hell of a lot harder of a time hiding what they do from the people they rule." Of course Philip remembered the book or, more accurately, he remembered it as yet another in a long line of books by humans Daniel found fascinating. He'd begun building a library, ostensibly for the pride but in reality primarily for him. Sure, Philip and the others occasionally enjoyed reading for enjoyment and Philip was particularly fond of Mark Twain, had silly ideas of meeting him when Justinian first announced the move to America. Daniel, though, loved the human philosophers, the thinkers.

"What does that mean? No nuclear catastrophe coming?"

Daniel shook his head and sat down on one of the now seemingly antiquated upholstered velvet chairs they'd brought with them from France. "There was probably some real risk in the fifties and the sixties. Now, it's highly unlikely. It would be like two elders fighting. Even if one won, the damage to both would be too great." He looked at Philip eagerly, and as he often did, Philip wondered why in the world he found the issues of humanity to be so interesting or even exciting.

"I think you think too much. We've watched humans for centuries, and there are always wars and always problems but we've thrived anyway."

Daniel shook his head. "You're missing the point. Things are changing just like they did when humans started gathering in cities and when they started with industry instead of agriculture." Philip shrugged, hoping a noncommittal gesture would hide at least a little bit that he was out of his depth in this particular conversation. Daniel didn't even slow down. "Think about it," he said. "They used to hunt and gather what plants they could. Then, they started raising goats and cattle and they started planting crops instead. Then, they made machines and even now, they can fly! They can fly so it's not safe to transform anywhere."

"Well, they have satellites, too, Daniel."

Daniel nodded eagerly. "That's exactly my point. Things keep changing, keep progressing so that humans today are nothing like what they were five hundred years ago. Really, they're nothing like what they were even a hundred years ago. We dra'acheck had made one major change in all of our history, one change! Humans are always changing and always moving forward."

"Jesus, Daniel!" Philip stood up and pointed his finger as his friend. "When was the last time you transformed? I think you've forgotten what it

270

means to be a dragon." He didn't feel anything about it, at least didn't feel it anywhere near as much to justify the vehemence in his voice. He supposed it was an attempt to goad. It was mean-spirited, he supposed, but it was fun to test Daniel's limits a bit, to lead him down the path until he realized he was being teased.

"I'm not taking the bait, Philip," Daniel said. "You should pay attention. Things are changing."

"Changing how?"

"We are entering a new age." Daniel's voice had the same eagerness it always displayed but somehow, to Philip, it had a great deal of significance added to the mix.

"Like the Age of Aquarius?"

"This isn't some fucking musical, Philip." Wow. Profanity. That was new. "I mean....sorry. No it's not some silly astrological thing, not something mystical. I mean there's a new revolution like the Industrial Revolution."

"You mean humans are entering a new age."

Daniel laughed and Philip couldn't help but smile at his friend's enthusiasm. "The lives of the dra'acheck and the lives of humanity are intertwined now, Philip. There is no age humans enter that we don't enter as well."

CHAPTER TWENTY-FOUR

NOW

Petros

He wondered why everyone else still looked pretty damned hurt when the soreness of his battle with Dimitri had already faded. It didn't make a great deal of sense at all. Surely, if they were full blooded dra'acheck, they'd heal faster than a half-breed like Petros.

Half breed.

He wondered why the others in his father's pride seemed to have no issue with him. He didn't think there was something nobler about dragons that they'd somehow be free of the prejudice that affected mankind. In fact, there was plenty of evidence with all that had just occurred that suggested the exact opposite.

He sat down and looked at them. Phineas seemed deflated, utterly deflated, and he wondered if it felt something like a zealot must feel when confronted by something outside of the scope of his religion. "When will me bury Dimitri's body?" he asked to nobody in particular. No one replied right away and when someone did, he was surprised it was Phineas.

"We don't bury our dead. We burn our dead."

"I thought you were... I thought we were immune to fire."

Justinian stood. "No. It has little effect in general but an older dra'acheck produces fire that can kill a hatchling and hurt a younger dragon. When we die, though, whatever protection our skin gives us from fire dies with us."

"So all those..." Petros cut off the words. It probably wasn't an appropriate time to talk about the legends of dragon hunters and dragon armor having magical properties. Instead he said, "When will we... do you make a pyre?"

"I have to think about it, Petros," Justinian said. "Agathon should be here."

272

"Are we just going to wait until the next meeting?"

"Should we at least unload him from the truck?" Daniel's voice was weary and Petros wondered why he hadn't rested. Daniel and Bernard had picked up the tractor trailer from one of his father's companies and arrived just this morning. Petros and the others had arrived yesterday. Petros wondered at everyone's demeanor. There was no relief at having prevailed, no joy at having overcome the attempt to murder Daniel. No celebration that this dragon mass murderer had been stopped and his plot to send humanity and dragons to war was stopped with him.

He realized with a bit of shock that all of those present grieved. He'd thought perhaps it had only to do with the necessity of changing their world view, of learning that indeed dragons killed other dragons on purpose and not out of emotions but because of cold and calculating plans. That wasn't it, though. He realized as he looked at their faces they were grieving, and not just for Philip but also for Dimitri. He wondered if it had to do with their lifespans. Even someone evil dying when that evil creature's lifespan was measured in centuries was a tragedy, he supposed.

"Yes. Put him in the barn for now."

"So you will be waiting until the council meeting? Until the vote?"

"There won't be a vote now," Justinian said softly. "Only tears."

Petros took a deep breath. He didn't really want to broach the subject that needed broaching so he was grateful when one of his father's men arrived with food. He pushed a cart into the room filled with breaded steaks, potatoes, and more. Nobody else moved but Petros realized suddenly he was ravenous, and he gratefully loaded a plate with half a dozen steaks and a mountain of mashed potatoes and gravy. He took a tray table with his other hand and sat. Nobody else moved to eat but he ignored the slight embarrassment of eating in front of them and began devouring the meal.

He finished two steaks before he finally asked, "Why do you think there won't be a vote?"

Everyone looked at him as though the question was insane and he took another breath but before he could answer, Daniel said, "We already know the truth. It wasn't humans killing dra'acheck. It was Dimitri trying to make it seem like they were."

He didn't know how to soften the blow, so Petros said, "He didn't act alone. You have to know that?"

The response was silence and half of the faces registered shock while the other half registered something more like knowing, patronizing understanding. He sighed and said, "Oh, sure. There couldn't have been more. I forgot that the dra'acheck don't behave that way. I forgot that the dra'acheck didn't kill each other either. I forgot that children of elders didn't attack people I love."

"It's unthinkable, Pete," Justinian said. "You just don't—"

"Perhaps the unthinkable is something we must consider." All eyes turned to Phineas, and Petros thought it strange that it was so easy now to forgive him for all of the imagined harms, to think of him as an ally and not Philip's adversary.

"For one to do such things," Daniel said, "was already incomprehensible. For you to suggest others colluded, Petros… It's just not possible."

"It's not possible that any of this happened. I just found out I'm a dragon or part dragon or whatever I am. I just killed a man. Okay, not a man but I just killed an intelligent being, a sentient being, and I killed him for killing my Uncle Philip. None of that is possible, and from what I understand it's not even possible that I should have been able to kill him in the first place, right? I'm just a baby lizard, right? What do you call me?"

"Hatchling," Justinian said. "But you're different, Pete."

"Yes, I know. I'm different. It seems to me that everything is different and it seems to me that your five thousand years on Earth hasn't been enough to help you see—"

"Not that long. A few thousand, and—"

"It was hyperbole, Dad." He sighed and mostly to organize his thoughts, he took another bite of the steak. "The point is that things have happened even since I found out about all of this, things that you would have bet your life couldn't and wouldn't ever happen. If I'm wrong, that's great. If I'm right, we have a real problem. This isn't a sad ending, this is just the beginning."

Justinian

Justinian watched as his son paused and let the words sink in for a moment. "There has to be someone else involved," he said. "Dimitri couldn't have thought this up, wouldn't have wanted to. Really though, that isn't the point. How does someone who really has no true interaction with humanity at all come up with a plan to derail all that your dispersal accomplished?" He gestured to Daniel. "He could have done it." Daniel looked shocked but before he could get angry, Petros added, "He didn't, of course, but the point is that he understands human nature. He understands humans not only as individuals but also as a collective species and—"

"But he spent his life among the elders," Phineas said. "He wouldn't have been able to have interactions with the prides."

"Why couldn't the conspirator's be elders?"

It was a fair question but Justinian didn't answer right away. Instead he motioned for Daniel to refill his drink. Phineas had no trouble whatsoever responding. "That's not possible. Dimitri was evil. He was evil pure and simple. He murdered dra'acheck without a second thought."

"But that's the point, isn't it? He murdered dra'acheck, the only creatures he knew. If he wanted to war with humanity, why didn't he just reveal himself and attack?"

Justinian pointed at Petros. "A month ago my son didn't know what he was. Hell, we still don't know what he is but he's right. If a dragon attacked people in Times Square, what would happen, Pete?"

Petros said, "Any dra'acheck that revealed himself after that would die." Daniel delivered a drink to Justinian and then handed one to Petros. Justinian found it interesting how easily he'd come to think of his son as one of the pride and not just one of the pride but a trusted member, even an advisor. "And yet…" Petros' face seemed lost for a moment and then he let out a low whistle.

"What is it?" Phineas said.

He still waited and Justinian added, "Tell us, son."

"If a dra'acheck attacked Times Square, any dra'acheck that showed himself would be killed. That would happen unless all of them showed themselves. That's the point you're all missing." Petros sighed. "It wasn't enough to reveal to humanity the existence of dragons. All dragons would have to be on board because one or two at a time, humans would win. Dimitri had to make sure the dragons believed—"

"To believe we were already under attack." Daniel said. Justinian noticed a number of those present nodding their heads.

"But who would do it?" Justinian asked.

Petros shook his head, shook it almost violently. "We all need to stop asking that. We need to stop because as far as you're concerned no one would do it just like no dra'acheck would kill another dra'acheck. I swear to God, you're all like Nero Wolfe."

It was strange to take him so seriously while he ate his food like he had a bottomless stomach. Justinian shrugged. "Nero who?"

"Nero Wolfe," Daniel answered. "It's a detective story."

"A whole set of them," Petros said. "The guy is fat and he hates to work and he never cooperates with the police and he never leaves his home. He has two periods of the day when he won't let himself be interrupted because he's working on his orchid greenhouse, and—"

"What does that have to do with anything?" Phineas asked.

"He has all these absolutes," Petros said, "Except every other story he's leaving his house and every other story he's cooperating with the police and he's always handling business even if he's supposed to be working on his orchids. That's what I mean. He's set up like there are all these unbreakable rules and he breaks every damned one all the time. You're all the same way."

Justinian shrugged again. "I don't follow what—"

"Dad, as far as I can tell the entire history of the dra'acheck is dragons doing things that dragon's just don't do. I'll never convince you that anyone intends to do anything. So, we need to stop asking who would do this and start asking who could."

Justinian didn't like at all where the conversation was going. He said slowly, "What do you mean?"

"I mean just what I asked. Who could do this? Who had the ability to figure out where the prides are located? Who had the ability to control Dimitri? For that matter..." He paused and looked directly Justinian. Justinian felt a terrible sense of foreboding because he knew what Petros would say next.

"Who had the power to call the dra'acheck to a meeting to cast the vote for war?"

"No!" The exclamation came from four of those present all at once. Justinian wondered why he didn't join in. He felt the same.

"What you're suggesting is impossible, Petros. Dimitri didn't act alone, okay. I think you've convinced me about that but there's no way it could be Agathon. It's not possible. He was the architect of the plan, the one who came up with our salvation in the first place." Justinian shook his head. "It can't be him. It might have been Katya before she was killed but it can't be Agathon."

Petros shoveled more food into his mouth, chewed it for a moment, and then swallowed it down. "You're blinded, Dad. He's changed the plan over and over, and…"

"He wouldn't do it," Phineas said. "He killed Yara to protect the dispersal. He killed him and—"

"And it's been a thousand years, right?"

Phineas shook his head. "Not quite. I know Agathon. There are times I despise him but I respect one thing. What he did, sending us into the human world, he did to save us and he did because he believes it's the hope for our salvation."

"Maybe he just changed his mind," Petros began. It was hard not to laugh at him.

"Son," Justinian began. "Dra'acheck don't…" He trailed off. Finally, he said lamely, "It's impossible, Petros."

"All men change their minds." Justinian turned his head, shocked to see Cheryl back from town already and even more shocked to see Patricia with her.

"They do," Patricia said. "It's a woman's prerogative but men have it down to a science."

Petros

Petros leapt to his feet, knocking his tray table over and sending a mound of chicken fried steak, mashed potatoes, and gravy to the floor. He stumbled awkwardly and almost fell over. That was embarrassing enough but when the assembled dra'acheck chuckled at him, he felt his cheeks grow hot. He knew at least some of that had to do with the realization that none of them had even arrived at the point to take his suggestion about Agathon seriously. They were condescending to allow him to talk but he wasn't making any headway.

"Well, if you want to hug me," Patricia said, "You'll have to come over here because there's no way I'm stepping in that just to get my arms around you." He stepped forward and promptly slipped on the mess on the floor but he righted himself just in time to avoid falling but not in time to avoid more laughter.

He didn't care once he held her.

"You believe you're eternal and unchanging," Cheryl continued. "You believe that but it's just not true. You just take longer to adjust. A man can believe firmly in something and then suddenly no longer believe in it. What makes you think Agathon is different?"

"He's no man," Daniel said softly as he rose. "I mean no offense." Petros realized he showed extra deference for the benefit of Phineas and his group, to ensure they knew of Cheryl's status as his father's wife.

Cheryl nodded and said, "I welcome your response, Daniel," and for the first time, Petros noticed there was something authoritative in the way she spoke, something always had been authoritative. "But I'm afraid you're wrong. He's no human, at least not any more than any of you are, but he's a man. He's a man who's led your kind for centuries and paid the price for it every single day. He's a man and he's changed his mind."

Phineas rose. "I beg your pardon…" He looked at Justinian.

"Cheryl."

He nodded and turned back to her. "I beg your pardon, Cheryl, but Agathon is unyielding, unchanging." Petros noted what appeared to be a grateful glance at Daniel for indicating her status.

"What is your name?"

"Phineas."

If she registered any shock from hearing his name, she didn't show it. "You think in terms of centuries because you are dra'acheck. His plan took effect more than a thousand years ago and he's probably changed his mind a thousand times. He's a dragon but he's also a man and he's seen his plan force his people into hiding, force young to grow up and never know what it really means to be a dragon. He's seen you, in many ways, subjugated by a race he certainly views as inferior. He's changed him mind, and like a man he couldn't just announce it. He had to come up with a scheme to make it seem he was pushed to act."

Nobody spoke for a moment and Petros wasn't sure if he should add to what his mother said. I may be smarter, but my parents are wiser. He remembered his thoughts when he was leaving for college and never had it been more evident than in his mother's words now.

Patricia still held him. He turned and looked at her. "Well," she said. "I had to come back. Look at all the trouble you get in without me."

It was strange to feel so damned elated despite the circumstances. He looked around. He was pretty sure Daniel was convinced. He was certain Phineas and company wouldn't require much more convincing at all. He turned to his father. He was convinced, Petros thought, but he couldn't admit it. "Dad," he said. "I was nine when I discovered I was smarter than you." There was few gasps, especially from the visitors.

"Petros Renault!" his mother said sharply.

"Wait," Petros said. "I don't mean that as an insult." He looked at his father. "I was ten when I started faking like I needed your help with my homework. It wasn't until I was a little older that I couldn't fake because the subject matter was beyond your abilities. I was nine when I realized it, and it was the hardest thing in the world for me to learn. I felt horrible, like acknowledging you were less than perfect was some kind of betrayal. I felt like a failure, a failure as a son."

He paused and looked at the assembled group. They all expected something brilliant to come out of his mouth but he found himself at a loss. Fortunately, Patricia took over. "But all you did in college was talk about your dad and his mom. Your father wasn't an idol but he was still everything to you."

He nodded. "Yes. That's true. At the time, though, realizing my father was less than perfect was the hardest thing I'd ever had to face." He fixed his gaze on Justinian and said, "Dad, I think I know what you're going through. I had to face that you weren't perfect. You have to face a lot more with the one you think of as a father."

Justinian took a long breath and let it out slowly. "We'll have to go to Tatras, confront him." Petros realized he still held out hope that Agathon

279

would be able to convince him or at least to… Petros wasn't sure what he hoped to accomplish but he knew his father wanted something from him.

Cheryl said, "I want to show Patricia the garden. Don't leave without saying goodbye." Petros held onto to Patricia and kissed her neck.

"Hey there," she said. "You don't get to kiss the bride anytime you want, you know."

He laughed and kissed her mouth before letting her go. She and Cheryl left and he turned back to his father. "When would we leave?"

"A few days. We should give everyone a chance to heal."

Petros nodded and said, "Okay. Let me know if—" He stopped short and felt his heart rate accelerate. "Nevermind, Dad. He's on his way here."

Daniel rose immediately. "You can sense him? I can't."

Justinian closed his eyes. "I think I can." Petros stared at his father's face and wished there was some button to press to eliminate the pain. "Yes. He's coming."

CHAPTER TWENTY-FIVE

THEN

Agathon

Were they all like that?

Before.

Were they all like Dimitri before the dispersal?

The thought was strange but he wondered if it were true. He tried to recall life before the first council. They were free, certainly, but were they like Dimitri? There was savagery in his son's movements and his actions, savagery that seemed appropriate and even noble but savagery nonetheless. He was savage like one of the wolves, one of the great cats. He was savage like the crocodiles or even like the sharks. Had that been all of them before this dispersal? Had all shown that kind of savagery? Was that the natural state? There were none among the dragons on Tatras untouched by man, none but Dimitri. There were none untouched and Dimitri moved with none of the hesitation all others seemed to have. Agathon watched him dive at a deer, watched the absolute efficiency of the kill, and saw in his son's eyes the excitement of the hunt, excitement Agathon hadn't experienced, at least not really, for far too long.

Did Agathon's eyes look the same when he first descended on that herd of pigs? Had all of them? He remembered their roars, remembered Bethuselah and Yara feasting, remembered sadly how he had to convince him to eat, so sure was Yara they took a portion that belonged to the others.

And Yara was dead.

"Come to me," he called and Dimitri descended, landing before him and dropping the carcass of the deer at his feet.

"Are you hungry, father?"

Agathon shook his head. "No. Eat." Dimitri lowered his head and snapped off the deer's hindquarters, gulping down the meat and bone in a single swallow. Agathon changed his mind and snapped up what remained. The blood was fresh and warm and Agathon tried again to remember that first real hunt, the taste of the pigs, the warmth of their blood. He couldn't recall, at least not clearly. "Katya knows. We'll leave soon."

Dimitri nodded. "And if she doesn't agree to give you the locations of the prides?" He didn't phrase it as a question, not really. There was regret in his voice but there was no question at all.

"I already know the locations. I've followed her over the years. I can see her, sense her from a great distance. Lionellek's pride is the only I don't know, and I will get it from her."

"Will she join us?"

"No. She's going to try to stop us."

Dimitri sighed and Agathon felt his sigh. "Then what must happen is already decided."

Of course it was but Agathon felt a burst of pain he'd hadn't felt since Yara. "I don't know if I can," Agathon began. He paused. "It must happen, my son but I don't—"

"I will do it." He said it simply but the import of the words weren't lost on Agathon. "Father, you have seen far too much death, far too many dra'acheck lost. If it comes to that, let her death be the last of your suffering."

Agathon nodded but he didn't enjoy the ease of his agreement. For thousands of years he'd borne the burden of his plan and to give it to another, his son no less, seemed to cheapen the years of sacrifice. He took a deep breath and let it out very slowly. "Have you ever wondered why you are purple?"

"Some would say I'm just a very deep red. Some would see the need for more blue to call me purple. There aren't many with my color."

"No." He lifted himself up and stretched his wings, enjoying the feel of the sun on him. "Not you in particular. I mean why are you purple? Why am I red? Why is your mother... He let his wings beat lazily as the sun warmed him. "No other creature is like this."

"Man has many colors."

Agathon nodded. "Fly with me." He leapt into the air and lazily ascended. It took little time for Dimitri to catch up. "Man has many colors but it seems to follow their geography. At least, it did. Now, though, if humans of two colors mate, they produce another in some combination. Not us. We all shared the same geography and even now... Can you explain to me how your mother and I produced purple?"

"There are no creatures like us, Father. None." Dimitri was right, of course, but the question still vexed Agathon. He didn't know why. The two flew higher in a wide circle. Dimitri snapped at a few birds, more out of annoyance than anything else.

Dimitri flew below him, and Agathon noted his strength, his power. Elderspawn. He didn't know why the word came to him now. He didn't know why the word seemed so sad.

No.

That he knew.

There was still a great deal about which he was unsure but not that. "How can I convince her?" he said softly.

He didn't intend to say the words audibly, didn't intend for Dimitri to hear them. He certainly didn't intend to hear what he knew to be the truth in response. "You can't."

Agathon nodded and began his descent. "But I have to try."

Katya

He'd flown at a breakneck pace, and Katya watched as he finally slowed and descended toward the lush green leaves. She was unfamiliar with this portion of the forest or even if this area was still part of the woods at the foot of the Tatras range. It was beautiful, though. It was beautiful and still unspoiled. She followed him and felt the heat on the sun on her back, a luscious kind of heat on a beautiful kind of day. She let her wings move lazily as they descended in circles and she noticed for perhaps the first time how the red of Agathon's scales contrasted with the green of the canopy and how perfect that seemed, how naturally the colors played against each other. The sight was magnificent but brutal somehow, magnificent in the way a cobra strike was magnificent.

She watched as he finally reached the canopy and then disappeared into it. She dove down after him, curiosity growing greater now. The smell of the underforest was pungent and powerful, loamy and filled with the strange juxtaposition of life and death that made up the forest floor. Agathon waited next to a stand of beech trees, and they shot up like thick needles around him so the color of his scales seemed like the base of some strange flower. He turned his head, craning his neck to follow her descent as she lighted on the forest floor. The ground was soft under her, and she made her way toward him slowly, enjoying the feel of the leaves and undergrowth beneath her claws.

He craned his neck and turned his face and she followed his gaze to a patch of ground. It was new, perhaps only a decade or two of growth. She watched as he opened his mouth and watched the flame shoot out toward that spot, lighting the ground afire and spilling over to light the bark of some of the nearby beech. The blast was controlled and short and it left a smoldering rather than a flaming patch of earth about a third of Katya's size. Strange. Strange how even a quick burst of destruction could be beautiful in this place.

"There was a hunting party, Katya," he said. "From the Hunt, I mean. A group of humans. I saw them here. The forest was a bit different back then."

"You were far from Tatras." He turned his head and Katya fought back the almost ever present awe that seemed to flow from every movement of his body. Even now among the birch trees he seemed like the source of life in the forest and not an outside force, not a guest among the worms crawling beneath the composting leaves or an interloper among the wolves just four miles north.

"Yes," he said. "Far from Tatras. It seems closer now, doesn't it? Even the humans at the foot of our range could be here in only hours, faster than some of us. Most of us."

"Perhaps all but you, Agathon."

He nodded. "About a mile from here, maybe two, I found the hatchling they killed. It was in their cart." He paused and gestured toward the still-smoking patch of ground. "Here I buried him, burned him. I... I sprinkled the blood of the leader of the humans on his body, a stupid thought, a fanciful idea that he'd know he'd been avenged when the flames reached him."

"He didn't know."

Agathon nodded. "He didn't know." He walked toward the smoldering ground. She heard the sounds of life returning to the forest. There weren't many left on the planet, places so old that the trees themselves seemed to tell the birds and the rodents and the insects that dragons belonged. "I return here from time to time and send fire where he once lay. I return here and imagine he knows."

"Was he avenged, Agathon?" The tone of her own voice surprised her. She already knew the answer and Agathon knew she knew the answer because he didn't reply. "From time to time," she said softly. "You return from time to time. Do you add more blood each time?"

He paused before he answered. "Not yet," he said softly.

She sighed. "And will he know now, Agathon? Will the hatchling know he's been avenged?"

"No." The word seemed out of place in the stillness of the forest. "But I will."

"And what fire will take the mighty Agathon? What fire will mingle with the blood of man to let you know?" He didn't reply but she didn't expect him to answer.

"Don't cleanse me with fire, Agathon. Let me lay where I fall."

"What?"

She wasn't happy at the hurt in his face, wasn't happy at the immediate and almost overwhelming grief that overtook his features. Still... "You have no choice, Agathon. You must kill me. You are as you always are. Lionellek is in Toronto." He stared at her in shock. She smiled. "There. I've spared you the hurt of torturing me."

For a moment brief hope showed in his eyes. "So you will join us?"

She shook her head sadly. "No. I will fight you and I will lose. I will fight you and die."

"But if you're just silent, you—"

She smiled again. "No. I will go to the elders and tell them. Leave me lie where I fall. No fire. Promise me, Agathon."

"Katya. You don't have to fight—"

"Is this now the fruition of the Great Plan of Agathon the Great, Agathon the Savior, Agathon the Red? Was this your plan from the outset, Agathon?"

"No!" he said sharply and then paused. "Maybe. Maybe it was and I didn't see it until the Second Council. I separated us, made us live among humanity to save us and then we came together again and as far I knew only two dra'acheck had died in almost a millennium. Yara." He paused and suddenly transformed. She stared at the change but saw him put his head in his hands. There was no equivalent gesture among the dra'acheck, and she felt his pain so viscerally that tears threatened to drop from her eyes. He didn't remain human for long but transformed back. "Only two dra'acheck had died but there was a sea of dragons there. It was then I realized it, then I understood that we didn't need to learn to live. We didn't need to keep alive, we needed..." He paused and Katya saw the doubt in his eyes. Only two dra'acheck. Two of them but both died at the hands of other dra'acheck. How many would be added to that sum?

"An army," she said.

"Yes," he replied almost defiantly. "The great plan worked. The dra'acheck survive. But it has left us as prisoners. It has left us denying who we are." Agathon paused, trying desperately to form his next words in a way that could bring both understanding and acceptance to Katya. "After Yara, who died at my hands, and after the second council I was lost. But then Dimitri was born and I saw it Katya! I saw the hope of our race! I saw a true dra'acheck again and what our people could be."

"And what can our people be, oh Agathon the great?" Katya retorted with power. She needed to remind Agathon he was not addressing some hatchling, but rather Katya, grand ancient of the dra'acheck and elder of their people. She needed to remind him that although he was Agathon, she was Katya, one of the most powerful beings on the earth. She didn't need to remind him in order to instill fear, because that was impossible. She needed to remind him that she was wise and her words should still hold sway with him.

A moment passed and Agathon finally said "Free."

"Freedom doesn't need to come through a passage of blood Agathon."

"Oh but it does Katya. Yara taught me that. Watching the humans these last few centuries has taught me that." Agathon turned from her, looked to the sky and continued. "There will be war Katya. There will be blood and there will be death. From that blood and death will then come understanding. Understanding that Dragons are here and have a place in this world. After some time a truce will be declared and dra'acheck will have a land of their own, a land free from the humans, and the humans will then be free from us."

There was such conviction in his voice that Katya knew this was a plan he had been designing for centuries and there would be no talking him out of it now. It was, after all, already in motion.

The red dragon turned back to face the mother of his son. "Please Katya, join us. You know the anguish I will suffer if you don't."

"No."

"Do you not see what it is I'm fighting for Katya?"

"I see it Agathon. It is a thing of beauty. But even things of great beauty can come with too high of a price. The price you are willing to pay is far to high. Far too high for humans. Far too high for the dra'acheck. Far too high for Katya the elder."

"Please don't make me do this Katya."

"I love you Agathon," The words shocked both of them for a moment since she couldn't recall ever speaking them before. "But it is already done." She said it with an uneasy acceptance of her fate. "Now do what you came here to do. But be warned, while I will surely die today, you will be healing your wounds for months. For never in your long life Agathon the Red have you faced one such as Katya."

CHAPTER TWENTY-SIX

NOW

Justinian

For just a moment, Justinian felt a rush of hope and security. Agathon the Red was here. Agathon was here and that meant the situation was fixed and everything was going to be fine.

One moment.

One beautiful moment.

Agathon didn't bother knocking but simply opened the front door and walked directly to where they were gathered.

One lovely moment of hope.

And then reality fell upon him and he sighed softly as a wave of terrible sadness washed over him. "It wasn't just Dimitri," he said softly. "Oh, Agathon. Oh, Agathon." The great red dragon hesitated for a moment and Justinian could see sadness in his eyes. The sadness offered no hope, though. There was resolve, the same resolve he'd shown centuries before creating the plan he was now intent on dismantling.

"And you won't join me," he said. "Will you?" For a brief moment, Justinian saw a vision of Agathon among the humans in the mountains, in the snow. He saw the same look in his eyes but there was something also unreadable there, something unreadable and unreachable. Agathon turned and looked at the room. He turned back to Justinian. "My son. He was very powerful. He was rash, though. I told him you could overcome him." Justinian stared at him, tears already threatening to flow. "He was in almost all ways my second son, Justinian. Come, old friend. Let us enter this new world together. Our numbers have grown and we no longer need hide among humans to win this war."

"War, Agathon?" Justinian stood. As he did he felt pain wash over his body. Dimitri had done damage. "What war? Your plan was always about peace." Agathon didn't respond and suddenly cold truth filled Justinian. "You didn't... Oh Agathon, why didn't you tell me? Why didn't you tell any of us?"

Agathon didn't respond immediately. Finally, he took a deep breath and said, "Say nothing. The war is inevitable. Say nothing and you will live. Say nothing and—"

"You killed Katya," Justinian whispered. "You killed her to learn where she'd put the prides."

Agathon looked wounded by the words, wounded as surely as if he'd been struck. The wounds, though, didn't come from false accusation. Justinian wished desperately that they did. "I knew where the prides were located," the red dragon said softly. "I always knew." He looked at the gathering and said softly. "Please. I have already lost so many I love. Say nothing. You need not attend the council. Say nothing and live."

Justinian looked at the group. Daniel was hurt but he stood resolute. Bernard was hurt, perhaps not as badly. Petros stood in human form. He was shaken. Justinian couldn't tell if he was hurt or... What the hell did it matter? Dimitri had nearly killed them all. A battle with Agathon would make what they'd just experienced seem easy. Phineas and his warriors were battered as well. One of them—Justinian thought his name was Cronees or something along those lines—was broken.

He was unlikely to live, certain not to live without immediate attention. His right arm was broken and not even cast yet but simply splinted. It had been twisted unnaturally and bent backward in a way that made Justinian feel sick. Nonetheless, the dragon rose shakily and stood. He turned to Phineas and nodded and then looked back at Agathon, looked back at him defiantly. "You are no dra'acheck, Agathon," Justinian said.

It seemed like the words hit Agathon as surely as a blow might have. "Please." Agathon said. "Dimitri was strong, a spawn of elders, but even if none of you were injured, you wouldn't find me as easy to dispatch."

Daniel rose shakily to his feet. "For my entire life I loved you. Only now do I learn I loved a lie."

The others rose as well and joined the one Justinian believed was Chronees. "I never loved you," he said. His breath came in gasps and his voice was punctuated with wheezing. "But every one of our pride respected you. We respected you on behalf of Yara." His form was broken so he shambled more than walked to stand right in front of Agathon. "I am thankful he didn't live to see you dishonor his memory."

The roar from Agathon was sudden and accompanied by a red blur Justinian only realized was his fist after it struck. Justinian heard the sound of bone breaking even as the man's body seemed to snap. Chronees crumpled to the ground and Justinian stared in shock. It was murder, simple murder. "Please," Agathon said, almost instantly recovered. "Please. I would not have this. No others need to die."

"You mean no others save me," Daniel said. "That's why you sent your son. That's why you're here. You need to silence me."

Agathon looked like he was about to speak but he sighed instead. Justinian took a step toward him and though he had no doubt of the outcome, he was thankful that the others stepped with him. Agathon looked sadly at him and Justinian fought back an almost overwhelming need to run to him, to embrace him, to beg. He swallowed down the urge and stared back defiantly. Agathon sighed again and said, "So be it." The great red dragon reared back and Justinian prepared for the end but instead heard a voice.

The voice of his son.

"I think I understand now why so many of my jokes fell flat," he said. "Dra'acheck have no sense of irony."

"Petros," Daniel said. "Stand down."

Petros ignored him and stepped forward and Justinian wondered at the sight of the dragons parting to allow him to stand in front of Agathon. "My father has spoken of Yara. Philip and Daniel have spoken of Yara. Of course, they've also spoken of Agathon the Great. Agathon the Wise. From the moment I knew the truth, they spoke of Agathon, the great defender of humanity and Yara, the misguided dragon with love so strong for the dra'acheck."

"Be careful how you speak, hatchling." Agathon's voice was filled with menace, filled with malice as he transformed, his body instantly crushing the walls by the door and making them crumble like dust.

"Petros, please," Justinian said but his son held up a hand. The hand seemed so weak. In fact, Petros's body seemed entirely weak, human and still bruised from the battle with Dimitri. Agathon's massive body, on the other hand, appeared to be the embodiment of strength.

"The irony is," Petros said. "That all along you had none of Yara's love and the hatred you bear for humanity is twice what he felt."

"I said be careful," Agathon roared. "I am Agathon. Neither man nor dra'acheck can stand against me." He inhaled deeply and Justinian's breath caught in his throat.

"Then it's good I'm neither," Petros said, transforming as Agathon let loose his fire.

Justinian screamed, "No!" as the flames engulfed his son. The heat was almost unbearable for him, and he imagined it would have been if the walls hadn't crumbled and given an outlet for it. He screamed in terror, and he felt like the scream lasted longer than any he'd screamed before but a moment later, Agathon cut off his flames and turned to Justinian.

"I didn't want this," he said. "I wanted us to stand together against..." Agathon's words trailed off but Justinian only barely heard them anyway. Petros still stood. He still stood and he was taller than before, at least a foot and a half taller. The second dragon from Phineas's pride was on the ground, and Chronees body was smoldering. Agathon followed Justinian's gaze and looked at Petros.

And Petros roared.

Justinian had never heard a roar he thought could equal Agathon's but the awe that had almost paralyzed him in Tatras flowed over him again and then suddenly, fire erupted from his son's mouth.

Fire.

Different fire.

It was blue, bluish green and it was hot, hellishly hot.

Justinian was perhaps five yards away but the heat from the blast was powerful and he turned his head and transformed involuntarily. He imagined it saved him because more of the room crumpled down. He heard the red dragon roar with rage and turned his head back. Petros stood, not even breathing hard, and Agathon lay on the floor, on his back on the floor. Justinian stared in shock. He was certain Agathon had never been felled. Agathon roared again and rolled back to his feet and then charged Petros. Again, Petros burst forth with flame and Justinian held his gaze firm despite the heat and watched Agathon fly through the air until he collided with the only standing wall in the room, shattering it as he fell back and out onto the sand, destroying a tall yucca plant on the way.

Agathon roared again and again flipped back over but this time he let loose with fire, and not the dismissive, fly-swatting heat of his first blast. Justinian dove toward his son, knocking him from his feet even as Bernard stepped in front of the stream. Petros cried out, "Damn it, Dad! I can take it!" even as Justinian watched Bernard burst into flames, flames not limited to those Agathon spewed.

Petros stood and threw his father away and Justinian gasped as he sailed through the air. Again, fire roared from Petros's mouth and Agathon roared again.

In pain.

The fire ceased and Agathon said, "With or without you," and leapt into the air.

Immediately, Petros turned toward him and said, "Dad, we have to follow him!"

Justinian couldn't move his wings. He looked at Daniel, who shook his head weakly. Bernard was already dead. Phineas and the others? They were in worse shape than Justinian and the thought of flight sickened him. He looked at Petros and said softly, "None of us can follow, son."

Petros roared and Justinian would have roared with him if he could have mustered the energy but then the roar changed to a scream and Justinian stared in shock as his son seemed to clench up, to bend together like some kind of stretch toy and then, still screaming, straighten up. He watched as Petros screamed and then suddenly shot into the sky, giving Justinian only a moment to see the wings that sprang from his son's back.

Petros

He could smell the salt from the ocean below and could sense the life beneath it and more than anything, Petros wished he could take a moment to reflect on that, to consider the school of tuna, the mackerel, the squid far below the surface, the crustaceans, and the lone shark with the injured dorsal fin. He could feel the outline of a wreck as well, something two or three hundred years old, not quite the age of Spanish galleons but probably filled with something exciting nonetheless. He could sense all of that, could almost see it, and he wished desperately he could stop and simply dive down to explore all of that and forget his chase.

As though he heard him, Agathon veered to the left suddenly and Petros realized his intention moments before Agathon acted. He wondered if there was something about his intelligence, the processing of thoughts so quickly it seemed intuitive, that made even this situation seem like some kind of a game of chess. He had to dive low, and he broke through the clouds and saw the ship before Agathon burst through above him. It was an oil tanker and it was empty, heading back to refill. There was only a skeleton crew and for an instant Petros considered just letting Agathon take it, considered letting Agathon believe Petros wouldn't waver even in the face of innocent deaths.

An instant.

He couldn't manage anything more than that. He let loose with his fire and the strange, unnatural color of the flame made him feel strangely queasy. He hadn't felt that way in the forest, perhaps just because of the air or perhaps because when it first came to him it came while Agathon's flames engulfed him. Agathon hadn't hurt him but there had nonetheless been heat, heat like the heat that billowed from an oven when the door was opened. Perhaps that heat held back the near nausea. He wasn't sure. He didn't care, not entirely.

Yes he did.

The nausea. It wasn't about the color of his flames. It had everything to do with the desire to kill, the absolute and unfiltered desire to end Agathon's life. The feeling was terrible, more than terrible. It grew worse as the greenish fire shot toward the red dragon and it howled with just as much pain as rage. He knew, at least he thought he knew, that in general dragon fire only hurt dra'acheck when there was a significant difference in age between them. It made

293

no sense that Petros should be immune to Agathon's fire and it made even less sense that the green flame should affect him at all.

But it did.

Smoke rose from Agathon's chest and it seemed also that steam billowed up from beneath his scales. He was wounded. He turned his head and looked at Petros, rage showing on his face but he only remained in the air for a moment before his face changed from anger to confusion and then disbelief as his wings crumpled to his body and he plummeted down. Petros shot out toward him, catching the dra'acheck's chest with his shoulder and sending him careening away so that they fell into the water a hundred yards or so from the oil tanker.

The impact of the water hit Petros harder than he expected, taking his breath from him momentarily. Worse, he watched as the glowing patch on Agathon's chest disappeared into the blue darkness of the sea. Agathon's jaws shot toward him, and it was only the added resistance of the ocean that kept the jaws from closing over his chest. Petros kicked to the left then back toward Agathon but he realized quickly the advantage here lay with the elder. Nonetheless, he swung a fist with all his might, a fist that bounced harmlessly off the dragon's chest.

Petros could sense a whale in the area and made a mental note to return to the sea at some point to see the life within but as Agathon lashed out with his tail, sending Petros a dozen yards through the water, he realized the foolishness of the idea. The blow to his chest reminded him he'd already lost his breath when he fell into the water and he needed oxygen. Shit. Was he supposed to die in the middle of the ocean?

Fortunately, Agathon erred. He shot up toward the surface and Petros beat his wings to follow, surfacing behind the red beast and drawing in air in great, heaving breaths. The sudden influx of oxygen made him lightheaded but fortunately, Agathon erred again and continued his mad flight. Where was he headed? North Africa was possible but Petros thought it more likely they'd end up somewhere in Europe. Why? Tatras was closer to Asia and...

Damn.

The answer was simple.

Agathon wanted to make the war inevitable. An attack on a human population would force the issue and no speech from Daniel could sway the rest of the dra'acheck if humanity took up arms. Still, why Europe rather than

America or even Canada? Petros was thankful for the chance to think about such things.

Agathon was a half mile ahead of him and he shot out the strange blue fire, more to see his range than for any other reason. The stream ended far too short but it gave Petros perspective. He willed his wings to beat faster though he was fairly sure he already beat them to their limits. Where the hell was he? He didn't have a very clear grasp of the distance or the time but he imagined they were closer to Europe than they were to the San Gabriel Mountains. He couldn't tell if he was faster than Agathon. He thought he might be but he wasn't sure.

No. Petros was faster.

He just wasn't fast enough. He imagined he could gain two or three feet per mile but that wasn't enough. He had to find more strength, more speed. He had to get closer, had to get within range of his fire, the nausea-inducing blue fire that hurt the dragon despite the effects on his stomach. Petros searched for reserves within himself but there were none. He was moving as fast as he could, and even gaining three feet per mile would put them, at their current speed, well over land before he got within range of Agathon.

Petros almost paused in flight when he realized penetrating the coast of Europe, wherever they crossed over it, would be the first time he'd actually entered another country. He roared, hoping to goad Agathon into slowing. No luck. Agathon continued to fly forward and Petros settled in to whatever time it would take to overtake the dragon.

Petros

It wasn't morning yet but it had to be coming. How far ahead was Poland? Warsaw. How far ahead? Seven hours? Eight hours. No. Nine hours, right. The sun was going to rise any moment now and Agathon's shadow would be large enough to cover an intersection or two. He had to get them farther away.

Exactly what Agathon didn't want.

Petros realized with an almost sudden and profoundly sad burst of understanding that Agathon didn't care if he died. He didn't care if he died as long as the presence of the dra'acheck was revealed. It was strangely admirable and made more strange because Petros felt, at least in part, some of that absolutism. He watched Agathon dive like one of the dragons in a fantasy film. He was preparing to breathe fire, to breathe it right down on a cluster of buildings probably filled with people. Petros shot forward and hit Agathon right beneath his left wing just as the fire loosed.

The night lit up as flame shot into the clouds and Petros clutched Agathon's chest and exerted what force he could to keep the dragon facing away from the ground. Agathon moved his head so that Petros felt the flames engulf him but he couldn't return the favor without engulfing the ground below as well. He had no idea how to halt the fire from the ancient. He supposed it was only a hunch that made him do it but he let go with one hand and brought his hand down hard on Agathon's throat. The fire sputtered and Petros grabbed hold of his neck and shot away.

If anyone looked up, they'd see the sputtering gouts of flame but they likely...

No. There was no if about it. There were already people looking up. Petros could sense them but for now they only saw flame in the darkness and a completely indistinct source. There would be UFO theorists and conspiracy theories but none would consider dragons except perhaps a few of the diehard role players, if any remained who didn't focus on werewolves and vampires these days. He wondered if the government of Poland would make some kind of announcement about military tests. He imagined an announcement from the Ministerstwo Obrony Narodowej about the great and glorious Siły Powietrzne and a comical image of the instructor who challenged him to learn the Eastern

European languages pointing his fingers and demanding he admit it came in handy after all.

Dawn would break at any moment, though, and Petros beat his wings as quickly as he could, trying desperately to remember which villages surrounded the Puszcza Białowieska. He knew he could get there, especially if Agathon remained stunned but could he get there before the sun broke over the horizon. It was about a hundred and thirty miles away. They'd traveled at speeds faster than a transatlantic flight, getting to Warsaw in about six hours. He wasn't sure of the speed but it had to be more than seven hundred and fifty miles per hour and even carrying Agathon, even fighting with him they could cross the distance to the forest in twenty minutes or so. How close was daybreak? They were headed East, which meant they were travelling toward the sunrise.

It didn't matter. He was committed and already a half dozen miles toward the destination. With any luck, if they were seen it would be by only a scattered few.

But he'd have to kill Agathon.

He felt suddenly foolish for realizing the inevitability of that end. He would have to kill Agathon or there would indeed be a war.

The dragon hadn't struggled since the punch to his throat, and for a moment Petros felt terrible fear that Agathon was already finished, that the end of this wouldn't be victory in a fight but instead the murder of a man already incapacitated. Well, not a man but certainly a murder. He sped toward the forest, making that goal somehow take precedence over all other thoughts and emotions. He could arrive there and do whatever had to be done but—Agathon suddenly began twisting in his grasp and Petros felt elated.

Elated and ashamed.

He'd be spared the indignity of simple murder but at the risk of a war that would cost far more than his self-assurance. He guessed they were a few miles from the edge of the forest and he drew back his fist again and struck once more for Agathon's throat. The dragon deflected but Petros tried a new course of action. It had worked with Dimitri. He wrapped his arms around Agathon's neck and squeezed, all the while thrusting forward with his wings. He was close. He knew that. He could sense the forest ahead, could sense the bison milling about. He held tightly and squeezed, flying blind. Only a few more miles.

Agathon twisted more urgently and once again sent fire spraying from his throat. Petros watched it sail in an arc, lighting up the ground, the sky, and… and trees. They were there. They were there, and it gave Petros a surge of energy and he shot ahead. He felt the trees give way before him, his body and Agathon's breaking through the trunks and sending leaves and splinters exploding through the air. Agathon stopped his fire and twisted wildly. "No!" the dragon screamed. "Not here!"

His movements almost dislodged Petros but he held tightly. By now, Agathon was righted and Petros, unsure of what to do, moved his body until he rode atop the red dragon, put his arms around his neck, and squeezed. Agathon breathed screamed again, almost begging, but Petros held as the dragon thrashed about. He held tightly, his arms cramping but holding as the dragon moved its body and each movement sent pressure against his arms. He thought he'd let go, was certain he'd let go, but he thought of Philip stabbed and broken on the floor in Nevada. He held tightly with his right arm to his left wrist and pulled, screaming unintelligibly as images of Philip filled his head. Oddly, when his voice formed a word, it was "Patricia" that exploded from his mouth. He screamed her name again as he squeezed and the two landed, no, crashed on the floor of the forest, sending moss and dirt hurtling to the sky.

Still Petros held, and still he screamed Patricia's name.

Agathon twisted his body again, rolling around so his body fell atop Petros and then dragged him back around until he fell atop him again. His fire shot up, lighting the trees so they wrestled under a canopy of flames but still Petros held. He felt his muscles straining and felt another burst of hate and tension from the dragon but he held and screamed Patricia's name again and he pulled his wrist and squeezed. Agathon lifted himself up and fell back, and Petros felt pain shoot through his body as the weight of the dragon fell over him. He squeezed and screamed but slackened when Agathon lifted his body up again. As the red dragon descended again, Petros jerked his hands, using Agathon's weight to add to the tension and the sickening snap that sounded when they hit the ground was profound. Agathon the Mighty went limp.

Still, Petros held.

He held tightly, not sure now if he could even move his arms to loosen his grip. He watched the flames slow until they only smoldered and watched he held tightly and watched the darkness in the sky gradually give way to light. He held and thought of Patricia and of Nevada and of Indiana and Los Angeles and mounds of potatoes and biscuits at his mother's breakfast table. He thought of Agathon and what Justinian must have seen in his centuries of life. He thought of these things and watched the skies and then sense approaching dra'acheck but still he held. "Come on Pete." The voice seemed to come from fog and distance but he forced his eyes to focus.

Justinian stared down at him. He realized he still held onto Agathon's neck and he let go. Daniel was there and someone from the other pride. It wasn't Phineas. He felt the weight of the body come off him and he forced himself to sit. "Why here?" Petros didn't respond. "Why did he come here?"

"He didn't want to." Petros said softly. "He wanted it to end over Warsaw." He rose to his feet. He was shaky but stood solidly. "I guess he wanted it to begin over Warsaw."

He turned and as he did he felt his body transform back to human. His father and the others, though, remained dragon and Petros watched as fire shot from their mouths and engulfed the red dragon. He watched silently and without intending it, he transformed again and let his fire join theirs. Far sooner than he might have expected, Agathon's body became a pile of ash. The four stood and stared at the pile and Petros said, "Can we fly home?" and then the world became black.

Petros

He woke to a strange rocking feeling and felt his father's arm. "He's waking now," he said. "As soon as we're there... You, too." Petros turned his head as his father returned the phone to its receiver.

"First class," he said. "Fancy."

"Hamaan went home," Daniel said from beside him. "Phineas will join him in a week or two."

His father looked grim. "We got back to the house with the wounded. Cimmran returned to bring Khroniss, the dra'acheck from Phineas's pride to the house so Phineas could arrange transport to Turkey. He also went to burn Dimitri's body. He was gone."

Petros nodded and then sat up straight. He felt a moment of dizziness at the sudden motion but he fought it down. "What do you mean Dimitri was gone?"

Daniel said softly, "Pete, what else can it possibly mean? He wasn't quite as dead as we thought he was."

"But Mom! Patricia!"

"They're fine," Justinian said. "They're fine and I just hung up with her. They're in Los Angeles and they're all protected. We would have had little trouble with Dimitri if Phineas and I had any experience fighting together. We didn't though and we ended up doing damage to each other. There are more than a dozen dra'acheck in Los Angeles with them and it would take no more than four of them to take Dimitri themselves."

"But what if he tries to do the same thing, just attacks humans." Justinian started to reply but Petros shook his head. "Nevermind. He can't. Agathon could but Dimitri can't. I mean, he can't now, not with Agathon gone. At least half of the dragons would be against him, maybe more if you—when you oppose it. There weren't many at that meeting who didn't look on you with respect that..." He stopped talking and shook his head. "But we'll still need to deal with him at some point."

Justinian nodded. "At some point. If he's anything like Agathon he's only going to get much stronger with age."

It made his future a bit more insecure but he felt strangely resigned to that future. "What now?"

Justinian signaled for the attendant and a moment later a tray of cocktails arrived. Petros took a soda. His father and his uncle took something stronger. He repeated the question. "What now?"

"We don't know," Daniel said. "The rest of the council will surely meet and they'll have to decide."

Petros nodded again. "Where are we?"

"Somewhere over the Atlantic."

"Did anyone see me? Agathon?" Daniel shrugged but Petros decided it didn't matter anyway.

"Can I use the phone?" he asked.

"Why?"

"I want to call Patricia."

Justinian smiled. "Sure."

EPILOGUE

TOMORROW

Light streamed through the trees, filtered so it seemed to drip like the soft rain running over the channels from the flat leaves and ending as tiny rivers in the dark soil. There were few places left where such a light could be seen. The air smelled of dampness but not the dampness of decay but the fresh dampness of dew. She turned to avoid a large boulder and then burst briefly from the vegetation, shooting up the side of the mountain and then swooping into the channel left centuries before from a burst of superheated steam. The steam carved a cave but the magma followed a different course and sealed the cave. It was warm and calm inside.

"He is dead?"

"Yes."

"And the youth survived."

"He did."

"Come. Rest. You have been away from home for too long."

The warmth was wonderful and filled her as she landed and breathed deeply of the sulfur and the charcoal and the water. "Agathon..." he didn't finish the sentence but she knew the sentiment. It was hard to lose a son.

"He saw a great deal," she said finally.

"But not enough."

"And the humans?"

"The humans?" He didn't respond right away. "Oh," she said. "Nothing. Radar, of course, but the images weren't clear. They assume technology, of course. Heated calls between nations, more distrust, posturing. Poland claimed a test flight caused the flames." There was no response so she sat in silence for a while before asking, "And the others?"

"They've set things in motion. I haven't seen farther." She knew he was lying but she said nothing.

"So it begins," she said.

Godon, the most ancient of all the dra'acheck, lifted his head and looked solemnly at her. "So it does."

THE END

SPECIAL THANKS

THE PRIDE would simply not have been possible had it not been for the generous contributions made by my supporters during the Kickstarter campaign. Words can not express my gratitude to you all:

Vic Holtreman, Jonny Green, Ryan Myers, Dennis Tzeng, Jon Schnepp, Jeremy Jahns, Robert Burke, Justin Gardner, Lindsey Ekwall, Andrew Ibarra, Graham newman, Lucia Massaro, Shaiful Kashem, Eduardo Herrera, Dylan Sherman, Kade Wiemerslage, Daniel Gamez, Connor Brown, Jakesplace, Katelynn, Rob Olin, Gregory Voigt, Jim McCann, Justin Sim, David Sherlock, Michael O., Chris Habersack, Brian Pinch, Mark Piland, Alex Hajna, Marco A Ramirez Gonzolez, Chris Martin, Shehbaz Ahmad, Jacob Bartley, Daniel M, Ricky Clayton, Adhithya Ravishankar, Raymond Alarcon, Dwayne Washington, MoonRift Entertainment, Corey Brown, Mike Lovins, Joe Geiger, Hussain Shishtari, Barkev Chaghlasian, Chad Bowden, Oscar Herrera, Colin Lauber, Katrina Massengale, Matt Randle, Tyler King, Wendy Lee, Roger Baker, Karen, Donald Saareste, Ezra Cubero, Martin Will, Michael Eaton, Julien Provencher, Christopher Rodriguez, Dave & Tricia Shrivastav, Scott Levasseur, Safiyya, Luke Heaton, David Carter, Matthew Mendez, Martin Ballard, Christopher M. Parsons, Matthew unruh, Tim Nunes, John Odigure, Renato Vieira, Dallas Richardson, Brock Emmerich, Michael Cachela, Matthew B, Brian Goubeaux, Dalton Lackey, Martin Edwards, Zuri Corbin, Ricky Burtrand, Scott Cooke, Troy Young, KingSalamander, Olly Cabot, Gary Allegra, Billy Ringer, Aaron Kataen, Adriel Velazquez, Brian Olson, David Rhoden, William (Micah) Greenhill, Shalen Cook, James Tyler, Sushan Shrestha, James Mellar, Paul Foster, Ryan Whittle, Adam Williams, Andrew Legner, Luis Chairz, Chris Doty, Mijo Vazquez, Thanh Ta, Simeon Leach, Darren Hanlon, Daniel Hurst, Joseph Bayer, Arturo Castro, Doug Johnson, Casper Gøtsche, Carl Byrne, Andreas Eduard, Aleksandar Zivaljevic, Christopher S. Harp, Brandon Labbree, Liz Jamora, Chris Sirmons, Yousif Zaman, Matt Ross, Shawn Schweinberg, Jacob Pullen, Brevin Smith, Minh Tran, Youngbin Park, Magnus Meling, Jeremy Martinez, Louie Carrizales, Samir Karim, Richard Begg, Justin Ayotte, Jorge Alegre, Dominik Batt, Tristan Lamey, Garrett A.M. Lee, Chris Ferrell, David Lasyone, Surya Swaroop, Stephen Blake, Tim Platte, Ariel Diaz-Torres, Addison Pettiford, Sean Northridge, Florian Ammann, Jayant Kashyap, Cameron LeeWong, Andrew Fox, Paul Mikhail, Marcus Kappel, Elias Bounader, Lee Hutchings, Nick Fin, André Broussard, Dakotah Barrows, Craig Manson, Toby Yawn, Jack T Crawford, Chris Parker, Michael Chamberlin, Ian Kramlich,

Jimmy Boyle, Dacian Predan-Hallabrin, David Derby, Kevin Boyle, Michael Arnold, Jimmy Olofsson, David Badrov, Daniel Drießen, Brad Snyder, Josh Aldwell, Grant Davis, Nick DiGiacomo, Albert Pizano, Tom Adams, Luke Pyburn, Darick Paul Petrik, Joshua Howerton, Jamal Pulliam, Noel Campos, Marcus Longoni, Juan, Daniel Kosonovich, Maro R Sirakie, Steven Foley, Dljones, Shaheer Naqvi, Davey Stevens, Patrick Hogue, Paul Daniel Kendrick, Yaniv Volpert, Nicolas Phelps, Jimmy Nordgren, ythejoshuatreey, Richard Crump, Jack Foxwell, Derek Santiago, Arturo Bardales Salguero, Joseph Loiacono, Pierre Johnny Vartanian, Jonathan Rowe, Brett Edwards, Bill Van Haun, Rony Vargas, Jordan Allen, Moses Avila, Richard Allen, Michael Eng, Diane Clark-Sutton, Benjamin Vinding Pedersen, Adam Power, Dwayne Gomboc, Adil Lebgue, Cody, Anthony Nugent, David Belarde, Ari Levine, Harold David Everly, Zachary Pushee, Rafael A. Rivera, Eduardo Posada Socarro, David Mcgill, Vincent Hie, Canon Smith, Kelsie Williams, Ricardo Huarte, Emanuel Ortiz, Marco Marchese, Jonathan Fung, Isaac Tha Dewd Phillips, Muadh Abdul-Hamid, Andy Daniel, Derrick Woodrin, Ben Atwater, Lukas ammann, Michael Gulick, Dustin Young, Meg Edwards, Tony Testa, Michael Yi Zhang, Steve Weiner, Patricia Banina, Jesse Torres, Linus Schill, Kory Leach, Eric Maher, Nathan Taylor, Hernan Castro, Nick Castagna, Jesus A. Ceballos Jr., Yannik Meinen, Louis Silvia, Skaj J. Céré, Arfan Naseem, Gerrard Cao, Anthony perez, Ricky Perez, Dylan James Doerksen, Clint Austin, Shawn Okeefe, Christopher Woychak, Steve Lawrence, Tomas Robles, Carlos G. Flores, Matt Paynter

CPSIA information can be obtained at www.ICGtesting.com
Printed in the USA
LVOW10s1739040316

477812LV00038B/1447/P